KINGDOMS OF SILENT SORROWS

A.G. HARRIS

KINGDOMS OF SILENT SORROWS

CROWNS FORGED IN CHAOS
BOOK ONE

A.G. HARRIS

A.G. HARRIS
— AUTHOR —

Cover design: Painted by A.G. Harris.

Page Art and Map by A.G. Harris

Edited by: EA co

❀ Formatted with Vellum

AUTHOR'S NOTE

Kingdoms of Silent Sorrows is a fantasy set in the time of war, which includes elements, situations, themes, language, and activities that may trigger or may be sensitive to some readers.

To my BETA readers, Jennifer, Lacey, and Ellie.

Your feedback and comments on my book are always so helpful. I know giving you my book means it's in safe hands. You always provide constructive feedback in a way that helps me grow as an author. Thank you!

I also want to thank the Cygnet groups who helped me when I was feeling lost during the formatting process. Author K.A. James, you are one of those authors who not only replied but also sent me voice messages and videos to help me when I needed them.

To my husband,

You always listen to me as I tell you all about all the characters and plots in my head. You're always supportive, uplifting, and my safety net. This especially came true when someone I hired on my team turned out to be a malicious person who scammed me out of money, weeks of my time, and worst, they played mind games with me.

You were there to listen as I vented, as I cried, you turned around my sorrows and made sure the joy of writing this book would outlive evil intent.

I've told you a lot of crazy plots, but you never once have sprayed water on my fire. You're always there to support me, help me, and guide me in whatever way I need. When I was so overwhelmed with trying to format this book (using a new program so more of my art could be within the pages), you even offered to learn how to format so you could help me.

Being an indie author means you will stumble, because you have to learn how to do everything by yourself, but I know if I fall, you'll be there to help me stand.

This is for every sheep that stumbled across a shepherd who didn't protect them but harmed them. You had to do whatever you could in order to survive being a sheep in a world of monsters.
You turned into a wolf.
You bit everyone, whether they tried to help you or showed you love.
It's okay to remain a wolf, but just remember, wolves survive longer when they are in a pack. You don't have to remain closed off, untrusting, and alone.
The characters in this book evolved into wolves. Some find a pack, and others.... you'll have to read to find out.

PROLOGUE

AMARIEL

Heat strokes my skin, pulling more and more sweat from my pores. The fire is relentless, as am I. Turning my back to the forge, I walk to the window and shove it open.

Breathe, calm down. Panicking does nothing.

I toss my long braid over my shoulder and press my palm to my heart. My chest is like firewood: rough, splitting open, and unable to stop the enemy—the truth of what I have done—seeking to devour it.

Every inhale is fueled by the aroma that surrounds me.

Death.

Spring flowers no longer bloom; their velvet petals decay under bloody boots.

"Don't do it. Why did you look up?" I hiss out loud. Falling ash masks the sun.

It's snow.

Why do you lie to yourself? I dream lies to keep the nightmare of my reality at bay.

The swelling in my throat feels like water transforming into ice. There is no more room to breathe; everything is solid. What's done is done.

This is why you should not take breaks. Stop concentrating on your mistakes and try to fix them!

Grabbing the latch, I slam the window shut, heaving a deep breath. My muscles tremble as I grab a shovel, ready to get back to work. Once I forged things of beauty, tools to shape our world, not destroy it.

Now, I make grotesque things. But in their ugliness, there's hope for survival.

Maybe that makes them beautiful in their own way. After all, how can we define survival without the existence of its antithesis? Destruction. Extinction.

This forge, which I hope will end this war, is also where the war started. The war caught us off guard, like a bolt of lightning on a clear sunny day. It should not have happened. The elves, who used to be loyal servants, knew they had to move fast. During our time of grief and shock over losing one of our own, they struck, killing another god.

The war against the elves, creatures lesser than us, has lasted only weeks. Victory is on their side. Our hope is as minuscule and slim as the eye of a needle. We try and try but can't thread it. I must find a way to sew us back together again. After all, discarded scraps can be turned into a quilt, something needed again, cherished, and loved.

My back bows and arches, my thighs scream with pain as I bend and shovel load after load of fuel into the fire. My biceps shake so badly I lose half the scoop on the floor. My pride persists, urging me to keep going.

Wait! I pull the next shovel back. *Don't overfeed the fire. You'll kill it. These hands will kill yet another thing.*

I plant the shovel's blade beside my boot and lean on the shaft, too tired to move, too exhausted to fall, yet too stubborn to sleep. The handle rests uncomfortably under my chin, propping my head up as I stare at everything I've done.

I forged thirteen swords as gifts for my fellow gods who desired peace. Those of us who didn't agree, or ignored matters altogether, received nothing. The swords were my version of a requiem.

I poured a piece of my core magic into the blades, a sacrifice most gods would not make lightly. I fell into a daze as I carved intricate designs into each sword, loving it as a mother cradles a child. I transformed a weapon into a piece of art to be admired rather than wielded. I wanted to show my fellow gods that an item's purpose could change.

We could change.

Peace lasted less than a season.

The extent of my creation came as a surprise, even to me. When I hammered my magic into the metal, I simply wanted the battles to end. Arguably, they did. The God Swords, the only weapons strong enough to kill us, were forged by my hands.

Mine.

I push the shovel aside, clenching my fists at my sides. If I didn't need my hands, I'd sever them from my body, ensuring I could no longer create anything ever again.

One wrong move changed everything.

It all happened during our celebration. It was meant to be a dance, a show of our blades. Not a fight.

No blade had ever pierced our skin before.

How could I have known that when I pressed the tip against my fellow god, his flesh would yield so easily?

Breaths were held, complexions blanched, mouths gaped, bones shuddered, bodies swayed, collective gasps and shouts severed the shock, and yes, the awe, for never before had a god fallen.

Then, one of us dropped to his knees. Dare I say a smile tugged at his lips. He knew death had finally found a way to claim him.

Gods were immortal no more.

His noble heart didn't resist. He reached up, gripped the blade, and drove it deeper into his chest.

Did he welcome death that much? Had we made life here so unbearable that he chose this ending over enduring us?

Or was it his way of telling me not to blame myself?

The world convulsed, the heavens groaned, and the balance was disrupted.

Those we viewed as friends saw an opportunity to become our foes, for they no longer feared the gods. One of the elves picked up the fallen sword; none of the other gods noticed, we were too stunned. During our shock, he drove the sword into another one of us, and chaos ran free.

I shake off the memory. I'm trying everything in my power to change the tides of war, but like any creature, I have come to learn we can't control the current. We must endure and fight during the flows; in the ebbs, we must plot and search for hope, even when all feels lost.

My skin is stretched so taut it burns as the heat from the starfire in my forge rages on. It has long hardened my hands, causing the ivory skin of my palms to turn a pinkish hue.

A lover's touch once smoothed my skin. Now everything is hard: my life, my heart, my gold-colored eyes, which have cried so much that the salt has practically turned them to calcified stone.

I flip my wrists and uncurl my fingers, letting out a slow breath. Thick black soot and oil etch so deeply into the lines of my skin, I fear they will never call me beautiful again. I'm the stitching of a war-torn blanket: threadbare, cut up, and ripped apart.

I look toward the god who's casting a vast, impenetrable shadow along the stone wall of my forge's corner. To Lucian, I'm still beautiful, innocent. But he's always been attracted to dark, broken things.

Lucian has attached himself to me just as his shadows stitch themselves to every creature. This god is a friend and foe, an enemy and lover. He's the mirror that reflects all angles—the things we love and parts of us we lust to change.

"This war will kill us all," I mutter to myself, yet Lucian, a god attuned to the faintest whispers, hears me. That man can hear the whispers of the northern winds, even when others can't feel them.

Lucian leans against a mountain of star rocks. The large pieces fell from the heavens, and they made the hottest fire. He resembles these stones—all muscle, hardness, and heat. His body has set me on fire many nights; I call upon those memories. I hope one day, my body will warm for him again.

His hair is as dark as the vast sky, but his skin is as pale as the untouched ice of the Crystal Mountains. He bears the hands of a killer, yet the mouth of a savior. His eyes are always plotting, but his smirk is the quill that pens the first strokes of peace.

But what is peace but a dance of seduction, anyway?

His heart is a soulless depth none have dared venture to chart.

Yet I have.

I have mapped out his peaks and valleys, discovered the monsters that lurk in his shadows; one might argue I have tamed them, but I am wise enough to know no wild animal can be broken.

Love is a game of trickery.

Some call Lucian's mind shallow. But they forget that even shallow waters can steal souls. Depths indeed hide many secrets, but shallow lands are the most treacherous; there is nowhere to hide from Lucian's mind, no escape once he sets his sights on you.

My head hangs, and a bead of sweat leaps off my cheek and dives into the sandy ground of my forge. I watch, mesmerized, as that tiny droplet sits on top of the small grains of sand, rejected from being absorbed.

My world has refused me for what I have done.

I raise my foot and step on the bead of moisture, forcing it to merge with the ground. I will fix this!

Lucian tips his chin up, ever the observer. His hands are caked with dried blood, making his skin tone indistinguishable. Bloodstains mar even the paleness of his prominent cheekbones. He wears the grime like the finest of silk, tailor-made for him.

He hates his beauty, which is why he's content with filth covering him. It keeps others at bay.

He is the God of Turbulence. He created darkness and light, two opposing forces that fight to swallow one another.

He opens his palms: one fills with a light so bright, I am momentarily blind. The other with a void so dark it pulls my body closer. With a wave of his fingers, the darkness and light clash.

His magic purrs as the battle in his palm takes center stage. It drowns out the sparks of my fire, a heat so intense no elf could survive entering this forge. I used to sit for hours after we made love, watching him make this symphony that lulled me to sleep.

"Such is life; what shall you have me do?" he murmurs in a relaxed tone, as if he's on a shore listening to waves, entirely untouched by the haunting purr of war drums pounding outside our walls.

When an immortal discovers they can be killed, they either swallow the pill like Lucian has or reject it like the others. I'm lost in the middle; the pill sits on my tongue, for I am unwilling to swallow it but not foolish enough to spit it out.

"Fight for it!" I hiss as I grab my hammer. *Fight for me! So we can have an eternity together!*

Water hitting molten steel is how his eyes douse me, begging me to stop, to cool. The steam his acknowledgment produces rolls off me. "I might have reached my end, but I'm still an ember. I still live!"

A tear rolls down my cheek. It pulls him up as his shadows reach to catch me. "I am lit, I am here! I'm trying to mend what I broke," I cry.

I blink and he's in front of me. "Do you wish me to lie to you, Amariel?" A rough hand cups my cheek as he speaks.

Quivering, I shake my head. "Don't start now."

He guides my eyes to his. "You move around this forge like sparks desperate for the hearth, for a purpose. But everything you touch is turning to ash. Fire, creation—it's wonderful, but sometimes that fire burns out of control. I do not blame you for what has happened. But we can not defeat the elves. Numbers *do* win a war. We..." he pauses, eyes blistering with rawness, "grow less each battle."

Not even Lucian can voice how many of us remain. The truth is too painful to declare.

Soon, we will be none.

"We cannot win. There is honor in truth, Amariel." He speaks as one sinks into a hot bath. Relaxed. At peace.

Yet all I feel is cold water. Another reminder: this is my fault.

Lucian has remained by my side, but I hate it. I deserve the death the other gods have faced.

"If whispers could shape truths, I'd press my lips to your ear and speak them into existence. But I am war; I am grit, terror, and honor. I am brutal honesty. It's time to accept that our time is coming to an end. Cushions do not help the blow; they make death more prolonged."

This is why I love him. He's not a lifeboat—sometimes boats never reach the final destination. He's the monster lurking beneath the waves, ready to carry me away.

How badly I wish to be plucked away from this life, to have all my mistakes wiped clean.

But I have a stubborn flaw: I'm a fixer. Another flaw is that I break the things I fix, which allows me to fix them again, then shatter them. It's a terrible cycle. So why can't I step back and let someone else fix my mistakes?

"What would you have me do?" I whisper, tasting salt on my lips. "Hand myself over?"

"No." He glides his lips over mine. I inhale sharply. "If I have one more night left to live, I want every moment to be spent holding you, tasting you, making love to you. I want the memory of you to transcend the trauma and agony of death."

He seizes my lips with a passion that invades my mind. The heat of his tongue curling and sucking on mine melts my willpower, but *I'm* a master at molding objects, not him. I know what he's trying to do. I won't allow it, but I indulge for one second.

I kiss him back, pushing up on my toes, snaking my hands around his muscular shoulders. His invisible chaos runs through my body, wetting my core, trembling my knees. My palms slide down his chest. I push him back, admiring him from a distance.

"I'm not ready to die," I declare, licking my lips and savoring his taste.

He's a tide that comes back; his arms ensnare me as an anchor halts a boat. "Neither am I, but hopes and dreams have no place in war." He lowers his mouth to mine.

How badly I want to have his lips silence me, to smother out my problems.

I twist free and walk back to the fire.

His growl is a hiss of metal that is quenched, hardening, but then he tempers himself, ensuring his determination is not too brittle after my rejection. His walk back to his spot is a long voyage.

"We are biding time, Amariel." Refusing to leave my forge, he glares at me. Those eyes, two orbs of pure black with streaks of light, have seduced me more times than I am willing to confess. "Life is precious, and if I have to kill a thousand to spend one more day, one more hour, or second with you, then I will, but I am not blinded by love like you. I know the outcome of this war. We can not win." He levels me with an honest stare. "I have come to terms with that because I know each day I survive is one more night with you. You can toil away in here, but before our two suns rise, I will have you under me and then on top. I will have you every way I can dream of. There is one thing the elves can not slaughter, and that is my dreams. For I will dream of you always. In life. In death. You are my dream, and I refuse to watch you transform into a nightmare, Amariel."

My bottom lip trembles with need. The door to my forge swings open. Erevan, God of Enchantment, enters. He has the power to alter things, whether it be moods or flesh and blood.

He's dressed in his finest clothes, as if there's a festive occasion and not a silent dinner. His brownish-yellow gaze rakes over me. He sees not the soot covering me but the imprint of his fingertips and the red hues left by his silken sheets.

Erevan longs to keep me a prisoner in his bed. I desire it, too.

Gold-spun threads around Erevan's collar are illuminated with his magic, casting rays of rainbow light in the forge. His hair resembles waves of a golden sunrise frozen in time for me to admire.

A feeling of calm tries to penetrate me, and for a moment, a mere blink of an eye, I allow it. I grant myself mercy and forget the wrongs I have done.

If Lucian is an unmoving stone, Erevan is sand.

Lucian wants people to see the beast. He wears white in battle so others can see the stains of death on him. Erevan hides his nature with beautiful clothes and wide smiles. Like sand, he invades the smallest cracks, slowly scratching away your defenses.

"Since when does turbulence settle?" Erevan eyes Lucian, mocking him with playful disdain.

The only time these men can withstand being in a room together is when I am here. When the gods were at war, I was sent to negotiate peace between them. I did, but it cost me my heart, which they both claimed as their own.

Erevan saunters over to me; his shadow blocks the heat of the fire that warms my cheeks. "My love," he purrs in a deep tone that settles into my body, causing an ache to sing throughout my very being.

Lucian flicks his fingers. The battle in his palm intensifies. "She might be your love, but she is my addiction. Everyone knows addiction outfights and outwits love on any battlefield." His smile sharpens coyly.

"I will be no one's if we do not think of something," I point out.

"Thus my appearance." Erevan places a lover's kiss upon my lips. My body betrays me as I part my mouth and accept eagerly. The weight of Lucian's stare presses into my skin with more heat than his fingers possessed a mere day ago.

I belong to neither of them yet both of them at the same time.

The three of us are pandemonium. I, the God of the Forge, created it. Lucian, being Turbulence, fueled our battling hearts. Erevan, the God of Enchantment, made us believe the three of us could be happy amidst conflict.

Erevan cups my face. "Even gods need rest, Amariel." His eyes roam my face with worry.

I look away. "How can I slumber when our world dies? This is my—"

In a sudden jolt, Erevan grabs my hips, soldering me to him. "Do not utter those words again. You made a gift; they used it as a weapon. It's their fault. You need to rest. Come to my bed tonight."

"I hardly think a night with you would grant her rest." Lucian's eyes turn smug. "I assume she must do all the work to get you off."

"If you wish to watch us, just ask." Erevan devilishly grins as he squeezes my ass, and my cheeks flush.

"I don't watch. I take heed," Lucian replies sharply. The challenge in his voice is as clear as the drums of war.

"A strong man knows when to comply," Erevan counters. "A weak man just continues to bark orders."

Lucian grinds his teeth.

I sense an argument stirring. "Stop it," I plead, stepping back so the fire of my forge ripples over my spine again.

"The enemy sleeps, thus their successes," Erevan tries to persuade me.

I raise my chin. "I will not close my eyes until I see hope, and if it can't be found, then my eyes will close for death."

"Enough of this talk." Erevan rolls his eyes, turning to Lucian with a rare spark of agreement. "I have a plan. We can not save our world, but that does not mark total defeat."

Lucian closes his palms, silencing his magic. "I'm listening," he says warily.

A chill ripples down my body. They're... agreeing. This truly is the end of times.

Erevan grabs my hand, pulls us closer to Lucian, and then he does something he usually doesn't; he lowers himself to the ground and sits next to Lucian. He places me on his lap and kisses my hair.

From down here, the weight of the world settles on my shoulders. I feel as tired and dry as bones, aged by the unrelenting suns.

"She was on *my* lap hours ago." Lucian winks with a wicked flare.

"Stop it!" I snap as I slide off Erevan's lap. "You two will be fighting over my bones if we can not find a way to end this war." That silences them. "What idea do you have, Erevan?"

"We regroup."

"You mean retreat?" Lucian mutters in disgust, propping an elbow on his raised leg.

"Yes." Erevan levels him with a glare.

"And where, pray tell, would we retreat to? The elvish armies have us cornered; they wait for one of us to show up and fight so they can stab us with one of the swords they stole. We fight to defend our wall every night and day. There is nowhere to run but into battle," Lucian scoffs, cracking his knuckles. Some of the dried blood flakes off, falling like snowflakes.

Those of us who survived now fight from a distance; Lucian is the only fool crazy enough to battle beyond these walls. I forge weapons for us while the others have been draining their magic dry to defend our last stronghold, but even then, it is not enough.

The enemy has too many soldiers. They know if they can get close enough to subdue us, hundreds will die, but one will get close enough to end us.

I've seen it happen.

Erevan clasps his hands. "Another world," he replies coolly. "I was thinking of Panthas, to be exact. We have been there before. We are familiar with the lands and creatures. It'd be the perfect place to gather again."

"What?" Lucian sputters.

I grab Erevan's hand; black soot stains his golden skin. "That is forbidden." My voice is a closed book. As gods, we discovered how to open up portals that lead to another world; it was deemed forbidden to corrupt lands not our own.

"By whom?"

"You know by whom," Lucian growls in warning.

"Panthas was made by the same creature, a Genesis, who made us. They will welcome us." Erevan argues.

"Panthas's maker is different." Lucian disputes, "She and our father have parted ways. Attkris is our world. Panthas is *hers*. I do not wish to anger one of the Genesis, Erevan."

"The Genesis made us! They have to help us. Our ways are about to be erased." Erevan's voice rises. "We have no other option. We can worry about the consequences, if there are any, later. Unlike our enemies, we can leave these lands. What I am suggesting is that we retreat and fall back. We hide in the other world and regroup. We build a new army."

"With what?" Lucian barks, shaking his head in disdain. "Our discovery of Panthas revealed only those who called each other human. They have no magic; they would be ants killed quickly under elvish boots. You'd doom another species to death."

"So we change them," Erevan counters. "As the God of Enchantment, I will give them magic."

"Erevan!" I gasp as I drop his hand. "That's forbidden..." Yet my words slowly die as realization hits home. He's right. Our old laws, etched in stone, no longer exist; our enemy has broken the rock.

War erases morality. But if we expunge it from our minds, we're no better than the enemy.

"Let's say we consider this," Lucian suggests, sitting taller. The mound of rocks behind him look like a throne. It's what our empire resembles now: rubble. "If humans can accept our magic and learn to wield it, and that is a huge if, who's to say they can stand a chance against the enemy who has inherited magic? You are condemning more to die."

"I have considered this. They will stand a chance; in the years to come, their magic will grow, and in time, they will master it as our enemy has. Humans would become new creatures. Our magic will transform them, but we will leave some untouched, so that their history is not erased. That seems fair." Erevan looks down and rubs invisible dust off his gold clothing. "I also recommend we don't just make an army of these magic-born humans."

"You sound insane," I whisper. I look to the scalding fire; the heat presses into my eyes, pulling water forth.

Erevan turns my face back to his, then twirls a lock of my fire-kissed golden hair around his finger. "Sometimes, one must be mad in order to see what the enemy doesn't. I am suggesting..." He pauses; his inhale is a lifetime long. His eyes fill with regret and a turbulence of pain I have never seen upon his brow. "I am suggesting the three of us have children."

"What?" Lucian and I both reply in shock.

"We cannot have children," I murmur. Thus, we'll never have the numbers our enemy has.

"Gods can't have children together." Erevan's gulp unlocks a terrible secret. "But we can have them with humans," he adds, voice quieter this time.

I flinch. "*That* is blasphemous."

He dips his fingers into the sandy floor, pinching a grain before he flicks it away. "The truth often is."

Lucian leans forward. Fury turns his brows into an archer's bow. "Have you—"

"No!" Erevan replies quickly. "Not I, but another has laid with a human and had a child. That child is alive, thriving, and possesses magic."

"How do you know this?" Lucian presses.

Erevan's jaw stiffens. "I am bound by an oath not to reveal which one of us has broken the old laws; all that matters is that we can have children with humans. These offspring have magic. We mate with these humans, produce offspring, create demigods."

His eyes cast downward, too ashamed to meet mine now. His hand reaches out for mine, taking it.

"It's the only way I can see survival. It is not what I want," he murmurs to me. "Deny me, and I will fight to the death here, my love."

My throat swells. "You'd bring innocents into this war."

"War does not distinguish between innocent and guilty," Erevan replies solemnly. "Think of it as a way to ensure our survival. If we had children, then isn't that a hope that a piece of us survives?"

I cover my mouth with my dirty hands. The more I try to fix what I've done, the muddier it seems to become.

"In time," Erevan voices softly, "we will have enough demigods and new creatures, these humans made with magic, to come back here and claim Attkris again. We can restore what we have lost."

Children. With others...

I look at Erevan and Lucian; their eyes sense mine. We all would have to sleep with others, with humans.

"Say something," Erevan whispers. When neither Lucian nor I do, Erevan continues, "What is the use of fighting to the death if our history will be erased? The winner writes the outcome; they plot the story. If we run, then at least we get to write our side of the story. Perhaps in centuries, we can return with an army, or remain hidden. At least our memories will not be erased."

Ding! Ding!

We all jerk at the sound of the bells. No!" I choke. I stand but slip. Lucian and Erevan grab me, locking eyes with one another.

As we were sitting and trying to find a way to bring peace back into our lives, the enemy found a way inside the inner walls.

Lucian looks down at me, his eyes are those of a painter admiring the next subject he will paint. But he's a piss-poor artist who has no canvas, brushes, or paints. So, I will live in his memory as his greatest unseen masterpiece.

"Get her out of here. Take her to Panthas," he orders Erevan.

"No!" I reach for him, but the dirt on my fingers causes my grip to slip free. Erevan slams me back into his chest, caging his arms around me.

Ding! Ding!

A new melody has been added. Death. Screams and cries that will forever haunt me. And then it happens... a horrendous, abrupt yank causes us all to stumble.

Another god is no more.

Shock holds us firm in its shackles. We sway, becoming soulless bodies held only by flesh, chained by bones. No hearts to give us strength or minds to seduce us with endurance. Just puppets.

"Who was it?" I manage to rasp.

"Go!" Lucian shouts. He opens his hands and two swords rage to life, one of pure light and the other of utter darkness. "I will find the last of us and try to take them to this world." He looks at me, lips parted in desperation.

I know he wants to kiss me, but he doesn't. It's a silent promise he will find me again; he will deliver his kiss when we are safe, hidden away from the mess I have created.

"I will find you, Amariel. In this life or the next. You. Are. Mine."

"She is ours," Erevan retorts with a dip of his chin.

Lucian locks eyes with him. "Then you better keep her safe. For us."

"For us," Erevan agrees.

A century later

I ran from war. It has chased me.

The enemy changed. The acts have not.

Blood, regardless of its color, makes rivers in the soil. "They will kill each other before we can build an army," I tell Erevan.

He stands as steady as a ship's mast, holding me together in these troubled waters.

Death surrounds us, so much so that the gold of his clothing has taken on a darker hue. "They will change," he murmurs, leaning closer to me.

I feel no comfort.

"It takes time. Power is feral at first. But it can be tamed, Amariel. Remember the wars we fought. War makes us respect and honor peace. These people are just figuring this out. They still use horses to ride into battle. And look at humans; they use candles to light their homes. Progression takes time," he declares as he looks at what his new creatures have done.

Bodies lay twisted and deformed, creating a roadmap neither of us wants to venture across.

The humans of this world lie dead, their skin turning to rot as the vultures above circle to feast. We don't have birds like this back home. They are a sight I wish to vanquish from my memory.

Erevan made his new creatures slightly different; this way, when we return with an army, they won't all share the same weakness.

"Many vampires died this time. See,"—Erevan points to a dead one —"the humans are getting stronger. Remember when no vampires lay dead? Humans are learning to defend themselves. In time, the vampires will be forced to acknowledge this. Eventually, they will have to seek peace."

Vampires fuel their magic through human blood. Erevan thought this would help them respect humans. Instead, they sought to enslave them. He also designed them to release pleasure or pain when they feed. It's his way of judging their character. Sadly, many vampires enjoy pain.

Erevan sees the glass half full, but I broke the glass. I see only the mistakes that spill out and stain my hands. "Eventually is time's greatest rival, Erevan. I fear it will win before time can correct the mistakes."

I pay my respects and glance at the dead vampire. He's as pale as the single moon in the sky.

How I miss our moons.

I find vampires most unsettling; their fangs resemble the elves. It's wrong of me to compare them, of course. I'm trying hard to distinguish between the two. We cared for the elves; fed and loved them, yet they killed us in the end.

Four other gods came here, making our total six, but the god I lusted for the most never walked through the portal, a fact which makes my heart ache even now.

Don't think of Lucian. Don't break.

The six of us agreed on a new tactic. Allowing these people to make their own kingdoms and laws. We want them to make mistakes, so they can understand our hardships. In time, we will make ourselves known. The Gods who are here want to be shadows, that watch over their children, in hopes they will follow our traditions, and defend Attkris. Hopefully, when the time comes, these creatures will realize they need shadows to protect them from the sun's heat.

"The mages and fae ceased fighting." Erevan's statement lands flat, despite the hope in his words.

"That's because they each need rest to fuel their magic. Rest has given them time to plot peace."

Each new creature has a flaw that limits its magic. Vampires need blood, mages and fae need rest, shifters need a full moon, and so on. Erevan had to ration his magic with each new creation, but now, after creating so many, his power has entered a state of dormancy. We knew this would happen; we planned and made friends to help protect him in this vulnerable state.

A huge shadow blankets the sun, making us glance up. A magnificent sapphire dragon circles overhead. The sun reflects off its hard scales, casting blue rays like the calm ocean waters.

Dragons are another of Erevan's creatures. Unfortunately, the creatures became too wild. I helped Erevan correct that by making dragon riders, a rare group of humans that can connect with the stunning animals with the help of a rune I drew in a book Erevan made for me. It wasn't the first gift he gave me since we arrived, but it is the most powerful and precious.

"They sent scouts." Erevan's mouth tugs up. He'd never admit it, but the dragon riders are his favorite. The riders have been the most well-behaved of his creations, which is such a juxtaposition since they ride the biggest beasts that roam these lands.

They are seen as the peacemakers and enforcers when needed. However, their numbers are small, so they mainly keep to themselves. We can relate to that fear.

"He's spotted us," I reply with a sigh.

Dragons can see us, no matter how well we veil ourselves, and since they can communicate with their riders, hiding from them is impossible. Consequently, Erevan and I conveyed much information to the riders and dragons.

But not everything. Our purpose here remains undisclosed. I don't feel guilty about the lie. Like any parent, we are merely trying to protect our children until they reach maturity.

The dragons and their riders know we are different; some of them whisper that we are the gods who brought magic to these lands. Perhaps that's why they want our favor. At least they have an inkling of knowledge of the truth.

Slowly, the dragon begins to descend. Looking down, I study another fallen human warrior for a long time. My heart aches.

"I need to help them. All of them. They fight for power, but what they lust for is safety," I admit. The original seed of guilt in my stomach has turned into a lush forest with deadly plants. I feel their thorns every time they spread.

"These things take time." Erevan gently pushes my hair off my shoulder.

"I understand that, but I cannot turn a blind eye to this. What good is an army if they hate each other? They must be equal."

"My magic still slumbers, but when it awakens, I can try to alter things," Erevan offers. His originals increased in number, producing offspring. Each new generation possesses stronger magic.

Then there are the demigods whom we kept hidden until this world finds peace.

"No, that's not what I mean," I say as I lead us out of the battlefield. "We must leave some humans untouched. It's cruel if we erase them, but that doesn't mean we can't help them. Give them a chance to fight back with equal power. Respect and fear are necessary for peace. Our new creatures need to learn they are not the most formidable monsters in these lands."

"Are you suggesting we reveal ourselves?" he asks cautiously.

Before I can reply, the ground shakes. The dragon lands in the small open space between the battlefield and the forest. The rider begins to make his way to us. His armor matches his dragon, making for perfect camouflage when he is on the beast's back.

As he comes closer, he removes his helmet and dips his chin in respect. "Erevan. Amariel." He bows, proving our assumptions are correct: they think we are gods.

"Rider," Erevan replies. He looks at the dragon and nods. It purrs back a compliment.

"The humans are marching back to reclaim their dead. But another vampire squadron lurks in the forest four miles south. I believe they plan to ambush the humans again," the rider informs us.

How can I help these humans? What can I forge for them that will make them as strong as Erevan's creatures? What can my hands create that will make them all equal, so the fighting stops? I press my palm to my stomach. Erevan steps closer, as if he can shield me from my inner pain.

"We can burn away their path," the rider offers.

"I think that is wise," Erevan agrees. We've been using the riders as a means of intervention. "There has been enough death for today." He reaches for my hand. I link our fingers, fearing that if I don't, my soul will be set adrift, bound to float endlessly with the countless dead that surround me.

The rider nods and then returns to his dragon. Erevan watches with pride as the huge beast launches into the air.

"Their hearts are pure," he says softly. "The others will learn in time to be like the dragons and their riders." He's correct; animals sense what humans can't. I think the dragons know it is Erevan who created them.

"What if they continue to fight until only the dragon riders are left? They alone can not be the army we seek," I voice.

Erevan rubs the back of his neck, hesitating.

I press on. "Dragon riders are still technically human. The rune I made bonds them and enhances them, but their core is human. Riders are chosen, not born." A memory of the fire of my forge presses into my skin; sweat beads on my brow. I will not build a forge again, but that doesn't mean I can't create something to help everyone. "I have an idea."

We travel back to the home we made here on Panthas. A safe place only the dragon riders can reach. The fae below do not know that this mountain, which blankets the land to the west in darkness, has been claimed by the gods. The fae have established two ruling courts. This mountain separates the Day Court from the Night Court.

I race up the last steps we carved into the mountain, past the near invisible veiled walls of our home. If you didn't look at the stars, you'd think you were in Attkris, in Silas's lands to be exact. Famed for his crystal walls, which are made of his veil magic. Walls the elves could peer right in. His kingdom was one of the first to be abandon. There was nowhere for Silas to hide.

We each had tasks when we arrived on Panthas. Erevan's was to make creatures. Silas's was to build our homes. The location we picked was tactical. The top of a cloudy mountain no human had dared to climb.

I appreciate Silas's hard work, but I miss the walls I forged. I made every brick from stardust, and they glowed at night. A beacon the elves thirsted for. Do any of those walls still stand?

Erevan's hot on my heels as I barge into our chambers. "The book you made for me," I announce eagerly, grabbing what I seek off my drawing desk. As I turn, I look at Erevan.

Is that a smile? A long time has passed since my lips curved up.

Erevan begged me to make a forge here once we arrived, but I refused. How could I work without Lucian sitting in the corner watching me as he leaned against the star rocks? Lucian was the one who ensured I did not work until I fainted; he'd pick me up, wash me, then carry me to his bed, where he consumed me.

After a few decades here on Panthas, Erevan came to me with a gift. A book he had created using his magic, making it indestructible compared to the books humans used. He didn't want me to lose another thing so he placed a piece of his core magic into this book.

Erevan did this when he made his creatures here. He shared a small piece of his core magic with them. We have to be careful not to give away too much of our core magic. But on occasion, it is required. All gods have done it, eventually. Sometimes, it involves the creation of things that are harmful to other gods. On occasion, it's assisting a god.

Erevan has never told me, but I know he has the core magic of fellow gods within him. I sense it when his guard is down. It is likely that he leveraged the other gods, striking a deal with them in order to keep their secrets from being exposed. After all, Erevan knew about the first demigod on Panthas.

For years, I drew nothing in the book until we watched the dragons burn the land. Charred bones surrounded me as I stood in the ruins of the burned mage city. With one touch, most of the bones would crumble. Burial was impossible.

These people would be nothing more than dust in the wind. No memory or place to grieve.

Nothing.

Defeated, I sat in the hot soil among the bones of mages who fought valiantly, only to be denied the sunrise. I held Erevan's book to my chest, wishing for tears that didn't come.

What's done is done. Tears didn't reverse it.

I pulled back the book's cover. I yearned to create a protective rune that would prevent a repeat of the horror. I had nothing to draw with so I searched, grabbing a shard of a bone that didn't crumble. The burnt end worked as a makeshift pencil.

The bone, once living, was brought back to life.

I last sacrificed core magic when forging the God Swords. The symbol represented my surrender and desire for peace.

I did it again when I held that book and drew the first rune.

This book he created was too precious to be just another sketchbook, so I used my core magic for the first time since we arrived. Forging something new, something to help bring peace. I changed the pages and glued my magic into the spine. The book became sentient, growing a mind of its own, just like one of Erevan's creations. I, too, made a living thing. Then I drew a rune similar to the ones I used to decorate my creations with. While sketching, I envisioned the rune's function and operation. The rune initially faded into the page. The book rejected it; it craved something more substantial. The pages desired more and more, a sliver of my mind.

I needed to give the rune more rules, a strong foundation to live upon. Hammer it, stretch it out, as a blacksmith does to steel when forging a sword to make it stronger.

The rune was a child I designed; I picked everything from the hair color to how tall it would be. I worked and reworked my drawing, making changes and additions. I had to keep my thoughts and intentions pure and focused. Only then did the symbol remain on the page. Together, our core magic created a book that had the power to transcend the pages and sink into whoever wrote the rune.

When Erevan asked what I made, I told him it was a rune that could be drawn onto humans. My intention with this first mark was to bind those strong enough to a dragon, thus giving the beast riders who could tame them.

I never wanted to endure the chaos caused by a wild dragon again.

And it worked. We created dragon riders.

That was how I made the first rune. A symbol strong enough to reforge Erevan's magic creatures.

Erevan's eyes smile, reliving the memory as I just did. I hug the gift he gave me to my heart. "You want to make another rune?" he asks.

The leather of the cover warms my hands as the magic-infused material glimmers in the light. Erevan magically ensured the book's pages would never deplete. The book purrs with delight at being held. Erevan's spine straightens as if he can feel my touch deep within his bones.

"Yes." I nod. "What if I made additional runes to aid humans in defending against magic? Victory won't be so simple anymore."

His eyes pull tight as he listens. "Wouldn't that create an imbalance?"

I rub my jaw, frowning in thought. He's right. Magic has a way of seeking balance. Focusing solely on humans risks harming other creatures, and magic may retaliate. Creation is fickle. Once you set it free, it's hard to catch again.

It's a wildflower; you can pluck it, but the seeds have escaped into the wind. Thus, some are forever on the run.

"I'll make runes for all of them to use," I finally say.

"That seems unwise, my love. Look at the battles they have fought because we gave some of them magic." He pushes off the door frame and comes closer.

I step back, keeping him in my full view. "We didn't regard the consequences because we were desperate when we came. Think about it, Erevan." My voice rises as I defend my vision. "All these wars are an imbalance. We gave them magic, but we didn't counterbalance it. The runes can be that opposition."

His brow lifts. "Or cause more wars," he counters.

"Think of it this way: giving them magic was like giving one clan metal; they used it as a weapon and a tool to grow. The other clan still has sticks and stones. If we give them all metal, that will teach them how to progress, how to make peace, and how to come to terms with the fact that no one is above the other. Then, in centuries, once they have allied, we can make our plea to them."

His lips press into a flat line. "But wouldn't that go against our original rule, my love? We vowed not to erase a species to save our own. If we allow humans to possess magic, it will alter them."

I turn and lick my lips. He's right. Glancing out the window, I feel the warmth of the now-rising sun. A new day has come.

"What if," I mumble, "I make the runes temporary? Some could last a day, while others could last longer. Like the dragon riders, whose runes last during their lifespan. Then the dragon is free for another rider to claim."

I whirl around when I'm greeted by his silence.

"It's a good idea," I insist, nodding as I close the distance.

His eyes sweep over the clean floor as if he's trying to find the dirt within my suggestion. "The others gods won't go for this." He reaches up and cups my cheek, his eyes full of a deep ache. "They don't know you drew the dragon rider rune. They will fear anything you create, my love."

My heart skips a beat. They are right to fear my hands. "Any tool can kill. It's the responsibility of those who wield it," I whisper as a tear slips free.

He tips my chin up and presses his forehead to mine. "I know." His inhale is deep. "And that is why we won't tell them." He pulls back. "My magic slumbers; I can't fix this, but your runes can. And the others will never suspect it. They think the rider's runes manifested naturally as our markings have."

He pushes up his sleeve, revealing the symbols that cover his forearms. I glance at the empty spot where he sacrificed his core magic to make the book for me, the gift we kept secret from the other gods.

I blink in surprise. "You... you agree?"

"I do. They will keep battling until one prevails, but equipping them with the same tool will leave them with no option but to reconcile. But more wars will come before peace. Humans will seek vengeance on magic users. Blood will be shed."

My throat tightens. We knew death would follow us, but we wanted to survive. It's selfish, but it's also survival of the fittest. "I understand," I force out.

Peace will come. I have to keep repeating that. It's what happened in our world. Every god commanded legions of devoted elves. We realized we'd have no kingdom left to rule if the battles raged on. We made peace; everyone was happy, or so we thought.

It was an ignorant belief that those who served us loved us.

We used them, but we also loved them. We learned the hard way that love is not equal.

"How do you intend to share these runes? The other gods can't know they are coming from us." He plucks the book out of my hand and sets it on the bed, then rubs my shoulders.

I bite my lip as I ponder. "We need those with pure hearts. I will teach the riders how to redraw the runes and use them. *They* can share the runes to everyone. Our fellow Gods will assume it's part of their magic, like the rider's mark."

"Power taints pure hearts, my love." He adds more pressure to melting the tension on my shoulders.

"When you cast a stone into the water, it's bound to ripple, but eventually, calmness will be restored." I grasp his face, willing hope into my touch. "This has to work; they must ally."

"I have no doubt it will, but remember, my love, alliances are only signed after much blood has been shed."

~

Two centuries later.

Swollen lips caress my blushed cheek. Erevan's warm breath stirs a purring in my body, but it can't erase all my tension. We made love all night, both of us filled with a deep anxiety and emotion over what the new day would bring.

I still think about what Erevan told me. He pressed a palm to my stomach and vowed that one day he'd find a way to give me a child of my own. A creature made of his magic and mine. I told him the book was that, for it was made of both our magic and love for one another. He promised to give me flesh and blood, not pages.

It's a lover's dream that can never be born into reality, but I will cherish the idea.

Dream.

Am I still your dream, Lucian? Are you able to dream where you are now?

I keep my eyes closed as the sunrise warms them, coaxing them out of hiding. My trembling hands grasp the balcony.

From this height, the world appears to be at our fingertips. A home above the clouds in a castle so high only our insight could have provided the creatures here the knowledge to build such a wonder.

Now, they build castles like this all over their lands. Eventually, all the wooden homes will be replaced with monuments that mimic our world.

They have come so far; I'm so proud of them.

Yet, just beyond these clouds, everything is about to change again. The castle we built here is surrounded.

By our army.

It's finally happening; we are returning home. Centuries later, our hope has come to fruition. We will return with an army of dragons, a few dozen demigods, and thousands of our other new creatures.

We didn't force them. Eventually, we revealed ourselves and gained devoted followers. At first, they called us gods. We refused to accept that title, asking only to be called by our names. They loved us even more. Respected us, unlike the elves.

When the elves called us gods, we smiled because it made us feel elevated and powerful.

We're trying so hard to learn from the past.

Slowly, I allow my eyes to open, like a child ready to explore a new world. I wonder how our lands have changed since we were forced out.

Flap! A leathery stretch pierces the silence. A gust of wind blows through the window. The dragon that sits perched on our stone roof is readying to fly soon. Its waking inhale sounds like wind rushing down a sunbaked dune.

"Do you think we have enough?" I whisper to Erevan as he moves my braided hair to the side so he can kiss my neck.

Once we leave this world, the balance will be offset again. This world and the creatures within it have been our children, but it's time for those who wish to remain to survive without us.

He nods. "Yes, and we have the act of surprise. The elves will have planned for our return, but not with an army like we have," Erevan replies as his arms snake around me, sending a warm shudder down my spine. "A part of me wants to demand you stay here." He runs his nose along my neck, the cold metal of his armor pressing into mine. "I want to put you in a crystal cage and make sure you are safe."

He nips at my skin, just above the armor that covers my shoulders.

Our armor was gifted by a dragon rider smith. The scales covering my armor are feminine and delicate, resembling lace, yet they are so numerous the lace looks more like a web that would ensnare you. It's a gift of such beauty it rivals even the book Erevan gave me, but I'd never tell him that.

Erevan's armor is equally stunning, cast in gold that has been forged under dragon fire, giving it swirls of red and burnish orange hues. It resembles the sun, with layers of fiery scales melting into one another.

I silently imagine Lucian here, standing on my other side, kissing my untouched cheek. His armor would be of pure white like he always wore it into battle. Untouched scales that blend in with the clouds.

My Lucian, you broke your promise. I never felt that final kiss. Perhaps if we fail, I will find him in the next life, as he vowed.

Erevan slides his hand along my back as he slowly comes to stand in front of me, blocking out the rising sun. "Stay behind until it is safe." He makes a lover's plea that falls on deaf ears.

I raise my chin. "You think we will lose?"

He cradles my jaw, tracing my lower lip with his thumb, as if he were the artist who made it. "No. I fear we will win," he admits, standing with such a glowing authority that he outshines that massive dying star.

"Fear has no invitation to dine with victory," I reply carefully. "What are you not telling me?" I step back.

Erevan licks his lips, weighing his next words carefully. "It's a worry I have had since the moment we first stepped through the portal and entered this land. The other gods hold a deep thirst for vengeance against you. They never acted on it because they needed me to create our army; they were forced to cooperate and accept you because I love you."

I was just a bow with no string or arrows. Useless in this new world.

The others would've abandoned me long ago.

Erevan gave me purpose. His magic became the arrow that kept the other gods away, his voice was the string. Because of his love for me, I was protected from their revenge.

"What will happen once we reclaim our lands, once we settle?" he whispers.

My armor conceals the tremble in my bones. Suddenly, everything feels too tight: my clothing, the braids in my hair. "You think they will come for me?"

His lips press into a thin line as his hand rests on his weapon.

"It's a risk I must take." I clear my throat. "I'm no coward. I will not stay behind. I will go back and fight for our lands. I will fix what I have done." I look at him through hooded eyes. "If you try to cage me, my love for you will melt like ice thrown onto fire."

His eyes skim over my face, but his hands swing behind his back as he grasps them. "Water and heat make steam, Amariel; the love is not lost but reborn into something else."

I touch my sword. "Do not test me, Erevan."

His chest rises and falls with a deep, steady breath. "I will not cage you here, my love." His shoulders roll back. "But I will kill anyone who tries to harm you."

I rub the hilt of my sword before I drop my hand. "No more talk of future wars, Erevan. We're still trying to end this one."

He steps to the side, causing the rising sun to illuminate half his face in a fiery glow. "Everything I do is out of my love for you," he declares, then nudges his head toward the door.

My feet remain firm, and a bead of sweat slowly rolls down my spine. For the first time, I don't turn my back on him. I stand still and wait, my eyes looking down at his arms, where he hides his hands behind his back.

"It is time," he urges as he takes the first step. "You need to open the portal. The army is waiting." His hands swing out, revealing nothing as he walks through the door.

When a god opens a portal to a new world, it subdues their magic for a few months, trapping the god in the world until their magic is recharged and they can open a portal again. Erevan opened the original portal to this world. During that time, we all worked to understand these lands and their people; then, when his magic was back, he started to create.

However, the others decided that I would open the portal ushering us back home. Putting me in a state with no magic to forge is a small price to pay. After all, it was my fault we had to flee in the first place.

Now I see the other side of the coin. I'll be defenseless against them... and Erevan.

I square my shoulders to the door. Was Erevan okay with this plan because I would have no magic, solely relying on him to defend me? I can fight, and I plan to, but I will be lesser until my power appears.

I shake the thought from my mind, steeling myself. Above all, I trust Erevan with my life.

I make my way outside, and Erevan holds his hand out for mine. His smile is warm and welcoming but also strained, like a pretty jacket that is slightly too tight.

"I'll be fine," I promise him as I take his hand.

"I know," he replies in a deeper tone.

Lord Thalis leaps down from the roof where his dragon is perched. Thalis is a fortress, tall and intimidating. Even I take caution and study him. His body bears scars equal in number to his dragon's scales. He refuses to use magic to remove them, as each is a memory of surviving death. His dark skin conceals his paleness about our leaving. A quick glance reveals the grief he hides.

He bows, greeting us, "Erevan and Amariel. Silas wishes to see you both before you leave."

My spine goes taut. Silas should be with the army of demigods; he is commanding them. Erevan and I are overseeing the dragons while the others command the rest.

"He is waiting for you in your office."

"*Our* office?" Erevan clarifies.

Thalis nods with a stiff glare. "I found it out of place. Evangeline wishes to stay close to you." He looks up at his dragon, who flares her wings.

Erevan waves his hand. "No, it's okay. I don't want him to see this as a threat. Silas always lets his suspicions control him. Amariel and I will speak with him. Make sure the dragons are ready. They will need to be fast."

Thalis nods and jumps up to the roof with ease. Riders can jump massive heights in order to reach their dragons' saddles.

I flex my fingers, pumping blood into the joints. It will drain me dry

31

to keep the portal open long enough for an entire army to pass through. I will need to hold it open longer than any god has. We're sending the dragons first since they're the largest; over time, my portal will grow smaller and smaller until it closes.

"What do you think Silas wishes to discuss?" I ask Erevan as we make our way down the stone stairs to our office.

As we descend, the clouds begin to clear. Erevan and I pause, finally glimpsing the armies below.

"Silas is like the wind; his thoughts blow in every direction," Erevan grunts as his eyes roam the warriors.

We expect Silas to be waiting outside, but he's entered uninvited. A glance at Erevan tells me he's pissed, but he's letting it slide since we must all stand united.

Silas has his back to us when we enter; his brown hair is pulled into a small braided bun. His armor is made of leather crafted by the fae. It stands no chance against the elves, but Silas is always the reckless one; his defense magic helps him create shields and veils that can deflect blows unless the attack is made with a God Sword.

"Making yourself at home," Erevan jabs, rolling his eyes.

"This was never our home," Silas fires back with a sneer. His palms are flattened on my desk as he looms over something of great interest.

Is he going over the maps again? None of us have forgotten our lands, but we continually drew maps to ensure the newcomers would not be lost to the great wonders of our world.

"I always had doubts," Silas adds with a measured calm.

Erevan shuts the door and pulls me close to his side, keeping one foot placed ahead of me.

"We have gone over the battle plan numerous times, Silas," Erevan sighs.

"Not of our return." Silas turns, revealing what held his interest.

My book sits open on the desk. Shock freezes me; I look up at Erevan, whose eyes scan my belongings, which we planned to bring.

"You overstepped!" Erevan rushes forward, about to grab Silas by the neck. A blink of Silas's eyes triggers his defense magic. Erevan's hand hits a veil.

"Your steps have been far more treacherous, Erevan." Silas's eyes loom over us, full of judgment. "I always doubted the runes were born naturally. They resembled Amariel's designs too closely. The lies you spun..." He flashes us a razor-sharp smirk. "The others were enchanted by them. You used your magic on them!" His laugh is more of a hiss. "They actually believed those designs were borne from your magic and that they resembled her art because you love her. But I had my suspicions; that's why I shielded my mind when you spoke."

The secret is finally out. "I had to make the runes in order to bring peace." I step forward, but Erevan blocks me. "I needed to create a balance. And I did. We have our army."

My palms sweat as I step out from behind Erevan.

"*You* are the imbalance, Amariel," Silas seethes. His shields rise, fully covering him. "If I had it my way, you'd be dead. It's your life that has disturbed everything. It can only be stilled when you die for your crimes. Only then can the requiems of war be sung."

"And what of your crimes?" Erevan spits back.

I swiftly avert my gaze, wiping away my tears. It's been centuries since the other gods cursed my hands and reminded me of what I made. Erevan's correct; the deep-seated anger towards me will quickly escalate after we gain control over Attkris. Once the elven war is over, I'll be their target.

"I never said I was without guilt." Silas slides his cold glare to Erevan, speaking coldly.

Erevan closes his fists and slams them into Silas's defensive magic. "Lower your shields and fight like a man," he growls.

"You forget, I am no man. I am a god." Silas chuckles when Erevan can't touch him.

"We left those titles behind when we felt the kiss of death. You can be killed. Threaten her again, and I will be the one to slay you."

"My debt to you is paid." Silas's smirk spreads slowly, then he points to my book of runes. "But that book will not be coming back with us." His eyes narrow.

"It's mine!" A precious gift that pulled me out of my depression. I lost my home and Lucian. That book gave me hope again.

"You lost the right to own anything!" Silas roars. "Your hands create nothing but tricks of death."

"The swords were a mistake," I cry. Erevan leaves my side, and from his belongings, he grabs *his* sword, the original blade I made for him. One of the last remaining God Swords in our possession. The sound of metal sliding against its sheath fills the air.

Yet Silas holds his ground. "You wish to kill me now? Do it." He tips his chin high. "All your efforts will be lost," he challenges.

We only have five God Swords here with us, but we all agreed they were too dangerous to bring back home, so we are leaving them here, gifting them to those who stay behind. Dragon fire has forged metal strong enough to withstand a few blows from a God Sword. Our armor and weapons are made from it.

However, there are still areas of vulnerability within its design. Should a God Sword pierce our flesh, we can still be slain.

"You cast a stone but forget your walls are made of air," Erevan seethes. "It was you who first mated with a human, so do not speak to me of our old and new laws."

Silas gave his sword away to his child last night. The first demigod. He bore children whom he will pass the sword down to, eventually. Erevan never confessed Silas's name to us; it was Silas's child who gave away his secret.

Silas's eye twitches. "The book stays behind, with the swords. Both are too dangerous if the elves get their hands on them."

Reaching out, I lower Erevan's hand, aiming the sword at the ground. "I can not leave the book behind. What if they abuse the pages?" *Endless pages.*

"You should have thought about that before you forged it." Silas crosses his arms; his eyes follow the tip of the sword as it presses into the stone floor.

"I created it," Erevan admits.

"It makes no difference. You gave her the material to create yet another weapon, you fool!" Silas bites. "Love has weakened you."

"And the loss of your love has hardened you," Erevan bites back.

I heard whispers of what happened to the human Silas mated with. Age stole her from him. But... "It can change, Silas. With this book, I can create a rune for you to use, a rune to grant prolonged life, to bind a human to you. You could find love again."

"I do not *want* love again! To you, love is a cut flower you trap in a vase; you admire it until it wilts, then replace it. I let my flowers grow untamed, refusing to confine them," he roars.

My knees falter. Before I fall, Erevan grabs me. I urge my legs to stand tall, then I say, "Flowers wilt and perish, but you forget they have seeds. I have never forgotten Lucian. I fight for him even now." I touch my heart, my chest caving in.

Silas leans forward, his voice but a hiss. "Your lips are unworthy of speaking his name."

"That is enough, Silas!" Erevan hollers.

Silas tilts his head. "You got what you wanted, didn't you, Erevan?"

Erevan exhales through clenched teeth. "What is that?"

Silas's sly smirk feels like scissors cutting thread. I look from Erevan to Silas. The air electrifies, and I step between them. "Let's stop arguing. Silas, I'm just trying to help. This book does that."

He angles his head towards me, but for too long, he watches Erevan. Finally, he speaks, "I don't doubt your passion when you forge items. I doubt your foresight. Rules, laws, and limits are still words you have not learned the definition of. I can not allow that book or anything else you created to come with us."

Erevan's earlier warning hits home. Once this war has ended, they will all try to cage me. Stop me from using my magic.

My hands yearn for my book. "Your love was of this world, Silas. If I leave the book behind, you damn her lands. There will always be someone who seeks to abuse. They will find my book and tarnish the good the runes have made."

"Then leave it here in these lands." Silas stomps his foot. "I will mask this kingdom with a veil of defense. Only the people we trust are here. Those who are staying behind are loyal. My veil will stop others from entering this land. If those inside wish to leave, they can, but the cost will be exile. The weapons we are leaving behind will be safe-guarded. You are not the only god who is forced to leave her tools behind."

"But what if it gets into the wrong hands..."

Silas aims an accusatory finger at me. "That's the question you should have pondered before you drew the first rune."

"What questions did you solve when you slept with the human? When she was pregnant with your child! You look down your nose at Erevan and I, but we were not the first to bring magic here! You were!" I shout back. My heart hammers against my armor. "You are to blame for the evil that is growing here. The evil the Genesis unleashed to purge our magic from her lands. A evil that hunts us all down!" This new evil is why so many of the magical creatures here wish to leave and come to Attkris. The only good is that its helped our army grow.

"How does it feel to know you started a war, Silas?" A menacing smile spreads over my lips. Our arrival on Panthas, did have repercus-sions. But that's another war story we can't take part in yet. I dread the day we do. It's unnatural for a child to kill their maker — for a God to murder a Genesis.

Silas's neck pulses. He blinks again. Erevan roars, fist pounding, but he can't reach me. Silas traps me in his shield. I raise my hand, trying to calm Erevan.

Silas steps closer. I hold my ground.

"I asked myself if watching her die of old age would be worth the few years of happiness, of freedom from you all. I asked myself the price our world would pay if I didn't return, if my absence disrupted the balance. I asked. I answered. I paid the price. For our world! I returned. I left my family behind for you. For our history. You dwell on fixing the past. I look to the future. That book will not be part of it, Amariel." He flicks his fingers, shoving me back into Erevan's arms.

Erevan holds me tight. "I think of the future," I whisper, voice broken.

Silas shakes his head, "If you did, you'd never pack that book. It is a weapon, just as the swords are. It stays behind. Who knows, maybe that book can help stop the evil that has taken root here. The army is ready," he barks, stepping to the side and staring at us down his nose.

Not once does he lower his shields.

Erevan nostrils flare. "Put the veil up first," he orders.

Silas's brow arches, but he agrees. He closes his eyes, jaw set firm. The air shifts as his body takes on a glowing hue of blue fire, like a star shooting through a night sky. The vein in his neck pulses as his muscles strain.

I know he's only doing this because this is where the love of his life lived. Where his son who has fallen in love with a fae lives. In the lands to the far northwest, under the shade of the mountains. Silas's first trip proved that leaving doesn't eliminate our magic from the lands. Magic can transcend distance. Therefore, returning with the book won't prevent the runes' effect on this world.

Two years of painstaking work went into copying my runes into a book, which now serves as my rune dictionary. Now, the people here can redraw existing runes. I presented the copied book as a gift to Lord Thalis, the dragon rider. However, if I must exchange books, those I've trained in rune drawing can create more. Runes I have not approved in the original book.

Erevan shifts. His armor is so lethally crafted it makes no sound when he moves. His eyes drift down to the God Sword in his hand.

"Perhaps..." I know what he's going to suggest before he utters it. "Perhaps the sword can destroy the book. It can kill us, so it should be able to kill our creations."

"You kill the book, and the runes will vanish. What of the dragon riders, of the humans who use these runes to remain equal? No! That is too cruel," I choke in horror. That book is like our child. Could he slay it so easily?

Erevan bites his lip. "I did not consider the riders."

I grab the sword from his hand. Silas's eyes snap open. "It is done. A veil of defense is up. It will hold." His eyes lock on my hands. "Give me the sword so I can give it to whom Erevan named last night." He comes forward, hand open.

Slowly, I raise the God Sword. I remember forging this one. For hours, I hammered the metal, pouring more strength into it. Too much. I cared for my creations too much.

I gasp when my fingers uncurl, and the sword falls into Silas's waiting hands. He holds Erevan's stare before he leaves the room, sword in hand.

Erevan glares at the book. It's the first time he's ever looked at it with disdain. He must feel as I did when I made those swords. It's shocking to be told your child is not only grotesque but also a tyrant. As parents, we try so hard to defend our creations, but sometimes that makes us blind.

I reach for the book and flip through the pages, recalling the moment I drew each rune. Then I reach the blank pages, knowing the book will never run out of them.

"Do you think they will draw new runes?" I ask as I flip the blank pages.

"I fear what we won't be able to draw. Silas does not realize this book is one of the strongest items ever made. It has the core magic of two gods fused." Erevan begins to pace the room, running a hand through his hair.

I pick up the book, press it to my chest, and kiss the front cover.

"Amariel." Erevan stops. "Give me the book."

"Why?" I hand it over, furrowing my brow.

He doesn't answer as he places it on the desk and starts taking deep breaths.

"What are you doing?" I whisper.

His eyes close, magic seeps out, but it is not his magic!

I knew it! He does harbor another god's core magic!

Shimmers of black grasp the page like spiderwebs, covering it entirely. "That's Tova's magic," A tear slides down my cheek. Tova, was the God of Replication. She was the third of us to be slayed.

Erevan sings his enchantment magic, forcing it to mix with Tova's; then, using his small dagger, he slices his palm, infusing his blood into it. He inhales sharply as the magic disintegrates, dancing in the air. The book shakes, then it stills.

Erevan grunts. Suddenly, he grabs my hand. His magic seeps into my skin, finding my magic. He tugs at my core.

I allow him to grab hold of it. To take a part of me without permission.

Erevan stumbles forward, crashing into the desk.

"What did you do?" I help steady him, but my stomach feels adrift.

Loving him gave him the key to my magic. He's never taken a piece of it before, but he did just now. I let him.

"I replicated the book," Erevan answers as he studies his hand, "It's magic to forge runes is within me now."

"You had Tova's magic." I whisper in a breathless horror. "Why did you not tell me?"

"I made a deal with Tova for a large piece of her core magic, long before you figured out how to master starfire, Amariel. I honestly forgot, it's been a hidden dagger I just remembered I had. This is good news, my love. We can still make runes."

"*You* can make runes," I correct him. I can't without my book. My eyes blur with painful tears from not having blinked. All of my blood has drained into the pits of my hollow stomach.

"Don't look at me like that. Everything I do is for you." The yellow in his brown eyes darkens.

I want to step back, but I'm frozen in place. My emotions are a thunderstorm coloring my cheeks in a hot red fire. "You stole a piece of my magic. My ability to forge was within those pages." I glare at his hands.

"Stole?" He recoils slightly. "I'm keeping it safe. *You* safe."

Me or my magic?

"We don't have time for this. Do not let Silas drive a wedge between us. He is jealous of our love." With visible effort, he stands tall. He takes a few deep breaths, and then his complexion returns to a healthy glow. Erevan takes my hand. "I will tell Lord Thalis of the book. He and his dragon shall watch over it. We will take the copy."

I can't stop looking at his fingers. What can he forge with them now?

"It's time." He guides me to the door. I look back at the book, just as I did with Lucian. Longing, regret over my decisions, a terrible feeling I'm about to lose again, bombard my mind, turning me into a shell that is easily occupied by others.

Just like last time, I numbly follow Erevan. Because I love him, just as I loved Lucian. I obey there orders.

"It's all going to work out as planned." Erevan squeezes my hand, but keeps his sights ahead.

Was coming to Panthas really ever our plan? Was it truly meant to save the gods?

Erevan presented it.

It's always been *his* plan.

Silas was wrong. It's not *me* who is the imbalance.

TORIN

I always thought my last breath would be painful, filled with lost dreams and the time needed to accomplish them. I thought I would have sealed my lips shut as I tried to hold that last exhale in my lungs. I would have begged the divine heavens to give me just one more day, one more hour.

I was wrong. Utterly, bitterly wrong.

A smile curls my lips as I push out every last drop of my dying breath into the stale air that crackles with my magic.

Having all my power ripped and forced out of my body will be...

unimaginable. There is beauty in debauchery; it's free, wild, and untamed. It's not delicately pretty and poised.

The sword hangs in my hand, covered in my blood, the ultimate show of my devotion to my world. The drip-drop of my blood echoes in these cavernous, hollowed-out walls that once belonged to a king. Now, the remnants of the castle lay buried in a cursed land. Once known as Caldara, famed for its outrageous luxuries, thanks to the mines hidden beneath its soil.

They dug too deep. Weakened the land. It swallowed them in return.

Most died the day it sank. Those who escaped whispered that the gods had cursed the land. A tale that serves me well—no one dares come here.

The ground is riddled with sinkholes that open into tapped-out mines. A few escape tunnels, buried deep in the mountain and unseen, are all that remain. A hidden location I discovered in a book I burned. These walls are nothing more than a skeleton. A perfect place to hide a terrible weapon.

I was born a fae, but I will die like a human—magicless, just flesh and bone.

Now I understand why so many humans want to remain in their natural state. It makes life more precious, less endless, more important.

In our lands, which rage and fester with war, the feeling of importance is hard to find when lives are snuffed out faster than eyes can blink.

My people never accepted me. I was an outcast, never understood. No one even tried. So I sank back, hid in the shadows, and tried my best to remain unseen.

That was better than being rejected.

What will they think of me now? Savior to all.

The stolen book, which we call the Vitalis, weighs heavily in my dying hands. A book the gods left for us. Some praise it, but I know the truth: it was a test we failed. It's a book meant to bring about our downfall. A book that houses all the runes and gives them life.

I was hardly the first thief who stole this book from the veiled lands now known as Lunestra. Therefore, my guilt is no more than a single leaf dancing in the wind.

The others are to blame; their guilt hangs as heavy as an age-old timber fallen to the scorched earth.

I, Torin Lochenhiem, am determined to end the War of Broken Oaths, an era in which rune magic runs rampant and laws are erased to create new runes. Balance has been severed by the excessive use of runes. Symbols that once brought peace can no longer be trusted, for whoever possesses this book controls everything.

More. *More.* They all want more, no matter the cost.

Our lands are dying; the sky is dark from the endless pyres, and the rivers have more cracks than the faces of elderly humans. Yet the leaders of our lands, the kings and queens, look the other way. Instead of putting laws and regulations around runes, they just create more, thinking that will fix the problem.

You can't fix a problem *with* the problem.

So, I dedicated my life to finding a way to stop the madness. I know it sounds insane, but I am a child of this mad world. It's the insanity I vow to stop.

I know that the gods are on my side; they are! We are their children, and the hardest plight a parent can endure is watching their child fail and die.

My first test was stealing the sword of Obryn, a demigod who preferred the pages of his books to his family's legacy. That sword, handed down throughout his powerful family, was covered in dust, having never been touched by his hands.

For years, I acted as his loyal servant. It was so simple to take it as he slumbered.

Getting my hands on the Vitalis was much harder, but I managed to do it. Me!

Once I had the Vitalis in my possession, I became the most wanted person in the world. I tried to destroy the book using Obryn's sword, which was said to have ungodly powers. But when I pressed the sharp blade into the cover, it did not yield. Instead, it released a magical pulse that almost killed me.

That's when I realized the book was not an object but a creature; its cover possessed some type of protection magic.

But what if I found its soft belly? What then?

I flipped open the book and glared at the pages, knowing they held power, but every creature had a weakness. In a fury, I struck the sword down onto the paper.

That worked!

A page was sliced free from the book, and as it fell to the floor, the rune on it vanished. But then another blank page appeared in its place. I cut the blank pages out, over and over again, but still it healed! I knew even if I cut out all the pages that were marked, more blank ones would appear, ready and waiting for another's hand to draw upon them.

That's when the gods blessed me with a new idea. The Vitalis is a beast that can't be killed, but... it can be caged. My first thought was to make a rune that would cage the book, sealing off its magic to those who have runes on their skin.

But if the magic were sealed off, then the cage made of a rune would stop working.

"Just a few... more..."

Ugh! Gods bless me.

"Steps!" I gasp as I stumble forward.

During my years of research, I discovered a truth the world tried to conceal from the fae. Fae magic differs from others. When a fae releases their dying breath, they can choose to give their magic to another or have it released back into our world.

But that's not all.

They can place rules over their magic, just like mixing ingredients before putting them in an oven to bake.

That's why the knowledge was hidden. It prevents one family line from inheriting multiple powers.

Since the Vitalis is a creature... I should be able to order my magic into it. But giving the book more magic isn't what I intend to do. I want to turn my magic into a cage that is strong enough to trap the most dangerous book in our world.

What better cage than death? The magic I happen to possess.

I just need the perfect location, one long forgotten and cursed, to hide the book in, and then I will stab the inner pages with Obryn's sword, cutting off the rune magic from the world.

With trembling hands and tired eyes, I set the Vitalis on the stone floor. *Thump!* The sheer magical weight of the book makes my toes curl and the ground tremble.

Drip, drip! My blood dribbles from my bleeding heart and onto the book. I felt little pain when I plunged the dagger into my heart. Only hope. For my death would release my magic and cast the world into light again.

Like a predator's wings, I extend the cover of the book back, exposing the soft pages. The book releases a whimper. I press the exposed pages against the cold, unforgiving stone. With them pinned, I lift Obryn's sword.

Touching the blade gives me a dangerous strength that makes my death feel farther away. I plunge the sword through the pages easily; to my amazement, the weapon buries itself into the stone floor as well.

For a moment, the book trembles like a cat's tail under my boot. It releases another whimper.

Then... *boom!*

The ground quakes as the entire world feels a tremor. The runes inked on the pages grow faint and sickly as the wound from the sword pins them down in a prolonged state of torture. I watch as the runes attempt to heal themselves, but the sword prevents them from doing so fully. For as long as this sword remains stabbing the pages, their magic will be cut off.

Letting go of the sword, I push up the sleeve of my tunic; the fabric is heavy from the weight of my blood. There on my inner wrist is the rune I used to help me steal the book. The thick lines slowly begin to fade until they are nothing more than an old scar, barely visible but certainly remembered.

"It worked!" I cry as my smile burns. I have cut off the magic of the runes from the world. "I did it. I saved us." Tears fall from my eyes, mixing with my lifeblood.

Then it happens: the last string that holds my magic to my soul is cut. The pain is so immense it rivals the fear of death itself. A wave of light leaps from my body. The shades of colors are unnamed in this world, spectrums of such beauty, I think not even the greatest poet could pen a name to them.

"Beautiful," I whisper in awe, my voice barely audible.

My magic swirls and roars as it seeks to be set free or attached again like a child unsure whether it should leave the nest or cling back to its mother's arms.

"I order you to cage this book, here on this slab, so it can never be moved; should anyone touch you, you shall strike them dead. For none can rival death but itself," I command.

My magic vibrates as it swirls, listening to me like a good, loyal pet. It surrounds the stone slab where the book is stabbed, forever stuck in a frozen state of life and death.

They will remember me as their hero!

Of course, some will call me a foe, but they will be erased from history. Sacrifices must be made.

Some will suffer more losses; for instance, the dragon riders will lose control of their winged beasts without the runes. Yes, that means the dragons will be hunted down and killed again, but what use do we have for those massive beasts?

Those riders sit so high and mighty on their scaly, overgrown lizards as if they were gods trying to make us see reason.

I never liked the dragons or their riders. They speak a strange language and don't teach others how to understand it. They are hiding things; I sense it. They patrol the skies and dig up the earth, searching for the book, but it was I, a fae without a dragon, who found it. Me!

The riders deserve a downfall. Many need to be humbled. And so they shall.

My back hits the floor, and the last sight I see is my magic encasing the Vitalis. It's like a flower. Its beauty tempts the thief, and when they lean in to take it, it releases its poison.

Now all the runes marked on their greedy flesh will be nothing more than faint scars. No magic flows through them.

Silence. Ah yes, that's it, nothing. I just want all their greed to be silent.

Now it will be.

ONE

SELENE

One thousand years later.

Hands grasp my hips, guiding them up and down with more force than I could have thrust them. "Gods, yes, Selene," Galen, my husband, groans as a sheen of sweat drips down his temple.

Even from this angle, with me on top and him lying flat on the bed, he looks like a king, taking what he wants with pride and confidence as he guides my hips.

The man doesn't fight on the battlefield; his face is too pretty. Seriously, it's stunning. Square jaw, clean-shaven, shiny brown hair cut to the perfect manly length. Not too long or short. His body—well, shit—look at it thrusting into me. Abs, biceps, those thighs. He's not an old, ugly toad.

Silver linings, right?

He's bred for this. Claiming a body.

I admit it's attractive to watch him like this.

Just like my husband, I prefer to take what I want. Just because I have the absence of a cock between my legs doesn't mean I don't want to enjoy life.

Stop lying; you're numbing yourself.

Trust me, the world would rather I be indifferent than emotional. The last time I looked deep inside my mind, I saw nothing but vengeance. It's still there, coating my tongue, tainting everything I swallow.

Seconds, minutes, and hours I have tolerated. I will continue to play this role until retribution arrives. I'll be the good, dutiful wife who flirts with her husband.

"There's that look of wildness in your eyes." Galen cups my cheeks. "It only comes out for me," he boasts.

He's right. Princesses are slightly off; we're taught to be persuasive, to disregard normalcy, to seek out rarities, to have our ears always listening but our smiles smooth and welcoming.

But then again, we are also taught to bend a knee.

Why should my knees bend? I have royal blood, just like my husband. He can press his knees into the soil and kiss my shoes! Shoes that have stepped on more battlefields than his!

That will never happen.

I know. Women have dreams. Men have crowns and freedom.

I can't help but wonder which reality is more forgiving?

"Selene," Galen grunts as his eyes roll back, his clean-shaven chin tipping up. If we were sweet and loving, I'd bend down and kiss his jawline. "If your muscles clench any tighter, my dick is going to snap in half," he chuckles deliriously.

Relax. Your pain is giving your prick of a husband more pleasure.

Am I scorned? Yes, you would be if you were in my shoes.

And my shoes? They are so tight that they only cause pain. Each step I take is meant to involve some form of suffering.

A lady's plight, that's what they call it.

Women are taught to endure pain; men are taught to hunt it down and end it.

They raised me to be like this, absolutely mad, seething with anger, yet that emotional instability makes me feel. That will be my undoing.

"Learn how to handle me, husband. Otherwise, I'll find a replacement." I roll my hips.

Oh, sex with him is good, I admit it.

Smack! His palm stings my ass. "I would love nothing more than to see you try." His grin's as wicked as a snake reeling back before it bites. Mesmerizing.

Did I mention my husband is off-kilter as well? Our poor children have no chance.

Let's just say our marriage is unconventional, but somehow it works. Usually, that's only when his cock is inside of me. It's a rare time Galen stops talking and just takes what I give him.

I'm going to win this round. Yes, round, because everything—every smile, frown, banter, kiss, hookup—is a game.

In the end, it's me versus him.

"I'm close," I purr as I press my palms on his hard chest. His muscles flex under my touch. He's on the edge.

Yes, right there. That's it! My head tips back as my climax hits me. My long black hair brushes against my ass as Galen joins me, grunting and cursing like the brute he is but often hides.

My body begs me to fall limp, exhausted from the pleasure. *Okay, he can leave now.* Finally, I collapse against him. We only talk if we bicker; it's fuel for our sexual banter. It's what got us into bed in the first place.

This is a marriage of arrangement, not of partnership. I have to guard my heart.

If I show it to Galen, he'll destroy it.

Do I hate my husband? Yes.

Do I hate him all the time? Debatable.

Do I want to fall in love with him and have a happy marriage? I don't know. Only one person ever hugged me, and he's dead.

Yes, Galen is trying much harder than I thought he would. I mean, the things he can do with his mouth are pleasantly surprising. But no matter how hot the sex is, we're enemies. He's a vampire, and I'm a fae.

Winning my heart is just another weapon he wants to use against my people. 'Look, I stole your princess's heart. I plundered something else from you.' That's what his kind gestures truly say.

The first two months of my arranged marriage were absolute anarchy; then, I thought, why can't I have sex as I suffer? Galen was sleeping around, after all.

So we sleep together.

We continue to. Each time I come moaning Galen's name, he thinks he's breaking me down. Slowly, he hopes and prays I'll love and worship him as everyone else does.

But marriage shouldn't prioritize one person's satisfaction over another's. There are two people, and Galen fails to see what would have truly satisfied my soul. He thinks his cock can bring world peace. Men forget it's their cocks that cause wars. Egos are the downfall of kingdoms.

"You know," Galen swings his hand under his head, "if you kill me, there will be another war."

"Kill you?" I roll off of him, allowing myself one minute to rest on the mattress.

"Yes." He turns toward me, eyes aimed at my bare chest, at the faint red marks where his lips sucked. "I thought I might die from how tight your sweet body was squeezing me, begging me for more, harder. You fuck me so good, Selene."

Yes, it does seem like I do all the work. "You're not just a king but a poet, I see." I roll my eyes. Gods, help me.

"There's that mouth. I missed it," he quips.

"It was wrapped around you only minutes ago."

He smirks. "Where it should always be."

"I don't know why I sleep with you," I grunt. I'm a failure as a woman. I should have been born a man.

"Because the sex is the best you've had." His lips meet mine, but the kiss is fast; he got what he wanted, and he's ready to go on his merry way.

As am I.

"How many women has that line worked on?"

He rolls off the bed with newfound energy. That's a fine-sculpted ass; a shame it's attached to a prick who wears a crown. I watch as he bends down and starts to collect his clothing.

"None as smart as you, wife." He winks at me over his broad shoulders.

"Are you still sleeping with others?"

He doesn't miss a beat, answering right away. "You keep me very occupied." He flashes me his famous smirk.

That's not a yes or no answer.

I stand and grab a sheet to cover myself.

"Where are you off to?" Galen asks, pulling up his pants and shoving his now soft cock inside.

I'm sure your spies will tell you.

"I have things to do," I mock. He refuses to include me in his schedule. I'm a trophy, not a wife.

I drop the sheet. His eyes lock onto my ass now.

Good. Suffer.

His footsteps close the distance, and then warmth covers my back. I have always been attracted to heat. Hot baths are a godsend; so is a man's hard chest.

His exhale presses into my spine as he hugs me from behind. "Is this your kingdom or mine?" he purrs in my ear. I can feel him growing hard again as his hands cup my breasts.

Hmm, I suppose I can fit in one more session. I tip my head back, resting it on his shoulder.

"Ours?" I challenge. *That shut you up fast, Galen. Is a crowned woman too frightening?* I wiggle my ass against him, testing him. "Scared?"

Cold air replaces the space where his hands were; my next breath is half as large as his fingers grip my neck. Is that meant to scare me?

He twists my neck like a doll, turning it so he can kiss me.

I go limp as I'm trapped between his hard muscles and flesh, not a bad place to be when I'm in the mood for it. His tongue is hot and angry, king-like, as it slips into my mouth, seizing my lips and then fighting my angry tongue back.

This kiss is a battle of willpower.

What will I do? I'll let him win; he can take over control now, but little does he know I won because I allowed him.

This is about survival. I will not be a mindless queen who eats cake, sits on a throne, zones out as she drinks her troubles away, and spreads her legs for her king to plant his seed, only to watch him leave to bed another.

If we want change, who do we expect will grant it to us? The men certainly won't. No one hands over power; it's too addictive.

Unlike the men surrounding this castle, I don't want more power. I just want one thing.

One tiny, insignificant life.

I want revenge, but not against an entire kingdom.

See? I can be agreeable.

I just want one life. One heart that doesn't deserve to produce another breath.

Not Galen. Not a king's head, nor a nobleman's neck. One tiny soldier is all I ask.

I need to wrap Galen around my finger. Then I'll ask him.

"You are the Queen of Blackthorn." His left hand slides down my stomach, teasing my hip bone before he inches it lower. "You can rule with me in front of my kingdom."

Your kingdom? Galen, hubby, you might want to revisit your understanding of possessive pronouns.

"But in this room,"—he pushes three fingers inside of me as he kisses and sucks my neck—"I rule; you will bend and bow down to me."

"What if I don't?" I start to move my hips, craving friction.

You see why I hate this man? He uses sex as a tool to torment me, but I learn fast. I can do the same to him.

Iron sharpens iron, right?

I'm giving Galen a taste of his own medicine. Using my body as a weapon.

"Then I'll keep giving you lessons until you learn."

We gave each other lessons all week long.

Ask, and you shall receive.

Not.

Warm rays of sunlight blanket my skin. I roll my shoulders back and sigh. I tip my chin up, almost tempted to open my eyes and look into the sun.

"Don't let him win." My whisper is a chisel carving my wrath into my heart.

My eyes snap open. My nostrils flare. A faint scent of spice drifts in the air. The cool stone presses into my skin as I lean against the balcony.

The royal gardens blur; my gaze darts, swifter than a hawk diving for prey.

There, the markets. Distance hums of songs and cheer stretch across the grounds to reach my ears. Stalls overflow with goods now that the borders have been reopened. Even the lower markets, too far to be seen from my vantage point, share in the festivities.

That is why my husband doesn't want me to leave the inner walls. The hatred between vampires and fae still lingers.

Sex with a vampire can only cure contempt for so long. Galen and I are not enemies-to-lovers; we are enemies-*and*-lovers. The 'and' is like a valley that keeps two mountains separated. It will never be filled. Mountains don't cross paths overnight; it takes centuries to inch closer.

That's a very long time. I'm willing to bet one of us will kill the other before then.

And after what my husband is about to do, his death is imminent.

No matter how many times I let Galen thrust into me, he still wants the attention of his people over the respect of his queen. So, I have no choice but to move on with my new plan.

Destroying the one thing he adores. His public image.

'*It's what the people want,*' he claimed.

It's been only one year since the vampires and fae declared peace. The era of The King's War was finally over. It's as if the soil of this world were mere fabric we assumed we could grab and sew into a quilt of our own desires.

Do those men who stole the land consider the plight women had to endure when sewing it back together? How mothers grieve sons and daughters who died in battle, how we are forced to be maidens again, who are hostesses that bring cheer to their guests, regardless of who the guests are?

That's why men are such great rulers. They take, they don't care. They lack the empathy that women possess. Women think and consider what we want, but by then, it's gone. We are left with nothing.

I did consider my marriage to Galen. Yes, we are enemies, but maybe if he saw how strong I was, that could change.

Galen was shocked at my demand.

What do men do when they face someone as strong as they are?

They test them and plunge a knife in their back. They get rid of them, or if they are truly tyrannical kings, they keep them, make them feel less than, force them to heel, like you would a dog.

As Galen meets with his council, he thinks I have bowed down and accepted his rejection.

"Think again," I whisper as I laugh bitterly under my breath.

"Queen Selene." My lady's maid steps out onto the balcony with a red velvet box in hand.

I don't know her name, and yes, that makes me a bitch, but she's also a spy for my husband, so that makes her a bitch, too.

I was not allowed to choose my ladies, but I was granted the choice of decorating my chambers, so there's that. That should make me happy and agreeable, right?

My chest sinks. *Don't be a spoiled brat. Smile. Wider, yes, show your teeth.*

It hurts my cheeks to smile this widely.

Too bad.

My eyes lock on the box she has in her hands. "Another gift from the king?" I ask.

I don't want his gifts. I want him to do one thing for *me* and not the crown!

This marriage isn't an alliance!

Don't let the term *alliance* trick you. It's always a precursor to war. Every other kingdom out there knows it, and they are preparing because kings like only two things. No, it's not women and ale, jewels and crowns.

They like armies and land.

And now that my husband has my father's backing, no other vampire king will dare challenge him. In fact, Galen will make it a point to march on our neighboring kingdoms to claim more land.

Soft fabric brushes my fingers as the maid gently pushes the gift into my hands. "He has sent an outfit for tonight's feast, as well," she says gently.

I eye the balcony. *Should I throw myself off?*

The number of feasts we have is causing my waist to grow. Even fae have to watch what we eat, just like the humans and mages do. "What is tonight's dinner for?" I ask as I stare at the box; the plush velvet is smooth as water, and the fabric alone is worth a gold coin.

It's heavy. Much too large to be earrings or a bracelet. Maybe he finally decided to collar me like the dog I feel like I am.

My maid glances down toward the market. "The feast is for the arrival of the Western squad. I believe a new general is to be named at the dinner." Her tone is sharp and fast, like a fox running for its life as wolves chase it.

Each time a new general or leader deserving of praise comes back to the castle, the king throws a feast in his or her honor. He usually gives them land or titles, which is followed by another feast. Then, one more feast to send them on their way.

"What new general?" I demand. My vision pulses in sync with my furious heart. The box begins to slide from my sweltering grip.

"General Titus Tarragon, my Queen."

You did it, Galen. You made sure I would never, ever love you!

My last hope that Galen would give in is choked off.

The box drops from my hands. My lady's maid dives for it as if it were a newborn.

And me? I am on the verge of collapsing.

She reaches for my trembling hands and places the gift back into them, forcing me to accept it. "I'm sorry," she whispers.

"You have nothing to be sorry for. This is the price of war." Kings, princes, fathers, sons, brothers... they all die.

Just like my brother did.

War ignores titles. It's the only time we're all equal and can show how monstrous we are. That's the only way to survive.

"Would you like me to start a bath for you? I can have a bottle of wine brought to you."

Is she offering me death? To drink myself into a slumber? The water can grant me an exit.

I know Galen parades me like his trophy. I can accept that, but I want his respect along with his cock. Oh, and one more thing. I don't want him to give a title to the man he was throwing a feast for tonight!

So many women often drink away their sorrows. I refuse to be one of them.

"Tell the smith to have my bow ready," I coldly declare.

The maid's face pales, but she nods and rushes out of the room. I scare the women in this court because I like to hold a bow more than a limp, drunken cock. My knife skills are better suited carving my arrows than chopping vegetables for dinner.

It earns me respect from many of my husband's soldiers, but it fuels gossip among the chattering females. Neither of which Galen likes. He doesn't want his men to respect me because I can fight, so he has built me a training field hidden from their eyes. A place of solace I actually do enjoy.

Sable, my twin, also wields weapons. Galen let's her roam this castle freely. Hers manifest in a sharp tongue and a wealth of hidden secrets. She endures the long parties, drinks with the wives, flirts, and fucks the men.

They fail to see how she stops drinking and listens, collecting all their secrets.

Blades dull with use, but secrets are like diamonds, never chipping as they strike. The only thing that can destroy them is another diamond, another secret.

Sable is a rock that absorbs everything: cold-hearted, unmoving, uncaring. Unlike a sponge, you can never squeeze Sable; you can never make her release anything unless it was on her terms. She's much better at playing the role of a royal woman, but make no mistake—she is as conniving and vicious as a kingslayer.

You think I'm bad? Sable's a new definition. As the second-born, she was taught she was less than, so she is determined to become more than everyone.

I slap my fist on the balcony, bracing it. "You knew this day would come and smack you in the face, so just make sure you don't turn your head from the force of the blow. Don't let them see how it affects you," I hiss.

I clench my abs tight and shove away my tears.

I have never seen the soldier named Titus; oh, apologies, I mean *General* Titus. Ballads about him have reached my ears.

They haunt me, keep me awake, which allowed me the endless nights I needed in order to form a plan to kill him.

I'm going to get my revenge, whether my husband agrees or not.

Ballad of the Heart Thief

Hair black as night, sword held tight; Titus charged forth with a soldiers might.

Target in sight, he was ready to fight.

He aimed his dagger, causing the fae prince to stagger.

With one firm slice, he cut the prince open nice. Tore out his heart with just one dice!

He shoved the prince back, dropped him like stone, then claimed victory for our king to own.

And just like that, the war was done. Another crown was claimed, and all was said and done.

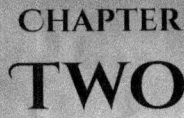

TITUS

Twelve months earlier.

Birds circle overhead. Hundreds, perhaps thousands. They dart through the sky, causing the last rays of light to flicker through their gliding wings in a frantic chaos of blinking madness. They wait more patiently than our kings do for their prey. Strong winds carry the stench of death over a large area.

I raise my foot and step over the arm of one of the fallen. Glancing downwards, I witness his last look towards the sky, where birds are poised to feast.

I have enough magic for one more body to burn. I wait one more moment, ensuring his soul leaves his body. I wish I could wait longer, but the battle rages on. I wave my hand over him, releasing my flames. The cotton fabric under his leather catches fire.

I turn my eyes away as it reaches his flesh. "Be at peace, brother."

Many of my fellow soldiers think I'm a fool for not using my magic as a weapon. I could have burned through my enemies with my magic instead of my sword. Maybe one day, if all my hope and morals vanish, I will.

Dying gasps are more familiar to my ears than genuine laughs these days. The battle rages around me; vampires and fae clash as swords and magic tear and dig into flesh, bone, and dirt. War renders even the soil unsafe.

This is my daily life. Blood washes my hands more often than water does. The war between the vampire territory of Blackthorn, ruled by King Galen, and the fae kingdom of Solaria, ruled by King Aridel, is as endless as the sun chasing the moon across the sky.

Unceasing.

I see no end in sight. So, I embrace it. My sword becomes an extension of my arm, my fire magic a way to apologize and send off the dead with respect.

I know I will perish like the men and women I kill. My last cries will go unheard; my tears of mercy will sink into the dirt.

No requiems are sung for the dead anymore.

I've come to terms with that.

I shove my sword into the belly of a fae that runs towards me and pull it out before he can blink.

Why didn't he wear armor? Was it ruined in the previous battles? Or is he perhaps a mere stable boy who had the hay held in his hands replaced with a dull blade?

Does Aridel's army lack supplies, or does this boy desire peace? Maybe death was his path to freedom.

We're ingredients in a boiling stew, forced to clang and clash, each one jostling against the other. We have been battling for hours, and the chill of the rising moon now replaces the burning sun. The majority of vampires and fae have long since used up their magic.

We are down to swords and fists. Hands can cause unimaginable damage, but our tongues can scar deeper.

Fae need hours to replenish their magic, and vampires need human blood. But it's hard to find a moment to drink blood when magic and swords are racing to kill you.

I spot my younger brother, Tristen, as he swings his sword, just like I taught him. Metal clashes, then screeches as the blades fight for victory.

Another body falls. Tristen adds another tally to his death sheet.

I wonder how Ryker is doing. Gods, I pray he's safe. He was sent on an ambush mission. I search the fields for Nero, Cyrus, and Ember, but the fighting has scattered us. Like the threads of a fraying sweater, we are barely able to stay connected and remain whole.

Another blade swings towards me. I deflect it and meet the eyes of a vampire. He swings again, his sword almost slicing my neck. His brown eyes are wild as mist, fogging his vision and thickening his terror.

"Hey!" I shout. "I'm on your side. I'm a vampire!"

He swings three more times until he blinks, lost and confused, his hands shaking. "I'm... I'm sorry," he mutters. A deep seed of emotion blooms in his eyes.

I don't like it.

I grab the back of his neck and press him to my chest, holding him as I try to steer us out of the thick of the fighting. "Go!" I push him. "Fall back. You're injured."

He looks down at his body. "But I'm not."

We lock eyes. *There, you understand. Your mind is gravely wounded, my friend.* "Go rest."

"Rest. I... I like the sound of that," he whispers to himself as his eyes comb through the sea of dead bodies littering the ground.

"Go," I order in a gentle tone.

He nods, stumbling as he walks a short distance. I want to grab him, to take him myself, but I can't risk leaving my brother on the field.

Why's he unbuckling his breastplate?

Our armor isn't terribly heavy, but my leather straps are so crusted and stiff with blood that it makes my movements challenging. Rumor has it that mages are trying to enhance fabric with magic, eliminating the need for metal armor. Unfortunately, that technology hasn't yet reached our land. Soon, it will. I hope it makes the fighting shorter and the death swifter. Any mercy helps.

Mages and humans are the best at innovation; it's fae and vampires who turn those inventions into weapons.

The vampire tosses his breastplate onto the bodies. He tips his chin up as he raises his hand.

"Wait!" I scream. "Don't!" I trip and land on something soft. My poleyns become warm and sticky, making my leathers wet and soaking my knees.

My throat tightens with dread when I look down. I've fallen on a fae corpse; my mouth parts as I gasp, pushing my chin into the sliced-open entrails. Stench and rot choke me. I stand up clumsily, trying to ignore the atrocities of war, and focus on helping my fellow soldier.

He thrust his sword down directly into his heart. A fatal blow to any magical creature. His knees fall before I can make it to him.

My eyes burn with dryness, but I can't blink. My hearing dulls into a sharp whistle. My body tingles. My throat rolls, but I can't swallow. "Rest now, brother," I manage to rasp.

I grip my sword. My morals leave. I want to lash out. I spot easy prey, a fae bent over a dying one, hands held as they voice their good-byes. I could raise my sword and allow him to join his friend. He'd be easy to ambush.

Stop!

Think!

Your wrath is misdirected.

Sparing souls will be what kills me. A clever man seizes opportunities to eliminate his foe.

The hairs on my neck stand on end, shaking the sweat that clings to them. It drips down my back.

Gods, I want to rip off my armor so my skin can find relief from the weight and rashes it causes.

I turn just in time to see a fae warrior staring me down. His green armor is stained red, where the embossed leaves have been etched into the metal, and now blood fills the pattern. His left arm's armor is torn off. His face is covered in grime like my own, but his eyes are sharp—a predator trying to survive a cruel winter in order to see spring flowers where easy prey roam.

Why do I feel like I'm looking into a mirror? What is scarier? Deep down, I know he feels the same way.

I inch back. *Don't do that; now he knows you're scared.*

A strange sense overtakes me. He's a kindred spirit.

I never pause during battle. The moment you do, you are dead, but like I allowed the fae to say goodbye to his fellow soldier, this fae allows me to watch him.

Why didn't he stab me in the back?

I pause; my breath is labored, and my muscles ache. I clutch my sword, willing my body to pour more adrenaline into my veins.

I desperately need a pint of blood!

That's why it's vital that vampires don't solely rely on blood. You need to be skilled with a sword in order to survive. The king often overlooks this, which costs him thousands of vampire soldiers.

I widen my stance, feeling the mud grow slick from all the blood covering it.

"You should have struck!" I shout, my mouth drier and more porous than the rocks volcanoes produce.

Can he even hear me over the fighting?

He continues to watch me, like an owl assessing something that caught its wide, ever-watchful eyes; his large sword is in one hand, but his other palm is open with the smallest hint of magic.

Shit! How the hell does he still have access to it?

Have the fae sent in reserves? If so, we're all dead.

My neck starts to turn in search of my brother, but years of training snap my focus onto the biggest threat.

"Why didn't *you*?" His reply surprises me.

I never talk to fae before I kill them. It makes them seem more like me: a soldier, duty-bound to follow orders, even when he loathes them. Killing your kind—I'm not talking fae or vampire. I mean, a person—that's never easy.

I won't blame, nor hate, the man or woman who bests me. It's just the way war is.

One day, it will slay you.

He moves his index finger.

What is that? I shake my arms out. Something odd seems to have feathered over my skin. All the cries and shouts of the battle become a faint buzzing in my ear.

He steps closer but maintains a fighting stance. Fae and vampires blur behind him as the fighting continues, but the soldiers move slowly; each hit and swing of their weapons is like lifting a mountain.

What's happening?

"You could have executed the fae easily," he states smoothly.

He's been stalking me. I nod and start pumping blood into my fingers. "He was saying goodbye."

"Why did you grant his desire?" he questions.

He really is like a goddamn owl! High and mighty, perched on a branch, just watching and questioning. He treats our conversation as if we are two nobles sitting at a table of finery; I imagine the scent of meats and ale instead of death and the battle surrounding us.

"Why do you assume I wouldn't?"

"This is war."

"War doesn't grant me permission to be a savage beast." I begin to circle him. We both understand: only one will remain. It is an unspoken vow we just made, a dance we enter, unknowing who will win.

"It seems so odd." The fae mirrors my steps. We've been reduced to two circling predators.

"What?" I ask.

"To murder so many just for land."

I almost stumble. Had that been his plan?

"The land is a symbol," I acknowledge.

"Some say symbols caused this war."

My mouth moves; words fly out without my permission. "Others argue symbols ended it."

Why did I say that?

It was a bedtime story my mother used to read. That was before her and my father were deployed. How did I remember that?

That book was about runes. The Era of Broken Oaths: runes ran unchecked, unbalanced, and untamed. Then, a counterbalance happened. The Great Stillness was a time of panic; runes stopped working. People had to go back to training their magic and not just relying on runes to enhance it.

But these are stories, long twisted by the old tongues who retell them endlessly. They teach children lessons.

The fae's eyes dip to my hands. "Why did you burn the dead?"

I don't want to talk about that!

"Why?" he repeats the question with such authority, like he's the author and I'm a sheet of paper, his question the ink I am forced to have absorbed within me. No matter how much I don't want that stain upon my mind, I am compelled to answer.

"We burn our dead," I force out.

"We are in the middle of a battle. You could have used your magic to kill."

"What does it matter to you?" I sneer as I place my boot firmly into the soil, readying myself.

"I watched as you looked at our dead, too. You looked like you wanted to do something."

Fuck this! I'm walking into a trap.

I make the first move, surging forward, my sword raised high. Steel catches the light of the rising moon and the setting sun. It is a strange time where light and dark meet.

I aim at his weak spot, his exposed arm. The speed at which I swing the arch makes a sharp whistling sound. He hesitates, lips pressed. Those wide eyes narrow with anger over my choice of replying with my sword and not my tongue.

Our blades collide with a sharp clang. I force all my power into my arms; my biceps are on fire, muscles burning and devouring all the energy I have. The force of the clash vibrates up my arm. We press against each other, faces inches apart.

"Why?" he persists with that bloody question.

He's really starting to piss me off! "Fae do not burn their dead!" I shout and spit. "That is why I do not burn every fallen soldier I walk past."

How does he know that if the fae did burn their dead, I would have set their bodies aflame, too?

His eyes are unmoving, shades of brown and green, rich like the tall forests in his lands. His hair is styled in the high fae tradition, braided on the sides and tied back. "But we are your enemy; why would you honor our bodies?"

"Alive, you are my enemy. Dead, you are my brother who is a casualty in this war." The surrounding battle grows dull. My nostrils flare, and I brace myself for the putrid scent of death, the sour tang of piss from the bodies now decaying, and the metallic sharpness of blood as it mixes with earthy soil.

I shake my arms, trying to fend off the chills that wrap around me, but... I smell nothing. Not death or life. The air feels strangely pure, though the sensation is so subtle I question its existence.

I twist my wrist; my blade slides down his. A terrible screech grates on my ears as the edges of our steel scrape. His grip holds firm, refusing to give ground. Our swords grind together until the tips hover near each other's necks, each one a hair's breadth away from ending the fight.

Our eyes lock; neither blinks. That would be the key that unlocks our next attack.

This isn't just a fight. It's something more.

If this is the last person I will speak to, I want to share my entire truth. "Our kings respect us when we hold a sword, honor us when we kill, and sing songs about our victories, but when we die... when we *die*,"—my voice grows colder than the death surrounding us—"we become nothing to them! Merely failures who should have fought harder! We're left to the birds and predators of these lands because using time and resources to honor our bodies is a waste."

"That's why you burn the bodies." He speaks to me with high respect and even dips his chin, which places his face closer to the edge of my blade.

Make no mistake, this is not him giving up; he will fight me to the death because, like any honorable warrior, he will give me the best fight he has until his dying breath. Or mine.

"That is why," I echo.

"You would bury my kind if you could," he states with assurance.

"I *have* buried them." Tristen, Ember, Ryker, Nero, Cyrus, and I did so when no one was looking. Instead of resting, we returned to the battlefield and dug graves. The sheer number of corpses overwhelmed us. We did the best we could.

I hope that one day, if my brother and I lie dead on a field, someone —it doesn't matter who—will take the time to burn my body and set my pain free.

A sword to the heart is a death I could accept, but knowing my flesh will be pecked open by the birds, then my inners ripped apart and devoured by the true beast of this world, that was a fate I didn't want attached to my name, whether my name was to be forgotten or sung throughout history.

He raises an eyebrow. "Night hides many secrets that your king would have killed you for."

How does he know we buried the bodies during the night? My swallow causes my neck to rub against his sword. "It kept the birds at bay." I admit as if the act was nothing. But it was everything to me. My apology for having killed another, so myself and my siblings could live. I am truly sorry.

He grunts. "Why do you cover up your honor with lies? You want their bodies to be respected."

"Why do you speak when we should be fighting?" Without warning, I push back and to the left, twisting sideways to avoid the tip of his sword.

We start the dance again, each of us circling for the next opening.

"They were wrong to erase the runes from our lands." He steps closer, forcing our dance to be intimate.

"You're mad!" I refuse to be killed by a lunatic. "Runes are myths."

He levels me with a stare that makes me feel stupid. "All things serve dual purposes. Perhaps I am mad, but I plead the truth. The runes brought stability and also gluttony. Balance and contrast make definitions. Look at you, for example."

"I'm a soldier. If I'm ordered to kill, I obey." Because my neck is on the line, and my brother's is too.

"But you also bury the dead. *All* the dead. You create a balance."

Continuing this conversation is a dangerous road to walk down, but it's trotting downhill; I'm forced to keep going rather than turn around and endure a more strenuous path. "It means nothing." I inhale; my lungs push against my stiff clothing, layers of leather and metal.

His laugh startles me. "It means everything," he declares.

What in the name of all the gods is happening? It is a risk, but I take it, moving my eyes off him to look around us. The longer I engage in this bizarre conversation, the farther and farther it is from my ears, yet it's right here next to me.

As I look, I watch fellow soldiers swing their swords; some miss their marks, while others land, and some fall to their knees as exhaustion claims victory. Lingering magic fades, mirroring the soldiers' demise.

I tilt my head and listen. Peace fills my ears instead of horrors.

Why can't I hear the battle?

I can see it. Wait, it's still moving slower. Or is it my tired eyes?

My gaze whip back to him as one would force a horse to run faster. My stomach knots so tight I fear it will never taste a meal that can settle it. The fear in my body spreads like a poison throughout my blood.

My eyes don't deceive me. It's *him* causing the soldiers

surrounding us to move more slowly. As if they are snowflakes, slowly drifting down instead of the strong, pelting rain.

"What magic is this?" I demand. He doesn't have to answer me, but he likes to talk to his prey.

His stained armor tells me he has been fighting for hours.

"How do you still have magic?" I press.

His mouth curls into a smile framed with dirt and grime from the day. "Like you, I choose to use my magic for other reasons—reasons other than killing. I've been looking for you."

His eyes shine like a monster's when entering the fog, or a hero who is unflinching in the unknown.

"I knew you'd be here," he continues, "but I needed to see if you were worthy. Only one who wishes to create balance can press pen to paper." His head tilts, like the weight of a scale. "I had to be sure your heart was pure. Not of vengeance like the huntress is."

He's a lunatic. I inch back, but shit! There is that force again, pushing at my back and tugging my chest closer to him.

"I'm a time-weaver," he claims with delight. "I can create pockets in time, slow things down for a few moments, keeping you trapped with me. But our time is almost up."

I snort, but the moment the sound huffs out of my nostrils, I start to doubt my next statement. "They do not exist."

He opens his left hand. "Am I not here?" He raises his sword. "Is my blade not made of metal? Has our conversation not taught you that things forgotten and feared *do* exist?"

"You like to toy with your prey," I counter, though I cannot help but shudder.

A time-weaver! Tristen won't believe it. The only good thing to come of the war was the travel. My brother and I have seen and met people and visited lands we never imagined. We witnessed magic we had only read about in books.

"Yes and no." His reply is instant, like a slap in the face. "I knew you'd be here, and yes, I cut my way through men and women to reach you on this battlefield."

My teeth clench. "You speak as if you have the magic to see the future."

"I never said I didn't." His smirk turns mocking.

I lift my sword like a shield, heart hammering beneath it. "Now I know you're mad with lies. Time-weaving is rare; foresight is impossible. No one person is gifted with both rarities."

With a sharp bark of laughter, he spreads his arms wide, sword dangling loosely in one hand. The weight of it seems more like that of a feather than of hard steel. "Who is mad?" His eyes become wild and unhinged, as if the battlefield itself has crawled into them. "I stand in front of you speaking and showing you the truth, yet you try to tell your mind that your eyes and ears are lying."

"Why are you telling me this?" I step back.

"Because you do both, kill and honor. You do what the runes once did before they were abused. Create balance."

"The runes did not create balance."

"Says who?" he challenges.

"Oh, I don't know, the wars they caused," I bark.

"Greed of the flesh was not the rune's fault. They were a gift from the gods; our lands need runes once again to bring peace. They make everyone equal. Humans without magic can stand a chance against us."

"I don't need more enemies coming at me." Humans with magic! No, thank you.

"Put yourself in the human's shoes. Or would you rather keep them as low as cattle?"

I point my sword at him. "I do not treat humans as such. I value them for the blood that feeds my magic. Call me a monster again, and I will carve out your tongue."

Not all vampires treat humans with respect, but I am not one of them.

This needs to end. "You've been fighting too long, my friend. Madness has claimed you," I tell him.

"Madness has claimed us all." His smile drops like a stone tossed into a calm river. "When the time comes, I need to know you'll be ready." His eyes feel like possessive chains around my ankles.

"Ready for what?" I widen my stance just to prove to my mind that I can move. His magic has no claim on me.

"To rule and to keep safe the runes."

"There are no runes! I'm not a king."

"You're not? I see a man more worthy of a crown than your king."

"Don't speak ill of King Galen."

"Try saying that with passion," he mocks, raising an arrogant eyebrow.

I swing my sword with everything I have; the force of my lunge has my boots sinking ankle deep into the ground. He meets my blow with confidence. A deafening clang pierces through the strange time bubble he has created.

For a split second, it shatters. The noise from the real battle wails and slashes through me, shocking me to my core, thrusting me into the chilling cold realization that he's telling the truth; he's a time-weaver, and shit, he must have the magic of foresight too.

Zap! The time bubble erects again, but this time, I hear more of the battle outside. It's not as strong.

"Now you believe me." He grins, taunting me, but I see the sweat beading on his brow. He's growing tired. His magic is fading.

I'm not going to enjoy killing him. It is a travesty to kill such a rare creature.

"A wiser man would let me finish our conversation," he says as if having heard my thoughts.

"I'm a soldier. It's not my duty to be a wise man." I move forward, aiming for his chest. "Only a deadly one!"

He blocks it! Dammit!

Our swords clash like two bickering lovers who hate to love each other.

He's the most skilled fighter I have struck metal with; there are no tricks I can produce that will best him. It will come down to who exhausts first. One small mistake will be the tiebreaker.

I sidestep his swing just in time, but the tip of his blade catches under my arm directly on my armor, where the metal turns to leather, allowing me more movement. Pain blooms, hot and sharp, but it is shallow enough that I can still swing my sword. It will heal slowly. Had I not used all my magic, I could have healed it in an instant.

I drive my knee into his stomach. The blow isn't strong enough to penetrate his armor, but it shakes his balance.

That's my opening.

He staggers; his boot slips on the bloody mud. I slash my blade down his exposed arm, cutting deep, to the bone. His sword falls to the ground.

Everything I do next is just a reflex of my training.

I don't mean to do it.

It's like blinking your eyes on a windy day; it just happens, a subconscious way to protect yourself.

I step in close, bringing my sword down in a brutal arc, aiming for the weakest spot in his fae armor. They love details. It's what kills them: all those etchings in the metal surrounding their collars and chest plates weaken the metal. Thinning it, and over time, if you hit it enough, it makes the metal more brittle.

Right as my sword hits the metal, I hear the crack.

I regret it. A part of me feels like my sword has pierced my own heart.

I just did something terrible; I have no idea what the consequences will be yet.

My sword breaks the metal. The rest is so easy, so light to the touch; it's like sinking my teeth into freshly baked sourdough bread. The armor's outside is hard and crusty, while beneath, his flesh is as soft and airy as bread's interior—no match for my bite. The taste is tangy, sour; my mind rejoices, because killing him means I get to live. Regret follows instantly, like the guilt after overeating on a strict no-carb diet—you want to vomit, but you don't, knowing it's wrong to start a new sickness. The urge to binge and purge lingers. My mind, convincing as ever, tells me it's okay: overeat carbs, kill if you must! Feel your heart beat. See, you're alive. You can walk it off.

I don't have to push as my sword sank into his heart.

It happens like breathing. Effortlessly.

"I'm sorry!" I choke. I let go of my sword as his flesh and bone now hold it in place. I grab him. He staggers for a moment, and then his knees give out, hitting mine before he falls into my arms.

No, no, no! I want to take it back, reverse time, pull my sword out, and not have his death on my conscience.

"I'm sorry!" A tear falls from my eyes. Its path down my cheek is slow as it pushes through the dried blood, dirt, and sweat, attempting to forge a bitter path.

"You were scared of the truth. I knew you would be. I saw how today would end, and I do not blame you for it." His confidence is now a whisper, each breath tight and pained, like fire that screams when water is poured over it.

"Then why didn't you run from me?" I hiss in outrage.

"We are soldiers. We don't run from what scares us. We embrace it." His lip twitches in agony.

I lower him to the ground, locking eyes with him. Magic creatures can heal faster than humans, but heart wounds are often fatal.

His eyes cry with discomfort. I look at my sword and begin to reach for it. Once I pull it free, he'll bleed out in seconds. His pain will vanish.

"Wait!" He seizes my wrist.

"Keeping it in only prolongs death," I gently admit.

"Let me finish."

I slowly nod. "What's your name?" I ask.

His teeth grind when he exhales. He lays his head back and looks up at the sky. I know the sight he sees.

"I won't let the birds have you, friend," I assure him.

"I know." He nods as tears roll down his cheeks. "My name is Everett."

There are those consequences.

"Prince Everett of Solaria?" I ask with dread, already knowing the truth. That's why he's a skilled fighter and wears such ornate armor.

"A prince is just a man, and a castle is merely stacked stones. We're all the same in the end." Everett's breathing slows. "My death will win you this war. My father will stop." He smirks. "One man's death can win a war or start it. One man can change everything."

I hold him closer. "My name is Titus."

He closes his eyes. "I know."

"So you can foresee."

Everett doesn't reply. I want to shake his shoulders. I crave his snarky rebuttals.

The surrounding battle is louder; the bubble he trapped us in is on the cusp of breaking because his time is almost up.

Instead, he asks, "Do you know what happens to a fae's magic when they die?"

I glance at my sword. The blood pouring from his chest slows now. His heart is barely pumping.

"We release our magic into the land again, but we have a choice, Titus. We can gift it to another."

Slowly, I push my hands on each side of my sword, trying to slow the bleeding, but it is a fool's folly. He and I both know it. He doesn't flinch when my hands press in. He has moments left now. "I don't understand." I lick my lips, feeling all the cuts that sting under my parched tongue.

Everett's hands grab me. I expect a sword to meet my flesh, but it is just his fingers. He speaks words I don't understand, and then a surge of icy cold numbness sinks into me. I hear my heart slow, and the blood in my veins sounds like a calm river brushing against a peaceful bank.

His eyes glow, locking me in place and binding my tongue shut so I cannot utter a word of defense. Then a massive, luminous shadow rips from his body and curls into a ball that rests on his chest.

"I give my magic of time-weaving to you, Titus Tarragon, to use until you find the Vitalis; then, I release my magic back into the lands."

His words spill free like a blow to the stomach. Too much at once, impossible to shove back in. My body sways like a sword, forced to endure and be responsible for its actions. His words keep pouring like blood into my mind. Echoing like a beast crawling out from a deep cave.

My inner magic is no more than a drop of water on dry, cracked earth—it tries so hard to rise, grow something to defend me, but it can't.

"But my magic of foresight, I release back into the world. If you were to see what you must endure, you would grab the sword from my heart and thrust it into yours," he rasps.

"Wait!" I shout as I jerk back. I expect his hands to pull me closer so this crazy conversation can continue. Instead, his glowing magic surges into my body, raising every hair, widening every pore, stretching every bone, muscle, and vein until I feel like I'm about to be ripped apart.

Did I die? No, the pain is too intense.

I fall forward onto Everett. "No!" I wince as I roll off of him in shock.

I want Everett's hands to grab me, but they fall by his sides, knuckles landing on the blood-soaked soil; it looks so peaceful, so... right, like a body buried in the soil, allowing multiple creatures to feed off it. Now they won't starve and die. Death fuels life; it's the ultimate life cycle.

His chest doesn't move, but his leg produces one final twitch. His eyes gaze up at the sky, and the smile on his lips falls slowly, like a boat drifting off into the sunset on calm waters. Peace washes over his face as I watch him pass over.

I lean closer to him, reaching out and running my palm down his face to close his eyes. "What did you do, Prince Everett? Why did you choose me?" I whisper.

THREE

TITUS

Flames dance over my cheek. I sit closer to the fire than most soldiers would. Unlike them, I can control the temperature. If I need to walk through fire, I can.

Tristen left to get us ale or, if we're lucky, something stronger.

Flexing my fingers, I glare at my hands. I thrust them into the fire, feeling nothing but joy as my magic grasps the flames. But I don't feel like myself. The skin that covers my body isn't mine anymore. It was stolen, taken, and used, then given back to me.

I see Everett's face in everything. In my dreams, in the clouds, even in the fire.

His words haunt me like needles constantly digging into my flesh. Urging me to take heed and acknowledge them.

"There you are," a soft, feminine voice pierces through my dark thoughts.

I pull my hand back and stand. I've tried so hard to distance myself from my friends, but in a war camp, finding a moment alone is impossible. Tristen and I have taken it upon ourselves to walk further from the camp, deep into the woods where enemies used to lurk.

Some still are.

"Sit down, you oaf. We need to talk," Ember says as she sits next to the spot I was just in.

She wiggles her hips as if the ground is as comfortable as a mattress. It is for us; our beds are not much thicker than the dirt.

"Thanks for warming the seat up for me." She smirks, then snatches the flames.

Like me, Ember possesses fire magic, but unlike me, she can't conjure it out of thin air. Some vampires call her a lesser. Lessers cannot produce their own magic; they need their element nearby so they can grab it and manipulate it. It doesn't make them less, but in the eyes of rankings, it marks them as such.

"I was just leaving. Long day." I grab the back of my neck and turn to leave, but she throws the flame at my feet, then wraps it around me.

Her eyes soften as the fire dance over her palms, warming her night-kissed skin. I watch, enchanted by her beauty, but I'm also worried I'll fail her, that one day some monster will lock his eyes on her and steal her away from us.

"Sit down," she repeats. "I just bathed, I swear. I don't stink like death anymore."

"We told you to keep that smell on you." I smirk as I cross my arms. "It fends the men off."

"And I told you," she looks down, sweeping her fingers over the dirt, "I like men. Therefore, I bathe frequently now."

If dragons were still alive, I imagine my exhale would sound like one. To me, Ember will always be my little sister who needs protecting. A child who would never have survived without us, and vice versa. We're a tight-knit group, like the ropes tying down the mast of a sail. Remove one rope, and the sail doesn't function the same.

I shouldn't reply, but Ember is hard to resist. "I'm tired." I wave my hand and kill the flames, cutting off her magic.

Her cheeks turn a burnt red color as she stands. "How long have we known each other, Titus?" She crosses her arms, which pushes her breasts closer together.

A reminder that she isn't a child anymore.

Neither am I.

When she first got breasts, she used to bind them, but one night, Ryker caught her in the act; he said her ribs were covered in bruises from how tightly she was pulling the wrappings. She told us she was scared we would treat her differently.

We put an end to that—fast. We made an oath and cut ourselves so we had scars in the same place. It was hard to control our natural healing abilities, but we managed to do it, ensuring the scar would not fade. A symbol that formed a unit; each line represented one of us.

The scars were nothing fancy, a simple hexagon over our hearts; we were kids with semi-sharp blades.

"I've seen you after a battle," Ember says. "I know you. You always seek solitude; you beat yourself up after those you killed. Unlike other soldiers, you don't boast about battlefield kills. You, Tristen, Ryker, Cyrus, and Nero, we're all the same. People, not weapons. You think Ryker, Cyrus, Nero, and I haven't noticed a change in you and Tristen since this last battle?"

This is also why I've tried to keep my distance. I don't want to involve them. I didn't want to involve Tristen either, but I had no choice after I used Everett's magic, wrapping him in a time bubble, moments after he found me on the battlefield.

"What's going on? You never take it this hard," Ember says softly.

"I killed a prince," I mutter.

"And he died a man." She shrugs. "Crowns make no difference in the end." Ember licks her lips.

We were forced to be child soldiers, but unlike the others, our friendship kept our hearts whole. We still have hope, whereas our fellow soldiers only have a thirst for battles and blood.

We're all very protective of Ember. Her beauty captivates the soldiers. That's why we made sure she was skilled with a sword. Fuck, she's better with a blade than I am.

I remember when she was tossed into our sleeping quarters. The army didn't care that she was a female forced to sleep with boys. We were all kids. That changed when we hit puberty, and other guys tried to sneak into our rooms to get to her. They lost some fingers in the process.

When Ember first arrived, she had no name. Her mother worked at a brothel but died during childbirth. They just called her kid. Once King Galen claimed her city, they recruited all eligible children for the army. Made no difference whether the child was male or female. Hands are hands, and they can all hold weapons in King Galen's eyes. He knows what he's doing. He takes kids who are invisible and makes them feel loved. He gives them a home, food, shelter, friends, and a purpose.

For years, Ember only allowed us to call her Kid. I think it was her way of trying to remember home. But then we came into our magic. She was drawn to the embers within my fire. The pretty glowing sparks on the verge of life or death. She was always playing with them, so the name Ember just stuck.

Ember looks long and hard at me now. Her brown hair is mixed with red strands, creating a pretty chestnut color in the sunlight, but at night, it looks more molten, dark, and brewing. Her hazel eyes are more golden orange than brownish green.

Her hand reaches out to touch me. I jerk back. "Don't!" I can't risk her touching me. What if Everett's magic flares and grabs her?

I have zero control. None. I'm a monster with teeth and claws that will destroy.

Her hand jerks back and hovers in the air. "I know what lies look like, Titus. They resemble a needle and thread. They sew us shut, stitch us up. Let me open you up again. Talk to me," she pleads.

"I don't want to talk. I want to be left alone," I snap as I frantically look through the woods, hoping to spot Tristen.

Ember's eyes narrow. "What the fuck is going on with you?"

"Like you said, some kills take time. I'm asking you to give me space." I step back.

Please, Ember, drop this.

She's not going to, so I say something I regret.

"I don't need a mother."

Her chest sinks in from her deep inhale. "Good," she bites, "because I'm not one." She spins on her heel and leaves.

I close my eyes. I want to run after her. Instead, I go and sit next to the dead fire. Soon, Tristen finally returns with a bottle of ale. "I spotted Ember," he says as he joins me and uncorks the bottle.

"I had to push her away."

He nods and hands me the bottle. "I sent Nero after her."

I blow out a breath. "How's Ryker?" I change the subject.

"The healer said he only needs to stay one more day before he's released. He's almost fully regenerated his magic. Fucker can't die." Tristen's smirk tries to erase the worry in his eyes, but I know better.

We came so close to losing Ryker during the last battle. A poisoned fae arrow struck him. He pulled it out and fought on, but the poisoned tip stayed inside, spreading the venom. He was less than an hour from the point of no return. He underwent surgery to remove the arrow and received a blood transfusion. A vampire's magic takes weeks to regenerate after such an experience.

"I'm going to lose everything, Tris. I have to push them all away. Ember, Ryker, Cyrus, and Nero. You, too. I can't grasp the magic Everett forced upon me. I can't control it."

"You will," he attempts to reassure me.

"It's different from my vampire magic." My fire magic was like a puppy: eager to come out and play, but if scolded, it obeyed me.

Everett's magic is like... a behemoth lurking in the shadows. I never fully see it, only flashes as it reaches out and grabs a hold of me. It feels so enormous and infinite, I can't wrap my hands around it. I feel like *I'm* the dog being trained, not the other way around.

It has no leash to grab and hold, nothing to tug it back. It runs wild and free, like time itself.

"I would presume." Tristen takes the bottle from my hand and drinks half of it.

I can't help but roll my eyes. "How do you sound so chill?"

"I have an idea," he announces as he scratches his scalp. We had to cut it short before the battle. Tristen detests his short hair; he says it makes his scalp itch. "But first, light the fire. My toes are getting chilly." He wiggles his boots and offers me a goofy grin.

I gently slap the back of his head. "Chilly?" I push my magic out. The hot wood crackles as it catches flame again.

"There are no women to warm my bed, so yeah, I'm cold." He sticks his hands out near the fire, then he uses his magic to encase us in his shadows. "I agree that you have to find a way to control Everett's magic," Tristen starts. "So let's find a way."

"What are you suggesting?"

"We find a fae to help us." He flexes his fingers, pushing the warmth between them.

"Find a fae? They're still our enemy."

He looks at me. "*Were* our enemies."

"What are you saying?"

"Mages portaled in a signed letter from King Galen. The war is officially over, brother. King Galen is marrying Princess Selene. That means we can return to Blackthorn at some point."

Over... it's finally done. Peace between vampires and fae has come!

Why do Everett's words feel like the start of a new war?

I shake my head, but Tristen grins. "Princess Selene will be our new queen, who also happens to be Everett's sister. Did you know that Everett had two sisters? Twins, I've been told. And guess who is coming to join our new queen? The twin. Everett's sisters must know how to decipher the crazy fucked-up things he told you. For starters, what the fuck is the Vitalis?

"We need to find that as soon as possible because once we do, you will be free of his magic. Things can go back to normal, Titus. That's the silver lining, right? Think of this as a battle; we just have to survive it. Whatever Everett did to you will end."

"That's..." I look into the flames, seeing the light. Mentally, I'm standing in the shadow of a mountain Prince Everett has forced me to climb. I can't flee, for the shadow stretches far and wide. Sunlight will never kiss my cheeks until I start to climb my way out of this mess. Tristen's helping plot the path. He thinks that's what is stressing me. It's not the trek up or the heights I must overcome. I fear the descent once I'm done.

"A fantastic idea," Tristen says with a fool's enthusiasm. "It's either that or sneak into enemy land, kidnap a fae, who hopefully is knowledgeable in time-weaving, then we must force them to teach you how to control it."

He raises a firm finger in the air. "I vote for option one. If anyone knows about his time-weaving magic, it's got to be one of his sisters."

Ryker leans against the bed while Ember is seated between his legs. He holds her so close it's hard to tell where one stops and the other begins. A perfect fit, but it's platonic.

Against her dark skin, his pale face and silver hair look like death, and the freezing river that leads to the next life.

My grip on the letter tightens so much that the edges tear under my fingertips, yet the words remain unaltered. Leaning on one another, Nero and Cyrus use each other's backs for support. Tristen sinks his fang into his lip as he reads Nero's letter again, and the other letters remain tossed in the middle of the dirt floor.

We're being separated. Tristen and I have orders to go to the capital, Blackthorn Castle, where I will receive my new title.

I am no longer a commander like Cyrus and Ryker. Each commander is given three hundred soldiers. Ember falls under Ryker's command, Nero under Cyrus's, and Tristen is one of my soldiers, but my duties as general are now requiring me to step away.

I should be happy that Tristen gets to come with me. I am, but... what about my family?

"It makes no sense," I hiss, grabbing Cyrus's letter off the floor.

Nero, Ember, Cyrus, and Ryker are to go to Lockhelm, a small human town that borders the western Fae kingdom of Lunestra. The humans call it the Night Court. The huge mountain ridge called the Cradle of Darkness separates Solaria in the East and Lunestra in the West, both of which are enemies. But unlike Solaria, which is bathed in light, Lunestra is bathed in shadow. I'm told their crops grow only with the help of magic, since sunlight doesn't touch their lands. Some even say that because the fae of Lunestra consume magic-infused food, they have strange and undocumented power.

The Night Court is a mystery to all, with its borders closed off by a massive veil. The human settlement of Lockhelm dares not roam near. Many people have tried to understand how Lunestra can produce a shield, let alone maintain it consistently.

The amount of power it would require is... mind-boggling. Some rumors claim they make sacrifices to a long-forgotten god, while others claim they traded their magic to a dark spirit.

"Why is King Galen sending you to the borders near Lunestra?" I mutter. It's a death trap, or a taunt to the Night Court now that we have aligned with the fae of Solaria.

"Because this war is never fucking done," Ryker grunts, hugging Ember tighter and closing his eyes, as if shielding himself from the fact.

"We're going to be separated," Nero mutters.

Ember reaches up and flattens her palm over her heart, where our matching scar is. "We're always together. Distance is an illusion. This war will end. One day, we will be together again," she whispers hopefully.

Ember reaches for Nero's hand, then, like a chain, he grabs Ryker's. Ryker takes Cyrus, and Cyrus grabs Tristen, waiting for me to take his other hand. I take Tristen, but I hesitate to touch Cyrus.

I may never hold his hand again. So I risk it, and that's when it happens. I feel the time-weaving magic grab hold of me and everyone in the room. I jolt and gasp, causing all eyes to look at me.

Shit! I'll have to explain what has happened to me. They'll be endangered because, like Tristen, they will put their lives on the line to help me.

A bead of sweat runs down my temple; it glides down my cheek at an irritating pace, as I hold my breath and wait.

One blink, then two. A sharp inhale.

I wait for them to realize what has happened. Frantically, I look around, but... it's just us, alone in the tent.

Oh, I've wrapped the entire tent in a bubble! They have no idea that just outside these thin fabric walls—shaking and bouncing from the strong wind tonight—everyone is moving in slow motion.

My lip twitches as I smile; a small amount of the weight on my shoulders lifts. In a way, it's like I've told them.

I look at Tristen. He leans closer to me, his left shoulder blocking some of me from their view. I think he knows what happened, so he coughs and says, "Distance doesn't matter."

"Distance doesn't matter," I repeat as I close my eyes and listen to them repeat our words.

SELENE

Is it too much to request a dress from my seamstress that's voluminous enough to conceal my bow? Perhaps a few spare arrows sewn into the layers of fabric? Someone imaginative enough to make it work must exist, I'm sure.

Damn this gown Galen picked! Yes, it's lovely, made of the finest red silk that feels incredibly soft against my skin. But honestly, I feel naked. Vulnerable and at Galen's mercy; that's what my husband wants me to feel. He wants me to cling to his side for protection.

My curves? They are more on display than Galen's most prized horses.

I pinch my stomach, feeling the food my maid brought earlier settle. Don't get me started on the cheese I had with the warm, fresh bread roll. Pieces of the crust are still flaked on my floor.

I stare at my fingers, still pruned from the long bath I took. What a queen I make tonight, bloated and wrinkled like a raisin.

I can host, regardless of the guest. "My looks need not be lethal, only my aim." Bending down, I gather up the dress, grab the single arrow I carved, and take gentle care when I tie it to the inside of my thigh. The sharp tip presses into my inner knee.

One single arrow. I'm a fine marksman. Everett taught me, after all.

Don't think about those memories now. Focus.

As the sun sets, the cool night air surrounds me as I walk through the gardens towards the grand hall for the feast. Roaring laughter and fine music penetrate the castle's stone. Even the scent of ale and wine sully the fragrant florals of the gardens.

During my time here, I studied all the hidden pathways. Killing Titus out in the open would be reckless; finding him in his sleep would also be unwise, since only whores enter the soldier's barracks.

I need to be a shadow that is both seen and ignored.

I stop at one of the famous Blackthorn rosebushes. Such ugly flowers; dark, deceitful, and riddled with numerous tiny thorns. Porcupines would look better in a vase than these roses. The black flower is a symbol of death to me. They grow all over these lands, devouring all the other florals, taking over everything. Killing and killing until only they survive.

Reaching for a lone one, I snap the stem in half and hold it gently, making sure the thorns do not pierce my skin.

Not yet. All in due time.

I walk off the path, and my heart skips a beat. I force it to settle when I slip into one of the hidden passages that the florist use. The scent of the black roses stifles my nostrils. Musky, velvety, woodsy notes. Elegant yet garish... like my husband.

A small set of stairs curls up towards the roof of the hall, resembling a tortured spine. It functions like a skeleton, allowing servants to hang the chandeliers and decorations without being seen.

Galen loves for the roses to line the rafters of the feast halls, and I intend to use their shadows as my cover. The passages are never used during the feast since everything is already set up.

A smile curls my lips. I'm alone here, with my thoughts and thirst for vengeance.

I run my fingers along the walls of the stairwell, pressing my fingertips into the cold stone. The stairway opens up onto a hallway. Large shelves line the walls, storing a variety of lighting options.

And what I hid last night.

Every few feet, narrow slits too small to be called windows line the walls. They're only big enough for a head to fit between; these small holes secure the ropes supporting the floral decorations hanging in the feast hall.

Or a hole big enough to shoot an arrow through.

"Finally." I bend down, hike up my red silk dress, and untie the arrow. The trembling in my fingers increases. "That won't do." I need a steady hand.

I push up on my tiptoes and tuck the arrow along the same ledge where I hid a bow I had stolen a few nights ago. I was wise enough not to use my bow but rather one from Galen's army barracks.

My heels hit the floor, and my exhalation is so heavy that it knocks me into the stone wall.

"It's almost time," I whisper, but first, I need to make my appearance.

Welcome to the den of vipers. Yes, they bite out in the open. They are vampires, after all.

Stiffen your spine. Okay, chin high.

I nod toward the guards. A loud groan signals to the guests inside that the doors are opening, but it feels like my lungs are closing. Each step I take is labored as the weight of the eyes in the room pivots towards me.

Whether they are looking at my face, the new necklace Galen gave me, the red silk dress, or my body, I don't care. They see I'm here, which is all I need.

Soon, they will be too drunk to remember when I leave. I never stay long at these parties, and everyone knows it.

The dancing stops, and the crowd parts so I can walk down the aisle towards the king's table.

I'm not a plague, I'm a fae. You can step closer. Unlike you, we don't bite.

There, in the center, my husband sits upon a large dais that houses his royal table. Arrangements of candles give his skin a magical glow. Black roses in polished vases create a receiving feel that Galen exploits down to the very last drop. His thick, curly brown hair wraps around a crown made of white-gold and embellished with black diamonds, like the vines of those thorny roses he adores, claiming it and ensuring no one will grab the item from his head.

Oh, look at that smile. Marble can't be carved that straight.

I admit, his smirk has fooled me until he flashes his two sharp fangs. He holds a goblet filled with blood, as he does a woman's hips with admiration and authority.

My masked smirk falters. Galen's always sipping blood, ensuring his magic is at peak reserves.

How has he not slipped into total bloodlust? It's a mystery we've all asked. The only work he does is with his dick, so his magic doesn't need to be recharged *that* much.

He raises the glass to his lips lazily as his eyes look me up and down. The red dress outlines every curve I possess, marking each asset as his.

I could have been yours, Galen. 'Could have' will be your final words.

I want to reach up and rub away the pain behind my ears. Even though the braids in my hair help cushion my crown, they still hurt like all fashionable things do.

Galen's throat rolls as he swallows. There is something sexy about a man swallowing, but then repulsing, knowing he is a vampire, and it's blood he's drinking. The civilized act of drinking blood from a cup is just a show. I know Galen drinks from the veins of willing women whom he houses in luxury and most likely fucks, too.

He never mentions the others. I just assume he has others, as my father does. He's king, so he's pardoned for the crime of welcoming others into our marriage. I grew up with men like this, so it's not shocking or news to me, and it wasn't like I could feed him *my* blood.

His brown eyes smile with each step I take. When he looks at me like this, it makes me want to smirk back, to push up on my toes and kiss him.

The way I sway my hips has him setting his goblet down. I might not have fangs, but I can be a viper, too. Snakes don't just bite; they squeeze. Hard. *Get ready, husband.*

His relaxed posture grows firm. He stands, and every eye shifts towards him as he rounds the table.

He has a power that brings others, including me, to their knees. He's charming. And that smile? It keeps people in a daze, too happy to realize how deceptive he is. He takes everything within his reach—women, men, a fork and knife, even a black rose—and turns it into a weapon.

Even me.

He forged me into a lethal one. His touch smelted me, his decisions were the hammer's blows that shaped me, and his silence to my pleas was the cold plunge that sealed his work, hardening the metal that replaced my heart.

Some weapons, when wielded improperly, inflict immeasurable pain, not just on their target, but on the one who holds them.

"My queen." He opens his arms, which swing past the sword he always wears. He sleeps next to it like a child clinging to a stuffed animal.

We meet in the middle of the hall, where I bow to him; the tightness of the silk dress makes the action hard, and I know every male and female is looking at how the material tightly hugs my ass like a second skin.

Look, but don't touch. That's what this dress says.

I keep my eyes downcast, watching the chandeliers illuminate the polished marble. His finger tucks under my chin as he guides my eyes up.

He's the captain and I the mere anchor. He commands me, lowers me when he wants me to stop, and dredges me up when it is time to set sail. He forgets that a ship needs an anchor or it can never make port, never be safely docked.

And this party? It has severed the rope, cutting the anchor free from the ship. There is no going back after this. My heart is forever under the pressure of the unrelenting water, and Galen's mind will be like a shipwrecked sailor: all his hope of a treasured future lost.

His eyes grow with lust as he looks from my red-painted lips to the ruby necklace he gifted me. It's so heavy around my neck that if I inhale too deeply, I worry it will choke me.

"Thank you for the gift," I whisper. "It's beautiful."

He holds my chin, measuring the value of my words. Galen thinks jewels will win my heart. "One day, I will find something worthy of your beauty to wear."

I know you are upset. That's what he means.

"All I need is you, my king," I reply, knowing everyone is listening, but only Galen knows the hidden meaning in my words.

Don't do this! My eyes scream at him.

His steady glare says, *I have no choice.*

Lies; the king makes the choices.

He steps closer; his soft velvet suit rubs against my dress, creating a sensation that has my nipples surely showing through the fabric. He presses his lips to my ear, "You can have every inch of me, Selene," he rasps. "Whenever you want." He sucks my earlobe between his teeth. "Just ask."

"Ask or beg?" *I begged you not to honor the man who murdered my brother!*

"The latter." He playfully grins.

You honestly think I'd forgive you this easily!

Words can be sweet, and Galen knows what letters to string together to get my lady-bits into a wet heat. But what men fail to learn is that women want more than just their cocks. We can get that at any corner. We want a heart to treasure us, arms to hold us, and ears to listen to us.

We seek a partner who can be both our shield and our sword.

"It's hard to be in the mood when you plan to honor the man who killed my brother this evening," I hiss.

Cold water. How do you like it, husband?

Galen and I's marriage is fucked up yet more normal than my parents'. We fuck, talk about surface-level things, we argue, but then we fuck again, and I guess it makes it bearable. I know that, over time, some marriages can evolve into loving ones. That's what we needed. Time.

He's about to shatter the hourglass. Time's up.

"Dance with me," he says in a hushed tone as he swipes his thumb near my bottom lip.

It's a kind gesture only I hear. He's giving me a choice without looking weak among his men. I look past him at the black roses hanging along the walls. There you are! My little window of salvation is barely seen because the florist stacked the roses so thickly.

I look around the room. Galen thinks I'm nervous. He allows me to leave these dreadful events early because he knows they make me uncomfortable, and also because he can flirt with other women.

I don't like being around people. I don't trust them. Too many have tried to kill me; some almost did.

Where are you? I look from soldier to soldier; every one of them is dressed in ceremonial leather, dyed grey, and embossed black roses decorate the collars.

Which of you killed my brother? Was it you, or you there, who only reaches my chin?

Galen's eyes shift. I reach for his hand. He grips mine with a force that does exactly as I plan. You see, Galen was so focused on that necklace that he didn't see the rose I held in my hand or how his grip pushed the thorns into our flesh, cutting his queen for everyone to see.

It's a reminder to all his court that those Galen claims to care about can bleed. No one is safe. Therefore, it will shake their trust in him.

That crown? It means nothing. Galen is flesh, blood, and bones like everyone else here. I intend to make his people remember that.

"Oops," I mutter. "I forgot." I flirtatiously smirk. His eyes emit heat as he gazes at the rose that wounded us both. "Sometimes things we admire can cause us harm. Fuck you," I speak fast and hushed.

The tip of his shoe hits mine. "What was that, my love?" His lip twitches.

"I said I plucked this for you."

"Plucked?" The arch of his brow rivals a staircase that reaches the sky.

"Yes, *you heard me right the first time.*" I nod.

I glance down and see his wound slowly start to heal. First, the blood slows, then comes to a halt. Next, the skin turns pink as it begins to knit shut. Vampires heal almost as fast as shifters. Fae and mages are only a step above humans.

Every eye watches as the king holds my now-bleeding palm.

"Heal yourself," he orders under his breath.

"The hour is late." My lips tug up. "All my magic is gone. I need rest." Unlike vampires, who can drink blood to fill their magic, fae and mages need rest in order to recharge.

His nostrils flare. He's trapped in a corner. Either look weak as his queen bleeds, or offer to slow my bleeding, but it will cost him.

"A very kind gesture." He speaks loudly as he takes the rose and tucks it into his front pocket. "I should see if others need plucking." An evil smirk graces his face. His long stare says, *Are you sure you want to threaten me, because I can kill more fae if you do so.*

"A lot of things need to be weeded from your garden," I murmur.

"I shall make sure you have the freshest of flowers, my love." *You will pay for this.*

Reaching out, I adjust the flower, making sure it's straight as an arrow, pun intended. "I think I'm allergic," I reply.

"You'll get used to it."

"Unlikely." I hiss. I glance at my palm and see some thorns are buried in my skin. His eyes, along with those of everyone in the room, follow mine.

His hand clamps around mine, holding it midair. *You just did exactly as I wanted, husband. Thank you.*

Our eyes clash, and suddenly, he is not the husband trying to woo me with fuck-you-banter; he is the king judging me. The music stops, so does the chatter. Every breath can be captured, held, and heard.

"Why did the music stop?" His tone is so heavy that it causes the onlookers to edge back. The musicians resume playing their instruments. The first note is offbeat, like hammers hitting glass; it pains the ears.

"One misstep can ruin everything, don't you think, husband?" *One small gesture, granting me my vengeance, could have stopped your downfall. One small gesture to show me you valued me and respected my heart. One small gesture, Galen.*

"Dance," he orders the crowd.

Bodies spin behind us, and we remain locked and forced onto the center of the dance floor. My large green eyes work in my favor. I force them to widen like a child who has done something naughty. "I know how much you love the roses," I say softly. "I just wanted to give you something you loved. I never want my husband to feel the ache of betrayal."

You want to play, I'll play. That's what his grin says. "The only gift I require from you is your heart, my queen."

My lips press into a flat line like an un-beating heart. "You could have it,"—I hold my chin high—"in time." *Call this off!*

His left hand presses against my lower back. I hiss when he forces our hips together. I'll need a peeler knife to scrape off a thin layer of my flesh after this dance. "That's all I ask for." *It's happening. Suck it up like a queen must do.*

But I'm not just a queen. I was once a sister to a brother.

His grip on my palm tightens, his eyes leaving mine to look at my blood.

He raises my palm, and as it ascends each inch, my heart beats faster. "You don't have to," I test him. I want him to hurt as much as I do tonight.

His eyes darken, his mouth parts, and then he kisses and licks away the small droplets. When his lips meet a thorn, he rips it from my flesh using his teeth. Our eyes lock as he swallows the thorn rather than spitting it out.

Sick bastard!

He continues to clutch my hand as he interlaces our fingers and begins to lead us into a dance.

"I'm sorry," I whisper, "I didn't mean to." *Oh, but I did.* Fae blood is toxic to vampires, and if drunk in a high enough dose, it could kill one.

"You should be more careful," he replies as he licks his lips with distaste. "I might need to assign you a personal guard." His eyes turn hard, but he's still eager to play this game with me.

I whisper in his ear, "I'd hate to see you lose more men." A personal guard? Absolutely not.

He catches my chin. "Do not test me, Selene. I like pain," he hisses before he presses a long, slow kiss to my unopened lips.

"You like pain with pleasure, which you will not be getting from me tonight."

What did he expect of me, to drink to the man who killed my brother?

Galen knew I would act out; thus, the fancy new necklace. "Was that what my brother's life was worth? Gold and rubies?" I challenge.

He looks away. At least he's remorseful. "I did not mean the gift to resemble that. I..." His jaw clenches. "I'm trying to make you happy, but it is you who needs to remember I was not the one who killed him, Selene."

"No, you're the one who praises the killer."

"This is politics. You were raised in this, so I'm warning you, my beautiful wife, to tread carefully. We are still learning how many buttons we can push, but I will not be tested in front of my court again."

"I'll watch where I step, knowing that if I fall, you'll catch me like any good husband would." I hold my breath, heart pounding as my face reddens. I look back at his handsome face and watch my threat sink in.

Isn't that right, husband? I'm your queen, after all, and my life is tied to a fragile, newly signed peace treaty. I hold his stare.

He holds mine with a firmness that resembles a hook in my cheek. *What are you up to?*

I'll never tell.

He runs his nose along my jaw. "I could have your tongue, but I'd much rather have it on my cock, so I will pretend you didn't just threaten my peace treaty," he purrs.

I snort. "You'll never have it again." I'd rather bite my tongue off and swallow it!

"Protection can come in many forms, Selene." His warning is clear. I'm granted many freedoms here, but he'll take them away if needed.

"If you cage me, I'll show you the animal hiding inside."

He flashes his teeth. "Taming wild animals is my speciality."

"You're insufferable."

"And you make the suffering of the crown so much more enjoyable, wife." He spins me, his hand dipping to the curve of my ass as he presses me tighter to him. "Some days, I think you want my hate more than my love."

"Says the man who is forcing me to hate him," I admit in a hushed whisper.

The stop in our dance is sudden, jarring me as he lowers his lips to mine. It's another test as he pushes his tongue into my mouth.

I kiss him back. I have to, since his whole court is watching. But when I open my eyes, his are already watching mine. Daring me to fall into line or else.

Life is short. Sometimes it pays to pick the other option.

Bite! I trap his tongue between my teeth. Hard. The taste of his blood hits both our lips, but he licks it away, ensuring no one notices my attack. I watch as he runs his now-bitten tongue over his teeth, satisfaction gleaming in my eyes.

A smirk tugs at his lips, torn somewhere between attraction and retribution. "I know you are upset about tonight, but this little stunt worked in my favor."

"It was not a stunt."

His lips pull into a cruel, mocking grin. He presses his lips to mine again, but this time, he bites my lip. I want to pull back, but I hold my ground as he proves yet again he'll drink my blood. He swipes his tongue over the cut, causing a sting before he pulls away.

He smiles, shoulders wide and worthy of the weight of the crown on his head. "Your father and the fae will learn of this. They will not see me as a monster who praises your brother's killer. I'll be seen as a man who is willing to risk myself in order to protect you. So please, my beauty, pluck all the roses you'd like. Bleed. Play games against me in front of my court, but Selene, remember that if I choose to screw you over in front of my court, it will be actual fucking. Weigh the cost before you make the move, my beauty. The game of a crown is long, and the road only grows more bloody and narrow."

My bones shake with fury. He holds my hand as he guides me off the dance floor and to his table. Instead of allowing me to sit in my chair, he places me on his lap. Fingers dance over my shoulders as he pushes back my hair, exposing my neck.

What is he doing? He wouldn't bite me!

"I am not the monster you think I am." He presses his lips to my skin. "But I will be the monster you make me, Selene," he croons.

"Another warning."

"You should heed it." One second, two, three, he holds my stare before he looks away and grabs his goblet, drinking down the rest of the blood.

"You want my heart, yet you give the man who killed my brother a title."

"What would you have me do?" Galen sets the goblet down firmly. "He helped end this war."

"When you recognize my sorrow, then and only then you may have my heart, Galen. Until then, you continue to crush it."

He's too stubborn to call this off now. "Stay and eat. Once you are finished, leave. I will wait to honor him with the title once you have left."

"How gracious of you," I sneer. I'm pushing him to every limit. It's foolish, but I have nothing else to lose. Everett was everything to me.

Galen's sigh sounds as heavy as an old ocean wave that's tired from the repetition of the tide. Soon, it might break free, swallowing land from the map, or perhaps it will continue the natural ebb and flow. One never knows what nature—or a mad king—will do.

Galen's hand reaches out to turn my neck. His touch is gentle. "I lost men who were like my brother, too," he admits as he cups my cheek.

His eyes dip, taking note of my trembling bottom lip. "And what would you do if my father held parties for the men who killed them?"

His honest answer remains unspoken. Only the lie is told: "I would remember this was war, and now we have peace, and I would do everything in my power to make sure that peace lasted."

He's so good at giving warnings and threats wrapped in pretty, loving words.

So am I.

"Peace is a prelude to war." I make sure each word I speak cuts like shattered glass.

"War is a prologue to a crown," Galen replies. His glare is meant to cut me like a blade, but I've been numb since my brother died.

"And the epilogue of a crown worn by an unworthy king," I slide off his lap and press a hand to his shoulder, "is an uprising."

I bow, acknowledging that he and I are officially at war.

As I saunter away, I bite my inner cheek, hiding my smile.

CHAPTER
FIVE

TITUS

Queen Selene is a sunrise after a battle that almost killed you. Awe-inspiring, breath-stealing.

You're so thankful to witness something this magnificent, but at the same time, reality hits you: you need to survive another day in order to be lucky enough to see the sun again.

How in the gods' holy names do I get close to her without risking my dick? Because he's perking up. Selene's as striking as a diamond trapped in a crown I can never afford to own or look at.

But I need her. Desperately. I need to free her so I can use her.

I'm a copy and paste of every male—shit, the women too—in the room. Mouths parted, eyes wide. It's a slap-me-silly moment to witness beauty at her level.

Galen and her dance like two skilled warriors, neither willing to back down. Her eyes smile darkly as she trades words meant for an intimate duel. The crowd's shadows inch in, hoping to eavesdrop, but the music swallows their conversation whole.

"I'd let a woman like that bend me backwards and—"

My fist hits hard abs. "Shut up!" I glare at Tristen. "Do you want to die?"

"If it were by her hands, after she rode my cock, I'd die happy."

Red stains my eyes. One blink removes it.

What was that? I never lose focus.

We travel faster than floodwaters ripping through a small ocean town as I drag my brother through the crowd, away from the dance floor, and towards the bar. I need a drink. I need the whole barrel!

Dying in battle is honorable, but maybe I should consider dying of toxicosis.

I grab a glass. Bloodwine spills over the rim, red drips down my fingers.

Is this a prelude to my time at court?

"Don't mind if I do," Tristen gingerly sings, reaching for a glass. I intercept, shoving water into his hand.

"Good idea." He speaks unfazed. "Hydration is key to killing a hangover."

"No more wine," I growl, rolling my eyes.

"See, you're always looking out for me." He raises his water, smirks, then chugs it down. "Wine hangovers are the worst. I'll stick to whiskey then."

"No more, Tristen."

He pouts. "You're like a guy who fails to get it up when you have a beautiful lady on her knees. Come on. Can I at least try to pump you up —I mean, talk you up?" He waggles his eyebrows.

My gulp sounds like a hammer.

"Fine." He rolls his eyes with a huff.

I shouldn't drink blood, not here; it could fuel Everett's magic, but I need to feel *my* magic calm me. One small sip can't hurt. I lift the glass with a grunt. Warm blood hits my tongue. Ah, yes. Fire magic kneads through my muscles, slow and steady.

We're so used to strict blood rationing when on duty. Blood wine is a rare delight. It makes our magic purr, along with other senses. But it can be addicting which, by the looks of it, our entire noble court is addicted.

Tristen presses into me like a bookend and whispers, "Please make sure I never fall in love; I will never willingly drink fae blood. Love makes you do crazy things. Then again, if a woman like that told me to drink from her, I would. I'm an idiot, but I have a huge cock, so there's the silver lining."

"You touch a woman like the queen, and you'll have no cock to brag about." I swat him.

"Don't be bashful; we're brothers. I know you're working with the same thickness and girth."

A doe-eyed female next to us blushes more cranberry than the wine. She giggles and bashfully scurries away. I pinch the bridge of my nose. "You did not just say thickness and girth," I groan.

"Ladies love words like that. Trust me." He puffs his chest out. "I happened to take a peek inside one of Ember's books. You can't imagine the shit she reads. Thick, aching, throbbing, pulsing heat. It's like a dictionary of what ladies want to hear. You want a language lesson 101? How about we start with the words that get them wet and aching," he jokes.

I turn away and cringe. "I don't want to hear this."

"Because you're the older brother to us all. But as the younger sibling, I must support all sexual exploration."

"You and Nero have spent too much time in the brothels."

"They're not brothels. Gods, you sound centuries old. Sex clubs are the hottest thing nowadays."

"It amazes me you find the time to visit them between battles."

"What's life worth living for if not to spend my last days between a willing lady's legs? They praise my tongue. Most call me a god." He winks.

I can't help but shake my head. "You're drunk."

"Absolutely. It's the only way to survive this. But some drunks spill only truths. I am one when it comes to my bedroom skills." Tristen leans closer. "What do you think fae blood tastes like? I mean, I don't mind trying new things, but I don't wanna risk poisoning my amazing body." He glances at his biceps and flexes.

He always does this, pretends to be self-centered and makes jokes; he's just trying to snap me out of my mood.

Don't get me wrong, Tris loves to fuck around, but he's not the hit-it-and-skip-out the next morning guy. He is a cuddler, but he'd never admit it.

"Taste is irrelevant. Galen can't let the queen bleed." I argue. What a queen she is, dripping in red, tempting us all, toying with the reminder that her blood is toxic to vampires, only to force the king to drink it.

Her actions remind me of Everett's. Both of them play games where they know the rules and you don't.

Queen Selene embodies the role perfectly. Tall and regal, her beauty is unparalleled. She has smooth golden skin, like most fae in Solaria, but Selene has an inner glow of confidence others lack.

She's only worthy of being touched by a king's hands.

Get down! I inwardly shout at my cock, an action I'm sure every male is also doing after witnessing Selene bow to the king. Her tight red dress makes her ass look so fucking... *Stop!*

My ribs press into my lungs when I look at Selene's face.

Tristen was right. I need Selene's help. Everett's magic has become a burdensome beast, and his words—mentions of runes—are a sweeping tide that threatens to wash away my sanity.

I hold the empty glass to my chest. The pressure of Tristen's eyes digs into my face. "It's going to be okay. They will help you." He places his hand on my shoulder.

Why does that hand feel more like a child begging me to listen rather than an adult trying to convince me to weigh all the costs?

"What if their help comes in the form of a knife?" That knot of dread Everett placed in my belly never died; it grew. Tristen tried to help me, but I was the older brother. I solved the problems, not him.

I have no idea how to control this time-weaving magic, and it's only a matter of time before someone else finds out. If the world discovers fae can gift their magic to other creatures, the world will fall into chaos and extortion.

"Make sure you smile widely, but not too widely. You don't want to look like an ax murderer. Women don't like that; they prefer swords. Long, hard, shapely steel cocks."

"I'm gonna stab you with my sword if you don't stop," I groan, running a hand down my face.

"If I were a woman who wasn't related to you, that would make me swoon. Although may I suggest, 'I'm going to plunge my sword into you with such a force you won't be able to walk for days.' It's got a vibe ladies would prefer." Tristen slaps my back, but before I can reply, the king is calling my name.

My skin turns into a tough shell I want to shake off. Run away. I don't want praise for killing. If only they knew I would have done anything, *anything*, to take back slaying Prince Everett.

They all smile and clap.

Miscreants, every single one of them.

I walk up to the king. Selene has left early, which messes up my plans because I was hoping to talk to her. I'd rarely have an opportunity to approach the queen.

Tristen thinks we should target Sable for help, and after seeing Selene this evening, I agree. But the other twin hasn't shown up at the party.

Maybe she's skinning bunnies for pleasure. I wouldn't put it past a royal-born fae.

Why the heck would Sable come here to honor me, the man who killed her brother?

All I hear is a buzzing as King Galen's lips move, his arms open, and he touches my shoulders and welcomes me.

Shit! It's happening! No! No! Not here!

Everett's time-weaving magic is complicated. I have no idea how to use it, but it certainly knows how to use me. There are signs, like the dimming of other senses. Sound is always first.

A soldier comes forward with a sword in hand, bows, and hands it to the king.

What is he saying?

Shit! Just nod. Oh, King Galen is giving me the sword.

Oh, it's a gift. I dip my chin and accept it, and then my eyes shoot to Tristen, but his clapping slows.

No!

Movement is the second sense to dim, just like it did the day of the battle. When these time bubbles trap me, I can move freely. Others who are not trapped have no idea. Tristen has witnessed it. He said it always appeared as if I were there, moving the same.

The first time I pulled Tristen into the bubble, he was so impressed he started brainstorming dozens of ways to use it to our advantage.

That's when I realized why Everett had given his magic to me.

I don't want to use it to aid me in killing kings when they have no idea I could move faster than them. I don't want crowns. All I want is safety and security for my family. I want to make sure no child is forced to become a soldier. I don't want a child to grow as Ember did, to have nothing, not even a name, for their first few years.

I want friendships to evolve into brotherhoods, not because they were forced to fight together or be killed, but because there was a genuine connection. I just... I know a better world is too much to ask for. I want a *different* world. A world where we respect life more than we value killing it.

I want land in a small village, where I know my neighbors and help them if need be. I want birds chirping and not men screaming as they die.

I think my heart is starting to sweat. I sink back, trying to distance myself without offending the king.

Snap! The time bubble traps me, and my breath turns to wet cement. Suffocating.

Wait, I'm... alone. How's that possible? Galen is so close. Did the time-weave listen to me?

I feel like I'm going to be sick, but then... a chill ripples down my body. That's not part of the time-weaving.

It's something else. A new sense I developed on the battlefield. This sense tells me one thing.

I'm prey.

Hair stands, sweat drips through the tiny strands, my throat tightens, palms grow slick. I have only a moment, one reaction, one chance to escape.

I look at Galen. He's not the predator that alerted my senses.

I start to turn my neck, but the time-weaving stops! My body jerks from the sudden inhale of all the sounds and movement again.

My eyes whip to Tristen, clashing with unspoken truths of what I just did. His smile drops faster than being told of a pregnancy scare, from a woman whose name he doesn't remember. His drunken state is now alert. He looks around and nods, assuring me my secret is safe.

I can't release the breath held in my lungs. "My newest General!" King Galen grabs my hand with the gifted sword and holds it high to the cheering crowd.

Their praises make my stomach revolt. My gaze shifts to the high ceilings and walls. Black roses line every inch, so many that you can't see the stones.

Why not just have the party outside in the gardens if you intend to bring them in?

Because that's what kings do, they cut and kill things, like these roses mounted and hung on their walls, for pleasure.

Like the darkness in Galen's eyes, the roses are layered. Not just shades of black, but deep violets and uncharted ocean blues. It's that tiny, insignificant glimpse of color that separates the sleek, dark depths that just move behind them.

There! It's a small window of sorts. Who's that lurking behind it?

You're the result of my uneasiness. The predator stalking me.

I found you!

King Galen lowers my hands and releases me. I grip the newly minted sword as I narrow my eyes at the predator.

Now would be an excellent time to time-weave! But no! Work when I don't need you.

There! I spot eyes peering at me through a small slit in the wall.

Holy shit!

I feel like ice being pelted with rain. Fracturing. Shocked. The predator steps closer, revealing her face through the small opening.

Silken black stands apart from the dark roses. What are you doing, Queen Selene?

Oh... Shit!

My sharp eyes catch sight of what's coming for me, an arrow, a weapon, hoping to shatter what is left of me.

Sounds vanish, people slow, but that's when I see it.

Death is coming, and it is aimed directly at my heart.

CHAPTER
SIX

SELENE

The stone walls don't swallow my breath. Each exhale bounces back, warming my face. My cheeks heat, but my hands are finally steady.

"I have you to protect me," I said to Galen. I can make threats just as well as he can!

But will he protect me after this?

The question is how badly Galen wants peace? If that's what he truly wants with my people, he'll let my transgressions go.

If he wants war, he'll kill me for my crime.

I don't see it as a crime.

It's justice.

A life for a life. If I have to sacrifice my life in order to avenge my brother, so be it.

What future do I have, anyway? Married to a prick with a huge cock—sexual pleasure doesn't make a marriage last. It helps, but love is the only way a marriage can truly survive. Love has the power to endure both good and bad times.

Love is both an ember and a fire. Some years, it roars, and others, it flickers but remains lit.

Galen and I don't have that. There's no fire, just sparks that never fully catch aflame.

Eventually, I'll be forced to bear his children. But what if those children are fae and not vampires? Never has a mixed-species child survived past birth before. It's one magic or the other, never both.

If our child is gifted with fae magic, Galen would not let them stay here. He will demand vampire children as his heirs. My child, if born fae, will be forced to return to fae lands. Since my brother is dead, my child, if male, will inherit my father's crown.

What if they are female? That was never mentioned. Will she be killed or traded like a playing card?

And if the child is a male fae, I cannot raise them. Galen would not let me leave to return home to watch them grow.

Death and loneliness. That's what defines my future.

So why not die with a purpose instead of a broken heart?

Galen will suspect me first. So I hid my tracks, returned to my room, changed in front of my maid, and slipped into bed. Deception began when she departed; I then secretly left my room, traversed the gardens, and reached my hiding place.

My arm is steady, but the weight of the weapon feels unfamiliar in my hands since it's not my usual hunting bow. The ash wood is rougher to the touch and in need of a good polish. It's smaller, better suited for close range.

"This is it," I breathe as I draw my elbow back; the weight of the string helps to steady my fingers. My biceps clench as I demand the string to pull tighter, but the hallway is so narrow that my elbow digs into the stone.

My eyes trace down the arrow I made. I sat by the fire and carved the wood, standing hunched under the light of the moon as I shaped the stone into a point, and polished it under the sun until it was so sharp that it rivaled my husband's fangs.

"There you are, the famous heart thief." That's what the songs call Titus. Ballads can turn monsters into heroes and heroes into villains.

Good, you're tall, taller than Galen, and easy to spot. That hair, rivaling my shade of black, shines under the chandeliers. His shoulders are wide, arms muscled in a way that proves he is more familiar with swinging a sword than lifting a fork.

His stance is steady and sure-footed. His jaw is square and hard, firmly clenched, unlike Galen's, which is used to seducing a crowd with a warm smirk.

Titus is every ounce a killing machine.

I move on from his face, because it makes him more human. Those hands belong to a beast. His fingers, which gripped my brother's heart as it still beat, are holding his newly gifted sword with confidence.

Did he cheer and laugh as Everett felt?

A dip of my arm has my arrow lining up directly to his heart.

"You don't want to meet him first?" My sister's voice startles me. I keep my bow aimed at Titus, but my neck turns to see Sable grinning at me, one perfectly plucked brow arched. "He's really handsome." Her lips curl up into sharp points, resembling the thorns that protrude from the rose stems.

Sable, my twin sister, looks exactly like me, but she wears a more voluminous dress with intricate black roses that draw attention to her pushed-up breasts.

Sable never lets an opportunity to dress up slip through her poisonous fingers. She likes fine things—jewels, dresses, crowns, cocks that are attached to men with titles, preferably crowns, but I got the king. Unfortunately.

"You disrespect our brother." I peer through the wall's narrow opening. "He killed him." I aim my elbow high. The string stings my finger from the tension as I pull it back with all my might.

Sable moves slowly, like a koi fish gently swimming closer.

I don't want her here ruining this memory as she usually does.

"Did you ever stop to think?" She pauses long enough for my arm to begin to ache. "Maybe Everett wasn't as skilled a fighter as you imagined him to be?" The sick joy in her voice bleeds through her next words, which are my final blow. "Maybe Everett deserved to die."

Clatter! The bow drops to the ground. I shove her back into the stone. Instead of grunting in pain, she grins. I raise my hand and press the arrow into her neck; the dark black stone I used to make the arrow's tip makes her skin look more luminous and tan.

The slight tremble my fingers had at the start of the evening is nothing compared to the earthquake-sized movements my hand now possesses.

Her smile spreads from ear to ear, but her eyes relax. The pulse in her neck pushes against the arrow's tip.

I want to pierce it, to slice the vein that supplies her brain with blood. I want to end her, just like she has tried to kill me.

So many times she has tried. It's a wonder either of us is still alive.

I never wanted it to be this way. She's my twin. Once, I did love her. However, things shifted at the age of five when she attempted to drown me. I knew then, even as a child, that Sable's magic controlled her. That fact motivated me to train my magic. It would never best me. I ruled it, not vice versa.

I tried a few more times to help her, but you can only pet a biting dog so many times before it gets lucky and delivers a deadly blow.

This is where we stand, always at odds, how we will forever be.

Like everything else in my life, I hate it, but I accept it. That's how I was taught to survive. Accept and move on.

However, I refuse to accept what Galen has done.

"That won't kill me," she purrs as if being on the verge of death seduces her. I want to shove knives in my ears. It's not enough that we look alike; no, we sound the same, too! She's my worst enemy, speaking my fears back in my own voice! "You'd have to plunge it into my heart."

"You don't have one," I hiss.

"True," she giggles. She leans into the stone wall as if it is a plush mattress. "But how poetic to die the same way our brother did. Pierced through the heart."

"One day you will die, and it will be alone. You won't beg. Your pride is strong, but deep down, fear will arise without a comforting hand to hold. Your fingers will grasp nothing but raw, deserted air, Sable. Because that's what your soul is. Frigid and barren." I lean closer, nose to nose with the version of myself that is truly the definition of evil. "You reap what you sow."

I push my feet back with force until my back hits the stone opposite her. This arrow is meant for one person, and it is not Sable.

"That is why I am spreading so many seeds, sister. You'd be wise to do the same. When the harvest time comes, you will be the one who is petrified."

I look at her feet, too sickened to meet her eyes again. Sable's always scheming and plotting something.

"I'm happy Everett is dead. He was always meddling in my business. He tried to stop me; he did for years. Now, I can't be stopped," she gloats. Her chest inhales wide like a dragon that finally landed on the pile of ashes it created.

"I'm free. My only regret is that I did not end Everett myself. I did enjoy all the attempts, though. Killing isn't the fun part; it's the plotting. The actual attack is just the blink of an eye. When the victim shoves out their last breath, it's always such a letdown. Then I have to start over again, choose a different target. It's like creating those needlepoints they forced us to do as children. Again and again. Select a design, make it, finalize the details, finish it, then start again."

She leans against the wall with relaxed ease. "You should see my next design, Selene; it will outshine everything in this world. Everything."

"A shine is just a reflection," I retort. "A reflection is a trick of angles and light. It makes something small appear grandiose. It's momentary, every light must dull, Sable; yours already is."

Do you like my wicked smile? You taught me how to make it.

I tip my chin up and add, "Oops, you just showed your temper. Put your mask on quickly. The beast inside you is too grotesque to be seen in court."

Her lips snarl back, showing off her white teeth. "You're a bitch!"

I shake out my arm, relaxing it so I can make the shot. "I could respond likewise, but I'd rather not share anything in common with you."

"You will fall one day, Selene."

I flick my hair back over my shoulder. "Tell me something I don't know. Fae have long lives, but eventually," I look at her, "everything dies, Sable."

"It's *how* they die." She rolls her shoulders back. "I have a feeling you will die with such heartache and agony, it will be unimaginable."

"That means I loved, and if I loved, then someone loved me. Someone will mourn for me. Who will mourn your death, Sable?" I tilt my head back, gazing down at her with disdain. "I know who will rejoice. It's how they die, right?"

There's your own medicine on a spoon. Open your evil lips and lap it down like the bitch you are.

I look out the window again. Good, my target is still there.

Go away, Sable! I employ my only known technique to encourage her exit. I keep talking. "You think you are free, but you are not. Your leash is long, but one day, it will snap back." I smirk. "And those people holding your leash, whom you think are your friends, you will be reminded they are not your friends but your masters."

"I'm freer than you." She argues in a weak defense. "I will be after tonight. Are you really planning on killing him?"

Turning, I try to ignore her, but Sable hunts down attention.

"You know," she begins as I bend down to grab the bow, "I think you'd do it. Kill me, but then you'd feel guilty and use your life magic to bring me back."

I have a rare gift; so do all my siblings. My family bred for that sole purpose. I have a form of life. My twin balances me. Sable's magic is death. One prolonged touch from her magic and death can set in and start to spread.

It works slowly, thank the gods. She needs contact for a few minutes to kill a grown man. My life magic is best at healing. One touch from me, and I can heal what she did to an extent.

Although I'll never admit that Sable is stronger, she can kill; I can't bring back the dead.

I have been cleaning up her mess my entire life. One time, she disliked the lettuce of the local farmer, so she went to the farm, poured her magic into the soil, and killed the crops.

Father allowed her to get away with it because one, Sable was learning how to use and control her magic, and two, I could heal the land and nourish the soil. That became the reckless cycle of how Sable and I mastered our magic.

Father forced her to sicken, and me to heal.

During the war, I spent my time in the healing tents. But the one person I wished I could have saved was Everett.

Sable is always one step ahead, one move ready to inflict pain, so my next statement shocks her. "Did you ever consider I'd only heal you so I could kill you again?" I hold my bow and peer through the narrow window as I take my aim. "Over and over again," I mutter.

Silence.

Thank the gods!

"Killing him won't fix anything, Selene." Why did she have to speak? "You'll only start another war."

Contentment lifts my lips into a smile, crinkling my eyes. "That's where you're wrong, Sable." I look at her one more time, watch the confusion wrinkle her forehead, and then her eyes dilate. Good, she is thinking about all the moves I'm playing. "You spoke to the guard who was on the northern wall; he saw you walking this way, not *me*."

Oh yes, it's clicking in her head.

You see, Galen will suspect me, but he won't know the truth.

Which twin was it?

I knew Sable would follow me here; she always likes to torture me. Galen has seen how Sable has been sucking up to his court, trying to win favor.

But why?

Was it so that Sable could kill the hero and be spared because the people would forgive her?

See, that's a smart suggestion. Sable just realized it, but wait, dear sister, there's more.

Galen thinks Sable and I disagree, but has he considered it all a game so we can trick him?

Oh, the plot thickens.

He must contemplate Sable's possible involvement. Which means... Sable's leash is about to be tugged back hard. Those freedoms she enjoys will vanish soon.

Ultimately, having an evil twin offers me one significant benefit. She can be a scapegoat.

"*You* will start this war." I look at Titus and release my arrow. "Not me."

CHAPTER
SEVEN

TITUS

The shock of the attack digs into me as a splinter dives under the nail.

Everett's time-waving magic wants to keep me alive—to be a pair of tweezers that plucks out the annoyance; it's like having an overprotective parent hovering over you.

Time slows now. I'm a lucky bastard because it's only me in the time bubble again. My secret is still safe. Noise turns into a distant hum.

Is this arrow intended for Galen or me?

Is our queen an assassin?

With each breath I take, the arrow draws closer. I'm unsure how long the time-weaving will last. I take a fighting stance. I raise the sword that Galen gifted me.

The crowd reacts. The bubble begins to crack!

Oh shit! They see me raising my sword next to their king.

See the arrow!

Good, Galen spots it.

Snap! The bubble breaks right as I swing down, slicing the arrow in half. I lock eyes with the assassin. She's already moving.

Screams erupt, guards shout. The hard stone floor collides with my chest as I'm tackled.

My fire magic roars against the assault. It slips into my palms, but two guards stomp on my hands. Pain explodes over my knuckles as three fingers break. The blood I just drank heals them.

"Stop!" Galen roars. "He saved me, you fool! Did you not see him cleave the arrow in two?"

Panic erupts. I'm used to shouts and chaos. My coiled muscles relax. My fire seeps back into my fingers.

"Bloody fucking heavens!" King Galen shouts.

Soldiers file into the party. My lips part, ready to confess. I slam my mouth shut. I don't have solid facts. An accusation could cost me my life.

If Galen believes me, he'd have to kill the queen.

I need her to help me.

It may have been her twin.

Fuck! Fuck! Fuck!

Galen regards me, chin held high. That crown on his head makes me take a step back. "Did you see who it was?" he questions with an authority that makes me feel like a young boy again.

The intensity of the glare his eyes hold is hotter than the very flames I can produce. His question is a multi-faceted game, and depending on my answer, I'll be granted life, death, or a chance to play again.

Shit! He knows it was the queen. He tilts his head as he places his palm on his sword. Answering him with the truth feels more dangerous than the arrow that was aimed at us.

Galen knows that Selene was trying to take my life.

Which means he could have stopped it. But he didn't. Why?

I shake my head. "No, my king."

His scowl sharpens. It practically scrapes across my neck. "I will deal with her," he mutters. A slight nod is the only apology I get.

My gulp gives away my youth. Galen is a seasoned tree; he knows how to weather storms. I am just a sapling.

"Search the grounds for the assassin. They likely headed to the main gates," King Galen orders the soldiers on duty. "I owe General Titus my sincerest apology. I heard whispers that the fae nobles were seeking the death of my warrior."

Everett's dying face flashes through my mind.

"I hoped these nobles would act with dignity, but emotions are still running high." King Galen makes a show of shaking his head.

My neck stiffens. I watch Galen weave a lie to excuse his wife, who wants me dead.

I glance at Tristen; if anyone looked at the angle of his feet, they would see he is ready to defend me, not King Galen.

Galen places a hand on my shoulder. *That's a hard grip.* "I will deal with them." His hold grows to bone-crushing strength before he drops his arm. "I am happy my beautiful wife did not bear witness to what her people did. Nobles whom I have allowed to live and dine in my court."

Shouts of anger bounce off the chandeliers.

He continues, "I know their actions would embarrass her deeply. Queen Selene, like me, just wants peace."

I doubt that.

"My lands will be safe for everyone. A place children can grow, laugh, and play without the fear of an invasion." More cheers. "Know this, I will have peace! I will punish anyone who dares to attack us." His hand rests on the hilt of his blade, not with rage; no, he sweeps his fingers over it with glee.

Then, Galen's gaze meets mine. "Come with me."

Stay away! I shake my head at Tristen. Fellow warriors clap my back and promise vengeance for the crime against me.

King Galen and I, along with a dozen men, exit the hall and make our way through the castle. "General Harold," the king thunders, "find Princess Sable. Bring her to the dungeons."

"The dungeons?"

"Did I stutter?"

"No, my king." Harold nods and rushes off.

"What of the queen? Should I go find her?" a soldier whose name I do not know asks.

It will cost him. He wants the queen to suffer in a way some vile men think.

Galen moves fluidly. A sharp intake of breath cuts through the air. Galen plunges his sword into the soldier's heart.

Some smile, and others, like me, carefully school their features.

Galen holds his sword there. We wait until death claims him.

"The price for questioning me," Galen states. He treats men as mere food he can toss aside. "Hold him," he orders the two closest soldiers.

Galen steps back, pulls his sword out, then wipes it clean on the soldier's shoulder.

In the end, that's what we are to King Galen. Nothing.

Every victory I had in battle, not counting Everett's death, is now sour. A nightmare that will haunt me.

"Get rid of him. If anyone asks, he was conspiring with the fae nobles."

I don't know how my feet move. Somehow they do. Eventually, we reach the end of the hall.

"Stay here," Galen orders the men. He pushes a stone. The wall groans like an elderly human whom sleep has yet to claim. They must endure another long, cold, lonely morning full of aches and pains.

The wall slides open, revealing a long, dark hallway.

Galen breezes inside. "Come, Titus."

I follow, unsure whether I'm heading to my death. But as Everett said, I'm a soldier. I don't run from what scares me.

Galen's fuming exhales echo off the hall. He pauses and presses another spot on the wall. This time, a large room is revealed. A fire crackles, and the scent of parchment, ink, and cedar fills the air. The only light is from the fire.

There are no windows to escape through. No one can see or hear what he will do to me.

It's clearly his office, lined with bookshelves and a large round desk with maps and notes. "You may sit," Galen grunts.

The fire in my veins itches to be set free. It senses a threat. I grab the chair and lower myself into it, but my ass remains on the edge.

I killed a prince. Will I have to kill a king in order to survive?

I would do so in order to reunite with my family. And to protect Everett's magic. I will not let his death be wasted.

Galen joins me with a bottle of amber liquid. His chair is a pair of warm hands he sinks into. His mouth tightens like wood submerged in icy waters, the corners cracking and splintering. He covers his fury with his cup as he swallows.

He tips his head back, exposing his neck to me as he drinks.

You're a stupid man. Maybe I'm the foolish one for thinking I can kill a king.

His gulp is thunderous; his hand moves like lightning, offering me the bottle. I grab it by the neck and drink. Each swallow is forced.

Galen rests his elbow on the arm of his chair as he rubs his temple. "My wife wants you dead," he states matter-of-factly. His tone makes me feel like a tree whose branches hinder the walker on a pathway. Galen likes the tree for the shade it provides—I won the war for him.

I'm his trophy. Selene wants me cut down.

"That's unfortunate," I respond. He has to protect his wife, so I make sure he can. "The killer had a sure aim. I'm sure the queen's hands are too delicate to pull a bow back with such force."

Galen's voice turns into a ghost's whisper. "Even tiny spiders can create remarkably intricate webs, Titus." He coughs and speaks loudly. "You're clever." Galen leans back, but his eyes seem to inch forward, attempting to peel me open. "Is that how you killed her brother?"

This is a fight, make no mistake. King Galen is testing me.

"To be honest, it was luck. Everett was highly skilled, but exhaustion weakens us all in the end."

He reaches for his crown and rubs it.

Like all vampires, Galen has elemental magic. His comes in the form of thorny vines that can lash out and cut through flesh as it grabs bone and snaps it in half.

If Galen knew I possessed magic from a fae, he'd never let me taste my next breath. It's already bad enough that I killed the prince and not him. But Galen would need to be on the battlefield, not tucked away in his castle.

His hand slips to conceal his mouth. "Why don't you lie to me? Embellish your story. You could have spun an elaborate tale of how weak the prince was and the pleasure you took in killing him."

Men who don't kill with their own hands take pleasure in it.

Soldiers don't.

"It's a crime to lie to you." *Don't flinch. That's right, stay humble and still.*

"Yet it happens every day." He props his head on his hand. His index finger traces the curve of his cheek. "Sometimes, I let crimes go unpunished. I assure you, this one will not be ignored."

"May I speak freely?"

He nods.

"I expect nothing less of the queen. I killed her brother. She wants my blood."

"Do you think she is owed it?"

"I'd rather she not. I did as my king commanded. I fought. It didn't matter if it was a prince in my way or a random soldier. They raised a sword against you."

"If only all my men were like you," he sighs.

If all your men were like me, you'd be dead.

"I can leave tonight," I offer. "Return to the border and keep watch. I don't want to cause unrest for the queen."

Maybe I can find another fae to help me.

"Leave?" He sits up straighter. "You're not leaving, Titus. If I bow down to her tantrums, I'll never be able to control her."

A man should not seek to control his wife. No wonder their marriage is so fucked up.

I avoid his face. *This* was what I fought for! Seeing it up close sickens me.

A more startling fact is that Galen isn't the worst king out there. He makes sure his people are fed, housed, and clothed. He gives humans a house and a job, making them feel dignified, so they want to donate their blood in return.

"Selene would take pleasure in a spanking. I must resort to other forms of punishment."

Now I'm picturing her over my knee, my hand coming down on her, with only that red silk dress as a barrier.

"You're staying." Galen's words wash away the fantasy. "You will be her personal guard."

I shift forward, almost falling off the chair. I grab the chair's arms tightly, too tightly! The wood starts to smoke under my fingers. "Pardon?" I bark. I force my magic to withdraw.

Galen raises a shocked brow. He spots his ruined chair.

"I mean, It's an honor I surely do not deserve," I hurry to say.

Everett, did you foresee this?

"You look ill." Galen's laugh slaps the shock off my face.

I am.

I'm just beginning to see how far ahead Everett has plotted.

You should look skittish, too, Galen.

"I do apologize, but this is the best course of action. Once I see that Selene has learned her lesson, you may have Everly Castle."

"Everly Castle?" *I don't want a castle.*

Galen nods. "I'll give you four hundred men to live on the land and guard the border, of course."

In other words, I'll oversee Everly Castle's conversion into a guard station.

I dip my chin. "What if she tries to kill me?"

He snickers, "Oh, she will, but I will kill the fae nobles tonight; that should make her think twice. Still, I'd watch your back. If she tries anything, let me know. Selene needs to learn that if she kicks and screams, she will not get her way."

How do I defend myself? Do I raise a hand to my queen?

His gift is a death sentence.

This is how a king thanks the hero who holds the public's praise. Kings are only kings when the attention is solely on them. If too many eyes look away, he's just a man with a pretty crown that means absolutely nothing.

CHAPTER
EIGHT

SELENE

With the same musical ease that the ballads detailed Titus slaying my brother, he sliced my arrow in half. Titus isn't just a soldier—an instrument of war—he's a composer.

I kick my feet, pushing the sheets off as I roll onto my side.

Polished boots walking down the hall reach my ears. Here he comes.

Boom! My door is kicked off its hinges.

Looks like you need better craftsmen, Galen.

Do I move from my bed? No, not addressing Galen's presence brings me joy.

"I know you're awake." His voice is a cold slither.

I press my fingertips into the mattress. I've pissed him off before. This is next level. Avenging Everett was worth it.

"Oh, silly me." I roll onto my back and stretch my arms above my head. "I thought I was dreaming." *Angering you makes me sleep soundly.*

Like a piece on a game board, he inches closer. His scent of blackcurrant and jasmine invades my nose. His eyes press into me like lips to a glass, drinking, slurping me down in a single gulp. Closer, closer. Only a thin sheet of paper can slip between our lips.

That little gap defines our relationship—a small separation, locking us in a constant state of love and war.

A bridge could have been built, but Galen burnt down all the forest that would have supplied the wood. Now, he will suffer as he shouts across the chasm.

And me? I'll simply watch as he struggles.

"Your dreams start wars." His eyes churn like soil being tilled.

"As. Do. Yours."

"Allow me to show you what a nightmare is." His hands shoot out. I yelp. Thorny vines seize me, clenching so tight they shred the sheets. Their thorns pierce the mattress and begin to make shallow cuts on my body.

Galen pauses.

I will not plead. "You're too used to me begging you, Galen." I lower my eyes to his cock. "It was my mistake to spoil you." I smirk.

"Oh, Selene," he purrs as he marvels at his vines, "you truly wish to turn me into a beast."

He shakes his head, then pulls the rose I gave him out of his pocket; he spins the stem between his index and thumb fingers. The vines holding me grow tighter. My blood seeps into the blankets.

"You need no help." I look away. He grows another vine that pushes my face back. A single thorn cuts my cheek in the process.

"I've heard you've come close to taking your own life," he begins. "During the war, you'd stay with the healers, working yourself into an exhaustive state of near death, trying to save your warriors. Pouring your life magic into them, regardless of your own life. Such a selfless act. A trait I wanted in my queen." He smells the rose.

"People are not ingredients at the market."

He chuckles, "You'd be surprised, my beauty; I can take everything away. I'll turn you into a mere object for my amusement, then store you away."

This was why hate-sex was bad, because you hate the person, Selene!

I grind my teeth to flat horizons. I wish I had never let him between my legs. Some monsters cannot be changed.

"Some items are deadly if used incorrectly. It's not the poison that is the killer, my sweet husband; it is the dosing. Careful, don't take too much of me, or too little. You need to determine the perfect amount. You realize that now, don't you?"

His cheeks redden, making his brown hair look more woodsy.

"You took too much. You will suffer the effects." I push against the vines holding me down. "How dare you praise Everett's killer!"

His inhalation is so deep, it steals the air from my lungs. "How dare you test me in front of my court!"

I sink back into my mattress, but I smile. Some animals can survive having an appendage cut off. They can regrow it. I'll just mimic them.

"You are right, Selene, you are poisonous." He sits on the edge of the bed. I try to edge away, but his vines dig into me. "Poisons can be mastered. I just need a small daily dose. He reaches out and slides a finger down my cheek. "A little taste." His touch glides down my neck, then lower, between my breasts. "Every day. Eventually, I will become accustomed to it."

"There is no more of me to take. We are finished. This marriage is over."

"Your death is the sole escape from this marriage. I've not tired of you yet." A flash of his fangs makes my stomach knot. "I'm well trained in control. I never give in to my lust."

"Lust and boredom got us into bed, not the need to make this marriage survive."

"It wasn't lust that made my cock hard. It was possession." He palms my breast, finding my nipple as he pinches it. "I own you, dear, sweet wife. That's what made my cock ache for you, and you liked that, being owned. That's why you spread your legs for me."

Cold air replaces his hand. He cups the rose in his palms now.

I spit back his own words. "It wasn't being owned that made me wet for you, my dear, sweet husband; it was purely boredom. Any cock would have done." I arch a brow, waiting for his rebuttal.

"If I had not seen you use your magic, I would have claimed your father tricked me, married me to the wrong twin." He looks down at me. "All you seek is death and war."

"That's what revenge is built on, Galen."

"Revenge should not be in your vocabulary."

"Oh, I'm sorry, silly me." I playfully roll my eyes. "Should only 'let me suck your cock, my king.' be the words I know."

Oh, Selene, you don't know when to stop. It's too late. I'll go down swinging.

"What shall I do with you?" Reaching out, he runs the rose down my cheek.

Stop petting me like a dog. Pets can bite, Galen.

I avert my gaze; escape proves impossible. His vines cover me. More crawl out from around him, covering the floor, then they creep up along the walls. They intertwine, forming a ceiling above us. No, a cage of thorns and roses.

"You seem to be quite the horticulturist; I'm sure you can set me aside in a pretty vase," I taunt.

His smile is filled with amusement. Tossing an insult back, he allows black roses to bloom on the vines holding me down. "That sharp tongue..." He looks away, admiring the vines as if they were his children. "There are so many uses for it."

"None that will please you," I retort. "I'd rather bite my tongue off!"

"Your mouth would still be a hole to use, Selene."

I buck against his vines. The thorns dig deeper. He twists and grabs my shoulders, trying to make me stop.

"I'll never forgive you!" I spit.

"I don't need your forgiveness, Selene. I am the king!" His shout causes his vines to squeeze me so tightly that I begin to panic.

He watches the fear seep into my eyes, allows it to linger like a fisherman watching a fish nibble on the bait, right before they reel it in; then he sweeps his thumb over my shoulder. His vines pull back an inch. I feel no relief.

My body shakes. "What we had before tonight will be the highlight of our marriage. Never again will I love you."

"You never loved me. You never gave me the chance!" he seethes.

"The chance was not something I needed to place into your kingly hands, Galen! It was to be earned, not given. For once in your life, you needed to do something yourself. I am not a soldier who bows down to you, nor am I a trinket you can adorn your body with! I am a queen. I have rights, opinions, and yes, demands. If that is too much for you to handle, you do not need a woman as a wife, but rather a dog. Find a bitch to train. I will put up with you no longer. It's my right as a woman to tell you, as demurely as I can, to kindly fuck off. This relationship is over."

His silence could easily delineate borders and establish new territories within its vast expanse.

"You're a queen. A pawn. You forget your place." *Is that hurt in your voice?* "That's okay. You will find it. I know you, Selene; I know how to make your body purr and hum, beg and shout. You think you crave love, but you need hate."

He smirks darkly. He raises the rose I gave him to his nose and inhales.

"You love my cock. You will beg for it again." He presses the rose to my lips before he places it between my breasts. "Vampires and fae live long, Selene. I've mastered how to play the long game."

"Being an old player makes you blind to the rules, Galen. They will come back to haunt you."

"I make the rules, Selene."

I chuckle. "The mere fact that you think you do shows how deluded you are. Kings who don't see reality don't see the knives aimed at them. Sleep tight, husband. Careful who you invite into your bed; even a whore can get lucky and land a deadly blow."

"It bothers you that I sleep with others."

"Oh no, not at all. It gives me a break from having to act like I enjoy our sex."

His lips press against my ear. "You need more acting lessons. Say that more passionately next time."

The mattress dips. He stands, legs wide, chest proud; his chin raises as though the world itself bends to his will.

I curl my fist, wishing I could smack him.

"You don't know the game you started, but in time, you'll learn the rules. You kicked and screamed, and yes, I heard you, but now you will hear my silence."

"Finally." I dismissively roll my eyes. "Careful, husband, your jaw is clenched so tight, we wouldn't want you to chip your pretty fangs."

He wants to step forward. His heels raise, but then he flattens them. "Mark my words, it will be *you* who comes crawling back to me." He runs a hand through his hair, watching me fume. "You're losing your composure. I suggest you find it."

Neither will concede. It will be our undoing.

I can't untie us fast enough.

"Define the word for me, Galen. I don't think you know its true meaning."

Galen slithers to the door. "A queen needs composure in order to remain alive. It's the impulsive ones who the people tend to overthrow and kill."

He raises his hands; vines grow, replacing the door.

"Sweet dreams, Selene, or should I say, welcome to the nightmare you begged me for?" He snickers. "If you scream loud enough, I might just come." He makes sure I understand every pun before he walks away in victory.

CHAPTER
NINE

TITUS

Not even the morning sun can lighten the dark circles under my eyes. The definition of sleep for me was sitting next to a dying fire, as I told Tristen everything Galen ordered me to do.

Sunlight leaks in through the small window, illuminating all the dirt and dust in the air. I flex my toes, stand, dress, and then... I panic.

My feet bring me to the window. I stick my head out and breathe deep. Black surrounds me. Towers of the famous Blackthorn stone comprise the houses and shops. The crudely cut blocks cause the sunlight to be trapped in all the nooks and crannies.

Do the people feel as trapped as the sunlight?

If I were not used to the scent of decay, I'd flinch. Galen should grow his roses here to counteract the sour smell of the soldiers' boots and the merchants' stale goods.

My elbows slide on the lacquered window frame. Why do kings never learn their opulent lifestyle has a vicious side effect called jealousy?

If I were king...

You're not king.

Everett thought I could be.

Thoughts like that will get you killed.

Why did he plant such thoughts if he wanted me to remain alive? Foresight sure would've been handy.

"I don't know what to do," I confess to Tristen. My breath is labored, my head dizzy. I slam the window shut.

"This isn't bad." Tristen rises from the creaky old chair in the corner and closes the gap between us. He claps my back as if his gesture were a cup of blood, giving me renewed hope and energy.

"It's not good." I stare at my boots. The leather is worn and dirty, but that's what makes them comfortable. You have to break things before they bend for you.

Tristen flashes me his goofy smirk. I want to take that smile, bottle it up, keep it safe, and ensure it can smile again. "It's great," he counters.

Tristen is my life. My purpose.

Our parents were soldiers. They died in the same battle, leaving Tristen and me to the kingdom. Like other orphans, we were tossed into the army, housed and trained, taught to love it.

We do love it to an extent. It's all we know.

Change is scary. That's why so many warriors chose to die a familiar death in battle. Opposed to uncharted territories like old age, where we hold a lover instead of the sword that has kept us alive.

"Our definitions differ." I turn and pace the small inn we rented for the night. I have a new room assignment, closer to Selene.

Tristen's squadron—a team I should have been in charge of—has a month off duty. He'll be reassigned. Maybe I can pull some strings and get him under Ryker?

"Stop being pissy. You need the queen's help." Tristen's hands spread open. "You have it now."

"Did you forget last night when she tried to kill me?" I retort.

"No." He shrugs. "I call it the evening's entertainment."

I rest my palm on my sword.

He snorts a laugh and raises his hands high. "Joking. But seriously, use this to your advantage."

"I see an uphill battle in front of me, Tris. No shortcuts."

"So climb it," he says, giving me a pointed look. "Obviously, Queen Selene cared about her brother. If not, she wouldn't have tried to kill you. What do you think will happen when you tell her that her dear, sweet brother gave you his magic?"

I lick my lips and wipe the sweat off my brow.

"Remember," Tristen stresses, "we can't steal magic, Titus. Everett gave it to you. *Gave* it. That has to mean something. That's the weapon that will save you, so I suggest you figure out how to wield it and use it against Selene or Sable. We still haven't met Sable."

"Nothing makes sense now." I hang my head and rub my neck.

"What do you mean?"

"You have another good idea; the world is coming to an end."

I glance at my dirty boots in shame. "You don't belong here," I whisper to myself.

Selene's wing of the castle is a separate tower. A gilded birdcage, Galen must admire as he peers at it through his window.

I advanced toward the tower's base. It's a skeleton-like structure. Like a rib cage holding a heart inside. The frame's design mimics the vines from Galen's famous roses. It wraps and weaves, enclosing the primary structure.

I wonder if I could climb this? Curiosity pulls me to the stone wall. I wedge my boot into the small opening with ease.

An assassin could use this to climb and kill Selene in her room. Why would Galen design her tower like this? If it's so easy to sneak in, then how many times has Selene snuck out?

The main door is blocked by four guards who are chatting. I can see my reflection perfectly in the flawlessly polished black door. Dirty boots and all.

Their chat stops, their eyes widen as if I'm their sung hero. One hurries to open the door; the others lower their eyes as I pass. Upon entering, I'm met with a spiral staircase. Tapestries depicting Blackthorn adorn the entire upstairs path. I pay them no mind. It's a pretty picture of Blackthorn, but I know the truth. I have endured the hardships so the kingdom can be painted in such colorful lies.

I reach the landing, feeling like a fish out of water. I rub the heels of my boots together. That's as good of a polish as they'll get.

The black stone walls are so shiny, I can't resist poking it with my finger. Wow, it's been ages since obsidian walls caged me. My inhale isn't filled with the wild wind of the war camps.

How can I adjust to this?

My face is reflected in the stone, dark shades of gritty grays and inky blacks. "Who are you? How did you manage to survive and become a men?" I mutter.

I avert my eyes, focusing on the black roses that create a pattern on the carpet.

Is that...? Yep, that is silver thread in the rug.

Tiny footsteps inch closer from the opposite end, barely heard since the carpet mutes them. The carpet should be removed. It makes an assassin's job easy as it swallows their footsteps.

I pause and brush the grime on my armor. Here it comes—the shitshow.

Will the queen be armed with her bow?

My chest widens. With practiced ease, my palm slips to my sword, ready to slice another arrow out of the air. But in order to stop an arrow, I need to slow time down.

Cotton fabric swirls around the corner first. That's too simple a dress for the queen. One of her lady's maids turns the corner. She stumbles when she sees me, then dips her chin. "General Titus."

General? I guess I am.

"Your name?" I ask as I approach her.

"Mary. I am the Queen's first hand. I..." She looks over her shoulder, down the hall, which I was told leads to the queen's bedroom. "I should warn you, she's in a mood."

When is she not?

"I'm sure my presence has upset her."

Mary steps closer and whispers, "Galen ordered me not to tell the queen she was assigned a personal guard. So be prepared."

My fingers curl around my sword. It's cruel to both Selene and me.

Mary reaches up and pulls at the collar of her dress. I spot a fresh bite mark. The skin is healed, but it still retains a light pink tone.

You're no friend of the queen. You're a spy.

I need to watch myself with this one. "Thanks for the warning, Mary."

She smiles. "Once you untie her, I'll bring up her breakfast."

"Untie her?" My brows furrow.

Mary clears her throat. "Yes," she replies as she scurries past me. I turn and watch as she heads down the hall.

Turn left. Don't be a rat. Shit!

Why couldn't I have been wrong about you, Mary?

She turns down the hall that leads to Galen's wing.

I scratch my jaw. "Untie?" I mutter. What the hell does that mean?

Wait, what's that? I spot the queen's door, only it's not a door.

I stop in front of a wall of vines and lean closer. They're so thick I can see nothing through the thin gaps.

Shit. Here goes nothing. I grab a vine and pull. These aren't your normal garden weeds. I flex my biceps and yank, but they don't budge.

I grab my sword. What if Selene is behind this wall?

Is this a trick?

My inhale scrapes up my throat, which feels like stale bread left out in the kitchen. "Queen Selene? Are you in there?"

An intake of breath reaches my ears. "Unfortunately." Her deep exhale almost shakes the vines. "Who are you?"

That's a nice voice—sweet yet firm, like unmelted chocolate. Too bad Selene wants to kill me.

132

I sink my fangs into my bottom lip. "I'm your new personal guard."

"That fucking prick," she growls.

I agree.

"Did he give you irons and chains?"

I look left and right. "No, my queen. Why?"

Was it out of place to question her?

"Because clearly, he wants you chained to my feet, so why not make a show of it?" she murmurs more curses before she shouts, "What are you waiting for? Get me out. I've got things to do and people to kill."

She's... a fucking tyrant. Typical fae.

"I was joking, guard. Come on, hurry up and untie me. No sense of humor, eh?"

This is so bizarre. Is this a kink they like to play?

I crack my neck. I don't belong within palace walls, where every action is a new move on a chess board.

"If I may be so bold, which part was the joke, your heavy schedule or the killing?"

"Good, you don't overlook the details. I would appreciate it if you could release me. I do need to use the bathroom and attend to the issues for today."

"Do the issues involve killing?"

"Tell Galen to come for a chat if he's curious. The last thing I need is another meager mouse, scampering to report every blink my eyes make to Galen."

I press my palm against the door of vines. "That sounds unbearable."

Her hesitation reveals her sorrow. "It is."

"Are you behind the... door, this wall of vines?"

"Clearly."

Her walls are back up, but they're cracked. Tristen would tell me this is good. I can make her feel some empathy for my situation.

"I mean, if I swing my sword into it, will I cut you? I value my neck and would like to keep my head attached to it." An impossible task.

Was that the sound of a smile? I start to pull my sword out.

"Swing away, guard."

I don't trust her. I put my sword back. Fire covers my fingers. I grab the vines. First, they smoke; the green waxy shine weathers away, like water wrung from a wet towel. It weakens them just enough for me to snap them in half.

Damp, mossy notes clash with cinder.

Once the hole is big enough, I slip through it.

I wish I hadn't.

As soon as I enter, I'm directly in her bed chambers. Another bad design in the castle. To protect the queen, a buffer zone—a waiting room—should separate her bed from potential entry points.

Shit! My boot catches on a vine. I shake it free as I stumble, almost twisting my ankle. Vines cover the room from floor to ceiling.

King Galen is skilled. It's a bird's nest, layers of vines to keep an egg safe. I should look away. Instead, my eyes remain locked ahead on the queen, bound by vines.

Our eyes lock. Selene's lips part, then pull into a tight snarl. "You!" she seethes, a sound hotter than the fire on my fingertips.

Oh shit! Here it comes.

CHAPTER
TEN

SELENE

O h, husband, you are next level.

You want to play dirty?

I'm not scared to break a nail.

My new guard enters. The control of his fire magic is impressive. The way he burned Galen's precious vines could come in handy.

His eyes take in the mess, particularly me, trapped in my bed.

It's not my best moment, certainly a first impression that will linger, though.

Will I beg to be cut free? No, I've mastered conspiring when trapped in a cage. Everyone thinks I want freedom. I'd rather show them what being caged feels like.

Pushing my spine into the mattress, I do my best to relax and ignore the tingling aches and pains groaning throughout my body.

Wait... tall, strong build, wide shoulders. That face wearing the mask of humble innocence, just like he wore when he received his new title!

Titus! The man who killed my brother is to be my new personal guard.

I push against the vines, fresh thorns cutting me as I do.

Oh, look, the murderer is concerned. He stumbles forward, tripping again. His eyes glare at the thorns cutting me.

"How can you protect me? You can't put one foot in front of the other," I bristle. He shifts from foot to foot, finding his balance on the foliage.

Suddenly, my body falls limp. My mind plots all the scenarios Galen must have calculated when he assigned Titus.

Galen expects me to kill Titus. He's handing him over to me on a silver platter.

Why? So he can declare war again? Or worse?

You know what Galen won't expect? Accepting my brother's killer as my guard.

That's what I'll do, but I intend to take it further. Galen, like any man, thinks with his cock. I never had a guard because Galen doesn't like men near me. I'm all his. It's only a matter of time before Galen starts to grow jealous of Titus's presence.

You see, I'm not going to be the one who kills Titus.

My dear, lovely husband will.

It's splendid!

How will Galen's people react when their beloved king slays their hero?

Trust will be broken. It will fracture the crown on Galen's head. Fear sickens everything from commoners to kings. His people will suspect he's a tyrant. His army will plot against him. Galen will fear, too. He'll sense the knife coming for his spine.

I never imagined this game with Galen would bring down an entire empire, but that's the price I demand for retribution against the man who killed my brother.

"I... I um..." Titus struggles to find words. At least watching him struggle brings a small bit of joy.

"General Titus." Uttering his name leaves a bitter stain on my tongue I don't think I'll ever get off.

Actually, I will once I stand over his dead body.

I paint on a mocking sneer. "It's such an honor that my husband named you as my guard." I press my body back into my mattress.

I expect his head to bow. What I don't expect is his glare. He looks back over his shoulder at the door, then walks back to it.

Great, he's going to leave me here.

Instead, he pokes his head out and looks down the hall. When he turns, the energy shifts. Each step he takes is measured; no more stumbling. His hand rests on his hilt, knuckles white.

Did I read this wrong? Did Galen send him to kill me?

We all know the truce between fae and vampires is like water; one toe dipped in, no matter how small, will cause a ripple.

Peace allows recuperation and preparation.

I should feel no guilt about using Galen to kill Titus, then turning his people against him.

No guilt.

But I do. Unlike my husband, who plotted behind his walls. I was there in the tents, witnessing the cost the soldiers paid. We all bled for the crown on Galen's head.

Every single one of us, except Galen and my father.

Stop; feel no guilt.

"Are you going to kill me?" I inquire. I press my fingers into the warm sheets.

"Why would I do that when you're so eager to kill me instead? What kind of soldier would I be to deny my queen pleasure?"

That deep rasp in his voice has a powerful effect on me. Why is my magic humming? My forehead wrinkles, my thighs clench.

He killed your brother!

I steer my chin up as high as my pillow allows. "A wise person would say Galen is punishing us both."

"I agree."

That's interesting. I almost believe he loathes my husband as much as I do. "Bold words for a king's guard."

He steps closer. His eyes are a deep shade of brown, but there is a sheen in them, an ember that draws you in as it tries to burn you. "I'm not *his* guard." He wavers. His voice dips so deep it touches my toes. "I am yours."

His eyes sweep over me, leveling me like a baker's hands flatten flour.

My lips part on my inhale.

A volatile intensity, a thirst for vengeance and answers, darkens in his eyes.

Answers to what?

There is also a hint of sorrow, an apology that has yet to be spoken.

My dry mouth snaps shut. I run my tongue over my teeth as I glare at his audacity. "You expect me to believe you're loyal to me?" I snort. "You're no more loyal than my lady's maid."

"I expect the queen to be wise enough to form her own opinions based on my actions."

Why can't he be a daft, humble doll like the maid is?

"Kings can form opinions. Not queens."

His head tilt highlights his unshaven jawline. Galen always has a clean face. I heard that beards can enhance sexual pleasure. The tickling sensation of their steel-like hairs can... stop!

What the hell is happening?

Yes, I enjoy sex, but I have control.

Yet in Titus's presence, I keep circling back to sex. The deep rasp of his voice; his vigilant eyes are not shovels tearing away at me—they are nets, catching me.

Just let me fall into the abyss of my yearning for retribution.

My toes curl. I need a mage tonic to assuage my mind.

My forearms stiffen. Did Galen slip something into my wine last night?

"That's funny." Titus breaks my train of thought. "The queen I protect has no problem voicing her opinions. I don't blame her." He peers over his shoulder again.

Now I understand; he was checking the hall to ensure no one was spying on us.

"I... we should talk," he whispers.

His aura shifts. *Are you scared, Titus? You look like a beggar. What's got your tongue twisted?*

The hair on my body rises, brushing against the hard, relentless vines holding me down. "Oh, trust me, Titus, the last thing we should do is talk. You killed my brother!" I shove my chest against the vines.

"It was an accident."

"An accident?"

"A reaction."

"Reaction?" My blood boils. "Don't insult my brother by declaring that murdering him was such an elementary task."

His eyes pinch shut. "I didn't mean that. I..." He looks at the vines. "Let me untie you so we can talk to one another with respect."

"You want my respect?" My eyes target his sword. "Take your sword and drive it into your heart." I glance away, pressing my cheek into the vine Galen used to push my face towards him. A tear slips free. "Leave me alone," I whisper.

I... let him see me cry.

Titus gulps. "I can't do that." The sound of metal scraping turns my neck to the threat.

Titus moves, sword in hand. Tenderly, he slips it under a vine next to my ankle and jerks up; the vine gives way, the dark brown green of it snapping open to reveal a lime green center.

"Why are you helping me?"

"It's the right thing to do."

"And if Galen ordered you to kill me, would you do that too?"

His blade freezes, caught between freeing itself from the greenery or keeping me trapped. "What do you think?"

I roll my lips. "I don't know," I admit. *You confuse me.*

I choke. Titus jostles the knife, slicing through the vine.

My raging heart skips a beat. Words turn to pebbles, weighing down my tongue.

He glides his fingers along my ankle. The rawness of the vine left its mark. Rage paints his face into a mask, a seasoned one would waver to fight.

Instead of removing his hand, he slides his fingers under my ankle and gently rubs a soothing touch to it. The sting from the vine dulls.

What is he doing?

Why am I not stopping it?

"Why do I get the feeling you are full of games and lies?" I mutter.

His touch is a tight line that is severed. He glares at his hand with a traitorous accusation.

He begins to cut my other ankle free. "I could say the same, Queen Selene." He turns and looks at me. The gleam is back in his eyes.

What secret are you hiding from me? I see it on your tongue, begging to be set free.

Titus's confidence falters. "I mean no disrespect, but I could say the same about your brother."

My blood runs cold. What does that mean?

"How dare you act like you knew my brother, beyond clashing blades with him!"

Titus's next inhale is so deep, it steals all the oxygen in the room. "I didn't." He replies. Our eyes connect, slowly, like a moon being pushed down, unwillingly, by the fiery sun. "But Everett knew me." His brow lifts.

Is he questioning me?

Certainly, he is. That's why he's watching as my chest rises and falls. Studying my pupils dilate—as if he can catch me in a lie!

"What's that supposed to mean?" I spit.

His sigh is full of despair. Disappointment breaks our glare. He continues to carefully cut the vines away from my legs. His hands glide to my hips, removing the last of Galen's green chains. The thick skin on his knuckles and the calluses on his palms are evident.

I compare his touch to Galen's.

You should mistrust a king with smooth hands. The ruler should fight beside his soldiers, knowing the cost of their suffering.

I feel... so dirty. I liked Galen's smooth hands because they felt like velvet against my body.

It was all a lie. Snakes are smooth. They need to slip in, strike, and then slither away.

How many deaths shaped those hands, Titus?

How many have you saved?

Warriors did both, didn't they? Killed an enemy. Saved a crown. A crown makes a king, but it embodies the kingdom, those who cannot fight and need others to save them.

Soldiers resemble clouds. They evoke a sense of security, but they also harbor lightning. They shade us, but blind us. Some are thunderous; others feather apart until they dissolve. They're a contradiction; they kill so we can live.

Titus continues to perplex me. He moves his sword with such talent and gentleness, it feels like a breeze wiping away the sweat from my brow.

My vision blurs. "Was it quick like some of the tavern songs suggest, or did you really carve out my brother's heart and hold it as it still beat?"

His knife slips for the first time, cutting my hip. "Fuck! I'm sorry!" His face pales with panic over the tiny cut.

Rapidly, I blink away the emotions and put my mask back on. "It's hard to believe you killed my brother. I think you'd cry over killing a bird," I retort. "It's merely a cut. Galen's thorns cut me deeper last night."

"I do cry over the death of innocents," he spits. "Maybe you should step out of the castle walls and witness it yourself, Queen Selene, or does the shadow from your fine-tipped fae ears stop you from seeing how people suffer?"

Deep, long breaths. That's all it takes for Titus to realize I could have his tongue for his insults.

His sword shakes in his hands; then he grabs the back of his neck. Sweat beads on his brow like morning dew.

What is wrong with him?

He drops the sword on my bed, steps back, and rubs his eyes. "I can't... you can. For him, you will," he whispers to himself. He hugs his hands to his chest, like they're a weapon.

My fingers claw the sheets. I try to drag the blade closer to me, but shit! It's too far to grasp.

"Are you ill from the effects of war? Do you have voices in your head?" I soften my tone.

He shakes his hands out. I expect to see his fire magic. All I see in his eyes is fear, as though something beyond his control is emerging from his fingertips. He scans the room as if he senses something I don't.

I've seen soldiers afflicted with this madness. If I can't talk him out of his visions, he might truly see me as the enemy.

If Galen cared, he wouldn't celebrate his men's return with a feast; he'd offer them compassionate ears and helpful hands. He'd offer them a place to dream. Being wild and angry is sometimes necessary; other times, we need a blank wall, a plain mattress, and a thick blanket. We need something rather than ignorance.

Sometimes, I feel like we lose more soldiers from the madness after the war than from the battle itself.

"You're not on the battlefield," I declare.

Why did I ask him about my brother? It triggered him. "You are here in my room. Observe your surroundings. You're not there, Titus. Titus, are you listening to me? Breathe in. That's it. Notice the scent. You're here, not there."

His chest sinks. "I know where I am." Violent eyes pin me down. "I wish I weren't here... I... fuck it." He comes closer and glares at me with a rage far greater than Galen has ever possessed. "I wish it were me! I didn't lie when I told you killing Everett was an accident. It was! And I wish he had killed me!"

My heart skips a beat. I lose another tear.

"It was a reaction! No, I didn't carve out his heart; how dare you compare me to a beast of the night! I'm a soldier; I did as I was ordered, but I still feel and react." He pounds his chest as if his heart had died the day my brother did. He's desperate to revive it. "I'd do anything to turn back time."

His lungs heave with an untold pain that has my ribs clenching.

"Time, Queen Selene." He grabs his sword, no longer moving gently, as he hacks away the vines holding me down. One by one, he slices and tosses them away in a fit of rage.

I'm free, but I'm too bewildered to move.

Titus moves around my room, grabbing vines and pouring his fire magic into them. The stone walls only allow the fire to spread so far.

He's... so broken; filled with agony that, I dare say, matches mine.

Stomp! Stomp! Someone's coming.

Titus and I look towards my door. His temper fizzles out. He sweeps his hand, extinguishing the flames, leaving charred vines scattered across my floor.

As the footsteps grow closer, Titus's eyes widen with sheer panic. "Not now," he growls at his hands, scolding them, like a father would punish a toddler.

Pressing my palms into my mattress, I push up with caution. Ugh. My spine aches in places I didn't know could hurt.

I know who is coming. Unlike Titus, she would have slain me in my bed when she had the chance.

"You bitch!"

ELEVEN

SELENE

Sable storms into my chambers, her face a mask of fury I've known since childhood. Dark, precise, and unforgiving.

Her long black hair-identical to mine-is braided so tightly that it yanks her eyebrows into a scowl. Her dress whooshes like torrents of foreboding wind. I wouldn't put it past her to wear a gown into battle. The number of jewels adorning her neck might confuse some into thinking she's the queen. She loves that.

Sable is a star that outshines every dying one around her. Little does she know that the stars that shine the faintest often hold the greatest potential, for when they finally burn out, their death sparks a power beyond measure.

All my light dimmed the day Everett died. I'm clinging to life like a tiny star. Surely my end will unleash a beast into this world so great it will force Sable to her knees.

Sable lowers her chin as if she were leveling a blade.

That's when I see it. Under all her finery is sweat stained with dirt.

Wow, Galen really did imprison her. She was so eager to seek her revenge that she'd forgone a bath.

I'm honored.

Sable's lips curl, as does her hand holding the arrow. She has no bow; she doesn't need one. Her words are a weapon more destructive.

Suddenly, the air in the room hisses, particles drift and tingle over my skin, causing the hair on my arms to rise.

Pop!

I recoil, my toes snagging on the sheets.

"Fuck! Shit!" Titus grunts. He steps towards Sable. That's when I notice her hand, how slowly it moves, like a single droplet of water clinging to a leaf. It's so close to falling off, moving, but it doesn't. "She didn't come in the bubble," Titus exhales in relief.

He reaches up and holds his neck, his worry evident.

This feeling... I know exactly what it is. How many times had Everett trapped me in his cage of unmoving time?

But my brother is dead.

My wide eyes target Titus.

No! No. No?

"You... you... you!" No, it could not be! I shove away. My back slams against the headboard of my bed. "You!"

"Yes," Titus says, as if reading my mind.

"How?" A vampire with fae magic? Impossible.

His hand drifts from his neck to his hair, fingers digging into the roots as he tries to remove the weeds from his mind. "I need you to tell me why Everett gave me his magic, because the few words he spoke to me make no sense."

Words he spoke? What words?

The shock causes my body to shake. I feel weightless. I grab my sheets, needing to hold something. Anything.

This makes no sense.

"Fae can't give their magic away."

"Yes, they can."

My throat thickens as I stare down at the sheets.

Titus steps to the invisible wall that blocks Sable. "I don't know how to pull her in?" he mutters. "I'd choose her instead of you, considering you want me dead."

He starts to reach out to Sable.

Oh.... now it makes sense. A final request Everett asked of me before he left. One I did not listen to, but now I realize I should have.

The past.

"*I need you to promise me something, Selene. Promise me you will not kill the man who kills me.*" *My older brother looks down his perfect nose at me; his face stern, yet his eyes are loving.*

"*Man? Do you assume a human can kill a fae?*" *I joke as I tug on the leather straps that hold his rerebraces in place.*

I frown. These straps are old. The smith made him new armor, but he offered it to a soldier.

"*Human, fae, no matter the magic, we are all the same. Forgetting that fact is what has caused these wars. Greed and self-proclamation, it all spiraled when the runes were stripped from these lands.*"

My sigh is heavier than the armor covering his body. "*Not the runes again, Everett. The gods banished them for a reason.*" *He's always so focused on these runes.*

Focus on the war and staying alive!

"*Selene, the gods did not remove them. We did, and one day, we shall help return them.*"

"*I don't care if the runes return; I just want you to.*" *Reaching up, I playfully pinch the tip of his pointy ears.*

"*Make me a promise: you won't try to kill whoever ends my life.*"

My hand drops as my forearms stiffen. "*Absolutely not. I will hunt them down.*"

"*Don't be a huntress,*" *he scorns, as if that title carries a bad omen.*

"*You were the one who taught me how to hold a bow.*"

"*I was teaching you how to survive, not kill. Do not forget that.*"

"*The two share the same meaning during times of war. Killing is surviv-*

ing, and surviving is killing, Everett," I retort. "You'd better survive, and yes, that means kill. I need you. I can't suffer this world alone."

His throat bobs, and his eyes cloud over. "Our suffering will end in a dark symmetry, my dearest sister."

I know that tone. He saw a vision of the future.

What weight must his shoulders bear, knowing the steps I will take before I have found the path to venture down?

"You saw my end," I admit in a hushed whisper.

He grabs my hands, trying to calm me. Everett could always tame wild animals. He failed only once, with our sister, Sable. No one could tame her.

"Selene," His grip tightens, hard enough to bruise.

My heart skips a beat. "What did you see?" Just tell me!

"I see many things. Outcomes always shift." A distant horn shatters our moment. It's the call to formation. "Wars are won by those who listen before they react, Selene. Listen first. Promise me you will not harm the one who slays me." He reaches up, grabs my chin, and forces my head to nod.

His eyes linger longer than his boots do.

I still feel Everett's eyes watching me. Judging me when I carved the arrow meant for Titus.

Everett saw the night I tried to kill Titus. He saw the moment when Titus wanted to choose Sable over me. All because I didn't follow Everett's order. I turned Titus against me.

Why is it so important that Titus trusts me?

"Wait!" I shriek. I leap off the bed, stumbling on the broken vines. I rush to Titus. He turns in time to catch me.

Wham!

Our chests collide, my thin dress presses into the warmth of his leather. Hard meets soft. Fury clashes with confusion.

Forgiveness smothers vengeance.

His rough hands grip me protectively before he gently lowers me to the dirty floor.

I grab his face, my fingers pressing into his beard; the coarse hair is rough beneath my fingertips. "Under no condition should you reveal your time-weaving ability to Sable."

His jaw clenches; the movement has the tips of my fingers pressing into his jaw, trying to grab hold of his bones to keep him safe.

Safe.

Here I am, trying to keep my brother's killer safe.

My eyes stretch into chasms of dread and fear. Titus looks deep into them, seeing every nightmare inside my mind.

So many questions need to be answered. So, so many.

His throat rolls. A chill slides over his skin like bladed shoes gliding over ice. It's graceful, cold, alluring, and a little scary. His time-weaving magic is about to break.

I look at Sable, who now has the arrow raised toward the bed. The bed I should be in! I step back. "I need you to trust me, Titus." I take another step.

"You tried to kill me last night."

I step back again until my thighs hit my mattress. I need to be in the same position when the bubble pops, or Sable will suspect time was frozen. She can not know Titus has Everett's magic!

"I did."

He studies at Sable. "Something tells me I should trust her instead."

"You know what is worse than death, Titus?" The mattress dips as I sink. "Being used," I answer.

His pupils dilate, right as a bead of sweat falls off his brow. "Sable will use you. She will take and take until you're just bones. Even then, she will crack them open and take what's hidden inside. She will drain you dry, leaving nothing behind. That's what she does. Think and be fast. Once she knows you can time-weave, everything, and I mean everything you hold dear will be her leverage."

"And it's not already yours?"

"I wanted an eye for an eye, Titus. You killed Everett; tell me, do you have any siblings you love? You would do the same."

"Is Sable not your sibling?"

"Not one I love. There is a difference."

"How can I trust you? You wanted my life. Fury like that does not fade. It's resilient and full of tricks."

"A piece of my brother is inside you. I'd give my life to protect him... that includes you now."

Titus looks at his hand. "I can't control it."

"That makes your circumstance as fragile as glass; press too hard and it shatters; expose it to heat and it melts; thrust it in ice and it cracks. You need to choose wisely what you will do, Titus."

Pop!

The time bubble bursts open. I keep my eyes on Titus, but from the corner of my eye, I watch Sable. She charges toward me, arrow in hand. She leaps into my bed like the beast she is, landing on top of me, swinging her hand back and thrusting the arrow down toward my heart.

Right before the tip can pierce my skin, she is lifted off of me. Titus's body blurs my view. His mighty hand plucks the arrow from hers.

Snap! He tosses it down.

"She's the queen," he roars. He positions himself between Sable and me.

A dangerous place to be.

His brown eyes bounce between us. His thoughts show confusion. I watch with bated breath as he weighs his options.

Then, oh no, Titus's eyes harden. His jaw clenches with a decision.

His swallow shows his worry as he begins to turn and look at Sable.

CHAPTER

TWELVE

TITUS

The passion in Selene's eyes heats my cheeks, but her fury crumbles. It turns into an anxiety so bottomless it leaps into my eyes, tangling my thoughts. I scratch and tug at my roots. *Get out!*

My nails dig deep; her dread slithers deeper. Coiling around my bones, capturing my muscles, inching into all the crevasses.

Being used. That's how Selene described what Sable would do to me.

And her point? It was a good one. Yes, Selene wants to kill me, but I can justify her reasons. I'd hunt down the person who killed my brother.

Sable, on the other hand, is the wild card. What are her intentions besides pushing the arrow meant for me into Selene's heart?

Fucking insane! That's what they all are.

I look at Sable, who's clueless. I could tell her. It would shift my odds.

For better or worse, I have no idea.

I turn, acknowledging Sable's murderous glare. The fear Selene thrust into my soul takes root because, in Sable's eyes, there is no passion.

There's nothing. It's like looking into uncharted waters in the middle of the night; even if the waves are churning with murderous intensity, I can't see them. It's all hidden under her dark intentions.

I force a swallow down, nearly choking on it.

There's too much at risk, not just my life and Everett's magic, but my family.

I know Selene cared about her brother. Does Sable care?

The only way to know what's in the murky, dark waters is to go fishing and see what I find.

"Everett thanked me when I killed him." Saying the lie hurts. "He was tired of putting up with the two of you. I understand now." I step to the back, watching the twins. Selene is shocked, enraged by my words, but there's a tear in her eyes.

Sable's eyes shift off her sister, pinning me down.

Good, she took the bait; I can practically see the hook in her jaw.

"I should thank you for ridding us of Everett. Could you do me another favor and kill her? I promise I won't tell a soul. It's in your right after she tried to kill you last night." Sable smirks.

Sable's a creature so grotesque, she should never breach the surface.

I don't care what transgressions have passed; I could never kill my brother.

Never.

I step between them again. It might not be the best idea to give Selene my back, but I'd rather the monster I semi-know than the twin, who has a serpent smile and usurper mindset. "You need to leave," I order Sable.

"Leave?" Her lips pull taut, like a fishing line. She's swimming, trying to run, but my hook is in, and I know who she is. "And I thought we could be friends," she croons.

Coating her poisonous words in honey doesn't mask the flavor. I know what she is trying to do.

"I don't need friends," I grunt.

"Oh, you poor fool. Without friends, you'll never survive this court."

"The people you spread your legs for are not your friends, Sable," Selene jabs, but hidden under her sharp tongue is a new tone, a warning laced with care.

"Jealous I get to open my legs for others? It must be boring to fuck the same man, knowing that man is fucking so many others." Sable's face glows like a rising sun.

"I don't fuck a man," Selene responds with no sign of insult. "Galen is a king, and he comes to *my* bed."

I cast my eyes down, but all I see are symbols of King Galen. I kick a vine with my boot. Anything can crumble: a marriage, a king, a peace treaty.

I feel bad for the queen, but it's the price of the crown, this castle, and the room she gets to live in.

Was it her choice? No.

That's the cost of fate. Some are born poppers, and others are royalty. But we all die the same; the breath leaves our lungs, our skin rots, and our bones decay all the same.

Better trapped in a gilded cage than a barren one.

"You two are worse than pups fighting for the nip. Leave, Sable!" I snap.

"He barks, but does he bite?" Sable steps closer and, in a patronizing manner, pats my chest. Her fingers might be smooth, but even velvet can hide a razor blade. Eventually, she will strike.

"I'm not scared of teeth, Titus; this is a vampire kingdom, after all."

"You threaten the queen; your crimes will be reported to King Galen. Leave before I make you," I command.

"Make me?" Sable's face gleams with twisted satisfaction. "I would love to have your hands on my body."

"I killed your brother," I snarl. How low can she go?

"Then I should thank you. Tell me how. I don't mind getting on my knees," she croons.

There is no pole long enough I'd touch her with. "Now I know why you are not the queen."

Before Sable drops her hands from my chest, she presses her fingers deep. The tips of her fingers blanch red and white, like the sclera of an angry god that now has its sights set on me.

"There's your first mistake, Titus. Insulting me. I wonder how much it will cost you?" Sable chuckles as she steps back. "Oh, there it is, a little drop of regret in your eyes. Don't worry, I accept apologies. I might let this pass. I know the adjustment to court life is hard, but if you think Selene will help you, think again. She failed last night, but she will try again."

Selene comes to my side. A strange warmth stirs in my belly. Comfort I haven't felt in years.

"Don't worry, we're leaving, Titus," Selene announces. "Sable feels more at home surrounded by discarded waste and trash." She glances around the room at the burnt vines strewn across the floor. "Isn't that right, Sable?"

"I will kill you," Sable confirms, voice like pure death.

"Upset your leash was shortened?" Selene crosses her arms. "I'd tell you to go run to Father, but you burned that bridge a long time ago. Yet again, your feet stand in ashes. One might think it's a most fitting end for you, to be left alone, surrounded by ash and dust until you wither away and join it."

"You might've had Everett's favor, but he would have traded it, killed you himself, to have what I do." Sable's golden skin practically glows.

Selene's posture relaxes, as if this back-and-forth were as serene as birds chirping. Maybe it is for them; as for me, I feel the need to purge my ears. "You have nothing but favors that will eventually run out." Selene's exhale is a ship that survived a storm, steady and calm.

Sable's brows raise slowly, like a feline pulling back her lips to expose sharp teeth. "It's funny how quickly nothing can turn into *something*. Value is like worth. It all depends on how you market it, and I, dear sister, have something that will bring you to your knees."

Selene rebuts as if this is a practiced game she's an expert in. "It will be an interesting and new viewpoint since I haven't sunk to my knees in order to find that worth you talk about."

Shit! Selene is good. Wicked but good.

A warm hand slips into mine. "Come, Titus, I have lots to show you if you are to make a good personal guard."

"Personal guard?" Sable's lip twitches. A rare sign she is caught off guard. Noted.

"Yes."

"I know what you are doing." Sable crosses her arms. "You're trying to make Galen think this is not a punishment. No matter what you do, it will be. Trapped with the man who killed your precious Everett. What did Galen leverage over your head to keep Titus alive? Is it your pretty neck? You kill Titus, his war hero, and he kills you."

"Maybe it was you?"

Sable hesitates for a fraction of a second. "No, he'd be dead already."

"Would he be?" Selene steals that sly smile off her twin's face and wears it. "Wasn't it you who mentioned, just hours ago, that I would be the one to kill you, only to bring you back? Maybe I am biding my time until I can kill two birds," Selene looks at me, then at Sable, "with one stone."

How can I keep up with the debauchery of the threats they sling at each other?

"Now, if you'll excuse me." Selene raises her chin. "I have a crown I need to put on my head." She shoves her shoulder into Sable's as she passes. "Come along, Titus, you can polish it while I brush my hair," Selene purrs, gracefully walking over the rubble and exiting her room.

Don't look. Why did you look? My eyes find Sable. Did I put my trust in the wrong twin? Each requires a mage to mend their twisted minds.

Sable's lips part. "Don't say I didn't warn you."

Is that another threat or words of wisdom I should heed?

SELENE

You're almost there! Almost free of her.

I rush into the room, part my lips, but where is my breath?

Breathing feels too hard an act to do.

I stumble further into the living room, where I usually eat my breakfast. It's large and grand, littered with chairs and couches, a fireplace, and a game table—a stupid place where I am meant to entertain nobles' wives.

I never have.

I'm not fake as fuck.

You want to gossip over tea and crumpets? Find someone else to bother.

I train in all my spare time. I would not let my skills falter now that a crown was placed upon my head. It's then that the real beasts emerge.

I press my palm against my ribs, giving my lungs more support. "I know why you didn't tell me all the details, Everett," I whisper. His words were always veiled and protected. Should he overshare, the future could shift. His gift of foresight was more affliction than blessing.

The closing of the door constricts the air trapped in my lungs. I gasp, struggling to catch my next breath. Titus steps closer but remains unaware of how to slay my inner beast.

"I'm fine," I rasp. A faint pink hue lines the walls as the silencing spell activates. All the royal rooms have them. I turn toward the wall.

I can't look at Titus. Not yet.

"If a torturous state is your definition of fine, we should reexamine it." The warmth in his voice thaws some of the frigid walls years of abuse have sculpted. "Are you okay?" he presses.

My breath quivers; my fragile reflection mocks me in the polished black stone wall I cling to. I hate these walls and the obsidian that makes them rise too high.

"Queen Selene?" Titus's steps are hesitant. He knows I'm a viper that will strike.

How could Everett do this?

My eyes seal shut. I refuse to cry in front of Titus again. I press my forehead to the cold stone, trying to allow the chill to calm me.

"Is it always like that?" Titus asks. How can such a gravelly tone feel smooth?

"What?" My warm breath heats my face.

"Your morning conversations," he answers.

Another step. Titus is at my side. I feel his eyes trying to dig between my forehead and the wall, to separate us.

"I'll need to start drinking coffee. One that is spiked in order to keep up with that," he jokes.

The corner of my lip twitches. I refuse my lips the smile they want to give him.

"We're surrounded by the seeds we sow, Titus." It's too late to speak to Sable with caring words. She never absorbed the meaning of love. All she knows is manipulation, hate, and treachery. Thus, my lone means of speaking with her is to reciprocate her decay.

The only reason I fight to keep the line of communication open with Sable is because Everett demanded I do.

The past.

"I can't stand her!" I rush towards Everett and bury my face in his chest. The scar on my stomach is still healing from where Sable stabbed me.

Everett's arm wraps around me. "You must try. Don't shut her out." His hand rubs small circles on my back.

"Talking to her only feeds her evil soul." My tears don't stop. I cry only in front of my brother. Father would punish me; Sable would mock me.

I hate this castle. My life. I'm a caged bird, forced to entertain with my voice—in the future, it will be with my body.

I can stretch my wings but never fly.

"The only way to understand Sable's soul is to keep peeling it back. The moment you ignore her is the moment you become deaf. You can't allow that to happen. Sable has a vision she wants to fulfill."

"Me dead?" I sniffle.

"No." Everett guides me back so he can look me in the eye. "She wants everyone to be brought to their knees, Selene. Everyone. She wants what she has been denied. Power. I need you to stay close to her."

I rub away the tears. "She'd never let me in." And I don't want her to.

"We keep our enemies closer than our loved ones. They are always on our minds and within our sight. Make sure you remain her enemy. Let me know what Sable is doing, where she goes, and who she visits."

"That's easy." I pull my shoulders back. "Sable spends all her free time in the library. I've always been better with a sword; Sable can't stand it, so she flees to her books."

"Knowledge can be a deadlier enemy than one with a sword at your neck, sister. And do not forget that Sable's magic is more feared than yours. Not many wish to fight death."

I pout. Everett's right. Father loves Sable's death magic.

Everett stands taller. "The most successful hunter doesn't chase their prey. They observe. They notice the details. They spot the telltale clues. They know where to go, when to strike, and how to get to the finish line first, Selene."

He wipes the tears off my cheeks. "What section of the library has Sable been visiting?" His chest leans closer. His face is graver and sculpted; the demands of adulthood are carving out his youth.

"The catacombs. She..."

"She what?" he presses.

I'd rather not discuss this with my brother. I look down at his boots. "She sleeps with others there."

"Who?"

"Who is she sleeping with?" I cringe. "This month, it happens to be a visiting mage."

"A mage." His gulp is deep and loud. "What kingdom is this mage from?"

"He has no kingdom. He's devoted himself to The Great Library of Ishmor." Ishmor is an island where the history of our world is housed in the greatest library; some say the gods helped build it.

"Every soul claims a kingdom, Selene; sometimes that kingdom is known, other times it's a selfish dream of a crown they wish to hold, but make no mistake, none of us are so noble to walk these lands without a thirst for acceptance. Even those who toil in Ishmor labor towards a cause. They all report to someone."

"You think this mage is reporting back to someone?"

"Yes."

"Who?" I question. Who in Ishmor wants to know what my sister is doing?

Everett arches a brow. "Turn the tables, Selene. The mage is working for Sable."

"Sable?" I repeat. "Sable has no power to command a spy."

"That is where you are wrong, my dearest sister. Those we overlook hide for a reason; they pull the strings. Sable is skilled at creating lies. Do you know what lies cover up, Selene?" He tips my chin up. "Terrible, awful truths." He cups my cheek. "Now I know where she is getting her knowledge. Don't worry. I'll handle it."

Everett leaves without telling me more. I know he's trying to protect me by keeping me in the dark, but it's in the dark that monsters lurk.

That old memory blankets my skin like a dress that is too tight. One week later, the catacombs caught fire. My father didn't know I saw my brother sneaking down there. Just before smoke poured from the staircase, Everett departed with some tomes and scrolls. The aged parchment appeared fragile, ready to tear if unwound.

What books did he collect?

What was in those scrolls?

Why did I never press?

That's why you trusted me, Everett. I didn't push. I waited until you confessed.

I regret that now.

"Why do you take all the blame? Sable is at fault, too," Titus questions.

"What?" I blink. I forgot where I was. My gilded cage surrounds us. Art hides the evil within the black walls. A gentle wind from my balcony cools my forehead. I peer outside as I turn my head. The floor is haunted by shadows from the skeleton tower Galen made me. The air smells too much like flowers here. I miss Solaria. The dense, humid, salty notes of the forest that framed the mountain range we call The Cradle of Darkness. The aroma always roused me from sleep. The Cradle's secrets made my nightmares seem like pleasant dreams.

"Why do you not fault Sable? Her tongue is just as wicked."

"We're twins. The same."

"Same?" Titus scoffs. "Coins share the same mold, but look closely and you'll spot the difference. Pressure shapes us in ways the surface doesn't show. You and Sable might've been cast in the same fire, but you are not identical images of one another."

I can see why Everett liked him. My brother would have voiced the same thing.

"I saw two very different people," Titus continues. "Both terribly pained and hurt, but their purpose differs." He turns, pressing his back against the wall, standing side by side with me like we're old friends. "I still don't know if I picked the right twin. Are you the best of both evils, Selene?"

He's trying to open me up.

"Best?" I snort. "We're cruel, grotesque, and ugly. That's what surviving has done to us, Titus." I study his square jaw, strong eyes, and broad shoulders. Why hasn't it deformed you?

"Sometimes thick skin is just hiding scars, not a monster," he retorts.

I lift my head off the wall. He's relaxed, leaning against it, but his shoulders are hunched.

I know the weight he feels. Everett knew how to pile it on.

His eyes? They look as tired as I feel. "Is that what you want to see? My scars?" I tilt my chin up to get a better view of him.

"You tell me. Am I brave enough?"

"No." Turning, I mimic his pose, then I allow myself to sink along the wall till my ass hits the stone floor.

He looks shocked to see his queen sitting in such a state. He waits until I nod, then he joins me. He's uncomfortable at first, then he forces himself to sit still. "Tell me how I can be," he gently presses.

I want to curl my legs in, hug them to my chest as a layer of protection. Instead, I kick them out. "Why would you want to? I tried to kill you last night."

"Because I need you to help me." He raises one knee, forming a small wall between us. He perches his elbow on it. "But I don't think you will until you can trust me. Trust is a river that flows both ways. I need your help, but I won't take it unless I can trust you. I'm desperate, not delusional. I will not trade the knowledge Everett confessed to me for peace of mind."

"You put my brother first. Why not your own life? You live. Everett is dead. Debts don't need to be paid." My voice dips, as do Titus's eyes.

"When Everett died, my life was altered. I'm not the same." Apprehension seeps through his plea. "I need your help because I am trying to survive."

"Why is it so important to see the next sunrise, Titus. Convince me. This land is cruel. Why should we beg to remain a part of a garden that only grows toxic fruit? I hear the after is a better place. Tell me why I should not seek my destiny this very moment."

"You've forgotten how to dream of the future could be," Titus murmurs. "You're stuck in the nightmare of the present."

"I didn't forget. I was never allowed to dream," I gulp.

"We must fight for the sunrise, not for ourselves but for those we love..." He tips his head back, searching the ceiling for answers.

"You love someone?"

"Yes."

My stomach clenches so hard it pulls my lips into a frown. Deep inside my heart, there is a sharp sting.

It's ridiculous. He killed my brother.

But... there is something odd happening, a feeling I push away. I fear that acknowledging it might yield more harm than good.

"She's lucky," I retort dryly.

"He," Titus replies. "It's not what you think."

"Aww, a sibling." I press my hand to my stomach. Titus loves his brother, as I did mine. I'd never wish the grief I felt over losing Everett on anyone. Now, I have to keep Titus and his brother both safe.

"I shouldn't have told you that."

"Why did you?"

"I'd rather you know than Sable."

"Good. You are smart."

He starts to smile. It's handsome, masculine, and firm, not devious like Galen's.

"Is he here in the castle?" I ask.

Titus nods.

"Get him out; send him away before dusk falls upon the land. Sable doesn't kill, Titus; she picks apart her prey. Slowly. She learns every detail; some they don't even notice. She uses that to torture them. She was doing that to Everett before he died. Everett never wanted to fight. He was using the war as a cover."

"A cover for what?"

"Something I considered a pathway to madness." I bite my lip.

Why am I telling him this?

"Everett was searching for a location," I confess. The scrolls Everett smuggled out were used in a time when we didn't etch our maps with magic but with paper and ink. "Everett and Sable were playing a game; racing to find the same thing," I admit in a hushed tone.

The question is, who started it? Did Sable find something that made Everett react, or vice versa?

Who threw the first stone?

"What location?" Titus's face lightens.

If I told you what my brother was searching for, you'd think me insane.

I turn toward him and lick my lips. "First, tell me what my brother told you. Tell me everything."

FOURTEEN

SELENE

The moment I ask, Titus's lips press into a thin line, like a coffin lid shutting. I roll my shoulders, but the walls still press in.

Knowing the memory of my brother's death pains him. A little.

We're forced to be friends because of what my brother plotted.

Titus's hands curl into fists. "I am sorry. I'm so, so sorry." His brown eyes cloud like thunder.

"You've expressed that," I declare. I slide over the polished stone floor and sit across from him. "Apologies get us nowhere now. Facts do. What did Everett tell you?"

My feet itch to stand and pace, but sitting lowers defenses. It makes this interrogation feel like a story shared around a campfire.

Titus pushes his hair back and rubs the back of his neck. "Prince Everett told me many things. Most of which made little sense." He glares at his hands as if they belong to a stranger he'd rather not associate with.

I reach up, cover my mouth, and rub my jaw. My brother's magic rests in these hands. I bite the inside of my cheek. How do I get him to cherish it?

"Do you feel the time magic?" I ask. He's a child running with adults. He needs to master this gift before someone more dangerous finds out.

What a waste that would be. My brother is dead, but his magic isn't. I'll do everything to keep it alive.

"No. Not at this moment; thank the gods. It... terrifies me." His sigh is a mountain that lost a piece of itself to the abyss. Another chunk cracks off, crumbling down and fracturing more parts. The agony of the fear, of the fact he's not the same person he once was, is palpable.

Titus coughs, but his voice only deepens. "During Everett's final battle, he caged me. Stopped time. My brother was on the outside, moving more slowly. I witnessed swords sink into flesh; I saw the prolonged confusion that death claimed them. I'd rather die instantly than watch the seconds pass."

The hand of my brother's killer slips into mine before I can stop myself. My actions shock us both. There's a spark that curls up our arms. His fingers hug mine.

"Some say a slow death is more precious; it gives you time to say your goodbyes," I murmur.

"What if I don't want goodbyes?" He studies our held hands much longer than is appropriate.

A chill sweeps over my body. I feel this moment has happened before. Humans call it déjà vu; the mages think it's a warning.

"Trust me,"—my heart aches—"I would rather have a goodbye than nothing but a last memory. I wish I were there watching my brother bleed out. I wished to be the hand that held his as he struggled to pass over. A hand that loved him, not this stranger."

"I wasn't a stranger to him," Titus whispers. It's his attempt at comfort.

Gradually, I nod. "We take goodbyes for granted."

Why did I just squeeze his hand? Why can't I let go?

"I guess we should voice everything." Titus looks up. "In case we don't get a last goodbye, that way the person knows our true feelings."

I slip my hand free and cross my arms so I can't reach for him again. This is too much.

Sitting taller, I force a swallow down. "You stopped the arrow with time-weaving."

He nods.

"If Galen saw..." Oh, what Galen would do if he knew Titus had fae magic! The unknown terrifies me.

Would Titus be his weapon? No, Galen is the ultimate weapon; he kills anyone who inches closer.

"I was lucky."

"That luck will run out."

"That's why I need your help. I tried to gain mastery over Everett's magic, but it always ends up dominating me.

"I didn't know a vampire could accept a fae's magic." What price did Everett pay for this knowledge?

"There was no accepting. Everett gave me no choice."

A deep need to comfort him possesses me. Again, my hands move without my consent. "I'm sorry for what my brother forced upon you." Taking his palm, I flip it over and uncurl his fingers. I trailed my finger across his palm, noticing his arm shake.

Heat radiates from him. I close his fingers, then squeeze them into a fist before I place his hand back on his lap.

I exhale, "Everett was adept at coercion. But he wasn't malicious. Everything he did was for the people."

"You mean his people. The fae of Solaria."

"No." I roll my lips so Titus can't see the tremble. "For *all* the people. That infuriated my father; he wanted him to grow angry, to hate the vampires who slaughtered us, so he sent him to the frontlines."

We sit in silence for so long that I count the dust particles that dance and float in the air.

"He would have been a righteous king."

My eyes water. "Thank you." I nod.

"It's the truth."

"I know," I whisper, hoping he doesn't hear the crack in my voice, "that is why it hurts."

"Only corrupt kings survive, never good ones."

"If only we could change that." I snort a bitter laugh.

Titus continues; he tells me how Everett stalked him on the battle-field and watched him burn the fallen bodies. Knowing that Titus has buried my people only expands the unfamiliar sensation inside my chest.

"He was testing you," I point out.

"He was," Titus huffs in annoyance. "All these questions about why I did this and not that. I knew what he was doing."

"Why did you reply?"

Titus drums his fingers on the polished floor; no sound echoes. These castle walls are the belly of a beast. Nothing, not screams or shouts of glee, escape. Everything is sacrificed for the crown.

"I don't know." Titus glances away. "I suppose having a conversa-tion made me feel civilized again."

What good is a kingdom if shattered minds fill it? How can I repair them, erase all the wrongs done to people like Titus?

"We forget soldiers are people. I am sorry for what you had to endure."

His eyes shift towards me, like brown timbers bracing a mountain of truth. "I killed many of your kind."

"You can't accept sympathy," I say.

"It's not owed to someone like me."

"Gifts are given, not owed. Titus, you're not the villain. There is no difference between you and a fae warrior. Your fight is to survive, return home, and live."

Why can't I look away? I want to hug him... hold him. I want to cry and feel his arms embrace me as I do.

Thump! Thump!

Does he feel it, too?

"It does not seem your wish but your fate that set you on this path." I confess, my tone somber and soft.

"It is." Titus's heavy exhale fills the space between us. "Sometimes I want to get off of it."

Determination settles on his brow; I need to wipe it off. "The path can be challenging, endless, but stepping a toe off of it is often what kills us."

"Now you sound like your brother."

I smile; it's stretched with heartache and honor. It's a kingdom's flag that withstood the entire war, threadbare and riddled with holes, but it survived only to realize its country did not. There's dignity in knowing you fought till the end, rather than lowering your flag and watching the enemy burn it.

Everett fought to his end. Titus was his flag. I shall carry him.

"Everett had his reasons; you have to do as he commanded, or you will change the outcome he died for."

Titus holds his breath. "I understand that now. I am trying hard, Selene, but I have my moments. Doubts tell me to run away from this mission. The only thing keeping one foot in front of the other is thinking like a soldier. This is just another order I must fulfill."

His words are a gust of wind that extinguishes a flame. My hatred of him is choked out. It's nothing more than smoke vanishing from my mind's eye.

Titus is of a noble heart, just as Everett predicted.

Did Everett foresee this very moment, when I forgive the act I once considered unforgivable?

A hard swallow thickens my throat, crashing down to my belly. "What else did Everett say?"

"He didn't say he was happy I killed him. I lied to Sable."

"I know. Go on." I look at the tapestries. Mentally, I erase their pictures; I repaint what Titus tells me.

"There was something odd, something I said, but it was as if someone else spoke it for me. Everett said, 'Some say symbols caused this war.' But my reply wasn't my own; I told him, 'Others argue symbols ended it.'"

Symbols? How much does Titus know?

"What does that mean?" I question him.

"Everett was referring to the wars that happened during the era of Broken Oaths."

My face wrinkles.

Titus smooths it out. "He was referring to runes, Selene." His tone is a line of chalk being stretched out along the board, emphasizing the point. He scoots forward, no longer leaning against the wall. Leaning closer, as a teacher would stand before a pupil.

"Runes," I whisper as I look at the door.

Everett told Titus about the runes!

This mad chase for forgotten knowledge killed my brother. It's worse knowing he died for bedtime stories.

"But you see, Selene, I think you knew this," Titus reports. Accusation weighs his voice down. "I watched you bite your tongue before you asked what Everett told me. You looked at the door because you wanted to flee. You knew the answer. You lied." His voice drops, low and gravelly. "Lying to me has consequences."

He shifts onto his knees. A defense position that has my spine pulling taut. His proximity makes me feel small, petite, and dainty. My hands feel unable to lift a sword. His eyes, now like cold brown dirt, press into me, like the hands of an undug grave, warning me he'll gobble me up if I lie again.

His intuition might be his most compelling weapon.

Titus is a blade with a hidden edge.

I press my tongue against my dry inner cheek. "I didn't want you to think Everett was mad," I confide in shame.

"Sometimes a monster lurks so deep in the woods that only one person sees it. They manage to escape and warn their village. But the people call them mad, crazy, delusional. They don't listen. When that monster comes, they all die, because they didn't heed the warning."

He rests his hand on my trembling knees. "We both need to be on the same page if we are going to survive. No more lies."

I can't look away from his hands. They are so large that they shield my knees, curling around the sides. "You're asking me to show you my heart, to trust my brother's memory with you, a stranger. I don't have one. The flesh your fingers press into," I flex my leg, but he holds firm, "is more like leather: dead and dried out, forced to be molded and reused."

Why did I tell him that?

"You have a heart. It's so deeply buried, you've forgotten what the sun feels like. You're scared of the warmth because you accepted the barren wastelands of the cold. I have fire magic. I control the heat, Selene. Unearth your emotions; step outside. I won't let the world burn you."

"What if you burn me?" What if you betray me and Everett?

"Don't give me a reason to."

That's fair.

His grip tightens. "And as for your flesh..." My heart skips a beat. "It's not dead, merely hardened. Do not hate it for that."

My eyes flick up, holding his sincere stare.

"That thickness kept you alive." His grin is gentle, revealing the tips of his fangs. He presses his thumb along the inner side of my knee. "With the right amount of pressure, you can soften hardness."

My insides melt, then flutter to life. The sensation is so raw my next heartbeat fractures me.

I drag my knees up, scared they were about to part for him.

"You only say that because you need my help." I hug my legs to my chest.

This means nothing; he's using you just as every man has.

"I do need your help, but I want you as a friend."

"Why?" My eyes follow his jaw to his full, firm lips.

"You were important to Everett, which makes you important to me. Also, I see my queen locked away, suffering. As *your* guard, I am duty-bound to keep you safe. From everyone." He looks at me through hooded eyes. "Do you understand what I'm saying, Selene? Give me the order and I'll free you from this castle."

"You would throw our people back into war. Break the peace treaty."

His smirk is a pair of scissors, cutting the lies of the peace treaty loose. "Peace? Peace isn't silent. It's agony—requiems cried and sung. Peace is fury, forced to dissolve into resolve. We live in times of silent sorrows, still caught in the clutches of war. Peace has yet to begin, Selene. You'll know when it does."

All my suffering has been for nothing. This marriage is a trick kings play so they can rebuild their armies. My eyes are dry. "How will I know?" I rasp. "I've never known peace, only the plots of war. What if it passes me by?"

"You'll feel a wrath so parched, no amount of blood can quench it. So you'll have no choice but to ignore it. Bury it just to start again. And pray that taste never bubbles up on your tongue."

"That doesn't sound peaceful." Memories flood my eyes, and I turn my head swiftly so Titus can't see more of my pain.

"Peace isn't always idealistic—it's raw. It's grounded; stability. The ache of closure. Sometimes it hurts more than the war did. Hey, look at me. If you want to leave this castle, I will help you. I just... I need you to know that."

"Why?"

He reaches up and rubs his chest. "I don't like to see you suffering."

Don't look at me like that, Titus, like I'm a trophy you'd never place on your shelf, because a man like you has honor.

You don't show off your kills; you melt them down and set them free. I can not be reforged. I am who this world has shaped me to be.

I peer out the window at the sunny day. "If freedom were my destiny, my brother would have granted it." A strange current swirls around us, like fingers trying to shove us closer. "My place is here, helping you."

"If helping me causes you pain, I will find another way."

"I'm strong. I can survive."

"I don't doubt you are." He looks around the room, taking in all the riches. "Do you love him?"

"It's hard to love a boat with no anchor. Galen sails away after he makes port. I... tried for the sake of our people."

"What about you?"

"Princesses are not born with space for happiness in their hearts. We're duty-bound."

"What did I say about lies? Don't spread more in hopes they will comfort you."

My breath sticks in my throat. He sees through me so easily. "We're getting off topic again."

"No. I asked to see your heart, and you showed it to me. I'll keep it safe. Just remember, whenever you want, I'll free you." His eyes turn sharp.

My throat thickens once more. "You didn't finish telling me what Everett said."

His eyes trace over me, judging. "Everett said they were wrong to erase the runes from our lands and that everything can be used for good or evil. He said runes create balance. Make us equal. He made it sound like runes were the answer, not the problem. But these were your brother's final words."

My heart stops as Titus speaks.

"'I give my magic of time-weaving to you, Titus, to use until you find the Vitalis; then, I release my magic back into the lands. But my magic of foresight, I release back into the world. If you were to see what you must endure, you would grab the sword from my heart and thrust it into yours,'"

My skin pebbles. Confusion, fear, and, yes, resentment take root.

"I... I'm sorry. I'm so terribly sorry."

Why, Everett?

"My brother wasn't wicked."

"One could argue he was a fanatic."

My shoulders curl in. All I can do is nod.

With a gentle finger under my chin, Titus tilts my face upward.

"I've seen the eyes of a madman. At first, I thought Everett was one. But it wasn't passion that stole his tongue, it was fear. He saw a future so terrible that he gave his life to prevent it.

"My anger toward him has passed; it does no good to harbor it. I did not choose this path, but I am forced to walk it." His tone sharpens, but his hand opens as he cradles my jaw.

It's a foolish move. If anyone saw him touching me like this...

"You will help me, Selene, because, like me, Everett has given you no choice. Do you understand?" The edge of his thumb swipes over my bottom lip as his hand drops.

Titus sits tall, shoulders back, jaw set firm. He could be sitting on a throne. I feel like he is. "Where is the Vitalis?" he demands.

"The..." I cough. He's cornered me like an animal in my room. A part of me wants to curl into him, as any scared animal would beg for shelter, food, and... love. "The Vitalis," I repeat.

"Do not play games with me. The word is not foreign to your tongue." His eyes lock onto my mouth.

In days long forgotten, the book that housed the runes was called the Vitalis. "That word means nothing now," I reply slowly. I know of it only because one day, I dared to look at the inner pages of a book Everett was reading, a book he stole.

"It's not a word," Titus growls. "It is a name. Every name holds a memory of those who bore it. What memory does it hold for you?"

I grind my teeth as I look at the corner. I wish I had never looked at that book! It set Everett's tongue into a frenzied, passionate fury. He spoke of the old book of runes, of the magic it possessed, of the gods who created it. He told me how the runes worked, how they were not everlasting.

They only stayed marked on the skin for as long as the flesh could endure the power. Some runes lasted only minutes, whereas those less powerful could remain for weeks or months.

What Everett confessed was a grain of rice, compared to the vast field of knowledge he kept hidden from me.

I knew if Father heard Everett speak like this, he'd cut his tongue out. My family no longer praised the gods, who vanished from our lands centuries ago. As for runes, only madmen spoke of them, and those men were hunted down for sport.

Fae were not dreamers; we left that to the mages and humans. Fae are sensible and factual in their thinking.

Titus shifts, widening his legs as he leans closer to me. "Answer me, Selene." His voice sounds like fog, thick, too deep to decipher the truth probing behind it. "Or do you wish me to pry the truth from your lovely lips?"

My hand flies up to cover my mouth. "You grow bold and forget your place," I retort. He's stopped calling me Queen Selene. Something that can not happen in public.

"Your brother blurred my place."

"I thought you wanted a friendship." *Why are your eyes so dark, Titus?*

"You're biting your tongue, not me."

"I'm processing."

"You're trying to cover up the truth with a lie. I'm trained to know when someone is dishonest. I can read your body like a book." His eyes sharpen with confidence.

My thighs clench. "Then you should know that my plot has been rewritten. I am duty-bound to protect you. No matter what."

"I know how to interrogate. Read between the lines. So let's try this again, as two friends who do not hold back. The Vitalis, where is it?"

I shove my emotions into the deep well where my heart used to be. Drowning them out is harder than usual. "How do you know what the Vitalis is? I'm asking as a friend who is concerned for your well-being."

His posture stiffens. "Whether by luck or Everett's planning, we took the Gates of Kalhiem on our way back to Blackthorn."

"That's past Blackthorn's main roads. Why did you divert?"

"The main road was underwater, a strange time of year for such heavy rain, which makes me think water magic was involved. Kalhiem provided the men with food, lodging, and amusement. However, Ishmor is near Kalhiem, a quick boat trip. The Kalhiem bartenders hear many rumors and old stories when the Ishmor scholars arrive. I spoke with some bartenders, and one told me about an old scholar's visits, and that she said a mage from the west came to Ishmor and enquired about a forgotten book, the Vitalis."

My smile fades. "Titus, I do not know the book's whereabouts or if it exists."

Some of the hope flees from his lungs. "It is real," he firmly states. "What do you know of runes, Selene?"

"I..." I lean my elbows on my knees. "I think they are madness. The Vitalis is likely a book written to read to children before they slumber. Nothing more than a tale of greed."

Greed. That's exactly what Sable would be after.

Why didn't I see the pattern before?

Does that mean there is a book?

"You think runes never existed?"

"I didn't say that," I bark. Reality settles into my bones. "I think they existed; you can't have smoke without a fire. I don't think they were ever as powerful as the stories claim."

"Why not?"

"Nothing that powerful can be silenced, which makes me question their power in the first place. Maybe a mage just cleverly crafted an enchantment, and people embellished it over time."

"I have to believe those bedtime stories are true, Selene. Everett said that when I find the Vitalis, his time-weaving magic will return to the land. I'll be free."

"And then what?" I question sternly.

His tongue twists. His answer is sour, but he's going to force it down. "Everett wanted me to rule and keep the runes safe," he admits bitterly.

"Rule?" My eyes blink more frequently than ripples dance across the water after someone throws a stone in. "So, it's a crown you seek," I spew.

"The crown Everett placed on my head is that of a melting delusion. If I could pull the crown off, I would. I never lusted for power, only freedom and safety for my family. I don't want castle walls made of slick, polished stone to cage me, Selene. I want a stone that is rough, not fancy. Porous, so memories of my family can seep into them. I want to sleep knowing that when I wake, I do not have to fight for a man who hides behind high walls and wears a crown, collecting more maps of land he owns, but never earned! But here I am!"

He slaps the floor of the castle.

"Tasked with finding an old book, but then what, Selene? If this book is so powerful, do I just cast it aside, give it to Galen to use? Or another king? I didn't want this! But I'm brave, or foolish enough, to see this task through. One battle at a time, I will end this. I will find the book, I will understand the runes, and I will keep them safe."

"You are one man against an army, Titus."

"That is the life of a soldier, Selene."

Why do I want to hug him, scoop him up, and place him somewhere safe?

His chest heaves. "I know my words are treason," he mutters in fear.

"That does not scare me." I smirk. "I plot to kill Galen daily."

Titus's nostrils flare as he shifts back an inch.

"Joking."

"Who is lying now?" His lips twitch in amusement.

For the next few moments, we both sit in silence as the weight of everything settles upon us. "I will help you," I voice, but he stays silent. His burden is so heavy, it's hard for him to talk, eat, or even see the rising sun and feel the freedom of a new day.

I think it was I who was meant to free you, Titus.

I try to make Titus laugh because his smile is like spotting a rainbow. "Your silence is spreading wider than a mistress's thighs, Titus. Say something. Amuse me." I poke his side, but all I feel is hard muscle.

Good, that caused some color to splash onto his pale cheeks again.

"Where is my 'thank you'?" I add.

"I feel like I owe you an apology, Queen Selene."

"Friends do not use fancy titles. When it is just us, I am Selene. But be careful. No one can suspect what our truth is," I warn.

"I am sorry." He hangs his head. His black hair brushes over his weary brows. "I've trapped you with me."

"I've been cornered with worst," I counter as I look at Galen's walls.

Titus's magic jumps from his hand, producing a fiery flame. He fists his hands, denying his magic.

"Seems you need help controlling your fire magic, too," I quip.

"Not usually."

"Everett's magic is to blame for this, I assume."

"No." He looks at me through hooded eyes.

"Me?" I whisper.

I'm to blame?

Knock! Knock!

My eyes flare wide, and I push to stand, as does Titus. I smooth down my hair and pray the blush on my face pales. "Come in," I shout.

My lady's maid enters with a tray in hand, bowing without spilling a drop. "Queen Selene. I have your morning tea, and King Galen has requested you dine with him for breakfast."

A silver vase on her tray catches my eye. It's polished so fine, it looks like pure liquid. Tucked inside is a plucked black rose.

Message received, Galen.

She sets the tray down on the corner table. "King Galen also sent this." She turns and grabs a box from a soldier in the hall. I glance at Titus, who studies the additional soldier.

"If I'm to be surprised hourly with an additional guard, our army will be weathered away by moonrise," I sneer.

The guard lowers his bald head. "I'm Titus's guard." He glares at me. He's a loyalist who doesn't agree with the peace treaty.

"What?" Titus and I say simultaneously.

Inhaling, I let my breath out slowly. "Whatever." I roll my eyes, open the box, and spot a lavish black velvet dress. Along the collar and sleeves is silver embroidery in the pattern of roses.

"King Galen said the color would be most fitting," my lady's maid whispers.

"Are you a parrot or my lady's maid?" The poor thing dips her head. I shouldn't be snappy with her; she is just trying to keep her head attached to her neck, a neck Galen unfortunately finds rather delicious.

"I apologize, Queen Selene, if I have upset you."

"Why is the color fitting for today?" I question.

Titus steps forward. "Thank you, Mary; I'll take it from here."

I reel back. Is he... trying to protect me?

Titus guides Mary—so that's her name—to the door. He nods at his new personal guard. Speaking with Titus will be difficult with another set of ears, unless I can manipulate Galen to replace the guard with someone Titus trusts.

"Black is fitting because..." Titus closes the distance. His words are hard and cruel. He's trying to make his guard think he detests me. With his back to the guard, he mouths, *'I'm sorry.'* "King Galen discovered who was behind my attempted assassination. It was your nobles who were acting as emissaries."

The guard flashes me a wicked grin.

"King Galen killed them as retribution. Thus, the black attire. King Galen assumed you would be in mourning over their deaths, but also horrified by the behavior of your people."

I clutch the dress, curling the velvet under my fingers. It feels like tiny thorns instead of something smooth. Digging, cutting, slicing, and then breaking off as they slip into me.

That's the cost of disagreeing with Galen. My people and I are objects. Whenever Galen wants a clean slate, or a new war, he can swat us off the game board.

If only peace weren't like water, ebbing and flowing. I wish it were as concrete as war.

That's okay. I can swim.

Maybe that's what Everett thought runes could deliver—not peace or war, something like clay, harder to mold and rip apart under the right conditions.

～

"Breathe, that's it. You can conquer this." I slap my face. "See? Now you have a blush on your pale cheeks. You look alive. Ready to fight."

I clutch the dress to my chest, fingers gouging like needles.

"Fight, Selene. Fight!" My whisper is a vow.

I feel claustrophobic in my closet.

That's okay; let this castle hug you too tight. You're not scared of anything. Not tight spaces or unsolved riddles. Nothing and no one!

The last pep talk I gave myself was before I walked down the aisle to marry a man I had never seen. Head high, back straight. I did my duty. Every duty a woman was meant to. I turned my mind into a shell, a place to crawl into. They could take my body, but I'd be damned if they plundered my mind. It was my last refuge. I would fight to the death in order to control it.

I glare at the door. Beyond it, Mary, Titus, and his new guard wait for me to emerge, dressed and ready to confront Galen.

Confront. Constantly confronting. Never comforting.

I am not designed to offer or receive comfort. I am a weapon. Forged from fire and cold plunges. I don't need soft landings. "Compose yourself now!" I command myself.

My world is water. Always shifting.

"Don't worry about breaking. You're already shattered." Racks of rich fabrics blur in front of me as I turn around. Soft and seductive designs. You can wrap me in pretty bows. Inside, I'm all sharp angles and rotting flesh. "So your brother lied. That's normal."

Harshly, I undress, ripping the fabric then leaving it discarded on the floor. I grab a dress, one I selected, and allow it to drop over my curves. "The man you wanted to kill must now keep you safe."

My fingers glide down my hips, smoothing out the fabric. It pools like liquid around my feet.

"You're used to changing tides. You will swim, Selene. You will not let Everett's death be for nothing!" I grab my hair like I do my sword, sweeping it off my shoulders. "You can do this. You must." I select my shoes and exit.

Titus meets my masked eyes.

He knows I just had a pep talk.

He sees my weakness.

Unlike an adversary, his eyes look like bandages, not daggers. He studies me, trying to see how he can mend me.

Some broken things shouldn't be fixed.

Some things are better left in ruin, Titus. That is a lesson you'll have to learn the hard way.

CHAPTER
FIFTEEN

TITUS

S elene didn't wear the dress. I didn't expect her to.

Galen is waiting to see if she will. If she does, that signals an apology.

Some concessions are signed with a dagger.

Blood-red fills my eyes as I drink in the sight of her. *She* wears the dress, not the other way around. Serenely, she sits, buckling the straps of her matching red heels. Her long black hair falls over her shoulder like a sheet on a bed, begging me to dive into it so I can unwind and relax.

I somehow convinced her to help me. Maybe I can sleep now.

I wonder what it would be like to have her silken hair draping over me?

Stop! Now! Turning, I put some distance between us and cough.

Everett thought you could be a king; he said nothing about fucking the queen.

But... I can't stop thinking about Selene naked, covered in my shadow as I hover over her. She looks good in dark colors. And her lips —they would be parted as I slide—*stop!*

I run my hand down my face. If Everett's magic doesn't kill me, images of Selene will.

"What do we do?" I whisper. My thoughts resemble a teenager.

"Well..." Selene stands. Her dress whooshes, sliding down her body, clinging to all her curves. "My initial plan is now useless." Kicking a foot out from her dress, she rolls her ankle, then glares at her shoes.

They're hurting her. I want to slide them off her feet.

"No more plotting my death?" I smirk in relief.

"Oh, there will be plenty of plotting." Facing the mirror, she assesses her reflection.

Gods, she is perfect, but her furrowed brow tells me she isn't happy.

It's so fucked up to be blessed with such beauty but think you're less. They should cast out whoever raised her.

She looks down and adjusts the draping of her dress. It's not as tight as the gown she wore to the feast, but it's no less attractive.

"I had formulated a plan when you first entered my room." Her hands slip under the neckline. My eyes widen. She shoves her breasts closer together, making sure her cleavage is mouthwatering.

She rolls her eyes when she notices me staring at her. "What?"

"N... nothing." *Look down! Now!*

"If men can adjust their balls out in the open, like feral beasts infested with fleas, a woman can adjust her bosom. Plus, Galen is a breast man. I want him to suffer." She glances down and smirks at how full they appear.

"Noted," I wheeze as I look away.

What were we talking about?

"Do I even want to know what your plans were?" I ask in a strained voice. Adjusting my cock sounds like a good idea right now.

How heavy do her breasts feel in her hands?

I scratch my palm. My hands are so calloused, I doubt I could recognize smoothness.

"It involved Galen losing his crown, then his head. Your death was thrown into the mix, but oh, the images of Galen losing the faith of his people. It would have been marvelous."

"You conjured up how to dethrone a king within a minute?"

"Yes." She smoothes out the wrinkles.

"You talk about killing kings as if we're picking out new paint colors."

Her eyes slide to me. What's she thinking? "Some colors don't deserve to grace the walls, Titus."

True, yet... vicious as fuck. That's how she got far in life.

"Are all fae like you?" *Lethally attractive.*

"Masters of skill, plotting, and world domination?" She lifts a brow and then giggles. "It is nurture in my case, Titus. I would apologize, but that word was carved off my tongue as a child."

Her smile flops like a fish tossed onto the shore, so close to the water, the salty scent fills its gills, yet it stands no prospect of returning.

What has she been through? "Why do I want to know the names of everyone who has harmed you?"

Oh shit! I said that out loud.

She freezes. The tall seductress in front of me turns timid. Her throat rolls, and her chest rises as she presses her palms against her thighs. "You feel it, too?"

"Feel what?"

"Nothing." She shakes her head. "You need no names. I handled them all myself." Her cough is tighter than the corset strings some women wear. "We have more than enough on our plate; no need to add weight to our ass and hips," she mutters.

Ass. Turn so I can see yours.

These thoughts are a serious problem. Something inside me is taking over.

"You will continue the act of a respected soldier, duty-bound to guard me. I will... I don't know how I will treat you in front of Galen yet. I'll figure it out as I go. It's probably best I act like I hate you. That means I'll need to attempt to kill you multiple times." Her eyes look to the ceiling. "Or I could pretend to accept my fate; that would piss Galen off.

"Yes, I like that. It will make him wonder what I'm up to. But then again, we don't want Galen's eyes on us until you figure out how to control your magic." A deep sigh rolls over her.

She said that all in a single breath.

"As much as I want to make Galen wait, I can't risk more of my people this sorrow-filled morning. Are you ready?" She cast a worried look at my hands.

"What if I time-weave?"

"I can't teach you how to control it within mere minutes, Titus. When you feel it coming on, look down. Everett targeted people by looking at them. Just keep your eyes down. Galen will see it as a sign of respect."

She grabs her crown. It's a smaller one, not the crown Galen gave her. The flower petals of the crown aren't soft or organic, but hard-edged and sculpted, carved from metal rather than stolen from a garden. They're faceted, angular, and deliberate, echoing the precision of fae craftsmanship. They represent forged symbols of fae strength and endurance.

Wearing that crown is a silent nod that she accepts the war against Galen.

CHAPTER
SIXTEEN

SELENE

The past.

There you are! "Everett!" I call as I approach the shore. With a stick in hand, he draws in the sand. His back is more curled than a creature clinging to its seashell. Everett's been gone for three long nights.

My feet stumble at the haunting image. He should have been able to do this as a child. Sit on the shoreline and play in the sand. Enjoy moments.

He was forced to play with swords. And when he roams too far from the castle, he is hunted down.

Shockwaves run through my arms because of the hounds' howls.

Everett always leaves me a clue before he vanishes. This time, he left a seashell.

Each step pains me as I close the distance. Salt and water fill the air, mixed with the jasmine flowers that line the shore. I wish we could set sail and leave this place—just the two of us.

Trudging forward, I wiggle my toes, driving out the sand from my sandals. "They're close," I warn him.

With a flick of his hand, the air pops. He traps us in a time bubble. "So is Sable," he mutters, but he remains engrossed in his doodles on the sand.

"Why did you run this time?"

"I never ran. That's not my fate. But one day I will. It will be towards my end, Selene." He blinks. The red in his eyes remains. "I needed time to think. To see all the outcomes." He shrugs.

"Outcomes of what?" I sink beside him. A coolness envelops my body. The sand welcomes me with open arms. Reaching out, I rub his back. My fingertips glide over bones, and I frown. "You haven't eaten." My hands freeze on his protruding ribs. Father will notice and force him to train harder.

"Seeing endless deaths makes food taste like ash."

"Everett... please. I need you." I rub harder, forcing heat into his numb body.

Everett's cursed with two magics. Time-weaving and foresight. And I'll let you in on a terrible secret: I am the only person who knows he has the latter.

It's a shared burden. If my father knew, he'd weaponize his son.

Everett's magic of time-weaving developed first. Father never thought he would gain a second power. Thankfully, foresight is not something others can see, only Everett.

"I see endless ends, Selene. Only one has the prospect of a beginning when all is done." His hand moves robotically, tracing lines in the sand.

I study his face; the circles under his eyes are too sunken and dark. The fae of Solaria have sun-kissed skin, but Everett has turned into a shadow; he resembles the fae of Lunestra, pale as the moon, but he does not glow.

"I have tried so many times to prevent a certain ending. I realize I have to let it happen. I have to allow many things to happen," he murmurs in defeat.

I run my hand through his hair. It helps Everett talk about what he sees, which is why he wrapped us in a bubble so no one else could hear.

It's hard to keep my voice tender when I ask, "You see your death?" I hate the gods for cursing him with this terrible fate.

"It's not my death I wish to stop. It's others."

Vines wrap around my heart, one of outrage and the other of compas-

186

sion. They intertwine and root deep, never separating. Everett always puts others before himself. I abhor that, but it's what will make him an admirable king.

"It's best not to meddle," I propose.

"I have no choice. If the gods didn't want me to impose, they wouldn't have gifted me this ability."

It's not a gift. It's eating you alive.

"Our family stopped caring about the gods long ago. Perhaps it is time you did."

"It is our lack of caring that put me on this path."

I drop my hand into the sand, burying my fingers beneath it. I indulge him as I ask, "What outcome are you referring to?"

He tries to lick his lips. They're so chapped that his tongue gets stuck.

Has he not drunk in the three days he's been gone?

"I have tried to stop someone from finding something."

"Who?"

He shakes his head. "I can't tell you. It would alter the path."

"What do you want to stay hidden?"

He shakes his head again.

I bite my inner cheek. "Okay," *I let out a breath.* "What's the reason you're trying to prevent this individual from finding this item?"

"In their hands, it will destroy everything we know. Everything," *Everett declares. His hand trembles with the weight of reality.* "I have to let them find the object. Only then can it be healed and awakened again." *His fist curls into a tight ball.* "I have to let so many horrid things pass in order to fix what was done. I have to lose so many people so we can win."

I'm often lost when he babbles like this. I figure out what he means; it's usually months later when it comes to pass.

"If this object is dangerous, maybe it should remain hidden."

"If it remains concealed, the world will crumble."

"Everett, you make no sense. If the object is hidden, the world ends, but if it is found, the world can also end."

"I just have to get it in the right hands. One outcome can save us all. One set of hands." *He nods to himself, blowing out a slow, measured breath.*

"*Unfortunately, the only way it can find the correct hands is through the wrong ones.*"

"*Why are you making yourself sick over something you cannot change?*"

"*Contrary to what you think, little sister, I am selfish, and I don't wish for both of us to die, but I have to come to terms with interpreting sacrifice.*"

Howl! Bark!

No! No to everything he said!

It's not the first time he has mentioned my death. His foresight saved me the day Sable tried to drown me. He's saved me many times, so hearing of my death isn't creepy. But this is the first time he sees no way around it.

"*We all must die at some point,*" *I whisper.*

"*I know.*" *He faces me for the first time. His eyes are wide yet taut with misery—a string pulled beyond its designed capabilities.* "*I just have to make sure you and I get to that point.*"

"*Is...*" *I already know the answer to my question.* "*Is the person who finds this terrible object Sable?*"

His swallow sticks in his throat. "*Promise me you won't stop Sable.*"

"*Everett, you should not force promises.*"

"*This one must be.*"

"*In the end, she's going to kill me,*" *I mutter.*

Everett doesn't reply.

A part of me floats away. I wish my relationship with my twin were different. I long for so many things to be different.

"*Does this have something to do with why she was in the library all those years ago?*"

"*Stop before you alter the future, Selene,*" *Everett bites.*

Bark! Snarl!

I glance towards the forest. Hounds gradually emerge. Their paws dig deep as they find purchase in the sand. Time's hourglass slows and traps every detail.

Everett pushes his stick back into the sand. I look down and see what he is drawing.

"*What is that?*" *I grab his hand.* "*What are you drawing?*" *It's not just random circles or lines. The sand is covered with odd symbols. Dozens he must have drawn over and over again. I watch in horror as his eyes trace the patterns, carving the images into the air.*

"I sent these to a new friend."

"Why?"

"He is a hook," he pokes the pattern with the stick, "these are bait."

I suck in my abs. "Everett..." I struggle to sound stern, "what are those?" It feels like some old power slumbers in them. I kick my foot out and rub one away.

He jerks his hand free and redraws what I expunged. "This is what will kill and save us." He stands, smirks at the designs, then kicks the sand, erasing his patterns with his boot.

Before I can ask him more, he lowers his time shield and surrenders to the guards.

~

The weight of someone's eyes has my head snapping up. Titus coughs and nudges his head to the right.

Oh... oh, shit!

The doors to Galen's private dining room are open. We've been announced, but here I am standing at the threshold of the entrance as if I'm petrified—me!

Not a successful start.

I wanted to strut inside with an air of confidence, a broad smirk, and narrowed, hateful eyes. I wanted to proclaim war. Again.

My dress gets trapped under my shoes, causing me to stumble. Ever the gentleman, Titus reaches out to balance me. His warm hands hold my biceps. For a split second, I take his strength as I lean in.

I look up, sensing Galen's eyes watching. I can't accept Titus, or Galen will grow suspicious. So I jerk my arm free, tip my nose up, and glare at Titus as I put on a show.

"Touch me again, and I'll take your fingers," I sneer aloud.

Titus steps back. He knows I'm acting.

"I apologize for my wife's tongue, General Titus. Fae can be so uncivilized; they take longer to grow accustomed to court behavior and manners." Galen leans back, smirking ear to ear. The morning light wraps around his brown hair and illuminates his clean-shaven jaw.

"Oh, dearest husband," I purr as I walk towards the long table filled with food; smelling fresh bread and breakfast sausages usually makes my stomach growl. "When will you realize your court is more huntsmen than handmaiden? One must wield a wicked tongue to survive."

So many seats, which shall I pick?

He'd expect me to sit across from him, forcing him to look at my anger head-on.

I round the table, allowing my fingertips to run along the smooth wood. Good, Galen's watching me.

"Interesting choice of color," he adds as his eyes undress me.

"Why would I mourn traitors?" I stop walking, loving that I'm standing and holding the higher ground. The irritation on his face is a small consolation. He wants to stand; perhaps bend me over the table in a poor man's attempt to show his power.

The ball is in my court now.

"That's what the fae nobles were, right?" I tilt my head and smirk. "We wouldn't want your people to think I am a sympathizer to traitors, even if they are fae. A queen must stand by her king through thick and thin."

Good, he's wondering what I'm up to.

"Although one must question how good your security is, Galen." I grab the chair next to him and step as close to him as I can before I sink into it.

Do I make sure my cleavage is at eye level with him for more than an intake of breath? Absolutely.

He uses all his tools to torture me, so I shall use mine.

"It must have your nobles covered with dark circles from the lack of sleep; their great and mighty king allowed an assassin so close to all of them. Nobles value gold and jewels, but they place their necks at a higher worth. Imagine if the arrow had not been stopped; it could have missed and hit something else." Reaching out, I grab the closest fruit, a blood orange.

Galen's eyes are sharper than an adolescent wolf's canine tooth; I can practically feel the moisture from their snarls.

"Once the nobles start to question a king's ability to protect them, it's a very bad sign, husband." My nails claw into the orange peel; the mist fills the air with a sweet scent of victory on my behalf.

I toss the peel onto his plate—the satisfaction it brings me should be illegal—then bring a slice to my mouth.

Before I eat it, I run it over my lips, savoring the sweet scent as I say, "I do hope you can quell their doubts before the roots spread. I'm sure you can. You have no problem spreading your weeds and vines throughout the land."

Juice coats my tongue, and I plop the slice into my mouth, never breaking eye contact as I swallow.

I lean in, my breasts against his shoulder, and whisper, "You're regretting crossing me." I kiss his ear and snicker. "I see it in your eyes, husband."

The smile on my lips curls around each of my letters, causing his jaw to clench.

It's so wonderful.

"Be careful." I kiss his jaw. "First, you let an assassin in, and now you're at war with your wife, which means our kingdoms are on the verge of war again. Don't let your nobles see your mistakes. That's two strikes; a third, and you're out."

Galen shoves his spine into his chair. *Perfect posture won't fix this mess, hubby.*

"Leave us, Titus," he orders.

That's exactly what I wanted you to say, Galen. Now Titus can leave the room in case he time-weaves.

As soon as the doors close, I sit back in my chair and croon, "Oh, Galen, you played right into my hands. I've wanted him gone from the moment he came to unbind me. I knew all I had to do was piss you off, so you'd excuse him."

You lose. Again.

He plucks the orange from my hand, rips off a slice, and swallows it whole.

"If you were a woman, your swallowing skills would impress me. Instead, you look like a gluttonous oaf." I giggle. The blush on his cheeks must chafe terribly.

"You think I underestimated you, but I know what you crave," he spits.

"A craving is a desire. Desires change faster than the sun can retreat from the sky." I grab my fork and stab a sausage with it. "You have no idea what I want now, what I am planning on doing. That terrifies you."

His eyes follow my hands as I slice the sausage into tiny pieces. *Yes, Galen, this is a symbol for your dick!*

"Naturally, you know I want your head after what you did to me, so you've put Titus in my path. Made him disposable. You want me to kill him so that you can declare war again." I sink my teeth into the meat and make sure to chew slowly.

He rubs his jaw. "I can't let what you did go unexcused."

"Neither could I." I set my fork down. "You wanted war; congratulations, you now have one." I stand and stab the knife into the polished wooden table. "Watch me end it," I declare.

"Don't you mean win it?"

"I'm the type of enemy that burns it all down, husband. No one wins. You should have considered that before the game began. I have nothing to lose. My brother is dead. I'm married to a prick who, yes, has a nice dick, but niceties only go so far. You've never fought a war like this, Galen. All your enemies had treasures they fought to keep safe. I don't, therefore I don't care who wins, only how it ends."

I round the table when he says, "If attempting to kill Titus costs you two dozen fae nobles, imagine how many more will die if you succeed the next time you try."

Good. In Galen's eyes, I have an excuse not to kill Titus, but to endure him.

Thank you, Galen, for making it easier for me, you fool.

I halt, then turn to face him. "If you never wanted the war between our people to end, then why did you agree to the marriage?" I ask.

He takes a slow sip of his goblet, making me wait as he cleans his lips. "Because I wanted you." He arches a brow. "The sole method to obtain you was to mislead your father into thinking I desired peace."

What?

"You never met me before the marriage." I want to hide my shock. I can't.

"Tales of your beauty have been the courtly gossip for months; kings collect beautiful things, Selene, so that's not alarming. But there was another truth woven into the rumors, one that made you stand out over your twin. Ask me what it is." He smirks. "Come on, I know you want to."

"You already told me. It was my magic."

"Your magic was just an added benefit my people would admire." He opens his hands as if he's unrolling a tapestry that reveals the picture he wants. "A queen who saves lives on the battlefield is more respected and embraced than one who uses her death magic to slaughter. Queens should be seen as affectionate mothers, not vicious bitches." He bites his lip as he grins. "Care to take another guess?"

I don't want to be silent, but he's managed to capture my tongue.

My skin tingles at the sound of his deep chuckle. "Fine, I'll tell you." He flutters his lashes like a feline seducing its target. "It was said you bowed down to no one. You don't use fake flattery as your weapon like most women do. You use your sharp tongue. You fight head-on, whereas your twin prefers a knife in the back. I like to fight head-to-head. I want to see those eyes as I force you into submission.

"And I did, and I will again, because like I said, you and I are the same; we crave each other; yes, cravings change; sometimes our cravings are desire, other times it's hate, and other times it's love."

"Love? Oh, Galen, I never loved you." My body is heavier than a stone pillar, unmoving, stuck, and forced to bear witness to the atrocities surrounding me. I must bear it, hold up the roof, and keep my head high. "Your mommy issues are deeper than I thought. She swaddled you too tightly. It wasn't out of love, Galen; she couldn't stand your cries; she was smothering you." I strike with my words, digging where I pray it hurts him.

You see, he's revealed an important card to me. He's obsessed with me, which means no matter what I do, he won't kill me.

He doesn't look as handsome with a red face. "You will," he replies. His smile is all teeth and fangs.

"You allowed thousands to die on both sides just to win me, and you think that will make me fall in love with you?"

"A soldier's duty is to obey his king, as is a wife's role."

A dozen ways to kill him run through my head. I'd be killed, too. Titus would turn to Sable for help; that would be disastrous.

I step one strong foot forward. "I. Am. No. Wife." I raise my chin high like a sword. "I am a queen."

"My queen. *Mine*, Selene."

"So I have led you to believe." I widen my stance. "The crown on my head isn't vampire-crafted. It is fae. I shall never fully belong to you, Galen," I state coldly.

His glare attacks the crown Everett had fashioned for me when I came of age.

Galen blinks as if he can flick it off. "It matters not." He steeples his hands. "You are here. You belong to me, and you will obey me. If I have to carve the pointy tips off your fae ears to make you understand you are no longer property of Solaria, I will. If you want someone to blame, don't look at me," he purrs. He nonchalantly picks up his goblet. "As you mentioned, I am a horticulturist. When something new is planted in my lands, I find the roots. Flowers don't grow without seeds, Selene. Rumors don't start without a tongue willing to spew them. Guess whose tongue spread the rumors of your wild temper?"

Galen waits until he spots my unmoving chest. My breath is locked tight in my lungs.

He leans in, jabbing his next words like a dagger. "Your dearest brother." His smirk is venom that invades my thoughts.

What?

"Everett planted all the seeds about how rare, strong, and untamable you were. Blame him, not me. Oh, wait, you can't. He's dead." Galen shrugs. He picks up the blood orange and continues to eat.

Then that means Everett needed me to be here, married to Galen, the king of bloody thorns and roses.

"Keep Sable close," Everett said. "Keep your enemies close."

Is Galen an enemy or a pawn?

I needed to be here to find Titus, and vice versa.

What other secrets lie within the castle walls?

We're all aligning. Coming together like pawns moving to the center of the board.

Why do I feel like the end is inching close to my heels?

My feet are stuck! I can't run; I don't know how, because there are too many missing pieces. I have to face it, just as Everett did when he saw the future.

Accept that I have no way to change the outcome just as Everett planned.

We all followed the breadcrumbs Everett planted. We all think we are playing games against one another, but the cold, hard truth is we are not the players.

We are the pieces Everett moved.

CHAPTER

SEVENTEEN

TITUS

A silent woman is a plotting one. When Selene plots, I worry.

We returned to her rooms. She ordered lunch but didn't eat. She now stands on her balcony, observing the land. She's a caged bird. Instead of the owner clipping her wings, he left them. It's savagery.

She knows she can fly, but her situation prevents her.

My offer to free her still stands. It's reckless. It could kill us both. It would set me back on my journey to find the Vitalis.

Seeing her suffer, trapped in a kingdom of vampires who whisper vehemently about how they detest her kind, married to a king who regards her as a trinket in his vaults. What kind of man would I be to allow this to stand?

Dishonorable. Unworthy.

Air slips between my fingers as I flex them. She'd look so magnificent if she could fly away.

Imagine if you could fly with her?

I swallow hard. *Stop dreaming before reality kills you.* I look away, knowing I'm left with the task of clipping Selene's wings, forcing her to stay and help me.

I roll back on my heels, too timid to approach her. The firmness of the stone floor pushes against my long-worn soles.

How in the world am I going to survive? I claw at the back of my neck. My flesh feels slathered with mud. There's no relief from the hardening layers, no way to sweat it off and cool down. It's a shell that's suffocating me. If I don't figure out how to flake off the layers, I'm fucked.

My palms itch; a dizzying chill slithers up my spine. Ugh! My body jerks as the time-weaving takes hold of me. I look at Selene. She's unmoving on the balcony, trapped on the other side.

Great, now I'm a voyeur.

Now's a good time to test the time magic. My approach is stagnant, achingly slow. I sense the size of the bubble wrapped around me, but when I stand next to Selene, it's as if the walls ignore her.

Selene said Everett looked at people to pull them in. That's what Everett did on the battlefield, and I did the same with the arrow. What if I touched them? My fingertips tremble, not from the magic. I'm restless to touch her, to feel her skin under my fingertips.

My attraction to her is immoral. I have to stop these thoughts.

How do you stop heat from warming your skin? If you add more layers, you only grow hotter. If you remove layers, the fever spreads faster.

These thoughts are something else. A new beast awakens deep inside my mind.

Magic, so rare and cherished, I dare not name it until I know for sure.

Quickly, I tap her shoulder. Her body recoils; she gasps as she stumbles back into me. I catch her in my arms. She's a mixture of soft and hard flesh. My hands cling to her, to this unfamiliar sensation that's foreign.

I'm used to grasping fallen bodies, rough steel swords, warm, wet blood.

"I'm sorry," I say.

Rather than letting go, I hold her closer. My muscles contract into iron, never wanting to release her. My magic pulses beneath my skin. It's like dipping a toe into warm, inviting water. The urge to dive in and relax is overwhelming. Dizzying. Precariously blurring the facts of my reality.

Selene isn't just any woman; she's a fae and my queen. Wife of Galen, my king.

Regardless, my magic wants to come out to mark her as mine. To steal her away, never to let Galen touch her again.

Step away!

I do as my mind orders me.

"You're time-weaving," she breathes.

I nod.

"What were you thinking before it started?"

"I was scared."

"The great General Titus scared of what?" Her tone's mocking. It's her defense.

"You know of what?" I bark. "Don't make me your enemy again."

Her eyes roam over my hold of her. "You're right." Her chest falls as she steps free, keeping her eyes downcast. "I didn't mean to attack you. It's going to take me time to adjust. I went from seeking your death to keeping you alive. Two sides of the coin. I keep forgetting to stop flipping it."

Her final words are a hushed whisper, water poured onto ice, cracking the frozen surface and letting the truth seep into her hardened heart.

I tug at the collar of my armor. "Adjustments don't have to be fast. Some take time, like reforging iron to recast it. Eventually, we'll fit."

Our eyes lock for dangerously long. It's like the sun shining directly in your eyes; you think you're strong enough to endure it, so you keep staring. We don't see the red flags. All we see is blinding white.

Light is a trick. It gives the illusion of gravity, causing you to walk towards it. But remember the trick: we have no idea what's hiding within its rays. It could be a beast or a savior.

Oh, how I want to let my heels dig in and my toes spring forward. I'm not afraid of monsters. I'm terrified of the other option—because saviors don't just save. They create bonds. Unbreakable ones, wrapped in love and devotion.

Saviors are weavers. Every emotion is a thread they use to craft a garment they cloak you in, one that makes you feel safe, seen, and loved.

There is something else happening here. I part my lips, ready to ask Selene, but she looks over my shoulder at the door. It's cracked open in case my guard needs to come to my rescue, but from where we are standing, he can't see us.

"Can you maintain the time-weaving for a few more minutes?"

"I can try."

She bites her lip and nods. "There are two pressing things we need to do, Titus."

Her tone holds the severity of a commander ordering a soldier to go to the front lines. Unforgiving. She avoids my eyes because she knows sending me to the front—ignoring whatever the heck is happening between us—might kill us both.

Step back. Take another step, you idiot.

I need to get laid. It's been too long.

That explains the source of this built-up sexual energy. Selene's beauty overwhelms me.

"Only two?" I counter. "I think you need to retake math. I can count a dozen issues we discussed this morning."

Yes! Score! There's that timid smirk she's scared to show in fear someone will carve it off.

"For now, yes." She crosses her arms. "One, we need to train your time-weaving magic. It can't wait; the mystery surrounding the runes and the Vitalis can. No one can find out you possess fae magic, Titus; that is a death I can not save you from."

"I agree."

"We need to figure out how the magic works. Does it respond like vampire magic or fae? Does it feed on blood, similar to your fire magic, or require rest to charge?"

"It's blood-based. When I deprive myself of blood, the time-weaving doesn't work."

"Can you go without blood?"

"Yes," I answer. Not every vampire can. "But not being attached to my fire magic within the castle makes me vulnerable. So, I've been having a small sip of my morning rations. It's enough to give me a minute of fire magic if I need it. Unfortunately, the time-weaving feeds off it, too."

"It was wise to allow yourself a little. Reflexes and a sword won't save you in this castle. Sometimes, nothing will."

Her chin tips up as she looks around her room. Old memories dance sadly in her eyes.

"I am sorry about Everett."

"Please," Her exhale sounds like it's being forced through the crack of a door. Painful and desperate to escape the room. "Stop saying that. What's done is done. This is what Everett wanted. We must play our parts."

I don't like that. Playing a part means I have no choice; the role has already been written. "Don't you mean figure it out?" I retort warily.

"No, Everett did figure it out. You and I just need to resume our roles." She reaches back and twists her hair into a low bun. She looks more like a warrior preparing for battle than a queen in royal silk.

"I'm not a toy to be picked up and played with, Selene. I had a life. I want it back."

"You also mention you have a new duty to these runes and Everett's magic." Her brow arches into the curve of a mountain that's withstood lightning strikes and torrential hail. "Like you said, adjustments take time. Adjust, Titus. You are a toy, one I will pick up and play with, one I will tuck away in a toy box to keep safe if I have to. Everett saw the future. He needed you and me to come together. The actions we take are not our choices; they're reactions Everett calculated, and took the burden of bearing."

Our breaths mingle in the silent air, two opposing forces that eventually succumb to one another. I slightly dip my chin. "You're right. But I have things to lose, Selene. Things I need to keep safe."

"Maybe the runes provide this safety net. But until we cast the line, we must read the waters. You need to train, and I need to dig into the past. Keep drinking a small ration of blood; we will work slowly; you'll learn the signs of the time-weaving. *You* are the master, not it. Once you get adjusted, we will increase your blood intake. This is good; we can control it." She speaks the latter more to herself.

I like the idea. It's smart and cautious, which means Selene does want to keep me safe.

"What's the second issue?" I ask, but the bubble around us ripples.

Her eyes peer up, giving me a perfect view of her long, smooth neck. My eyes hone in on her pulse point. My mouth waters, and my head starts to dip closer with an uncontrollable need to bite her.

"Your guard," she replies, but her voice grows distant.

Thump! Beat! Thump!

What does she taste like?

"Titus! Are you listening? We need to plan this before your time-waving stops and your guard can hear."

Stop looking at her neck! Stop! But it's so lovely and long...

Hold your breath, stop smelling her.

I blink. It takes Selene stepping back in order for me to peel my eyes off her neck.

I rub my eyes. *What the fuck was that?* I never have the urge to get drunk on blood. The side effects of bloodlust are a perilous path. As a teen, Sergeant Vivienne swiftly corrected us, ensuring we'd be soldiers who drank blood only to power magic, not to get drunk.

"My guard?" I repeat as I roll my tongue. I fail to swallow. I'm so thirsty now.

"Yes, we need to get rid of him."

"You want to kill him?" I'm not okay with that.

"No. I mean, that would be lovely, but I was suggesting we replace him. Of course, this will have to come from you, so Galen is not suspicious. When your shift is over, seek an audience with Galen; tell him you wish to have a man with whom you can communicate through a mere glance. This way, I am left in the dark. Galen will like that."

"Who is this man?"

Pop!

The time weaving vanishes. Internally, I pull for my fire magic, but nothing comes. Losing a sense is disorienting. I'm tapped out until I get more blood.

Selene can see my thoughts, so she steps closer and pushes up on her toes. I almost groan when her chest pushes into mine, but all my desires stop when she speaks. "Your brother."

CHAPTER
EIGHTEEN

TITUS

"I don't like this," I grunt and slam the door. My fingers curl around the knob, not wanting to let go.

Turning, I look at my brother, at his black hair that mirrors mine. It used to be longer before they made us child soldiers. I used to ruffle it when we played tackle. After our parents died, we were sent to the castle as wards of the kingdom. They shaved our hair, replaced our carved wooden action figures with dull blades to train with.

We never tackled for fun again.

I believed, with naïve optimism, that after the war ended, my family could look at a field and imagine building homes on it, not battles.

Everett altered that.

I battle the stages of grief. At this moment, I abhor what Everett forced upon me.

"I know. It's too goddamn early," Tristen, my brother, sighs as he rubs his eyes. The hickey on his neck is cherry red with purple spots.

That reminds me, I need to get laid. I sink into the bed and tell Tristen everything Selene and I discussed.

I kept one secret. My desire for her.

Could the attraction be a trick fae use? I want to see if Tristen falls prey to it today.

Galen agreed with my suggestion of having my brother as my guard. It's genius of Selene. Reckless of me to accept.

I hope it wasn't a misstep.

That's what Selene is wearing! Her leathers are so tight that they practically replace her skin. Her leggings wrap and curl around her thighs, stretching over her feminine hips. This war could have been ended in a day. All Selene had to do was walk into battle wearing that. Men would have thrown down their swords and bowed down.

Fuck me.

Please fuck me. Pretty, pretty please.

I look over at my brother. Oh shit! Tristen's head is tipped down, eyes glued to the floor. I know my brother; he sleeps around. He's a flirt, regardless of whether the woman has a crown or knots in her hair.

Were Selene to wield such power, Tristen's reaction would mirror mine.

I kick his shoe.

He arches a brow. *What?*

I nudge my head. *Look at her? Do you feel it too?*

His lips press stubbornly. *What are you talking about?*

He clears his throat. Selene knows we're here; Mary, her maid, is helping equip her weapons.

"Is there a war?" I break the silence.

Selene glares at me, keeping up the charade in front of Mary that she detests my presence.

"War is a horizon that never fades from the sky, General. It is a constant burning sun. Its light and heat will always warm the flesh. There is no peace from it, General."

General.

I hate that name. Call me Titus; let me hear my name on your lips.

Shit! What the heck! Why can't it stop?

My gulp is as loud as a hammer digging into the stone. My stomach is in a knot so tight Tristen can feel the tension.

Selene's eyes narrow. "That's all, Mary. You may go. I know Galen demands your whispers, so tell him I'm off to train. His general will be my target. Let's hope he survives until sundown."

Tristen spreads his legs wide and steps an inch closer to me. It's a talent to know when Selene is acting. At times, the knowledge eludes my comprehension.

Mary nods and leaves.

"Close the door," Selene orders in a hushed whisper.

Tristen moves, and as soon as the door shuts, the silencing spell ignites. "You're the brother," Selene states with a lackluster tone.

Nothing about Tristen is lacking. Nothing. Yes, he's a goof, but I would be wary of challenging him in a duel. That smile he wears? It's sociable and playful. It hides his fangs, which he will use in a fight. If need be.

He's not ruthless. Each deed undergoes evaluation, though frequently he deems the assessment worth the gamble. Tristen is a predator who finds satisfaction in beguiling his prey into thinking they're acquaintances.

Each time you laugh, he sees behind your walls.

Every time you smirk at his joke, he peels another layer off your defenses.

Tristen, bless his foolish heart, tries to lighten the mood. "Challenge accepted." He flashes his trademark half-smirk.

"What challenge?" Selene crosses her arms.

"The battle to make you see me as a friend."

"I need allies with armies. Not best friend bracelets."

"My queen." Tristen slaps his palm to his heart, "I assure you I make the finest bestie trinkets. They shall outshine your crown." He smiles, and so does Selene.

That smile. Why hasn't Selene shown it to me before?

"He knows everything? Titus, hello? Have you told Tristen everything?"

Thump, thump! I glare at her pulse. How would it feel to have it tenderly hum against my lips as I drank her down?

"Titus!" Selene snaps.

Bloodlust. Again.

I turn abruptly and grab a vial of blood from my pocket. I drank only half a ration this morning. I packed this in case I need to recharge.

"Titus?" Tristen steps closer.

I shake my head. "I'm fine. It's Everett's magic." I gulp down the small vial.

Lies. It has nothing to do with Everett's magic.

"That's not fae magic in your eyes, brother," Tristen whispers; his concern corners me to answer for my crimes.

Selene's sigh sinks into my skin, relaxing me. "We will get this under control," she assures me. "We're leaving the castle. I can't risk these walls. We'll train every day we're able to."

"Training?" I turn back around.

Yeah, I see you, brother. Tris knows I'm lying. I didn't need that blood because of the magic. I needed it because I was about to sink my teeth into the queen's neck.

Tristen steps closer, ready to tackle me.

Yesterday I felt the need to taste her. Today it's worse; it's spreading like a rash. I see it. Feel it. I'm trying not to itch it. Once I do, I won't be able to stop.

At this point, Tristen is going to cling to me like a monkey on a branch. He knows the signs of bloodlust.

Shit, he is questioning why I'm having it.

Am I deprived of blood? Marginally, but that doesn't provoke urges this strong. A vampire would need weeks without blood to trigger blood-lust, or they would have to be regulars who binge on blood to get drunk.

I'm neither.

Which means the urge to drink from Selene is claiming.

Claiming? Admit the actual word behind it.

I can't. Not yet.

Sometimes the need to claim is apparent. It grips you so profoundly that each side knows what is happening.

Occasionally, fate is wicked. It prefers to play games. The need to claim can be tedious, like a predator stepping out from an uncharted forest. Hesitant, careful to make sure it survives.

"Holy shit!" Tristen mutters, but the fool says it loud enough to capture Selena's attention.

"What?"

"Nothing?" I bark, my eyes dig into Tristen like a nail pressing a warning sign into soft wood. *Shut up! It is not that!*

His forehead wrinkles. *Tell me, what is it then?*

"You two truly can speak without words," Selene remarks. "This can come in handy."

"We're brothers," I mutter. Regret coats my tongue as soon as the words slip free. I hang my head. "I'm sorry." I didn't mean to bring up Everett.

"Tristen, please help your brother," Selene sneers. "He has a sickening need to apologize after every utterance. An odd trait for a soldier. An annoying one. Our boat is built; we're all inside. No more regrets. We must learn how to paddle. If not, we all shall sink."

"Speaking of navigating waters. What about Sable?" I ask.

Selene crosses her arms, her gaze flicking towards the door. "What about her?"

A cloud shifts, and morning light pours into the room. Strands of her black hair catch the glow, turning the edges gold.

"I picked *you*," I say.

A flicker of blush blooms on her cheeks, but it's gone as suddenly as it comes.

"Sable's got a bone to pick with me." I shift so my back is to the door, blocking her exit. "We're not leaving until you assure me my brother is safe from Sable."

Her unflinching eyes lock with mine. "She will not attack you. She'll aim for me. Consider me your shield, Titus."

"I don't need a shield." My chest stiffens as my brows pull together.

"Then call me your sword." She speaks loud enough to turn this into a duel of titles and power.

You want me to bend a knee? Fine. I can fight when on the ground, my queen. I'll protect you, my brother, and Everett's magic.

"Don't question me," she commands.

I step close enough to feel her body tremor. "That's not how this friendship works, Selene." My voice drops low. "My brother's life is on the line now! I ask, you answer."

"Now you sound like my husband."

It's a slap in the face, "Never compare me to a man who deceives and cheats. I'll kneel for you, obey your demands, but unlike Galen, I expect you to do the same. If you ask me, I answer truthfully. Show me equal respect."

The steel in her posture melts; her arms drop to her side.

"When I sense Sable's attack, I will let you know. I promise. We have time before this happens. Galen already put her in the dungeons. She'll be cautious now. The most important thing is getting a handle on your new magic."

"No, that is not the most important thing. It is you. You're my queen," I retort.

"Did you forget about me, big brother?" Tristen steps closer, wedging himself between us. His tone is light, but his eyes are full of concern as he glares at me.

"He's right."

I don't reply. I memorize all of her unique features, like those sharp, angled eyes that the fae of Solaria are known for, along with their sun-kissed skin and rich, dark hair.

Selene clasps her hands, "We will train everyday. If Galen comes to watch, which he never does, we'll pretend it's my normal sparing routine. Tristen, you'll need to stay vigilant while on guard and alert Titus if you sense anyone approaching."

Just like that, she's all hard edges and impenetrable walls once more.

I square my shoulders, facing her. A braid holds her hair in a tight, high ponytail. Her face is bare, green eyes cold and serious like an age-old tree that belongs in shadowy lands.

No matter the garment, Selene has the power to silence.

"That's your training uniform?" My words are more of a wheeze.

"This is a traditional fae uniform," she deadpans.

"I like it," Tristen coughs. "Vampires should adopt a similar fashion." He's provoking me. Testing if what he thinks is happening between Selene and me truly is the word I won't utter yet.

"Leathers like these can not be fitted to form to beasts," Selene jabs. "One must have sophistication, not feral instincts."

"Every beast can be pacified." Tristen smirks.

I elbow Tristen.

"Now I know why my brother picked you, Titus. Tristen and I would have gotten along."

"And that's a bad thing?" I grunt. Jealousy sits on the tip of my tongue.

"Yes. When you get along with someone, you become relaxed. You let your guard down. We need all our senses on high alert. There is a storm coming. It has inched over our horizon. The time to prepare is growing slim. When it comes upon us, I fear it will change everything." Her last words fade into a smoky whisper, like frost on a windowpane, blurring the view.

I try to breathe some hope into the narrative. "We'll survive."

Why does she look away?

Her grasp shifts toward her dagger's hilt. "Not every storm is about survival, Titus. Some storms are a lesson in endurance, as I fear this one may be. Come along." Selene strides past us.

I reach out and grab her hand. Searing heat floods me. Her eyes widen, then narrow.

She feels it, too.

Flames erupt. The fragrance of magic pollutes the air. My fire magic springs free, covering her hand in flames. Selene's inhale is so alarmed, it stabs my gut.

She tugs her hand back, trying to break my hold.

Tristen rushes forward.

"It's okay!" I insist. "It just wants to feel you." I can't hide the grin on my lips as my flames hug her hand.

Selene tries to pull her hand free again. This time, I let her, but my magic stays cocooned in the palm of her hands just as dust clings to cracks. It doesn't want to be swept out; it wants to remain tucked away in this embrace.

Happiness engulfs me, ripples down my spine as land quakes to move. Whatever these feelings are, they have migrated, inching us closer. In doing so, they're causing harm to everyone.

Selene's panic vanishes once she realizes my flames mean no harm. The fire transfixes her eyes. For one moment, that gets lost between her inhale and exhale, she smiles, a smirk so stunning that my knees tremble.

"You can control the temperature," she states in awe.

She's impressed. Why does her approval feel so damn gratifying?

I nod. "It comes in handy if I need to conceal myself in flames."

"That's enough, Titus." Tristen smacks my forearm.

I don't want to let go. But I do. My flames leap from her hand and land in mine. I force them into hiding again.

Selene examines her palm, rotating it, as if she seeks the maker's mark on a valuable plate.

I wish I had marked her.

Tristen's eyes burn into me hotter than any flame my fire could produce.

I know. That was odd. My fire has never investigated others as it did Selene.

I clear my throat and shove my hands behind my back. "The training field is filled with soldiers who report everything back to the king. How can I train there?"

"You think Galen would allow me to train near his men?" she scoffs. "Of course not, because that would show them how big a threat I am. I'm not the demure queen they believe me to be. You can drape me in silk to hide my scars. You can slide rings on my fingers to obscure the calluses from holding a weapon, but every mask can be removed."

I'd never define you as demure, more like a lethal attraction.

Selene continues, "Galen made me private training fields to the east of Daria Hills."

"Daria Hills?" My breath hitches. "That's outside the castle walls."

"I am well aware of the location." She pulls at her belt strap, tucking it into place. "We use the king's passage to leave the castle walls." She opens the door and enters the hallway.

"A queen wielding a blade shouldn't remain concealed," I blurt out as I cross through the doorway.

She turns, eyes scanning me from boot to chin. "Why is that, Titus?" A step closer has my nostrils flaring. Her scent isn't sweet, but rather spicy, like a chili just ripped off the vine. I know it's going to burn, but my magic is fire, so I'm not scared.

"I would respect a queen with a sword."

She tilts her head, eyes roaming over my wide shoulders, down to my leather chest plate. It's not the one I wear into battle. This one is softer, lighter, and more casual. She shocks me when she reaches up and presses her palm to my chest.

Tristen's jaw grinds, then he scans the hallway. We're alone. He glares at me and shakes his head. It's not out of vexation, but sympathy. My situation just reached treacherous depths.

"Galen doesn't want my respect, Titus." She glides her palm to my heart.

Thump! Oh no, we're slipping into overdrive. My fangs press into my bottom lip, ready to sink into her.

"He wants my submission." *Oomph!* She pushes me against the wall before proceeding down the hallway.

Tristen enters my sight, his eyes taking on an uncharacteristic seriousness.

I drop my chin. *I know.*

His chest expands. *I don't think you do!*

I shrug. *I agree. I'm royally fucked.*

CHAPTER
NINETEEN

TITUS

Eating was one of my greatest joys. Stale bread or a hot out-of-the-oven baked sourdough meant I was alive. I appreciated stale bread; it soaked up all the flavors of the stews we were given on the field; it proved you could take something discarded, better labeled as trash, and turn it into something purposeful.

Like an orphan turned into a soldier.

I rub my stomach, suppressing the growls. Selene's aid has given me reason to eat again. We've been training for a few days, skipping lunch, which Selene said was usual for her.

I keep waiting for Galen to check on her, or for Sable to jump out from around a corner and try to stab my heart. Neither has happened, which makes sleeping a most difficult task. Selene, however, wakes looking refreshed, as if the constant state of chaos is her peace.

Lack of sleep is nothing crispy bacon can't fix. Speaking of which, yum! My nostrils flare following the aroma. I glide my tongue over my fangs, anticipating the crunch of the meat; it'll bounce through my ears and then dive to my belly. My boots glide eagerly, like rocks skipping water, along the polished floors of Blackthorn Castle.

But a glance at my shirt sleeve makes me frown. I glare at the hole in my hem as I would at an enemy I spotted. I should have bought a new one. I'm not used to luxuries.

It's nice walking on clean floors, having boots that don't dirty everything.

Yet it feels like a limited-time attraction not suited for this battle-worn soldier.

I'd rather have rips in my shirts than gaping, bleeding wounds in my back that came at the hand of my royal advisors. I run a hand through my hair, making sure I don't feel the imaginative weight of the crown Everett told me I could have.

I don't think men should pledge allegiance to another man. They should fight to the death for a purpose far beyond that.

"General." Two soldiers dip their chins as they pass me. Breakfast scents linger on their clothing.

Red flashes in front of me. I dodge to the right to avoid the collision."Titus, my man." A grinning warrior with curly red hair rushes to my side and tackles me in a hug.

I stiffen. It feels too... fatherly. Caring.

Enough with the hugs and welcomes. I want food.

I clap his back in acknowledgement. The sting in my palm surprises me. He's got the physique of a bull: stocky, shorter, but wider than I am. I'm like Ryker when it comes to socializing with others. I prefer the shadows.

I grit my teeth, step back, and listen to him babble. *Hurry so I can eat, please.* "My wife just had our first child," he tells me. His glow highlights his freckles.

His arms are bigger than tree trunks. I step back. He smiles, and the hulking tree turns into the kind you'd want to sit under.

"Thanks to you killing that pointy-eared fuck, I got to be home to hold my son. I owe you my life."

His eyes don't share the joy of his words. What are you searching for?

Grind your teeth; don't defend Everett.

Why not? If I agree with this speech, I'm just a sword, no longer a man.

I touch his shoulder. "I am happy you can hold your son." It takes those born with magic much longer to have children compared to humans. Some vampires try lifetimes only to be refused by the gods.

"But Prince Everett was a man, the same as you and I; he fought for his family as you do yours."

Defending others will be what kills me.

His eyes narrow.

Yeah, I see all your weapons. The small dagger on your back, the two long swords at your side, they are a bit overkill, eh? The breakfast meat is already slaughtered.

My lips set in a firm line. "I have witnessed evil and vanquished it in battle. Everett was not that."

"He was a fae."

My toes flex against my boots. "As you are a vampire. Prince Everett followed his king's commands, as we do ours. We're warriors; it makes no difference in the shape of our ears. I do not blame the sword for how sharp it is. I blame the maker for how he swung it."

"Are you not the man who holds the sword?"

"My hands have never been my own." I fear they never will be.

I'm a cog in a machine. Alone, I do nothing; I am nothing. But with my fellow warriors, we can accomplish much. The problem is that all Galen seeks is more land.

"You sound like a fae sympathizer." He doesn't step back in offense; he's firm as dungeon irons.

Tristen would have me by the balls over this conversation.

"What's your son's name?" I ask.

His eyes soften as a smile touches his lips. "Griffen," he replies with pride.

"I don't want Griffen to grow up in a world where death is his neighbor. The only way to change that is to start looking at fae as our friends."

"Some would argue killing them is safer," he counters.

Why are you looking at me that way? As if you're waiting for me to bite the bait?

I'll bite; sometimes, that's the only way to catch the predator by surprise. Be warned, I fight back when lured in. "I'm sure fae think the same of us. Years living in a war camp taught me that chain reactions topple everyone. If we don't break that mindset, we're all bound to end up buried."

"What if some fae don't want to be friends?"

Now I know you're fishing for something. What is it?

"Some see a rock in the road as an enemy, whereas others simply walk around it. I chose to judge character. Is it the rock's fault that it was kicked around and landed there, or is it the fault of whose boots punted it? Everett obeyed orders because he hoped the war would end."

His head tilts. "You think that's what their prince wanted? An end?"

Everett's sharp jaw, plotting eyes, and pointy ears flash in my mind. My lip tugs up. "No. He wanted a new beginning. That's why he let me kill him." I begin to turn, but he grabs me. Hard.

"You're too modest, Titus. You bested him."

"I'd rather be a modest man than one who exaggerates." I glare at his hand on me. Instead of letting go, he presses another hand to my chest.

He peers over his shoulder with sharp eyes, then says words considered treasonous, "I'd stand by your side over the king's, because I've seen you fight by mine."

I scan the hall. The fact that we're alone brings no relief.

I feel bad I don't know his name, but that's a soldier's life. We're not blessed to live long enough to sit by the fire and learn each other's stories. Those who do live that long don't speak of the horrors they survived.

I study his hands, his stance, the corners of his eyes as I search for wrinkles.

How old is he? His red hair has no grey. He speaks with a youth's foolish tongue, but with the manner he carries himself and all those weapons, he's seen enough shit to fill a library.

Vampires age like humans until they're thirty years old. After that, we age one human year for every twenty-five vampire years. So by the time we're 1000 years old, we'd look like a seventy-year-old human, give or take.

I'm twenty-eight. This guy looks in his thirties. He could be thirty human years or nearly 200 years for a vampire. King Galen looks a solid thirty-seven. Last time I checked, he was 205 years of age.

His fingers turn into needles, sticking my clothing into his palm. He's holding me as if I'm a shiny new weapon he seeks to strap onto his heavy belt. "Do you understand what I'm saying?"

You'd commit treason, stand by my side, and not our king's. Yeah, I get your point, but I'm not going to repeat it out loud.

"You're a father now; you have a son to consider," I warn him. "I'm not worth dying for."

He snorts a laugh. "Your worth is more than your hands that hold your sword, son." He jabs a finger over my heart. "You and I know peace is an intermission before the next act. I've lived through a lot of acts, Titus. I'd like to see a new show." He slowly nods.

"There will always be war."

"Let me rephrase that: I'd like to see a show where war for land is not the main plot. Give me a war with a purpose that doesn't just benefit a king; give me a war in which it is an honor to fight. As you said, we're all the same. If we don't all stand as one, we will die as many.

"I'm not the only one who feels this way, so I'll ask again: do you understand what I am saying?" Even though I'm looking down at him, his authoritative tone makes me feel like a child again.

What rank is he?

He's dressed similarly to others, in battle-worn leather. The marks and weathering shine like badges of honor. But he carries himself the same way a wild cat moves: with pride.

A feline whose mane is torn, patches of fur ripped away in ancient feuds; arms, shoulders, and back scored with wounds, yet the massive beast moves smoothly, with unshaken grace.

"I understand," I respond hesitantly.

"Good." He presses my leather sleeve smooth. "Soldiers were raised to have each other's backs. We're different from kings." He gives me a side hug.

I whisper in his ear, "Be careful no one hears you speak like this."

"I was going to tell you the same thing." He smirks. His friendly pat on my back steals the air from my lungs. "The nobles have no idea what's going on; they don't leave these walls. The majority of us are sick of that. I thought it was time you knew how others felt."

"They praise me as a hero who killed a prince." I hate it.

"They praise you as a brother who let them come home, Titus. We're watching as you sit in silence on the side. We weighed your character. I want to hold my son tonight, so I hope you know the risk I'm taking when I tell you this: you have the majority of support when the time comes."

He's scaring the shit out of me. He shouldn't be talking like this.

Maybe it's a trick I walked into. My face must convey that. He steps so close I can count all his freckles. "You know what's funny? Some vampires think all fae look the same. I don't." The air starts to push in on me.

He's got air magic! He can hush conversations.

My fire magic dances up my spine, warming me, eagerly waiting to defend me. Something more dangerous awakens. The time-weaving. My chest widens as I fight to suppress it. *Not now! Please!*

"I remember their faces. In particular, a young boy," he continues. I smell his morning blood on his warm breath. "At the time, I didn't know he was a prince. He was just a boy with pointed ears, but as you said, all I saw was a boy who sought me out; it made no difference that he was fae. I didn't know he would grow into a man who was destined to wear an enemy crown."

"Everett," I whisper. Shock defeats me. My knees tremble; the time-weaving surrenders to my pleas and sinks away.

He uses his magic to nudge me closer. "I had to know where you stood. After all, you killed Everett." His eyes grow distant. "I got a feeling our pointy-eared friend didn't give you a choice. I didn't get one either."

Footsteps sound, another group approaches the breakfast hall. My skin burns. He peels his air magic back with a force that leaves a cooling burn over my exposed skin.

"I just want you to know you have friends here, Titus." He winks and begins to turn.

Yeah, not happening. I grab him and drag him further down another corridor. "You'd better start speaking."

"I've spoken a lot; I'm much more conversational with my sword."

I try and fail to shove him into the wall. Are his feet roots? "You knew him," I hiss. My fingers curl into his leather.

"I knew him," he agrees in a solemn tone. "He looked a mere sixteen years old, but he spoke as if he possessed the sands of time. That boy said such funny things. Didn't believe him. Marked him off as bonkers. Turns out I was crazy not to listen. Everything Everett told me has come to pass."

My grip drains of rage and possesses a vagrant. "Tell me," I plead.

He covers my hands as a father would, peeling my fingers back and cradling them. "I made a vow to Everett. Don't ask me to break it. I just wanted you to know that your back is covered. Let things unfold as they should. You'll hear from me again, Titus." He steps to the side.

"Covered for what?"

His stare makes me feel like a silly boy who cried when he fell. His eyes urge me to get back up and conquer what anguished me. "Breakfast is getting cold. You'd best drink up; keep your magic charged here."

He winks, turns, and leaves before I can reply.

I fall against the wall like a brick no longer needed. My ass hits the floor, and the back of my head smacks against the pillar. All I see is polished black stone reflecting my face in shades of darkness. No guiding light.

How many more spies did Everett make? How many slumber within Galen's walls?

Tristen appears, stopping at the entrance of the corridor. "I thought I sensed you here," he declares. His smile drops when he spots me.

He covers us in his shadows, then I whisper what happened.

"I don't think it's a bad thing," Tristen mutters, legs kicked out wide, faking confidence for my sake.

"It's treason," I bite out with a shake of my head.

"This is my fault. I was the one who suggested that we come here. Maybe we should leave." He watches me closely, waiting for me to admit what is happening between Selene and me. We're both too terrified to admit the truth, so we keep poking it.

"Running away from a problem doesn't fix it."

Tristen nudges me. "Are you sure about that? Nero and I got away with a lot of shit as teens."

"No, you didn't; Ryker and I cleaned it up."

"Those were the good times." He whistles. "Come on, let's eat and focus on the biggest problem we have which, by the way, you controlled your time-weaving. That's great." Tristen stands, extending his hand and pulling me up.

"Controlled is a big word. I think when he mentioned Everett, the time magic grew calm. It was odd."

He drags me toward the hall. "It's still something to be happy about. Speaking of the fam, I'm gonna send a message to them, see how they're doing. The mail goes out this afternoon. Want me to add anything from you?"

You can peer at me for hours. I refuse to tell you what I fear is happening, Tris. I'll handle it. I always do.

"Just tell them everything is good." I swing the door open. My cheeks grow red from the heat of the kitchen. The scent of oven-baked meats fans out. But now I'm not hungry.

"Your definition of good scares the shit out of me," Tristen replies warily.

"General!" I flinch. "Just the man I was looking for. Come." King Galen strides down the hall, waving me over. The soldiers cafeteria is within easy walking distance of his dining room. It's not so he can eat with his soldiers on rare occasions. The location was strategic, ensuring his men were nearby if needed.

The shine of his leather causes my eyes to squint. "I wanted to invite you to the war council this morning."

"War council?" *I thought I had ended your war.*

Galen pauses at the insinuation in my tone. A group of nobles stands behind him, watching.

Tristen coughs. I dip my chin. "That is a high honor, King Galen. I fear I'm not worthy of such knowledge," I say to ease the blow of my words.

Galen plays it off by laughing. "I suppose I should rename it now that the war is finished, but it has such a nice ring to it."

War often does, until the bodies pile up and the scent of rotting flesh breaches Blackthorn's high walls.

"Come, you might provide valuable insight," Galen demands.

Shit!

"What of Queen Selene?" I ask. *I need to be with her!*

Galen's eyes find Tristen. "Cover her security until the General returns."

"Absolutely." Tristen bows.

Galen and his entourage leave, filling the hall with chuckles and morning gossip. I peer at Tristen. "I'm good with the ladies, don't worry," he assures me as his goofy, lopsided smile fills my eyes. "Hey, it's fine. Go." He nods, but his hand is on his sword.

I fear the trenches of Blackthorn will alter me far more indefinitely than the battlefield did.

CHAPTER

TWENTY

TITUS

My lungs shudder as the massive doors slide shut. I've never been so out of my element. This guy's hands are so smooth they look like butter. What the heck is he wearing? His purple velvet suit looks more suited for an armchair.

War's requiem is blocked by the castle walls, allowing them to dance like nothing matters. The insult coats my tongue with a sour tang.

I peer at their knees. Have they felt the weight of blood-soaked armor? Of course they haven't.

The fragrance of the roses in the vases along the walls gives an odd illusion of tranquility. My chin tips up toward the massive stained-glass windows, making the war room feel like a place of worship. Reds and blacks paint a scheme of the landscape of Blackthorn. The vaulted ceilings allow for plenty of nooks for the light to slip into.

The scent of fresh blood in the air has my hand resting on my sword. There! Every pitcher on the large table is full of blood. The smooth, deep red silken surface, filled to the brim, draws my eyes.

My fangs throb, but I've long controlled the need to drink in excess.

I stand back as they all clamor towards the table. What about rations and a proper blood diet? We're taught as kids about overconsumption, which leads to bloodlust.

Consuming too much human blood doesn't strengthen your magic. It gives you a sense of pseudo-strength. It's an addictive high.

It seems the nobles were handed different books. Binge all you want; we'll rehab you and make you fit as new again.

Galen saunters over to the only chair—it's more of a throne, really. The trunk of a tree was gutted, hollowed, and then carved into a chair. The back of it curls up into braided vines with fresh black roses. I follow the others as we stand around the table. They're comfortable as they grab goblets and gulp down their fill.

The hairs on the back of my neck raise. That one has air magic; a fresh scent of air circulates around him. The vampire next to me must have water; the air feels more humid.

"Lieutenant Ferdinand, tell me—" The door swings open, and Galen hesitates with insult.

"I apologize. I was late in getting word from the scouts." The man stands tall with a note in hand.

Fuck!

It's Griffen's father. Everett's spy/friend/I-don't-know-what-the-fuck-to-call-him.

He's not a random soldier if he's here. And he just interrupted King Galen's meeting without much concern.

"Vice Admiral Adrian," Galen guides his crown to fit more snugly. "I would call upon you next. What news have you?" he inquires.

Vice Admiral Adrian Airendale! He's in charge of Galen's whole damn army! Gods!

Of course, I know his name. I've never met him, but stories about him rushing to battle, laying siege as if death itself could not claim him, are endless. He's so valuable, King Galen ordered him back to Blackthorn, no longer allowed to fight on the field.

If Galen lost Adrian, he'd be fucked. Adrian knows how others think, where they will attack or retreat. He's a mastermind.

"I have troubling news." Adrian hands Galen the note. His eyes lock onto me and lighten, the only sign he's a friend not a foe. He refrains from drinking, adhering to the warriors' dietary habits.

"Troubles are nothing more than morning gossip." Galen smirks. "Go ahead, enlighten us with your tales." He drops the letter, not bothering to read it.

Adrian must be used to the insults, for he doesn't flinch. "We found another body."

"Not this again." Galen rolls his eyes. "I don't care about bodies; they offer me no value, Adrian."

"A body of the creature, not its victim."

I look from noble to noble; some wear ignorance, like Galen, while others pale.

If I'm part of this council, I intend to use my voice. I clear my throat. "What creature?"

"I apologize, General Titus, for this is a nuisance you must now endure." Galen waves his hand at Adrian to continue, but the gesture is akin to swatting a fly.

"Nuisances, if not dealt with, can steal crowns, Galen," Adrian responds, purposely forgoing the title of king.

Galen touches his crown again. Adrian's disregard for decorum clearly vexes him.

The king's spine presses into his chair for protection. "Let them try." He mocks the looming threat of battle, comparing it to mere pages of a story, not real horrors.

I run my tongue over my fangs.

"This is nothing more than mage magic. Shadows and light molded into the silhouette of flesh," Galen adds. "Mages have tried to merge their magic with creatures before; the fools never learn. They are as stubborn and persistent as humans."

"Mage magic or not, these creatures are strong. One can take out four vampires and over two dozen humans." Adrian's eyes hold mine.

"I told you," Galen grabs his goblet, smirking at his reflection in the glass, "let some other kingdom deal with this. I have enough to worry about."

"I have brought the body of the creature here and a witness," Adrian states.

The room erupts with cries of excitement. I keep my features carefully blank.

"I want to see!"

"I don't!"

"Come on, let's see."

The ceiling captures Galen's unfocused attention. The cost of such a sheer scale of artwork could feed a town for a year. I don't know what's grander, the art or the white-gold gilded frames that are fighting for the viewers' affection.

It's so overwhelming I look down at my worn clothing to remind me what the reality of the majority of the people in this kingdom face.

"Let's see this body and interrogate the witness," Galen groans.

"The witness is just a child."

"I do not care. Bring them."

Adrian hesitates, then lifts a shoulder. Air draws in, followed by a shrug, causing more air to hit the entrance. The soldiers outside open at his signal. "Bring them," Adrian orders.

"This had better be worth my time, Adrian," the king says snidely.

"I trust my king knows what holds value when it comes to protecting his people," Adrian retorts.

Moments later, four men appear, carrying what appears to be the small shape of a body covered in tattered blankets.

Why are there no bloodstains?

Wait, if this beast is dead, where is the smell of rotting flesh? I smell... nothing.

The men make to toss the sack on the table, but Galen shouts, "Not on my table, you fools! There, on the floor will do."

We all move around for a better view; Galen sits as he watches.

They drop the sack. "Why was there no sound?" I wonder, furrowing my brows.

"These creatures have weight, but they make no sound. That's how they are so successful in ambushing. I am told that when they grab a hold of their prey, the victim can make no sound either," Adrian informs me. "Gossip has reveal they are called Shades."

"Do not give them a name, Adrian," Galen barks.

Adrian dips his chin, then motions for his men to remove the cloth. Some nobles gasp. Others stand dumbfounded, like me. Air presses into the metal of my sword as I unsheathe it a few inches.

I lean closer to study it. It's just shadows, lumped and grouped into the shape of a figure that resembles a human form. It should not exist, yet it's before my eyes, like waves tucking into ocean waters. No longer moving, but you feel their strength and know any second they can rise again.

"It looks like a shadow," one of the nobles claims.

Galen moves for the first time, planting his elbow on his knee. "You," he points to the noble wearing the purple velvet, "touch it."

"Touch?" The man shudders and fearfully stumbles forward.

"I'll do it." I step forward. I don't want to, but this man is about to piss himself.

"Look! That is why we won the war. Brave men," Galen speaks. "Come, Titus, prince slayer." He waves me over.

Adrian subconsciously steps closer. Is he worried?

Gods help me. The closer I get to this... thing, the more the air shifts. "The air is colder near it. That is a sign we can use if one lurks nearby."

"Very wise observation, General." Adrian widens his chest.

"Yes, yes, now, go on," Galen huffs.

This is a different version of Galen. I'm so used to the showmen, the friendly king who woos the crowd as he holds feasts and parties. This version is just a spoiled brat who would rather be fucking a line of women than defending his empire.

Slowly, I bend down; I expect my fingers to slip right through it, but instead, I hit a form that feels hard yet moldable. "How was it killed?" I ask.

"They kept stabbing it. I surmise one of the cuts must've hit its heart, but as you can see, it remains solid. It does not tear open, nor bleed, yet it can be killed when the correct spot is struck."

"That's enough touching, Titus. When was the last time you fucked a woman? I'm worried," Galen jokes, and the room laughs, except Adrian.

"It's hard to find a woman when you're readying for battle, King," I bite. I cast my gaze downward, too ill to view the individual I slew for.

"That's the best time to search for pussy."

My jaw ticks.

"Make sure you bed someone soon. You caused me concern that you would request seclusion with the beast."

More laughs.

Would he mind if I used the sword he gifted me to kill him? Right here, right now?

"Where is this witness?" Galen shouts.

Two more guards usher in a girl, perhaps eight years of age. Her feet are bare, covered in dirt and blood. Her clothing is in the same terrible state.

"She's a human," Adrian states by way of explanation. "Her family lived in Noria; they were killed on the premises with all the other humans and vampires."

"Come here, child." Galen orders. She takes one step before Galen says, "That's far enough." He sneers down at her rags for clothing. It was a test to see if she'd obey him.

Adrian and I exchanged a glance of disillusion.

"Tell me what happened," Galen orders in a cold, authoritative voice.

She steps closer to the creature. Adrian and I remove our weapons in sync. She doesn't flinch. She's shocked like Ember was, mute and dazed when she was thrown to us.

"She needs a healer," I mutter.

"Resources are costly. Let's see if she can pay in the form of valuable information," Galen sneers.

Adrian's glare tells me to bite my tongue.

But even tongueless men can conjure a scream.

She bends down, stealing my attention. With a smile on her lips, she begins to stroke the shadowy creature.

The room's atmosphere crackles with more magic. Every noble pull their sword out, all untrained. Their fragile wrists couldn't endure over five minutes of combat.

"I am not scared of a child; put your blades back," Galen grunts. He scoots back with ease. "Speak," he demands.

She presses a long touch to the cold form, then stands. With dirt-filled nails, she pushes her knotted brown hair back, giving us a perfect view of her face. Her stained cheeks suggest she tumbled into blood face-first.

"I am not from Noria." Her voice lacks a child's playful optimism.

"You were found in the village."

She digs her thumb into her index finger, picking away at the grime. "Wind can carry a leaf. That does not mean the leaf is from a tree rooted in that land," she snaps, eyes turning cold as she glares at Galen.

My lip twitch at her boldness. Had she been born at another time, she could have been with me and my family.

"Where are you from?" Adrian inquires gently.

"The Valley of Sand and Bones," she answers. Adrian pales. "They thought the fire killed me, but they were wrong."

"Lies. You'd never survive the journey from those lands. Childish nonsense," Galen snaps. "It's clear you know nothing of manners. Tell me what happened in Noria?" Galen demands.

"They said I was a mistake. I have no control over it. It's a lie." She digs into her fingertip so harshly that it will break the skin any second.

Stop! I want to shout. *Someone cares if you hurt. I care. I want to help.*

"I was chosen because I was good." She nods to herself.

"Who chose you?" Adrian inquires in a gentle but unwavering tone.

Ignoring him, she looks at the creature. "We were hungry."

"You? You mean you and this creature?" Galen clarifies.

She smirks, sending a bead of sweat down my temple. A second later, two fangs appear.

"Impossible," a noble whispers, and her head snaps to him. She lunges, jumping onto him, sinking her fangs into his neck.

Shock chains us all to the floor.

"She's a vampire!" someone shouts.

"No." I shake my head in horror. Vampires' fangs don't retract. She said she was hungry. We don't drink blood to satiate hunger, only magic.

"She's something else," I whisper in horror.

Suddenly, every noble panics. I look at Adrian. He nods. I unsheathe my sword, and Adrian sends his magic out, squeezing the child's neck. She drops from the noble, her hands curling around his force. Her fangs disappear.

I move in. Don't ask me to kill this child, whatever she may be. I won't be able to.

Galen lunges; his vines pin the child down, and then he raises his sword. He's going to kill her without a second thought. I step forward to stop him, but air pushes me back.

I find Adrian's eyes, a delay that gives Galen the time he needs to ram his sword through the child's heart.

How could you? I glare at Adrian.

He shakes his head and glances at Galen. He was trying to keep me safe from Galen's wrath.

Gushing hot blood fills the air as it slams against the blade, freeing it. Galen pushes his sword deeper and deeper, twisting and churning it, until the child takes her last painful breath.

Clang! The gifted sword Galen gave me clatters to the floor.

A pool of blood seeps out of the child. Black blood! I want to rush to her side, push it back in. But it's too late. I need to kill Galen so this doesn't keep happening.

I get it, Everett. I understand, and I accept.

Adrian watches as I bend down, grabbing my sword. I glare at Galen as I rise.

I can't kill Galen now; that would be foolish. I need to plot this wisely.

The noble cries, his hands slapping to his neck, "She... she fed from me!"

"Close the doors!" Galen shouts to his men. He whirls on the noble. "Drop your hands. Show me the bite." The noble does. "Heal it."

The noble gulps. Vampires, mages, and fae have accelerated healing, but we need to focus on it; it's like a state of meditation, which is hard to do in battle.

"I said, heal it."

"I... I can't."

Galen's jaw clenches. "You," he points to another noble, "Cut your palm and stop his bleeding."

The noble does as ordered and covers his friend's bite. Vampire blood has clotting properties, but when he removes his hand, the wound still bleeds.

"I feel faint." In seconds, the nobleman collapses.

"Put pressure on it, as humans do." Adrian steps forward. "You," he orders the soldier, "go get a healer. He's suffering blood loss."

"Wait!" I step forward and glance at the child. She didn't deserve heart stabbing... regardless of her being a monster. There are kinder ways to kill. "Try her blood," I suggest.

"What?" the king exclaims incredulously.

"Maybe it clots as ours does."

"You heard him!"

We wait with bated breath as one of the soldiers presses her blood to the wound. When he removes his hand, the bleeding slows.

The noble's eyes land on me. "Hero! You saved me."

Shit! Galen's eyes dig into my side. "Thinking fast does not warrant the title of hero," I respond humbly.

"Nonsense." The noble staggers to stand.

"What the fuck was she, Adrian?" Galen roars so loudly he has to reach up and steady his crown. His outburst takes the attention off me, thankfully.

"She acted as a human, smelled as a human."

"Clearly," he jabs a finger at her, "she is not human!"

"You are very wise, King." Adrian remains calm, but I can read his insult from here.

"Enough with the pissy mood because I called you back to the castle!"

Adrian dips his chin and adds, "It seems our nuisance has escalated into a problem."

Galen flashes his fangs. "Solve it!" he roars. "Eject those *things* from this castle!" He glares at the Shade and the girl. "If I hear one single word, a single mention, or a whisper of gossip over what happened, I will hang you from the vines on my walls. Do you understand? This will never be mentioned! The last thing I need are whispers of a plague, or whatever the fuck she was. Do you understand?"

We all nod.

Galen storms to the door. "And clean up this mess!" he hollers over his shoulder.

I stalk Adrian down the halls. Does he think I'll let him go?

He soon reaches his office and waves me in; the door closes, activating a silencing spell. He unstraps his longswords, then sinks into his chair, head in hand. "I did not know he would kill her."

I have no wise reply.

Bookshelves cover one wall. Beside the tiny window, a ledger rests upon a small desk, along with mage ink, plus a vial containing mage power used to mix into wax seals. The powder enchants the letter so it can fly as a bird does across the lands.

I lick my lips. "Explain." I block the door. This is a pinch-me

231

moment. I am ordering Vice Admiral Adrian Airendale. Tristen won't believe this!

"I can't." He rubs his temple. "All I can tell you is Everett warned me something was coming, and I presume this is it."

"The girl or the Shade?"

"Both, one or the other, I do not know." He hunches over his desk. "She was human, Titus. I smelt her."

"She had fangs." I pause. "We need to figure out what she was." I rub my jaw.

Adrian shakes his head. "You have a queen to guard. Let me dig into this matter."

Selene. *Thump!* My palms sweat. The need to see Selene floods my mind, consuming me.

"The tides are changing; only seasoned fishers know how to read the waters, Titus. Galen hasn't sensed it, but he will, and when he does, be prepared."

"How do I do that?" I grate out.

"Follow Everett's orders." He looks at the door. "You should go. Galen will arrive soon to continue his bitch-fest."

"Where do the Shades originate?" I inquire.

"There is no set place. I hear whispers of their sightings all over the land."

I glance at his mage ink. "I have family stationed near Lunestra," I admit. "Is this why Galen sent half the army there?" I cautiously step forward.

Are my sister and brothers about to face an unknown enemy?

I look at the mage ink again. I can steal some and warn them.

"He sent his army there for another reason."

"What reason?" I come to stand in front of his desk.

"I can't tell you that. I will admit that I acknowledge I know those you consider family. I made sure they were sent to Lunestra."

My bones feel hollow. My family is my biggest weakness. "Why?" I rasp.

"Because the last thing you need is more leverage within this castle for Sable or Galen to use against you. Keep Tristen in your sights. You need to go. Go! Let me handle this." Adrian grunts, stands, and walks to the door.

My lungs release a hiss before I turn.

"And drink some blood." Adrian's order is full of concern. "Never leave yourself vulnerable within these walls."

I have no choice but to tell Tristen and Selene as soon as I arrive for guard duty. It delays Selene's scheduled training, so in order not to arouse suspicion, she tells her maid she's still hungry. The new plate of eggs and pancakes sits untouched as she paces her room.

Her palm presses into her stomach. "My brother knew Adrian," she whispers. She feels betrayed. Again. It fractures trust, which we need to have in Everett.

I step in her path. Her hips feather over mine. She has the willpower to step back.

I don't. I want to grab her, to shield her from this additional pain.

"I'm sorry." Looking upon her is like staring at a star—all fire and blinding light, a fighting force trying so desperately to keep everyone at a distance, yet it does the opposite. It draws attention.

"Stop. Apologizing." She glares at me through hooded eyes. That wicked, sharp tongue makes me want to punish it with mine. Instead of yelling, I want to coax it into my mouth and show it what love can feel like.

"I'm comforting you," I snap, stepping closer. Too close. Our hips touch once more, like two docked ships recklessly close to sinking one another.

And... fuck! I'm hard. *Think of battle, of the guts, piss, and shit. Don't think of her warm, soft curves.*

She gasps and steps back. "I don't want comfort."

Run and I'll chase.

I grab her by the shoulders and anchor her to me. Fuck, that feels...

perfect. She was always meant to be molded to my side. "You *need* it," I rasp.

Gods be damned, this woman will be the end of me!

Her lips part, pupils dilate. "Let me," I urge.

"Titus," Tristen warns. I ignore him.

"Why?" she whispers. Her chest rises and falls with urgency.

"Because I want to. I need to."

She remains silent, leaning closer. I meet her halfway and pull her into me. My chest rumbles when her breasts push into my hard torso. The hug is awkward, like two swords stopping mid-battle to talk instead of killing. But it's a start.

A dangerous fucking start, Titus.

I know, but I don't give a shit.

Turning her face, she rests her cheek on my chest. Utter peace fills me. "I'm so furious at Everett," Selene confides.

"I am too." I push my fingers into her hair. "But I am not Everett. Don't give me your hate."

"That's all I have left inside me."

I slip my finger under her chin, tipping her eyes up. "I can find something else."

"That would be unwise." Her lips part.

Her lips. Kiss her. Claim her! Now! Do it!

"Titus!" Tristen shouts. It shatters the hold I had on Selene.

Oh fuck! What was that? My heart possessed my mind. I had no control.

The look on her face says she felt the same. She raises a sharp finger at me. "You need to focus on my brother's magic. Adrian is right. We have our path; he has his. If they collide in the future, so be it. Until then, we remained focused on what we had planned. We're allies, nothing more," she stresses.

The icy stare in her eyes is an arrow piercing my heart. Turning, she walks to the wall, takes a few deep breaths, and then she walks into her hallway pretending all is fine and she's ready to train.

Tristen steps into view, dagger out, pressing it to my cock. "I will cut your dick off when you sleep if I have to. What the ever-loving-fuck, Titus? Do I need to get Ryker here? I will. I will tell him and the others everything."

"Don't you dare endanger them!" I hiss.

"Endanger? Bro, are you blind? You almost kissed the queen."

"I did not. I was comforting her."

"Is that what we call fucking these days? In that case, consider me the gold standard bestie in comforting women. I love to comfort. I can do it all night long. For days! But I'm smart enough to know *who* to comfort."

I avert my gaze. "I have it under control."

"*It?*" He presses the dagger against my balls.

I grab his wrist and twist the dagger away with a scowl. "I know what to focus on for now. Come on, Selene waits for no one."

I brush past him.

"Don't think I didn't hear that word, Titus, 'for now'. Just consider the latter when you allow your dick to comfort her. Her husband is king."

"A king I will kill when the time is right."

CHAPTER
TWENTY-ONE

SELENE

Nausea churns my stomach. The rose-lined walls aid the sickness.

Why did I hug Titus?

I keep letting him see me cry.

I feel faint.

Stupid, stupid girl!

You don't behave like this. You're a mold; you do not bend or break!

Picking up my pace, I nearly fall into the door. Fresh air slaps me in the face as I emerge onto the rose-covered path. The thick vines could be mistaken for marble pillars. Their braided patterns knot so tight, a fly could not buzz through.

This hidden exit from the castle is Galen's safety net, and a cage he gave me.

My foot meets the path with familiarity. It's twists and winds, not disclosing the final destination until you're brave enough to enter it.

When Galen first led me here, I was at his mercy. Exactly what he wanted, it wasn't until I released my captive breath that he revealed the training field, which he enclosed in more rose bushes. The faster I walk, the fresher the air becomes.

I crave release from these roses! From this cage! From the chemistry that sparks when I look at Titus's face.

The wider the path splits open, the more my heart cries. It's so damaged that it should have evolved not to weep.

I glance over my shoulder, seeing Titus and Tristen follow suit. They look like twins, but Tristen's face has a lightness to it. Blackthorn will expunge it.

Titus is all haunting eyes that lure the predator into his emotional depths. If he wishes to survive, he must resemble a stone. Let things soak into him but not change shape.

The brothers share a heated glance, jaws set firm, eyes locked in a silent argument as they hunt me through the caged path towards my field.

Shit, Tristen knows. He sees the bubbles dancing in the air when Titus and I are close.

He's wise enough to pop them.

As must I.

I have to stand tall, numb everything. Reaching for a rose, I rip it from its vine, crushing it in the palm of my hand.

I sprint towards my refuge. Running as fast as I can away from the desire I feel for Titus.

There's a problem. Those feelings are a predator; they have one purpose. To claim. To mark.

I run, they give chase.

I tell them no, I see their claws ready to hook me, dragging me to their jaws, no matter what the repercussions are.

I must discover an alternative tactic to defeat them. Snuffing the flame is impossible, but I don't have to fan it.

Stepping free from the pathway, I enter my field, a wide-open cage that traps the sloped hills and pastures. Behind it, mountains frame the landscape, feathery skies, and a bright sunny day masks the corruption on these lands.

You are ice. You do not melt under Titus's flames. Stomp on the swelling emotions!

Feelings so dangerous, empires would topple. Kingdoms would be no more.

Tossing the rose aside, I walk to the center of the field and grab my sword, pressing it to my lips. This is who you should love. Metal. Weapons.

Not men trying to save you.

I'll never admit what is happening between Titus and me, why I inch closer when I should shove back, why I dreamt of him last night.

It can't happen.

Spinning, I aim my sword at the man who has caused my heart to beat again.

It's time to train, to stay steady on our course. At sea, an island looks inviting. It was never the final destination.

I can not divert.

Our emotions are nothing compared to the grand scheme. I will not let my brother's death be for nothing.

"Let's begin," I declare. My eyes swim along the metal of my blade, the sky above reflecting on it. It's time to vanquish these emotions so they remain forever hidden.

CHAPTER
TWENTY-TWO

TITUS

One week later.

Training with Selene is both my torment and salvation.

She's a guiding light that leads you off the edge of a cliff. Pushing. Shoving. Forcing your toes to uncurl so she can plow you off. As I free-fall, I sense Everett's magic. Time is curious; it pursues knowledge. It halts everything so it can gobble it down.

Keeping Everett's magic asleep is a battle of masking my emotions.

There's another problem. A separate magic is blossoming inside of me. A sensation flows up my spine when I'm near Selene.

Selene senses it yet tips her chin up. I want to curl my fingers around her slim neck, guide her jaw to mine, and force her to acknowledge it.

Tell me I am not the only one! Tell me, Selene.

My fangs throb with a thirst the blinding sun cannot extinguish. A swipe of my tongue over them only tickles it, as my eyes lock onto the temptress.

239

It's getting worse, this curse inside of me.

How do I rebuke it?

Tell me how?

Our blades clash as I deflect her attempted attack. She moves around me with a fury, allowing me to stand still and watch as she searches for her next opening.

Mistake. Don't search. Demand an opportunity. That's how you defeat your enemy.

Selene's black hair lashes like ropes in a harbor, forcing me to dock and to look her in the eye. She spins around, blade held high, creating a small whistle in the air. She lets out a growl as she lunges. I force my smirk into a straight line.

She's not a poor fighter; she's brilliant, but there's a sense inside of me that seems to know where she is going to strike next.

Pulverized grass, a light humidity, and the faintest hint of rain scent the field. A light sweat beads on my brow. Not from the exercise. No, proximity to Selene is the cause.

Driving the heel of my boot into the soil, I stand firm. Selene glares up at me; the angle of her eyes looks sharper. I peer at her as I do a flame, admiring its shades and the levels of heat.

With a hiss, Selene slides her blade down mine. "You're holding back." Metal screeches like a cat plunged into icy water. That sound transports me back to the battlefield. The ground is so slick that your heels stick. You look down, thinking it's mud.

How can that be? It didn't rain.

Oh. Puddles of blood—so many, the earth can not drink them down fast enough—trap the soles of your boots.

Your mind stops fighting. You look around. Trauma forces you to inhale. The smell repulses you more than the swamp of blood and guts did. Sweat, urine, and shit. So much shit.

When you're handed a sword as a kid and told to fight, no one tells you about the shit, or how the body purges everything from it when it dies. They speak only of glory.

I breathe again. Selene's faint scent works like an elixir, calming my mind.

"You're my queen," I answer. I can never fight her as I would another. "You don't toss a diamond into the dirt and trample it."

"A diamond was born in the dirt, under pressure. That is how it's made—by being pressed, nudged, forced to accept more and more weight. A diamond is more comfortable in difficult times than joyful moments when it's forced to be nothing but a sparkling object in a crown. So feel free to toss it in the dirt, stomp on it again, Titus; pressure will not chip or mar it, it will only make it grow stronger." She swings her blade; the movement is as magnificent as a rainbow spotted in the thunderous sky. The sunlight bounces off the steel, blinding me.

I twist, then lunge forward, close enough for her to sense the warmth of my body, before I parry her next strike. "Not anymore," I murmur.

You are no longer just my queen. You're something else.

Her next three hits are hard, sending tremors up her arm. Her muscles are fatiguing. She isn't pacing herself. "The lack of a dick between my legs does not mean I can't be the one tossing you down!" she shouts in frustration.

My spontaneous laughter startles both of us. She attacks. I lean into my next block, so my lips hover over her ear. "Careful, some men would consider that an open invitation to check."

The blush on her face makes me hard. She swings, but it's slow. I catch the blade in my hand and stare into her eyes. "Here's your chance," I taunt her.

Her eyes move from her blade to my palm. Her breath hitches as the air crackles. My fingers close on the blade and draw her near.

"Titus!" she pants. My gaze drops to her full lips. Moving my hand off her blade, I grab her wrist.

Air rushes between us, wedging us apart as she steps back. My mouth dries as my gulp sticks in my throat.

Rejected. Rightfully so.

What was I thinking?

Shit! "Selene—"

She replies with another attack. This time, I let her land a few blows on my armor.

"This isn't the palace," she pushes back, chin low, eyes sharp. "Fight me as you do on the battlefield."

I'd have your back on the ground in less than sixty seconds. I'd have you right where the creature inside of me wants you, at my mercy. Defenseless so that I can carry you away. "As you wish." I nod.

She points her toe with grace as she takes her next plotted step. Her elegance has no place in battle. When you're inches from the next brawling duo, you have no room for trained luxuries, like perfect footing.

We start circling each other. I like this type of dancing. Blade to blade. Heart to heart. Life and death. All or nothing.

Her foot stumbles. It's a trick.

She's baiting me. I don't bite.

The anger on her face is as hot as the sun above. "Treat me as your equal," she demands as she lunges again.

I'll never be your equal. I'm not worthy.

"Which is it you want? For me to fight you as my equal or as my enemy?"

Her nostrils flare, but her lips don't reply.

"You don't want me to fight you." Behind her, the castle is a blur, like fast-moving water. My heartbeat tries to escape through my ears. "You want me to save you. All you have to do is ask." The fire inside me is whispering to be unleashed.

Her lips separate, eyes dilate, but then she hides it with a stern look. "It was *you* who needed my help, Titus."

"I don't deny that." I dig the tip of my fang into my lip. "But you renounce what I have spoken, and one day you will regret it."

"I can live with regrets. I can't go on living with unsung sorrows."

"So sing them!" *Tell me you wish to escape this life! Beg me to help you.*

"I was never meant to be a maiden who sang songs. I'm a tempest who destroys hearts."

"You are not your twin."

She averts her gaze, gripping her sword tightly as her deepest fears surface. "Sometimes I fear I am." She attacks again. We spar until Selene makes an uncalculated error. She stretches her wrist too far, giving me a brief window to strike her sword with mine. Unable to flex her wrist, her weapon falls.

One mistake makes killing another so easy, like pressing a mold into dough. The more you fight, the more experience you gain. You notice the mistakes, see the moment to strike. Before you know it, you've punched out a dozen cookies. A dozen kills effortlessly made.

If this were an actual battle, she'd be dead.

What happens next is a mistake.

Or a mercy.

I advance, grabbing Selene by her collar, chest to chest. Hard muscle to soft cleavage. My sword kisses her neck. I glare at the edge of the blade, wishing the sharp edge were my parting lips.

Her soft exhale hooks me in the cheek, reeling me in.

My shadow masks her face. Such a lovely portrait, I should commission someone to paint, but I have no walls to call home to hang it on.

Our lips... by the gods, our mouths are so close. It's so tempting, like looking at an open treasure chest. I want to proceed. Ignore the obstacles that litter the path to that treasure.

I want to dream, to imagine how my life would change if I had that treasure in my hands.

"Selene," my sigh is a prayer a dying man makes. An appeal for clemency and redemption.

Save me from this feeling inside me. Tell me I'm not mad!

Her eyes twinkle like unpolished emeralds—shades of cloudy greens, forces of dark and light, battling to gain my affection so they can slaughter it.

Nobody truly loved her. They used her.

My actions toward her are foreign, so she's safeguarding her mind from them.

There's no space between us. We cannot separate or distinguish our breaths. Selene's pupils dilate into pools of darkness. It's easy to dive in. Unexplored waters call out to forgotten souls like mine. It's the light we stay away from; it illuminates all the caution signs and repercussions of our actions.

"What would you do next?" she whispers.

It's not us speaking; it's that thing inside of us we both are ignoring.

We're failing. It purrs in delight.

My mind screams at me to stop. The beast takes over.

Her muscles soften into me like butter on hot bread. You can never separate or scrape it off, because you would ruin both objects. It's best to gobble it down.

I want to devour her.

Fuck.

If you were not a queen, I'd kiss you. Were I not a gentleman, I'd do far more than steal a kiss from your desiring lips. I'd use your moans and cries to stake a claim upon this field. I'd use your fingers—that dig into my back as I claim you—like a shovel. I'd build a home here, on this field where I first made love to you—where I savored every inch of you, where your tears of pleasure watered the soil for more of our love to grow.

I would completely erase you. Then, I would redraw your definitions. I'd show you what affection is, what love and respect are. I'd make every man I stood next to look less than.

Selene's eyes glance at my mouth. "I wish we had different lives."

Why didn't you want me to hear that, Selene?

With a hard gulp, she tries to swallow her words down. The pain of it parts her lips, inviting me to slip my tongue inside and soothe her.

This is wrong.

I need to stop these thoughts.

How do you stop a shooting star? The only way is to collide with it. But then you destroy the star.

It's best to let it shine until it leaves your horizon, or it burns out.

I need these feelings to fizzle out!

My nostrils flare wide. Blood.

Shit! My blade cut her.

It's small, only a paper cut. The drop hangs onto her skin, like a child begging me to catch it as it jumps.

I've scented fae blood plenty of times. It's repulsive. Nature's warning: consuming it is toxic.

Why does she smell so tantalizing?

Even though I haven't tasted her, it feels like honey is coating my tongue.

Air fills my palms. My sword drops. My tongue darts out.

Closer, one more inch, and I can taste her. One drop on my tongue would answer all my questions. One drop and my magic and body would know if she was my mate, or if this is a game of seduction she's playing.

There, I said it. Mate.

Is she my mate?

The beast inside me roars. *Claim her. Mine, mine, she's mine.*

"Mine." I watch the droplet slide down her neck. The hunger that growls up my throat isn't from my stomach. It's from the mate magic swirling deep, waking up, stretching, readying to fight. It's dormant inside us all. Sometimes it wakes; other times, you live life without ever finding your fated mate.

"Titus," she hisses a warning.

"Do you feel it?" My voice is feral, claws scratching against stone, in a deep, dark cavern.

"Our feelings are irrelevant." She presses her palm to my chest, blinking away tears. "Control yourself."

Control? If I drank from my mate, my magic would grow tenfold.

Magic. Would Everett's magic grow?

That's why she is denying this. To protect me.

Her hand slides down my torso until she peels it free.

Just one tiny lick would subdue my urges. "Just one taste."

Metal presses against my lips instead.

Does she think her dagger would stop me?

The game of chase entices my predator.

Oh yes, she sees the truth in my eyes.

"Don't make me hurt you." She tilts the dagger up, parting my lips with it. One flick of her wrist and she could carve a permanent smile.

Denying this hurts more than her dagger would. I close my lips around the blade and kiss it.

"You need to stop," she whispers. Instead of a detached tone, she sounds worried.

Where is the treat?

Wait, it's me. I caused her alarm.

I stagger back.

Shit! I lost control. The magic between us consumed me.

I turn my back to her, too ashamed to look upon her. My ribs stab my lungs. I can't take a deep enough breath. Denying this is suffocating me.

"It's for the best, Titus." She touches my back. Her words are a bucket of water on my flames. I flinch. Her hand drops.

"Is there a problem?" Tristen shouts as he enters the sparring field, having left his spot near the entrance.

Selene rasps a curt, "No." Internally, she's screaming.

I rush towards Tristen. "Give me a vial, please!"

"Titus," he warns as he hands me a vial of blood.

"I'm fine."

"Drinking this won't stop what you feel," he mumbles. His gaze shifts to Selene as he speaks to me. "You need to admit it."

"What good would that do?" I rasp.

"It would make you realize we need to leave. What good is finding the Vitalis if you're marked as a dead man? She's a fae, and she's our queen; she can be nothing more to you. I'm... sorry. I wish it were different."

My eyes skim down my unpolished armor, down to my dirty old boots.

I am nothing; unworthy of having a mate like Selene.

Tris is right. I need to ignore this, as Selene is.

I swallow down the blood, tasting nothing. My eyes met his. "I can't leave." All the answers are here. Tris knows this. He prefers risking it.

His lips formed a thin line.

"Again!" Selene shouts.

"I can spar this time," Tristen offers.

"No, Titus will."

I run my hand down my face. I'm losing my mind; each day I'm near her, the attraction grows.

"Come on," she snaps.

"He needs a break." Tristen steps forward. He thinks she's torturing me. She isn't.

She's protecting me, even at the cost of hurting me. It's noble, a sign of an affectionate leader.

"He needs to learn control. The only way is to confront the issue head-on."

Deny my need to claim her.

Deny, reject, ignore.

~

Three days later.

Sometimes, hurting yourself strengthens you. It's like lifting weights. You justify the ache in your muscles when you see results.

Training with Selene has yielded results. Just not the kind my heart wants.

We learned that time-weaving feeds off my emotions. This week, Selene has plotted a new task for me: teaching the magic *I'm* the boss.

My fire magic is like a puppy. It's eager to play, but if I scold it, it listens. Time is like water. You think you can bottle it up, build a dam around it, but it can always find a crevice to drip free from. I have to figure out how to soothe it, convince it to listen to me, not control it.

"Well done," Selene announces. She settles onto the grass with such grace you'd think the soil was a silken pillow.

Her usual post-training routine is to sit still until the sun sets. She doesn't want to return to the castle. She skips lunch, spending all her time outside. She's been eating dinner by herself, avoiding Galen, whom I saw with two different women this week alone.

Her eyes mirror a flower aware of its fleeting season.

"Thank you," I mutter.

Do it. Sit down. Talk.

Selene and I speak only about Everett's magic; we've yet to discuss runes. Selene still struggles to accept that her brother died for a long-forgotten magic.

Tris and I give her space. We stand guard on the edge of the field, but I can't allow that to happen today. I need things to move faster. We need to find the Vitalis, understand the runes... and I need to know if she is my mate.

I lower myself to sit beside her. Her eyes silently question me. Our chemistry is an immense shadow that looms over us. It darkens each day; now it thunders.

"I should have asked your permission to sit," I murmur.

"We are beyond asking, Titus."

I love the way she says my name. It sounds stronger than I feel.

Maybe I am. Everett picked me, after all.

"I enjoy sparring," she begins. The tenderness in her voice shocks me. Its rarity increases its value in my eyes. "Being outside the castle walls. It's only then that titles do not matter. The tip of a blade does not change its shape when it pierces a king or a soldier. We're all the same to the weapon, just flesh and bone."

She longs to be equal to her people, nothing special, just a peasant who wants to see the sunrise. "If you allowed the people to hear you speak like this, they would love you," I say.

"I don't want their affection." She rips a blade of grass from the soil and tears it into tiny bits.

"Do you act so cold to protect King Galen?"

"What?" She reels back. The sunlight glints off her black hair, making it look like expensive oil.

"They would cherish you more than they worship him. Is that why you do not show them your heart?"

She rolls her lips. "Love is an illusion. Those who cherish monarchs are the first to light the torches and throw them on the pyre. I do not need love from others, as Galen does."

Bite your tongue.

It's harder and harder to do. This thing between Selene and me started as a caterpillar, wiggling and crawling. Less than a week later, we have cocooned ourselves in order to remain safe. We try not to feel.

Deep down, I long to taste her lips, to kiss her whole body, to watch her fly as I set her free.

This cocoon we have built is cracking.

Will a butterfly emerge? If so, how long will it soar? Will it feel the air under its wings, or will someone else, like Galen, crush it?

She is married to the king! But... if she is my mate, that changes everything. It happens more often than expected. Bonds form, sealed in magic, unable to be broken. Mating bonds take precedence over marriage contracts. Galen would not be the first king to lose his queen to her mate.

Crossing my legs, I sit and face her. "What do you need?"

She looks at me. Long. Is it a silent answer?

"The truth is," she swallows, "I fear I will only find out when I release my last breath. Everett knew, that's why we're both on this path together."

She's changing subjects.

Frustrated, I cast my eyes forward and scan her training field. It's ideal for keeping her hidden. Tucked down in the middle of a valley shielded by towering rose bushes. A manicured cage.

If it weren't trapping her, I'd be in awe of the magic. Instead, I contemplate the amount of fire required to destroy it.

I could do it. I'd burn through my first supply, needing a second dose of human blood to fuel me up again. Drinking blood back to back after magic has been depleted is safe; there is no risk of bloodlust.

With an annoyed sigh, Selene closes her eyes. "It's clear you want to chit-chat, so do it, Titus." Her walls are back up.

"How do you think everything is going?" I ask.

How do you remain strong, neglecting the heat within us that ignites when our eyes connect?

"Don't tell me you're the type of man that needs to be praised and worshiped." She flicks her long hair off her shoulder.

"I'm not." I smirk, but it deflates like a cake pulled too early from the oven. The words fly out before I can stop them. "Your walls are so hardened, I fear no amount of screams or hushed whispers can penetrate you, Selene. I lay awake at night, formulating the correct way to arrange my words for you, because every time I ask you something, you act like I'm stealing the crown from your head." I flash my fangs. "Why is it so hard for you to speak to me like we're friends?"

She looks away as if I had slapped her. "Friends are uncovered enemies, Titus," she mutters.

Closing my eyes, I massage my forehead, hoping I can push out the throbbing pressure.

"If you are sick, then it's best to vomit it all out, Titus. Say what else needs to be said so we can move on."

She's fighting, denying the potential of this bond.

Does she expect me to shut up and surrender?

Here is more of my heart. Look at it! See what's inside me before you stab it!

"I have these thoughts in my head." I tap my temple, shaking them free.

"You should keep them there," she rebuttals, looking my way again.

"There is not a cage large enough to hold them, Selene. If your walls were visible, I'd tear them down. I'd force you to be free."

"Free or with you?"

"Free. And in your freedom, I'd crawl to you, on my hands and fucking knees. I'd find you and beg you to accept this bond. Tell me how to prove myself?"

"You of all people have nothing to prove. If dreams of a future could exist, you would be mine. And I should not tell you this because dreamers die young. I need you to live." Her eyes are not gentle like a woven blanket; they are chain mail, linked and unbreakable. "Speaking to me is only fueling this fire. Talk to your brother."

"I did," I confide. "He told me to run." I kick one leg out, and she frowns. "Do you want me to go, Selene? To leave and never look back?"

Her eyes study Tristen as he guards the entrance. His hand is always on his sword, ready to kill for this secret. He keeps his magic filled to the brim in case he needs to use it.

"Fine, talk." She rolls her eyes. Does she think I don't notice the tears she shoved back inside?

Oh no, I'm not sweeping half the shit I just told you under a rug.

I'm going to make you trust me. Need me!

"A conversation with you is like gazing into dark waters. I never know what creature will emerge."

Her lips thin into a pressed line. "That method keeps me alive."

"I realize that, and I don't blame you." My heart turns to lead as it sinks. Her tongue is a sword that saves you, but haunts you with the memory of every kill you forced it to make.

"That's not a question." She tips her chin up like a warrior raises a shield, ready to deflect my words if they intend to cause harm. "Just ask what you seek."

"My questions destroy foundations. I have a suspicion you don't want to build yourself up again, even if it's with indestructible materials like a mate bond. You're tired, and you wish to fall and be left alone."

I don't think you want my love, even though I crave yours.

No reply. There's my answer. I convinced her to help me; I can't persuade her to live for me.

Her lip eventually twitches, "Dig a grave far away from the lands

Galen rules and bury your feelings, Titus. Blackthorn has no place for them. *I* have no home for them."

Wow, how many years of suffering did she endure to be able to look me in the eye without wavering?

"We have a task at hand," she stresses.

"I will bury them," I bite, "alive. But that doesn't mean you won't be haunted by their screams as they suffocate."

"Titus," her voice is full of regret over her decision, but she doesn't beg for forgiveness.

Rejection hurts like a motherfucker. "But be warned, over time, soil weathers away, revealing the bones of what once was."

She looks down her nose at me, green eyes thick as foliage concealing a wounded beast. "If we both survive, perhaps we can reexamine what we find. Until then, it is wise to keep this attraction dead in the water."

I grind my teeth. "I shall try."

"You've kept my brother's magic hidden, so I have high hopes."

"This is a string; it's held by two hands, Selene." *How can you be so cold-hearted?*

She crosses her arms. "My hand is not the one tugging on it, Titus."

"You lured me into this conversation to wound my pride," I grunt as I kick my boots out and scoot further away from her.

"Pride often causes one's downfall. Consider this a lesson." She leans back, faking ease, as she allows the sun to tan her face.

Fine. I can pretend our sparks don't burn. "I was wondering if you had someone you trusted, someone we could send to The Great Library of Ishmor."

Selene's stony stare slides over the field until it lands on me. How can those eyes be so frigid yet inviting?

"What do you seek there?" She looks sharper than a fiddle in a master musician's hands. I never know what tune she will play—one of sympathy or sinister appeal.

"You know what I seek." I lick my lips and straighten my spine.

"The Vitalis. Once I find it, I'm free of Everett's magic. I have no duty here."

She runs her tongue over her teeth. The wind stirs, sending a cooling sensation down my spine. The sun inches lower, readying to set. Vivid oranges and pinks swirl, painting a relaxing picture that contrasts with the look on her face.

That hurt. Good. Learn to understand you can't live without me, Selene.

"What of the runes and the future of a crown for your head?" she hisses.

"I can accomplish that somewhere else. No need to burden you and Galen."

"You strike low."

I raise my knee and prop my elbow on it, creating a wall between us. "I attack where I see opportunity, as do you."

Glare at me as long as you like.

"The Vitalis is not in Ishmor," she admits.

My muscles tense. "How are you so certain?" *What are you not telling me?*

"Everett spent time in Ishmor. If the Vitalis were there, he would have found it. He wanted us all here." She pounds a fist to the ground. "The book must be nearby."

"So what the heck are we doing?" I throw my hands up. "Let's go search the castle."

"Sable would have found it if it lurked within the walls. Calm down," Selene huffs. "I told you we need to work on your magic before we delve into the runes. Baby steps."

"Why do I get the feeling you're stalling? You're forcing me to accept the path Everett put me on. You must do the same."

"I am."

"But—" Why do you look so vacant when you stare into the future? What are you not telling me?

"But what?" she heaves.

"I fear waiting until I master the time magic is a mistake. I have a sick feeling in my gut. I had it the moment Everett gave me his power."

"What feeling?" She scoots back so she can look at me more clearly.

"Someone wrote my story. I have no power or authorship to change it. Everett chained our futures in iron. I'm stuck, forced to fulfill this role." I press my palm against the soil. "I want liberation, but it would destroy everything. I'm trying not to be selfish, but this is my life."

I want to tell her it's her life, too. What she fears does not have to come to pass. If Everett played with the future, so can we.

She mimics my pose but hugs her legs to her chest. "It's not about us, Titus. Our wants and needs are but a drop in the ocean."

I'd swim those perilous waters in order to find you, Selene.

She continues, having no idea of the thoughts in my mind. "Everett saw the future, thousands and thousands of lives. I'm willing to sacrifice my life and my happiness for the good of others. You can, too. I know you can." Her voice deepens to a plea. "When I look at you, I see a man who wants to do good, but you've been denied. The only order that has been spoken into your ear has been to kill. Then Everett demanded you save. Change is hard, but it's often a force we can not control."

I inch my hand closer to her leg, filling the small space between us. Her eyes hug my hand with compassion, but her fingers do not move. "How do you sleep at night?" I question.

"Women have always been forced to accept their fate, Titus."

My biceps flex. "Let's get a step ahead! Stop waiting for Everett's spies to find us. Send someone you trust to Ishmor. Let's read all we can about runes. There's got to be something about where the book was housed and what happened to it."

A smile touches her lips before she snuffs out. "First, I have no one I trust, Titus."

"You can trust me."

"I'm not meant to trust you," she replies. Her eyes flit to my lips. She glances away before she sees that I've pulled my hand away, no longer expecting her to reach for it. "Galen wouldn't let us leave. Secondly, Ishmor's Great Library would be a waste.

"It's the biggest library in all the land. If any place held books regarding runes, it would be there."

"You seek the wrong book, Titus." An aura curls around her, one of knowledge and authority. "The library will house thousands of books regarding runes. They have been woven into fables and tales for far too long to be of value."

"What are you not telling me?"

"Before this war escalated, Everett did not lead the army. He spent two years in Ishmor as a dignitary scholar. When he returned, he had a book with him. Before you jump like a child grabbing a toy, it was not the Vitalis."

"Removing items from Ishmor is illegal," I point out, voice sour.

"Everett was a prince; they do not pause for laws, Titus."

"Nor do they hesitate to ask if you will accept their magic," I spit. "What book?"

Her eyes lose their green as recollections surface. "The Great Curse of Caldara." Her voice slinks away until it's nothing more than a hushed whisper.

"What's that?"

"Precisely," she replies. "That is where we start, Titus. The runes shall follow suit."

CHAPTER
TWENTY-THREE

SELENE

T he past.

    I crash into Everett, my arms coiling around him. The sand embraces my feet as I rise on my toes. The portal's magical scent clings to his clothes.

He's here, alive and safe.

But for how long? The only reason he returned was because of the war. I close my eyes, resting my cheek on his chest as he embraces me, his fingers combing through my hair. I sense him creating a time bubble, isolating us from the shore, granting us privacy from the escort.

Tipping my chin up, I study him. His eyes, a blend of brown and green, resemble the forests that guard the mountains known as The Cradle of Darkness.

"When's the last time you stepped into the sun?" I glide my knuckles along his jaw, feeling the sharp prickle of freshly shaven hair. His skin tone, once similar to mine, has become gray. He looks like a rubber band pulled too far, forced to blanch a lighter tone.

My touch makes him close his eyes. He's been in Ishmor, studying and working as a spy for our father. But I know my brother; he has his agenda.

"Light does not always save us, sister. Sometimes darkness does," he mutters as his shoulders relax.

Cool sand surges through my toes, grounding me as I take a step back. "Is the price you're paying worth the deal with this darkness?" I grab his hand and squeeze hard. "Look at you. You're flesh and bone. You need to be solid muscle, callus hands, and a stony heart for the war that is to come."

He flips his wrist, trapping my hands in his, "The wars of our past and present will be child's play compared to what I have seen. I'd pay any price to stop what is coming."

"It is not your sole duty to vanquish evil, Everett," I stress. "Remove the weight from your shoulders." Ask for help! I'll help.

My gulp forces those words down, trapping them in my belly. They raised us to be vaults. Keyless; nothing can crack us open except the correct combination. Everett will never reveal his code, for he doesn't know it. His magic of foresight has jumbled his mind, like a child coloring outside the lines. The original picture is lost. It's merely scribbles now.

"I do not wish to rid the world of evil. That is an impossible task. I just need to create a symmetry. Balance."

Not this again. Mindless babbling. I want words. Yes or no. Yes, I am fine. No, I'm not deteriorating.

I hug him again, but my fingers dig into something hard at his back. "What's that?" Those are not ribs.

Instead of replying, he drops the time shield and addresses the guards. "I'll change before I see my father." He grabs my hand and walks quickly, not allowing them to reply.

The guards create a formation as we walk through the port village, up the winding wall that leads to our castle. The water reflecting off the ocean bounces off the polished sandstone, making the castle appear to be one giant gem. Everett and I know the flaws hidden within the light.

The guards remain on our heels until we reach his room. Once the door closes, he peels off his traveling cloak and pulls out an old leather book from behind his back.

"*A book! Wait!*" *I choke. "Is that for The Great Library of Ishmor? Please tell me it's not." Stealing from the library is a high crime.*

"*No one saw me.*"

Which means he used his time-weaving magic.

"*Everett," I step closer to look at the book's title. The letters on the front used to be gilded, but the foil has been worn off, creating an outline as speckled as the night sky. He hugs the title to his chest, but not before I read it. "What's the curse of Caldara?*"

"*Nothing," he waves me off.*

"*What do you mean, nothing?" I lower my voice. "You stole a book from the great library, so it is not nothing.*"

"*My words are true. The Kingdom of Caldara is nothing now. It's a grave. No one returns to clean gravestones, Selene. No one will miss this book," he replies as he turns and walks to his bookshelf.*

"*You're hiding it here, out in the open?" I deadpan as he slides it onto a shelf.*

"*If I hide it anywhere else, Sable would seek it out. Some treasures are best hidden under your nose.*"

"*Why would Sable want that book?*"

"*I told you, Sable seeks everything." He walks to his bench and pulls off his riding boots. Sand begins to shake loose. Wait, why is the sand a deep orange hue? That is not from our shores, or Ishmor.*

Unless he didn't portal directly from Ishmor to here. Where did you go?

His fingers become red as he tugs his laces with force. Without bothering to change, he just slips on his formal boots. Walking to the sink, he splashes his face. "Everything is happening as I saw it." He looks into the mirror, studying his haunted stare.

You don't look relieved. Shouldn't you be happy if this is the ending you seek?

"*Then stop it," I whisper. I sense a great dread chasing us all.*

"*I told you, if I stop, we all die. Every single person, Selene. Look what's already passed. Dragons have died; their riders. Humans will be next, then mages, vampires, and fae. Someone ripped away the balance, and we must restore it.*"

"*Dragons? I inhale sharply. "Dragons died because their riders forgot the beasts were wild. They are uncontrollable. Men hunted them down to stop them from burning down their cities."*

"*Why, Selene?" he shouts so passionately that the tips of his pointed ears redden.*

He keeps his back to me as he stares me down through the mirror.

"*Why did dragon riders lose the ability to control them? Because someone ripped away the runes. That is what I am trying to fix. Dragon riders used to control dragons. Humans used to be able to defend against magical attacks. There was a level of fear that kept people calm because we all knew everyone had a defense."*

He grabs a towel and dries his hands. "Now we don't. Humans have to barter their inventions to get respect. Mages must sell their enchanted objects to stave off the fae, and don't get me started on the false sense of power faes and vampires fight over.

"*We fight for metal crowns and ink on paper that hands over the rights of land. We fight for objects when we should fight for the safety of flesh."*

I step back, keeping a distance. I've never seen him so... desperate. "You don't have to be the one to fix this. Let others," I plead.

"*Others?" he questions with disappointment. "Selene, if I see a crime and do nothing to stop it, then I am no better than the aggressor. My actions might be no more than a drop in the water, but I would rather die knowing I tried to help instead of sitting on the sidelines, praying I stay alive so I can sell a book of tales about what I witnessed. I am no coward."*

"*I never said you were," I breathe.*

He cast his eyes down into the drain of the sink. "There is a darkness coming, Selene; I have seen it."

A tremor ripples over his skin, then jumps onto me.

"*Beasts are being born as we speak," he continues. "Monsters so terrifying that even a dragon would hesitate. They will claim us all if we do not unite, and the only way we can do so is with runes. I have seen a future where we conquer them, Selene. We still bicker and fight, but like a family, we're united. We train together and form armies to hunt down these creatures. But*

I have also seen a future where the monsters rule, a future I will never speak of."

"Stop!" I stomp forward. "You are going in circles. Everett, you mention things long dead. You sound mad! Now you talk of dragons and riders, armies and monsters?" I desperately grasp his face. "Please stop whatever this is. Let's seek an elder. Tell them about your foresight. There must be a way to stop it. To soothe your mind."

He jerks back from my hold and, for the first time, looks at me with distrust. "We all have sacrifices to make," he says firmly.

He's never going to change his mind. That much is clear to see.

His chin lowers as water drips down his face. He wants to cry, I know it, but he can't, so he lets the water he splashed upon his face mimic the action.

"What is the book for, Everett? What's Caldara?" I demand.

"If you look now, Sable will know. Do not look before your time, Selene."

"And when is my time?"

"When this conversation becomes an old memory."

"Where will you be then?" Reaching out, I grab his shoulders, anchoring him to me.

His eyes shift to mine.

I press again. "Where will you be, Everett?"

He licks his lips. "Whether we are in the same room or leagues apart, I'm always with you. Remember that."

I grab my chest as tears spill from my eyes. "I can not do this anymore, brother. I can't play this game of guessing. It's tearing me apart, and you as well."

Each step I take back is like a knife to my lungs.

My heart still beats, but it's missing what defines it. "I'm finished. No more. Keep me out of it."

His throat bobs as he swallows.

"You knew I would say this," I state.

He nods. "I'm not mad."

"You... you wanted this. You want me to hate you so that I won't stop you."

"If you love me, you'll follow me—through thick and thin, life and

death. If you detest me, you will leave me alone." He keeps his eyes on my feet. "*Sister, you'll grasp the significance of these words eventually.*" His raw yet tender stare locks onto me as I stagger back to the door. "*If you are smart, repeat what I said to save the one you love.*"

I lean against the door for extra stability. "You've demonstrated to me that nobody in this family understands love. We exploit." I turn fast so he won't see me cry. I fling the door open and slam it shut, but not before his reply reaches my ears.

"*We exploit people because we love them. If we didn't, we'd just discard them.*"

~

The present.

Some seeds remain dormant for years. For them to sprout, conditions must be right. Everett seeds are starting to awaken. I fear the flowers they grow will be of deadly beauty.

"Caldara," I whisper. I trace the name onto the stone of my balcony. "What and where are you?"

Do you house the Vitalis or just more breadcrumbs for us to follow?

I did as you said, brother. I didn't look because I knew if I did, it would be disastrous.

I stopped asking Everett questions after that awful day, which was easy because of the war. I worked as a healer, Sable as a dealer in death, poisoning the lands so the vampires could not grow crops for their army, which forced them to invade human lands again. Everett left as a warrior who never returned.

I turned my back on my brother. I felt like his madness was seeping into me, so I had to wring myself dry of it.

"I'm meant to look now, am I? And, yet again, you were right. You are not with me." I bring my hand to my chest. "But I feel you. Your magic. If that is meant to be a source of solace for me, I beg to differ. Why Titus? Actually, don't answer that. I know why. I'm strong. You made me so, but strength has its limits, brother. I will bend, and if I don't get the answers, I fear I will break."

The door to my living room opens. Galen's strong footsteps carry him to my balcony.

"Bored already, husband?" I titter. Reaching up, I pretend to tuck my hair behind my ear, but in truth, I'm swiping away a lone tear. It vanishes before Galen comes to lean beside me.

"You haven't killed him yet," Galen comments as he looks over his land. His head is held high, ensuring his crown won't fall over the edge.

"Is that permission to do so?" I raise an eyebrow.

"Why haven't you?" His lips curl back, revealing his fangs. The red stain on his mouth causes his teeth to look pristine white. His blood intake is rising. There is a fine line that Galen no longer sees. He's addicted.

"Eager to punish me, Galen?" It makes me sick to pretend with him, but I will endure it to keep Titus's secret safe.

"Always," he twists his neck and smirks.

Everyone thinks monsters are scary, ugly creatures who hide in uncharted lands.

They're wrong.

Monsters are cunning, beautiful. Seductive. They make themselves known. That's how they get so far in life.

His eyes darken as he looks at my body. "I thought you were good at the long game, Galen," I retort, pushing off the balcony and giving him a look that finds him lacking. "It seems your judgment of length is as inaccurate as your manhood." I glance down at his cock. "It's merely average."

Turning, I make to leave, but he grabs me, pins me to the ledge so my torso hovers over it. His lips press against mine, pushing and forcing mine open.

He wants my fight. I do the opposite. I kiss him back until his walls lower and his cock hardens, pressing between my thighs, and then I shove him hard, catching him off guard.

He reaches up to balance the crown that almost fell off his head. A shame it didn't.

"Careful; your lack of control is showing. People don't like angry kings. That's when they start whispering about replacing them."

His fang sinks into his bottom lip. "I know what you crave."

"A bar of soap to scrub your taste off my tongue." I begin to applaud him. "Bravo, you figured it out." I can't help it. I dig further. "Add in a bottle of wine so my vision blurs. This way, I need not clearly see how insecure you are."

His eyes turn sharper than his fangs. "I could make you." He juts his chin out like an iron, trying to warn me it will brand me if I wander too far off the pasture.

"Of course you could." *You, terrible, vile man. I regret every kiss. Even the one just now, where I pretended so your eyes would stay on me and not Titus.* "But that's not what you crave. You want my knees to sink of their own accord. You want my submission, not my resignation. You had a chance, Galen, and you squandered it."

"All this because I denied you one kill."

Calm down. Breathe, that's it. "It was never about the kill, Galen; it was about respect."

His shoulders widen, as does his stance. "You are under the delusion that you hold a string that controls me, wife."

"Delusion?" I mock. "I've cut our strings. It is you who seeks to re-knot them. Once cut, the relationship is never the same. It can't endure what it once did, Galen. The knot merely tries to cover up the weakness. Your mistakes are sealed in stone now. You can try to chisel it free, but the more you dig, the less stone remains. In the end, you'll have nothing left but pebbles and soot under your feet. You are the one who came here seeking me out, stealing a taste. Not me. I never craved you. I ate out of boredom, just as most of your nobles do."

That look on your face tells me you finally realize I played you. I never fucked you because I loved you. You never tricked me.

"You cannot deny me forever," he growls as he looks at my lips.

Reaching up, I wipe his taste from my mouth and smirk. "Careful.

Fae are immune to many poisons; next time, you might find my lips coated in one that strikes you down."

He takes a step closer. "I'd love to see you try to kill me."

"Oh, Galen," I tip my head back and laugh in his face. "Not all falls are deadly." Reaching up, I straighten his crown and then run my hand down his chest. "Who's to say I will not knock the crown off your head and relish watching you struggle to stand again?"

I step back and pretend to admire the vision.

"You forget your place," he growls in warning.

He sounds as strong as a puppy.

I turn lazily, forcing him to watch the sway of my hips. I walk to the door and glance over my shoulder as I reply, "You're mistaken. I just found it."

TWENTY-FOUR

TITUS

"You can slap glasses on my face and put a cloak over my amazing body, but I'm not fooling anyone, Titus." Tristen playfully fixes his hair as he sits at Selene's vanity. He picks up a bottle of perfume and smells it before he sets it down and continues to snoop, opening the small drawers.

Selene and I plotted; Everett must have wanted us to look in Blackthorn's library. We don't want Galen to grow suspicious since Selene has never visited the library, so we're sending Tristen tonight.

"Have you ever seen scholars?" He grabs her hair comb and brushes the sides of his hair. "They are not muscled and sexy like me." He sinks a fang into his lip, as if I'm the target he's seducing.

I snatch the comb from his hand. "Stop touching Selene's things." *Stop putting your scent all over what's mine!*

The color drains from my face. That's why he's doing this.

Tristen's eyes narrow. "We need to leave before you make a public mistake," he hisses.

"I can't leave."

His sigh is a mountain of disappointment that kicks me in the gut. Turning, he grabs one of her makeup brushes and spins it between his fingers. He's trapped in a role, as am I.

"I will not fit in," Tristen shrugs dramatically. "And you know me. I hate missions where I'm doomed to fail."

I look him up and down. "Just pretend you're chasing tail," I suggest.

"You want me to sleep with the librarians?" Tristen flashes a flirtatious smirk. "That's a mission I can nail down, pun intended."

Scratch that. I've had the unfortunate circumstance of being in a room next to Tristen when he has company. No wall is thick enough to stop the screams of pleasure my brother causes. If he does that in the library, he'll be kicked out and banned.

"No, just pretend," I correct him.

"Pretend what? That my dick is a bookmark they can slip between their pages—I mean legs?" He winks, then looks back in the bathroom mirror and grins haughtily at his reflection.

"Tristen," I sigh and close my eyes as I lean against the door.

All I smell is Selene when I inhale. I hear her grabbing clothes off the hanger in her closet.

"We need this. Use your magic, hide in the shadows, and find us any books on Caldara that you can. If you have to flirt to get help, then do it, but keep your dick in your pants," I order. "I don't want them to remember you."

He stands suddenly, grabs my shoulders, and jerks me forward until the tip of my nose hits the mirror of Selene's vanity.

"Hey!" I shove back. The gold foil of the mirror frame catches my eye. It's adorned with carved roses. I'm starting to hate those flowers. They're everywhere, reminding the people that Galen is always watching.

Tristen nudges my eyes towards our reflection. "Have you seen my face?" He grins from ear to ear. "No one can forget perfection."

I spin around. "You're an idiot. I take it back; don't ask for help. Hide in the shadows and look for any books on Caldara you can find."

He crosses his arms in protest. "The library is huge. Do you know how long it will take me without asking for help?"

"Do what you must." I walk back to the wall and stand like the guard I am supposed to be portraying.

Selene exits her closet, dressed in her leathers again. "If you two are done bickering, I am ready to go train."

Look up. Don't look at her hips. My chest feels too tight for my heart. She's the key to unleashing the tension, but she'd rather keep me bottled up.

Our eyes clash, feet planted firmly. I wait for Selene to crumble, to admit what's happening; she waits for me to acknowledge we can never be.

Tristen steps in front of me, blocking my view. He tries to open the door, but Selene grabs his hand. My forearms flex with a need to switch places with my brother. She touches him so easily, like his skin isn't fire that burns her.

"Tristen, I've been thinking," Selene states, head held high, eyes ignoring me, "when you go to the library tonight, start in the map section."

"Map?" he asks. "I thought we needed a book."

"Caldara is a location. The curse is irrelevant, I think." She bites her inner cheek.

"You think?" Tristen raises a shoulder. "If I break out in nasty oozing hives, you'd better run, because I will hunt you down."

Selene's eyes bounce from the door to Tristen. "I do hope you can control your replies when you're in the king's presence. He'd have your tongue for speaking back to me," she warns him.

"There is a long list of people who wish to play with my tongue, Queen Selene." He steps back and bows mockingly. "Oh, my mistake." He bows again, more formal this time.

Selene glances at me with concern. "Children have better manners."

"He's trying to make you smile."

Her lips form a line. "Why?"

I glance at my brother. The truth is, he's triggered by tense, quiet atmospheres. After we lost our parents, each of us was tossed on a horse, forced to ride for hours with our new guardian until we reached the training orphanage we'd call home. The wind was so strong it stole voices.

We rode, letting nature carve us into shells. My eyes were raw from the wind, but I kept them fixed on my brother's hands. I was so worried he'd let go of the reins and fall off.

We didn't have accelerated healing then. We were no better than humans until we came into our magic. The cold caused his hands to shudder; his knuckles looked as delicate as thin white eggshells. Then, the shaking stopped; his hands turned to iron, numb and unmoving.

Each time I get on a horse and hold the reins, I recall his little hands.

Now, when the mood becomes too much, Tristen makes people laugh, scream, or shout, anything but silent thinking.

"Because when you're stressed, it makes my brother react." Tristen's voice is all sharp edges now.

Selene turns her head and stares at her bed. "I think better in silence," she mutters as she clasps her hands behind her back. That's her form of apology.

"Oh, my lovely queen, it would be a travesty to deny you my voice, especially when you have been caged for so long. I'm trying to redefine how entertaining vampires can be."

"I make my own definitions," Selene responds. "Trust me, you do not wish to hear what I think of you."

"Oh, but I do." Tristen playfully tries to link his elbow with hers.

He's testing me again. Touching and flirting with Selene, so when it happens in front of an audience, I will not react.

She slips her arm free but doesn't scold him. There is a new light in her eyes. Tristen has a unique ability to make anyone feel at ease. Sometimes, I wonder if it's untrained magic that he never focused on.

She rests her hand on the doorknob, looks at me, and asks, "Ready?"

In other words, do I have my emotions under control?

"I'm ready to do a lot of things, my queen," I hiss under my breath, shoving my gulp down. How can she be so strong, fighting against the pull?

"Let's go train and get some fresh air," Tristen suggests, but his eyes push into me like hands shaking sense into me.

"Wait," I step forward. "Why are you so sure we need a map?"

"It's a location," Selene firmly states, avoiding my eyes.

I slide between her and Tristen. "I've been honest with you, Selene. I've told you everything. My life is in your hands. My brother's life is in your hands."

"I know."

Wow, she actually looks concerned.

"Then be honest with me. How are you certain it's a location?"

Her tongue runs over her teeth. "Because Everett told me it used to be a kingdom. He rambled many things; some I can reveal, others I cannot."

My nostrils flare with her sweet scent. "And why is that?" *What are you hiding from me?*

She's good at masking her face so others can't see her genuine emotions. "Everett told you if you were aware of the end, you would change it," she says carefully.

I banish the air between us so our hips press against one another. Selene's eyes widen, and the tips of her pointed ears turn a faint cranberry hue. Her lips part with a moan I wish I caught on my tongue. Her foot slides forward, trying to move her closer. She looks good covered in my shadow. "And do you know how this ends?" I urge. I can't help it; I reach up and cup her jaw, tilting it up.

Her next breath is sharp, quick, and... full of lust I wish I could sink my teeth into.

"Titus," I listen to Tristen's warning and disregard it.

"N... no," Selene says. "I recognize we all will have to make sacrifices." Her words falter as her lips part and inch towards mine.

That's it.

269

Deep in my gut, I know she's my mate. We're unfortunate that our mark remains hidden, but sometimes mating marks take time to appear. Other times, they scar your skin when your eyes first meet.

"Stop fighting me. You won't win." I flatten my palm over the curve of her ass.

There, she's surrendering. She pushes up on her toes so she can kiss me.

Before it happens, before we both commit a high crime, Tristen shoves us apart. Selene gasps, caught off guard, then recovers.

He flashes his fangs. "Stop! Now!" he commands me.

"What the fuck are you doing?" Selene sneers.

Is she snapping at Tristen for stopping us, me for forgetting my place, or herself?

"I could ask you the same!" Tristen shouts as he steps between us.

The truth is painfully clear. I almost kissed the queen. It doesn't matter that she was meeting me halfway. They would find me guilty and kill me.

"Are you my mate?" I ask. I need her to say it.

"Titus!" Tristan rushes me and slaps his hand over my mouth. His eyes beg me to take back the words, just as he did when I told him our parents died.

I grab his wrist and tug it down. *Say it!* I glare at Selene. Meet me halfway.

Selene covers her mouth and turns away. "I don't love people, Titus. I don't know how."

Let me teach you.

Gods, I want to say it out loud. I want to steal her away, forgetting everything we have to focus on.

Did Everett anticipate this outcome? Did he warn her? Is that why she denies me?

She presses her palm to her stomach. "Tristen is correct. We need to be careful." She slips on her infamous mask—cold, detached, and unreasonable. "Anything you believe you are feeling is just a fabrication. I'm sure bedding another will quell the sparks." She coughs again.

"Tristen, I will spar with you today. I need to be more mindful of the distance Titus and I need to have."

"You want me to sleep with someone else?" I snort. "Yeah, I didn't think so."

Tristen hangs his head.

"I hear you, Selene, but I'm listening with my eyes, too. I saw you flinch. How long can you keep this deception going?" I fume. "How long do you think your fingers can keep the need at bay. You need me! Every inch of me, every part. Me, your mate."

"Stop," she breathlessly whispers as her cheeks redden.

"Are you telling yourself to stop? It sounds like it. Stop slipping your fingers into your aching core when you bathe, stop thinking of me and how I will claim every inch of your body. Stop Selene. Go on, stop fantasizing about me because I know you are."

"Stop,"

I chuckle, "That sounds like a whine a beggar makes. A plea. Beg me to make it stop and I will, Selene. Beg me to do something. Gods! Anything. Claim you! Reject you. Beg! I'm imploring you for anything but this current state."

"I can not change it," she snaps as she presses her thighs closer together.

I grab her wrist and hold her hands high, "For far too long, men have tried to make women think they can not do anything. I'm not that type of man. These hands," I shake them vigorously, "can change anything. Do anything. I wish they would. How do I convince a bird that's been caged all its life to learn to fly? Jump! Yes, we might fall, but eventually we will soar."

Her bottom lip trembles, shaking tears free from her eyes. I kiss her knuckles, then swiftly drop them.

Her gasp of agony over my abandoned touch will haunt me. But I will never force her. I am not Galen. *She* has to want this.

"Sometimes we lie to protect those we," her breath catches. She was about to say a word she claimed never to have known.

Love.

Turning, she swings open the door, shattering the silencing spell over the room. "Come, we have more important things to focus on."

Tristen strides forward and slaps me. "If Everett's magic didn't kill you, this will. What the fuck? I warned you." He tugs his hair. "We need to leave. Now."

"She's my mate."

He punches my jaw. His lips curl back, revealing his fangs. "You're dooming yourself."

"Mating bonds have laws," I dispute, losing my patience.

His gaze rakes over me. "Laws?" he spits. "You think Galen respects the laws?"

"This is not the first time in history a royal has been bonded to someone lesser."

His eyes search my face, and then he grabs my shirt with an iron grip. "You are not lesser, brother. It matters that she is married to a raving, murderous lunatic who has armies. We might be soldiers, killers without a home or titles of value, but we have things to lose."

The plea in his voice would make a monster see reason. But the bond in my chest doesn't care.

"We have Ember, Ryker, Nero, and Cyrus. Think of them when you want to sink your fangs into her." He pulls me into a hug.

Slowly, I hug him back. "I can keep it hidden." I say.

It's not true.

Tristen breaks our hold and snorts as he shakes his head. "Here's a tip, brother. Learn to lie better." He stomps to the door. "She's the queen; she cannot be your mate."

Why can't she be both? Everett said I was meant to be a king. Therefore, Selene could still be a queen.

My queen.

CHAPTER
TWENTY-FIVE

TRISTEN

I'd do anything for my older brother because he has done everything for me.

I feel like a parent doing something my child won't like, but I must. Like all loving parents, I'll do anything to save my child.

Our time in this castle has turned Titus from a block of granite into shale—flaking layers that Selene's chipping away to find his fossilized heart so she can shatter it.

Is my brother's happiness something I desire? Yes. Gods, yes!

Selene's hands don't love you; they kill you.

Brother, a knife cannot become a needle that mends you. This bond with Selene will stab everything we love to death.

Yes, mating bonds take precedence over marriage contracts, but this is... disastrous.

I watched Titus stumble, even fall, when Everett forced his magic into him. I can't let him fall again because this stumble will end with a knife in his back.

I know Galen. He's ruthless, and he'd give zero fucks about the mating bond law.

Sweat drips down the nape of my neck. I push the cloak off my head, needing more air to cool me down. I walk the winding streets, exquisitely paved with stones. Each step is harmonized, unlike running through dirt and debris on the battlefield. It's unusual to be surrounded by walls and not trees or camping tents.

Crossing the pathway to avoid the loud tavern, I glare at the drunken patrons laughing outside. "Why couldn't it be you?" I mumble as I spot a female vampire.

You would have been easy to bond with.

Shaking my head, I pick up my pace. "Mated to a fae," I hiss under my breath.

I've never fucked a fae, never had pillow talk with one. It's not that I hate them; I love women of all shapes, forms, colors, sizes, and species. The more hips, the better! I just haven't had the time to wander into a fae tavern, and most fae women on the battlefield only want to fuck their swords up my ass.

No, thank you.

I'm reluctant to risk a hair on Titus's body. What I'm about to do is going to piss him off.

That's okay. I'll sacrifice his friendship to save his life.

"There you are," I whisper when I spot the library.

It's a tall building, with four floors framed in black stone columns that are lined in vines and roses. Its darkness slows my steps; the sheer magnitude of the place makes me feel stupid, unworthy to step inside.

"You've overcome that weakness," I growl.

Have you?

Yes, that's why Titus gave me this mission. He knows books don't scare me!

My head tips back as I study the ominous building. The light of the moon bounces off the angled roof, making it feel like the tip of a sword swinging down upon me.

I touch my dagger for comfort. The sad truth is, I am stupid. I can read, but I take longer. The words used to appear backwards when I was a child. Titus made me work so hard, and I improved, but then our parents died, and we were tossed to the state. Titus resumed my lessons three years later. We were older, and I was so insecure and embarrassed that I often lashed out at him.

But he dragged me to a hiding spot and helped teach me to see the words properly. Ember found out and helped, too; she stole romance books from the small towns we passed through. She forced me to read it out loud as she lay back and daydreamed of a star-crossed lover who would take her far away from the battlefield.

All those lessons and years of struggle, and I still feel unworthy of holding a book in my hand.

My stomach churns with nerves, and I grab my small bag of dried berries and swallow a mouthful without chewing. I have a nervous habit of snacking in private.

It developed when I was on a scouting mission, deep in enemy territory. I was hiding in a blueberry bush, and when the mission ended, Nero had to roll me out of the secret spot I made because my belly was so full of berries. I always keep a bag of nuts, dried jerky, or berries with me.

Some nights I dreamed of dying in battle, but right before I took my last breath, I fished out my snack bag and gobbled down one last meal.

"Okay, let's do this." I shove my snacks back in my pocket and approach the library, ready to commit a crime Titus and Selene didn't order me to. Instead of looking for Caldara, I seek something more pressing. Yes, it's more urgent than this business regarding runes.

The scent of old paper and ink has me craving a vial of blood to wash it away with. I walk up to the desk and drum my fingers on the wood until someone appears. *Please be someone hot.* I'm a flirt with my eyes. Ladies can't resist me.

No such luck. An old man rounds the aisle with a dozen books in hand. He spots me through grey eyelashes but makes no haste in coming. Taking his time, he puts the books onto his cart categorically.

"How can I help you?" he grumbles.

"I'm looking for a book." I press my elbows onto the desk as I keep my voice down.

"Congratulations, you're in the right place," the old vampire mocks. He must be well into his ninth hundred year of life. I grimace. Is that what I'll look like? A hunched back and skin like cracked leather?

Death in battle seems... sexier.

Vain.

I'm vain. I admit it.

I like it. I'm not apologizing for liking my youth. I love women, and seeing this old man makes me want to bed more of them, because one day, it's going to end. No one wants to fuck a raisin.

And those that do... I'm not letting them near my cock.

Or, you can be an adult and fall in love, find a woman who loves you, regardless.

Nah. The path Everett put us on is likely to end in a premature death, so I might as well live life to the fullest.

Leaning forward, I ignore his rude reply and flash my best smirk. "It should be in the mage section regarding spells to break bonds." Wow, the closer I look, I can see his wrinkles have wrinkles. Surely a mage cream can repair that.

"What kind of bond?" His brows resemble furry caterpillars.

Nosey, are we? "You know," I wave my hands in the air, regretting the action because it wafts the old book smell. "This and that."

"What if I give you a book on that and this?" he playfully spits. "Be specific. We have thousands of books here, boy."

Asshole.

Leaning closer, I whisper, "Mating bonds."

Even if the word gets back to the king, he'll have no idea this book refers to Selene and Titus. I'll just lie and tell him I found my mate during the war, but our views are different, thus my need to sever the bond.

He jerks back, his cloudy eyes swinging up and down like I'm old meat flies are swarming at the butcher's market. "You have a mate bond you wish to break?" He's short but manages to look down his hooked nose at me.

I shrug. "I have commitment issues," I lie.

"Fix them."

"Don't want to." *Dude, what is your problem?*

"Breaking a mating bond is a crime." He crosses his arms and tips his nose higher to reveal his grey nose hair.

I flinch. Gross. So bloody nasty! You don't need a mage to fix that; just grab wax from a candle. That's what humans do.

I push off the counter and stand tall. "Not if it's voluntary."

"It's also a myth," he grunts as he trudges back to his cart.

"Myths have seeds of truth," I argue as I rush after him. *Listen, asshole, just point me in the right direction.*

"A mating bond is magic. Magic is the only true immortal. You can't kill it; it may take a new form, but its roots are vast, and they never fully sever. Bonds are never broken." He grabs a stack of books.

"Let's put it to sleep then. Cage it. Taint it. Take your pick. I need the bond dulled," I argue.

He waves his hand dismissively. "It's a waste of time. Putting things to slumber has consequences. It's better to dream than have nightmares, boy."

I clench my jaw. "Which section will the book be in?" I'll find it myself.

Shaking his head, he pushes the books toward me.

"Hey!" My hands dart out, grasping the stack.

"Follow me." He sounds more annoyed than a horse that has to deal with gnats swarming its face. I'm just about ready to toss the books down when he glares at me from over his bony shoulder. "Carry those. Help isn't free here."

Our descent through the first aisle is slow and irksome. If Galen has this many books, I wonder what Ishmor is like. The shadows from the aisles cover us. It's relaxing, like the hands of a woman rubbing your shoulders as you sink into a hot salt bath.

I can do this; linger in libraries. There's got to be a hot librarian hiding here somewhere.

The light from the chandeliers barely illuminates the path now, but each aisle has gold switches that turn on wall sconces attached to each shelf.

"There are so many light bulbs. It's impressive," I mutter. The barracks now have human-made glass bulbs, and some village houses have adopted human engineering.

Humans love to build cities of light powered by their version of engineered magic called electricity. They make it with light from the sun and windmills, and store it on large panels. Some vampires think human engineering will change our world entirely since we don't have to rely on candles or magic lights now.

"Give a human a stick and they will make fire with which they will clear a forest; they will use the fallen timber to build a village. They are impressive creatures."

"We could use it to make fire, too," I remind him.

"But we don't, boy. Vampires use others. It's the way it's always been. Perhaps it will change. It once did." He grumbles the last part under his breath.

We soon reach a set of winding stairs that leads to a lower level.

"You're quiet," he huffs.

"Miss my voice?" I reply as we descend. Oh, look, *another* room filled with books.

"It was an observation, not a question. I'm simply wondering whether your lack of voice is due to you not knowing any more words or if it is a blessing from the gods not to be burdened with your incessant comments."

"Why are you so rude?"

Stopping, he grabs three books, grins, and adds them to my stack, saying, "Because I can be."

"I see maturity isn't gained with age," I shoot back. He's a total fucker, but... I think he'd be fun to drink with. The bitchy ones always are.

"Neither is it with youth."

We continue to walk, then reach more stairs—again and again. *Fuck. My. Life.*

This is boring. I take it back. No more libraries.

His endurance is impressive, though. "How old are you?" I ask.

"Old enough to know a pompous prick when I spot one."

My back straightens. "I'm not pompous."

We reach a door, which he kicks open forcefully. Stale, moldy air comes rushing out. What's down there? Old cheese?

Okay, I'll follow, but there'd better be wine with that stinky cheese.

"You put your wants over others' needs. That's pompous." He nods his head for me to follow.

I peek over the stack in my hands. I've walked on hills with smoother inclines. We must be far beneath the surface. My guard goes up. "No books are housed down there. The mold would eat at the paper." I step back, fingers uncurling, ready to drop the books and grab my sword.

Whoosh!

A strong shove knocks the breath out of my lungs. Yuck! My inhale is filled with musky notes. I stumble, missing the first step. Fuck, here it comes! I tumble down the stairs, my shin and back hitting the hard corners of the stone. I'll heal faster than a human and a fae would, but it still hurts.

He set me up!

But why?

As soon as I stop rolling, I stagger to find purchase and stand. With a wave of my hands, my magic flares to a dark, shadowy life. Darkness. It consumes me, covers me as my shadows curl around me like ringlets of hair.

"That was a mistake," I growl as I unsheathe my sword.

Whoosh! Another attack assaults me, shoving my back into the stone wall.

Slowly, footsteps approach me. "You have earth magic, too," the old man states. "Shadows."

"And you have wind." Lucky for me, I've trained with Ryker. I know how to fight against the wind.

"Yes. Now lower your shadows so I don't trip and break my hip again."

"You think I'm a fool. You tried to kill me." I push my shadows out, blinding his path, until his steps halt.

"Kill?" he questions. "I merely gave you a little shove."

"Down a set of stairs!"

I can hear his hand sliding over the wall, feeling for the path as he takes another step. "It's not my fault you lost your balance."

"What game are you playing?"

"I could ask you the same, boy. Mating bonds, my ass. If you did find your mate, it would be *them* who was running for the hills, not you. You'd be lucky to land a fish as a mate."

"Then why did you lie and let me follow you?"

"Those books are heavy; I didn't want to carry them." He waits a moment until he releases an old bellow. "Joking. Pull back your shadows and lower your blade. I heard you pull it forth. I have what you need."

My balls are starting to sweat. I don't like this. Not one bit. Should I risk grabbing my snack bag?

I hear him take another three steps. I take a defensive position. He knows these stairs. Each step in the dark is controlled and measured. It's I who is the prey.

Hiss. Hiss.

My shadow makes a slithering sound that echoes off the narrow stairway until the old man comes face to face with my sword.

Does he flinch? Nope. He still looks bored.

"Ahh, there's the prick," the old vampire grunts. "A man speaks before he pulls his sword. A prick thinks his sword will save him."

He nudges his head like I'm a dog, then has the audacity to squeeze himself past me and my sword with the grace of a paperclip slipping onto a sheet of paper—so gentle it leaves no mark behind.

I hope I didn't make a mistake by not driving my blade through him.

"Adolescent fool," he grumbles as he raises his palm to the stone wall. "You pissed yourself," he comments.

"What?" I raise my blade. "I did not!" Seriously, I didn't! I look at my pants to double-check.

He laughs as he taps his foot. Sure enough, at the bottom of the stairs is a puddle of water. I... I did not! I've faced endless battles, and I've never pissed myself.

"You actually think you did." His laugh hits me like cold water. "The walls leak; these old stones drink everything up; water, whispers. But eventually, everything hits rock bottom. Everything comes to my doorstep." The old vampire raises his hand and chants a mage spell over the wall. The ring on his finger glows.

Aww, he's got an enchanted ring. It allows others who are not mages to do simple mage spells, like opening mage-locked doors. The ring is rare. I've never seen one in person before.

Turn around. It's a trap.

A door magically appears. *Whoosh!* His wind magic flares behind me. *Splash!* My feet stumble through the puddle as I barrel into the small room.

He rolls his eyes at my sword as if it were a loaf of stale bread and not a weapon.

"Do you even know which end is the pointy one?" he ridicules.

"Would you like me to show you?" My shadows purr around my feet, eager to be set free again.

"Perhaps," he rolls with my punches. "Talking to you is rather painful. If I were wise, I would just have you end it before nightfall does." His choice of words feels like a sketch an artist makes before they commit to the design.

Does he think he's dying tonight? The grin spreading on his lips tells me he wants death.

He closes the door, and then a silencing spell snaps into place.

"What is the meaning of this?" I demand. My palms grow sweaty as I clutch my blade.

"I could ask you the same." He tilts his head and then shakes it.

I look around. Is this a room or a closet? The space contains only a bed, a dresser, a chair, and a trunk. "Is this your bedroom?" Surely not. There is nothing personal. Where are all his knick-knacks? This guy looks like a hoarder.

"Not good enough for you, boy?"

This asshole! "This bed is better than the one I received when my brother and I became wards of the kingdom."

His lip twitches. "Good. You're not scared of losing everything because you have before."

"What's that supposed to mean?"

"Nothing." He rubs his jaw. "Didn't Titus order you to pretend to bed the librarians?" He lifts a snarky eyebrow. "There is a bed. And if our conversation has been you seducing me," he laughs, "I fear for the future of our young men."

Seduce! Wait... what did he say?

My mouth fills with a sour taste. "Wait a minute!" Driving my elbow back, I prepare to strike. "How did you know what Titus and I discussed?"

He grabs the only chair in the room and sinks confidently into it, taking his time to cross his weary old legs before he smirks. "Because Everett told me."

CHAPTER
TWENTY-SIX

TRISTEN

Everett! That prick is like sunlight; he seeps into the smallest of cracks, bending and refracting, sneaking his way into all layers of life, both past, present, and future.

Chills cover my skin.

I want to shave them off. Wipe the slate clean.

The old librarian leans over and drops his head into his hands. "You pompous prick, you fool," he mutters through his dry, cracked lips.

"Stop calling me that!" I aim my sword at his liver.

In the end, we're all the same. If we bleed too much or can't heal fast enough, we're dead. It makes fighting simple. Whether you have fae magic, vampire, shifter, mage, or human, we're just thin flesh wrapped around bone. It cuts open easily; if you can't heal in time, then you're done.

Humans have proven that point time and time again. We've killed so many of them, but they survive. Heck, they even manage to defeat us in battle with their machines and tactics.

"That's what you are!" the old man snaps. His fists raise as they shake with small tremors.

I can't help but feel bad for him. I lower my sword and let him grab me by the collar. My eyes zero in on his inflamed white knuckles, which he can't fully curl closed.

I don't know why we fight so hard to live long lives. Time is the cruelest master; it makes you crave more of it, yet the longer it grants you, the more it slowly devours you. First, your smooth complexion, then your stable lungs, each stride you take as you age becomes as unbalanced as a flag being held as it's charged into battle.

It's an abusive relationship. I just want to enjoy my youth. If time doesn't slowly eat me, a battle will consume me.

I pick the battle, dying fast and young over this man's poor state.

But I can't die until I know my brother is safe.

"You could have ruined everything! Everything because you're pompous. You were supposed to come here and wander aimlessly; then I was to find you, bring you here, and give you this." He shoves me into the damp stone wall, then rummages through the trunk at the foot of his bed.

He grabs a small piece of paper, rolled tightly, and then swats me over the head with it.

"Hey!" I fuss as I snatch it from his hand.

"Leave. I did my part." He waves his hand dismissively in the air.

"I'm not a fly you can so easily swat away!"

"More like an imbecile who needs a kick in the ass," he heckles as he slams the trunk shut. "Do you comprehend only the moans of women? I said, leave."

"I'm not leaving!" I snap as I unravel the paper. It's clearly been ripped out of a binding. "What is this?" I demand.

"It's called parchment. You use it to write on." Turning his back, he slowly strides to the opposite corner of the room, where the single chair is. I've seen thicker toothpicks than the legs on that chair.

"Stop being an asshole!" I fire back.

"It takes one to know one," he grumbles as he crosses his arms.

"I might be a pompous prick, but you're a petulant child." I practically shave off a layer of my teeth as I grind my jaw. As I smooth out the paper, some of the ink flakes off. Tavern tables are less stained, and the smell... let's not comment on the scent.

"It's a map," I state.

"Wow, he knows pictures." He claps. "Can he do one plus one?"

I give him a dirty look. "You really want to die, don't you?"

"Yes. I do. I'm tired." The wood moans and aches as he adjusts his position.

"Not soon enough," I hiss under my breath, tracing my fingers over the old parchment.

So many of the borderlines are faded, and the kingdom's names I can make out are not known to me. Most have been conquered and claimed, their history rewritten. Maps this old are usually held in Ishmor.

"Where did you get this?" I ask, voice low.

"I didn't get it. It was given to me."

I can't help but roll my eyes. "Pulling teeth out is easier than conversing with you."

"I feel the same."

"Who gave it to you?" I demand.

"Who do you think?" He grins.

"Everett," I hiss. "Where did he get it?" I mumble as I look back at the map.

"That doesn't matter, but he got it from a book he stole from Ishmor."

My head snaps up. *Click!* Answers slide into place. Tristen told me that Selene had told him Everett had stolen a book from the Great Library of Ishmor. This paper must have been ripped from a book.

"Why did he give it to you?"

"Because he needed me to give it to you," he deadpans.

"Why not my brother?"

"Stop asking and start looking, boy."

I roll my eyes. Looking back at the paper, I memorize it. There, that mountain line looks familiar. "It's the land of Blackthorn, Galen's kingdom," I state. Only on this map it's called... holy shit.

"Caldara," I whisper. Blackthorn is Caldara!

"No one alive knows the Kingdom of Blackthorn was Caldara," he states with a gleam in his eye. "It's had many other names since then." His spine curls in like a snail seeking the walls of its shell as he exhales and leans back in the chair. "Don't you find it so frustrating that we can never remember a name? Details haunt us, but a name is like water; we don't value it until we need it."

My heart slows, my ears open, and every hair on my body stands. The pressure shifts, as it does when a storm is coming. Everything cools down. I raise the paper closer as if a new angle will reveal hidden details.

"The mountains surrounding us provide more than a barrier to our enemies; they are loaded with minerals." He stands, wipes the sweat from his brow, and unbuttons his cloak.

Glancing back at the map, I notice an error. The mountain to the north was drawn twice the size it is on our maps today, and the western entrance into our land was significantly smaller.

"Shall I continue?" he asks as he tosses his cloak onto the bed. Small clouds of dust billow in the stale air.

When's the last time he washed that?

I step back an inch. Who knows what plagues linger here? He's never cleaned the surfaces, of that I am certain.

"I never asked you to start," I dispute. "You're like a pipe leaking water. You'll drip regardless."

"It's irritating, but it alerts you to what is broken. Perhaps that is why Everett picked me." He lowers himself back into that old chair and crosses his arms. Now, instead of looking like mite-eaten wood, that chair looks like a throne.

He holds power, and he knows it. I have to play his game if I want answers.

"I'm listening." I dip my chin.

"When I mention Everett, irritation prickles over your skin like fire. Why?"

"Fire burns," I bite out.

"Everett did nothing to you."

I stride forward, grinding the soles of my boots into the stone floor, hoping it scuffs. "He stole my brother from me!"

His eyebrows furrow like a rabbit raccoon's tail. "Maybe you're looking at it wrong. Perhaps he saved him."

I look down my nose at him. "We don't see eye to eye. Continue your tale about Caldara," I order.

He crosses a leg and steeples his fingers. "Some people find the drip-drop of a leak annoying; others find it soothing, like music. Remember that. Your perception is like the hands of a sculptor. It shapes everything. Regard Everett's actions as beneficial, not detrimental."

He takes his time settling into a comfortable position, knowing I must wait if I want answers.

"Caldara's king was wise. He built his castle along the northern mountains, offering him a bird's-eye view of his surroundings. If an enemy marched through the narrow strait, he'd be first to know. The problem is that we forget to look at the enemy hiding under our noses or, rather, under our feet.

"The king allowed his people to mine, digging deeper into the mountain. What happens when you continue to remove the foundation of your house?" He looks at me knowingly.

My stance widens. "It crumbles."

He nods. "The mountain to the north is only half as grand as it once was. The land caved in; the mountain swallowed the king's castle, along with his people. Those who survived lost trust in the land. They said that a curse had befallen it. For the king built his castle in the mountain's shadow; he should have assembled it within the light so that the gods could see and judge him."

A smirk ghosts his lips as an uneasy shudder snakes down my spine.

"Humans spin such beautiful tales, don't you think? Instead of saying the king was a fool, they tried to appease the gods. But," he lifts a finger, "by labeling the land to the north as cursed, it made it so no one would dare to enter. Fear is like the wind." He huffs out a heavy breath to emphasize his point. "We cannot see it, but oh, how we feel it. Aren't you going to ask where they rebuilt?" His brow nearly meets his hairline.

My gaze sweeps toward the ancient stones that enclose us. "Here," I mutter. The mountains still act as a border that is only a short horse ride away, but Galen's castle is bathed in sunlight; thus, his black roses grow so dutifully.

"Yes," he taps his foot, kicking up more dust.

I've never had allergies, but all the soot is going to test my limits. Raising my hand, I wipe my nose.

"Right here. The old castle of Caldara had become a skeleton, long dead and buried. However, bones take a long time to weather away and return to the earth. If one knows where to look, they can still find a passage through the old mining caves that survived. The hidden tunnels the king built deep in the heart of his castle, a heart that's not dead, but slumbering."

Thump! Boom! Thump! Control your breathing; consider this a battle where your tongue is your sword and your mind is your shield.

His words feel like the tip of a sword that gently glides over my lashes. Each statement takes one of my senses. My sight. My hearing. My ability to move.

I planned that once Titus found the Vitalis, we'd just burn it or sell it. I just want him free of this shitstorm. That look in the old man's eyes tells me we're all stuck in this terrible web Everett weaved. There is no escape.

"Why would we want to find the heart?" I ask as dread coils through my muscles.

"Because it gives life, and life is what evil seeks. It thrives on it." He stoops, pulls his shoes off, and flexes his toes.

"Then it's best to let it sleep." I inch back, map in hand. Titus is starting to control the time-weaving. He can live with it. There's no need to find this book.

"You think you are the only one with a scent in the air? Others know; they have been looking. Why do you think Everett sowed so many seeds? He needed to ensure that we all developed in a certain way. So sit your ass down, yes, right there on the stone floor, and listen because I'm tired and want to sleep, but I promised I would retell a tale."

CHAPTER
TWENTY-SEVEN

TRISTEN

I don't realize I'm running my tongue over my fangs until they slice it. Shoot!

Leave.

Run to Titus and drag him here, or better yet, force him away from this mission.

"Sit that pompous ass down. I'm sure you've let filthier things touch you," he huffs. "Oh, but wait, before you do, be a good lad and get me the aged bottle of human whiskey there." He points to the trunk.

I fall into the role of callboy. He's lucky I don't smash this thing over his wrinkly head.

"I'll stand," I bite out as I lean against the wall.

He mutters under his breath, too low for me to hear.

"Tell me," I press. Smelling all this mold is making me dizzy.

"Do not," he says, lifting the bottle like a dagger, "intervene again. Do as you're told." He takes a swig from the bottle.

"I've seen swines swallow with more grace," I grumble. "Why is Caldara so important?"

"It's a cursed place I wish we could forget, but evil seeks evil."

"Everett wanted my brother to find this place. Titus isn't evil," I point out.

His eyes look longingly into the bottle. "Not Titus."

"Selene, then?"

He rolls his eyes and releases a fed-up huff. "You need not find Caldara, boy. You're already here. You seek the wrong questions. The night grows late. Let me tell you the story I was told as a boy, the same story Everett asked me to tell him."

He kicks his feet out and leans back in the chair. "Long ago—"

"Shouldn't you start with 'Once upon a time'?" I cut off, raising a brow.

He rubs his temples. "It's rude to interrupt your elders."

"You're well past elder age," I jab.

He levels me with a glare. "Do you wish for me to continue?"

"Yes, fine." I cross my arms loosely and let one of my shoulders rest against the wall.

"It's not 'once upon a time' because the story was never finished. So, I'll say it again: long ago, a war between what you call the gods and the creatures they call elves revealed a terrible truth. The gods were no longer immortal. Since the elvish army was larger, the gods withdrew and then reformed."

I tap my boot on the floor with an impatient beat. "They don't sound like gods to me."

"Ignorant," he grumbles, running his hand down his face. "Wise creatures take refuge when the storm is too strong. Fools stand out in the open. The gods had no other option. You'd do the same."

"I'd rather fight till the end, but whatever," I shrug, waving a dismissive hand.

"That's a hero's story, boy, but what if only the enemy survived to tell your tale? I doubt they would write you as a hero who fought to the end."

I hate to admit it, but... "Point made. I stand corrected. So, these gods and whatever the heck an elf is are at war; the gods run. Then what?"

"Like you, gods seek vengeance."

"I seek justice." Freedom for my brother, a life away from Selene's fucked-up family.

"Some say it is the same," he counters. "They came here to build an army, but humans were like paper; they could hold great wonders written within their pages, but they were so fragile. The gods needed to create something stronger. They infused their power into the humans, and over the centuries, you were born."

"Me?" I push my spine into the icy wall. "You're suggesting I'm the descendant of a god."

"*You*?" He tips his head back and chuckles. "No." He slaps his knee. "You're like a mangy mutt compared to a demigod. You have a god's *magic*, not their blood."

"What's the difference?" I bark.

"Meet a demigod on the battlefield and find out."

"Demigods aren't real. They're myths."

His laughter dies. "You're in for a rude awakening. Myths are like dried flowers pressed between old pages. But a flower came from a seed, boy. Hands plant seeds. There is truth in every myth."

He pats his thigh. "As I was saying, wars between the new creatures and the humans grew vastly. So in secret, two of the gods tried to correct their mistake. They created a new creature; they didn't know this, but things forged with love are no less deserving of being called a child.

"One created a book with endless pages, but it was the other god who altered the book; she took a piece of her magic and fused it into the book, then she forged the first rune."

"The Vitalis," I declare. The book that will free my brother from Everett's magic.

"Wow, he knows some history. Color me surprised."

"I was told runes are nothing more than mage magic."

"Lies spread faster than truths. Unfortunately, people believe them quickly. Here I am, telling you the facts, yet you narrow your eyes at me like I'm the delusional one."

"Color me skeptical."

"Spread your legs and accept it."

"Fuck you."

"Not my type." He smirks.

I prop my foot against the wall and glare at him through my thick lashes. Is that steam coming out of my ears? It feels like it. "So anything drawn in the Vitalis has magic?" I retort.

"It's not a book for toddlers. If you scribble down letters, you can call it a name, but a name is not defined until it is earned. To function, a rune requires nurturing, much like a child. One must have a clean mind; they have to think of many circumstances, time limits, magic limitations, and how the magic will react. It's like making a feast rather than a simple sandwich.

"Then, and only then, once the pages are satisfied, will the rune remain on the page. After that, the rune can be copied onto flesh, and through magic, the rune will work as the artist intended."

"So far-fetched," I mutter.

"So is the fact that you have survived countless wars yet are so clueless."

I tip my chin up. Does he want me to end him? This way, his secrets die before they reach my ears.

I've got news for you, old man; that old crusty heart will keep beating until I say so, and that sharp, bitter tongue will keep talking.

"Think of the runes like a virus," he continues. "They enter your body and change it. But instead of fevers and aches, you get magic. Eventually, your body returns to normal, and the rune disappears."

"So they have to be inked onto the skin?" I clarify.

"Ink is preferable, but some used to be tattooed and burned in. Just as your magic needs to be recharged, the runes do as well. The tattoo remained, but the rune would rest until it charged and reactivated itself. Tattoo runes can be dangerous. I would proceed with caution.

You can wear less complex runes, like simple shields, as pendants or carve them into walls. They activate only when threatened. They could withstand many blows until the rune deactivated."

"What happened to the book?" I need to find it to free my brother.

"Eventually, the gods returned with their army, but they left the book behind. It presented too much danger should the elves obtain it."

"Now they sound more like the gods I know."

"Why is that?" His interest sounds genuine for once.

"Because leaving a book so powerful is cruel. We kill for land that has dead soil. Imagine what we'd do for a book of power."

His eyes drop. Is that guilt heavy on his brow?

"Taking it away would have been crueler." He licks his dry, cracked lips. "Sometimes we try to do a good deed, but it results in a terrible one instead. Interpretations are like options; opinions are like taste. We all seek different ones, digest them differently."

"That's not an answer." He speaks in so many riddles, it makes my head hurt.

"We will always fight over silly things, boy. Caging people won't change that, nor will stripping them of their freedoms. One must allow everyone liberty, even if that liberty involves initiating conflicts. It's a balance," he replies in a solemn tone.

"What happened to the book, old man?" I press.

He answers me without a fight. "A man named Torin tried to fix the balance. He lived in a time when runes were abused. He thought his actions were heroic."

Why does it sound like you were there?

"You never told me your name?" I say warily.

"I am not him." He grunts and continues, "Torin stole the Vitalis in the hopes that one day he could destroy it. It was born of two gods. Only one thing is known to have killed a god." He looks down at his hands and tries to flex them. "When the gods returned to their world, they left the God Swords here. Torin happened to have that in his possession as well."

"Wait... if Torin used this sword to kill the book, then..." That means Titus will never be free. "I don't understand."

"A God Sword can kill a god, but this book is different. The god who made it did not realize that some of the materials he used were not of this land."

"What land were they from?"

He looks to the corner of the room, gazes deep, as one does at a night sky. "You know... I don't recall the name anymore, but I still remember the heat of the rising suns." He smirks. Is he going to cry?

"Suns?" We have only one sun. This man makes no sense.

His hand shoots up faster than I thought it could, covering his mouth as he scrambles to filter his words. "That detail isn't important to this story. All you need to know is that he was given material to help him make the book. He simply desired to see her smile again."

"Who gave him the material?"

"How should I know?" he grumbles as he looks down.

Liar.

"It's important to your story, isn't it?" I acknowledge. He looks at me with respect for the first time.

"Indeed." His eyes snap to mine. "Back to Torin. He tried to stab the book, but the cover was like an impenetrable skin. However, if he pulled back the cover, he could cut the pages free."

"So all that's left of the Vitalis is just a front and back cover?"

"No, like you, the Vitalis, can heal. Its pages regenerate." He holds up a crooked finger, weathered with age. "When a page was removed, the rune on it vanished from the paper, killing the magic link to those who wore the mark. Torin discovered he could erase all the runes by removing the pages. However, the book itself was still an issue. Anyone who possessed it could redraw the runes. So Torin had few choices. Hunted and desperate, he hid it somewhere no one would think to look."

"Caldara," I answer. It's smart; curses make people—even greedy ones—hesitate.

He nods, "Torin found an old entrance that hadn't collapsed. He opened the book, held back the covers, and stabbed it with the God Sword. Since the pages were not ripped free, no new pages regenerated, but the runes were wounded, their magic cut off. Removing the sword will probably require redrawing many pages unless someone can heal them."

"Redrawn?"

"You sound like a parrot. That is what I said."

So Titus needs to find this book, free it of the God Sword, and then... I laugh. My brother can't draw for shit!

"That's it? That's your grand story's ending?" I sputter.

"Did you want mage fireworks, boy? Let me guess, you wanted a 'happily ever after'?"

"Who told you this story?" I push off the wall. "You said it was told to you as a boy. How do I know if any of it is true? It could all be a myth."

"Wasn't it you who, upon first meeting me, said, 'Myths have seeds of truth,' and later I repeated that? By the gods, boy, how dim and daft can you be?"

He's got me.

He narrows his eyes at me. "Find the seeds."

"What if I don't like what they grow?" I challenge, folding up the map and placing it in my pocket. This story is as heavy a burden as Everett's fae magic. I can choose to harbor it as Titus did or... I can pick a different path.

I can decide not to tell Titus. Force him far away from these lands.

"Do not blame the flower for the color of its petals. It has no choice. If you tell it that it is ugly, it will become so. If you choose to use runes to create evil, they will be seen as corruption. Create good. Do good. Evil will grow regardless. Look at how some wield their magic; we kill without blinking. Bringing runes back into the world will not stop that."

"Why should we let them return?"

"You were born a vampire, boy; you had an advantage over others."

How dare he judge me!

"I was an orphan at an early age. I had no mother to love me when I woke with night terrors. I was given a sword and forced to kill. The only luxury I possessed were the skills that were forced into my hands so I could survive, but it was not without a heavy cost. The kingdom only cared about my survival if I was good at killing."

"What if you were born a human?" he rebuttals. "No magic, just skin and bones."

"I was skin and bones as a boy," I scoff. "My magic didn't manifest until adolescence, like all vampires do. Yes, humans have no magic later in life, but that taught them to be resourceful. Look at what humans have invented."

It is because of humans that we have machines without the use of magic. They have built cities made of metal and not stone. On the contrary, I respect humans for all they have accomplished without magic, but in the end, we were all born the same, and this old man will not make me feel guilty for being born a vampire!

"Would you trade your circumstances to be a human?"

My shadow magic hisses under my skin. I can't imagine a life without magic. My anxiety is what humans must have felt when they were given runes. A taste that was eventually stolen from them by Torin.

He raises his chin. "No, I didn't think so. When you are standing on a higher step, it's easy to look down into the eyes of the people looking up. But have you looked at their feet and the path they walked in order to remain standing?

"The time is coming, boy. Evil will always have roots here, but if we are all even, then we stand a better chance of not being tempted by it. Runes make us even."

"You never answered my question, *old man*. Who told you this story?"

He stands and walks to his bed. "I told you, I was told the story as a boy."

I impatiently run my tongue over my fangs. "By whom?"

He touches the post of his bed, as if this matter pains him. "I'm orphaned like you. Only back then, the bed I had made this one look like it was worthy of a king." He pats the blankets and smiles at them. "When I was a boy, my keepers traded me to a fae. She was a gentle soul. That's when I realized what we were—vampire, fae, human—didn't matter; it was who we were. This fae was caring, loving, and she became my mother."

Turning lazily, he sits on the bed and looks long at his old, withered hands.

"Each night, she told me a bedtime story from the days of old. It wasn't until later in my life that I realized they were not stories. She had the magic of hindsight. But the past didn't matter, so they never deemed her useful and cast her aside. So she wrote many books, concealing the past's truths with twisted plots that sold. For decades, the Vitalis was guarded, but over time, the guards grew too relaxed. People stole, used, abused, traded, and won the book of runes in battles."

The old bedtime stories we were told about runes were true. There was once a time when everyone used them.

"But how did the world just forget about runes? You said there were hundreds of runes. Surely a symbol is marked somewhere," I argue.

He flips his hands over and gazes into his palms. "When Torin cut off the magic, tattoos became a symbol, symbols turned into meaningless patterns, then nothing at all. Why ink your flesh if the drawing has no meaning? The crest of a kingdom became more powerful."

He clears a congested cough from his lungs. "Who's to say a symbol marked on these old castle walls was not once a rune? I'll tell you this, boy, I'd bet my life runes surround us; they just don't work anymore. We consider the pattern just a decoration."

I scan his walls, but they are barren.

"It's time for me to sleep, but I should warn you of one other thing my mother saw. This changed Everett's plans; it forced him to keep certain people alive. Torin placed his magic over the Vitalis. Caged it," the old man states.

My brows furrow. "You can't turn magic into an object."

"We turn people into objects all the time, boy. Mages can store their magic in objects, and now they have figured out a way to infuse those gemstones into swords, making magical weapons. Haven't you asked yourself why King Galen is so worried? He has the numbers, but imagine a human and mage army stocked with magic weapons that deliver a blow ten times stronger? That scares our king, and it should scare you."

I can see it. The vision hollows out my stomach and scrapes clean my tongue. I'm unsure if food will have the same sensation again.

Death. So much death.

"We're on the precipice of killing ourselves off. And as we kill each other, a new beast is born."

I flex my forearms, hoping to dispel the fear that covers them. "What precisely was Torin's magic?"

"Aww, he finally asked the correct question," the old vampire purrs, and I roll my eyes. "It was what I wish to claim me, to free me from these weary bones. *Death*."

A frown tugs at my lips. I hate the old man, but he's kind of fun to banter with, and the idea of him dying... yeah, I don't like it.

"Death," I echo, the word sour on my tongue.

He nods. "Just as Everett gave his magic to Titus, Torin spoke this to his magic, 'I order you to cage this book, here on this slab, so it can never be moved; should anyone touch you, you shall strike them dead.'"

"That doesn't sound like a friendly welcome mat. How the fuck can Titus get the book then?"

"There is one more thing Torin said you need to know..."

"Why can't we just end this story here?" I rasp. "Never mind; don't reply. Continue,"

"Say please." He crosses his arms.

"*Now*," I deadpan.

"In this kingdom, we spell 'please' with different letters." He snorts. "Fine, fine, I'll tell you. Torin didn't realize his magic was still obeying his demand when he said, 'For none can rival death but itself.'" He tilts his head as he waits for me to understand.

"So you're telling me I need to find someone with death magic?"

Oh shit...

He replies before I can. "You don't need to find them. They are already here."

His mage ring glows as he waves his hand. The wall behind me grumbles as the door opens.

"That is all I can tell you, so unless you plan on trying to seduce me and sleep with a librarian, as Titus suggested, I'm headed to bed. Good night, pompous prick." When he reaches for the buckle of his belt, I grimace and edge towards the door.

"I'll be back," I warn him.

"I knew you'd say that." He chuckles to himself as he slips into bed.

CHAPTER
TWENTY-EIGHT

SELENE

The scent of velvet and flowers fills my nose, stirring me awake. My eyes snap open. "I'd ask what you're doing here, but in truth, I know how weak of a man you are, Galen. You're showing your cracks, and soon they will fester into flaws." I sit up and stare at him. He's perched on the edge of my bed. The grin that was painted on his lips slips off like watercolor paint that was doused with too much liquid. He's just a sad mess now.

"I know you're lonely." He pushes me to stand so he can look down at me. He thinks this gives him the upper hand. Newsflash: I can turn my neck and look elsewhere.

"Only a weak mind grows antsy in silent times, Galen. It is you who is lonely. I am content." I stretch my legs out, proving my point. A glance outside tells me it's still early morning. "Did your whore last night not exhaust you? You should still be sleeping," I jab as I uncurl my spine.

There is no going back to sleep now.

His lips twitch. "Most women would be jealous."

"Most women are fools. Why would I be jealous of a husband who breaks multiple vows? Murderous is more like it," I sneer.

He opens the palm of his hand, magic flaring as he grows a shiny black stem, thorns sharpening like a knife on a whetstone. A red flower blooms as he stretches his hand toward me.

"And that is why, my sweet wife, I will always crave you. You're a huntress, and that makes the game more fun." His magic cuts the vine in half. He alters it more, and I watch as the flower turns the dark purplish-black color I know best.

He brings the rose to his nose, glides it over his lips, and then places it on my pillow.

"I only hunt prey that is worthy." I swat the rose off my pillow and climb out of bed. I'll have all the bedding washed now. "Small bunnies mean nothing to me. You were fun until you became annoying. The bridge we made will never be rebuilt. The chasm is too wide. And I don't care to make an effort with a liar who seeks to kill my people. What do you want?"

He flashes his fangs as he grins. "I want to go catch bunnies, Selene. Unlike you, I enjoy hunting all prey." He lunges forward and grabs me.

Not involving Titus was the best part of Galen's impromptu visit. His time weaving is emotionally provoked, and Galen is a master at plucking the string and playing with other emotions. The man's tongue is a fiddle that can make even the most uncoordinated dance.

Magic snaps and swirls around us, creating a static that charges the air until the portal closes. "Why are we here?" I press my palm against my stomach, holding back my nausea.

I hate portals. The sensation is something I can't get used to. Give me a horse so the wind can fill my hair any day. I also don't trust portals. You need to have complete faith in the mage who opens it. We could have walked into a dungeon in some other kingdom.

I can't help but wonder what Galen has on this mage. It's rare for mages to work with vampires. They don't want to be dragged into our war with the fae, which has made the alliance between mages and humans dangerously strong.

In front of us, a wide-open field runs endlessly, like an ocean. It's untouched; the wild grass dances and sings as the morning sunlight and gentle breeze awaken it. Fresh dew drops still cling to the blades. It would be a beautiful sight if my husband were not looming over me like a rain cloud. Three dozen men gather on the far right, standing at attention, waiting for Galen's orders.

"We're hunting," Galen smirks. He pulls off his leather gloves, which are embossed with black roses. For a man who gardens so much, he has only smooth, clean skin.

"You see, bunnies are useful. They can do so many things, sweet wife. You can use them for food." Galen takes a flask out of his breast pocket and flips open the cap. "As pets, weapons, even prey to catch something bigger." His brown hair soaks in the sunlight, making it look like strands of gold are hiding in the woodsy brown shades.

It's a built-in trap, luring prey closer. Galen's soul isn't black; it's a void that swallows everything, every shade of color, till none exists. He's been sucking away my spirit.

But then Titus came. He colored me with a new palette, thanks to Everett. I have a purpose again.

I watch as Galen's lips close around the flask. A single droplet of blood escapes and dribbles down his chin.

He's powering up. What for?

My neck stiffens, my fingers itch to reach for my weapon, but I only have my hands at my disposal. I look out at the field again. I understand. This is bait—free food humans eagerly accept—concealing Galen's sharp hook.

"What do you want with humans?"

Gulp. "You're so smart. I love that about you." He drinks the flask like the sun slurps up the moisture from the soil. Leaving not one drop behind. "I have a use for them."

"Your blood banks are full. If you welcome more humans, your people will think you are slipping into bloodlust."

"That's true," Galen replies, offering an easy shrug. "So I have found another way to welcome more humans without spreading rumors. That's why we are here." He opens his palms and thrusts his hands forward. Long vines shoot forth from under the earth. Tearing and ripping through the peaceful field. Grinding and thrashing open the soil.

I step back. The wild grass is churned into the soil and swallowed. It's disgusting and impressive, in the same way vultures wait patiently for a dead animal to fester.

"Humans need food," Galen adds. His vines continue to till the land for miles. Then it stops. He's labored. He turns to the side so his people don't see. Galen waves his hand, and a woman steps out from the crowd. He readjusts his crown, letting his fingers linger on it.

Does he fuck his crown? He's caressing it like a lover.

He lowers his hand when the woman reaches our side. I stay silent. She has the manners to bow. Galen grabs her by the shoulders and tips her head to the side. His eyes hold mine as he grins, then sinks his teeth into her neck. She moans with pleasure. Courtesy of him, of course. A vampire can choose to inflict pain or pleasure with their bite.

His throat rolls as he swallows, gulp after gulp of her essence.

I want to grab her. If Galen doesn't stop soon, she'll be dead. Instead, I hold his stare. If he wants my resentment or jealousy, he shall see none. Instead, I wear a mask of apathy.

Truly, I feel... nothing. I'm delighted he's got his playthings. After all his confessions about his lies to trick me into being his wife, how could I not?

Titus.

He pops into my mind. What would it feel like to have his lips on my neck?

You can never know. You're stuck in a marriage you didn't choose.

Love was never in my future, only death. Everett knew this. He embraced it, as must I.

Turning suddenly, I try to hide the blush on my cheeks. Why do I keep thinking of Titus?

You know why. For the first time in your life, you are entirely terrified.

My brother's death ripped out my heart. The only thing left is my mind. I can't give that to Titus. In someone else's hands, our minds can play tricks on us; they can make us think we have a heart again, believe we have a future, and have hopes about escaping.

I know the truth.

I have no future.

Everett knew this. He warned me about what was to come. I understand now. That's why I keep Titus at bay. That, and Galen would kill him. The last thing we need is another problem on our plate. Everett gave Titus and me a mission that I intend to see through.

Galen licks his lips. He pulls away and presses his fingertip to a fang. He cuts himself and smears his blood, which has blood-clotting and healing properties, over her wound.

The human walks back to the crowd like a bee, dizzy and darting as she sways and wobbles.

"Nothing like freshly squeezed juice in the morning," Galen comments with a chuckle.

"Some courts consider drinking from the vein to be a hedonistic act. They have reformed ways you might learn from." I lift my chin higher and look back out at the field. The scent of dirt that has never felt the sun fills my nose. Musky, and wet, its layers are much darker than the topsoil.

The soldiers form a line as they drag huge bags closer to the tilled land. They flash their daggers as they slice open the bags. Whatever is within, they scoop it into their palms and begin to toss —what looks like grains from this distance—into the air. Four more vampires stand behind them, hands raised, and then the winds begin to howl.

"Seeds," Galen mutters. He stands shoulder to shoulder with me. He's as annoying as a button that is holding the fabric too tightly around you. I just want to rip it open and be free.

It makes sense now. Galen tilled the land. The soldiers throw seeds into the air, which the wind magic spreads.

I know why he needs me here.

What I don't know is why he needs more humans. "Why?" I whisper.

"Because humans need food, and I can provide that endlessly," he retorts.

Galen wouldn't lessen his barracks to hold human warriors unless he was plotting a battle I could never have predicted. Capable of not only dethroning a king, but setting siege upon the entire species.

"Now tell me the real reason you want more humans."

Galen slides in front of me like a cornerstone, holding up all the weight and knowledge. I'm just a small brick in this grand scheme. However, removing just one brick can have a significant impact. It might not cause the wall to crumble, but it will affect its longevity. That's what Everett would have told me.

"I told you we are hunting bunnies." His smooth fingers snake around my neck like phantoms. "Humans procreate like rabbits."

I wish I could stop the chills that flare over my skin as he runs his nose over my flesh.

"Your father received the news of my killing spree. He's quite upset." His hot lips press a kiss over my pulse. "Hmmm, do you smell that?" He runs his tongue along my throat. "War. I love that smell."

"You've never smelt it." I try to jerk away, but his left hand grabs my lower back, and his right digs into my neck as he holds firm. "When were you on the battlefield?" I challenge.

"Why would I need to be? Soon, I'll have humans in my army. I will far outnumber your father."

It all makes sense. He's luring humans here with farmlands, but the cost will be their lives, either as a blood bag or a soldier.

I don't have the magic of foresight, but I do see the future if Galen succeeds. He will kill my father, invade the fae territories, and slowly, both our people will be killed off. Vampires will grow desperate and start hoarding humans as cattle.

Humans will revolt. More death.

So much more.

Then, the mages will strike because we will all be weak. Those who are left will fight; they will have no choice.

I look out at the field. Death is here, taking root in the soil, and we are all nourishing it.

This is the outcome Everett saw.

But runes can balance that.

I want to cry, scream, and shout. To tell Everett that I understand. I know why he never flat-out told me. I had to see it to believe it—not just me, but everyone else. We had to endure the wars and suffering; we had to learn so that in the future, we never slip this far off the scales of balance again.

Clouds eclipse the sun in a poetic moment of realization and symmetry. Two more vampires step out onto the field, their hands raised high as they tug on the clouds that do not want to cry today. They have water magic, forcing the clouds to bleed and suffuse the land.

Darkness blinds me as my sight is taken in an instant. Galen blocks my view; his lips cover mine. It's a long kiss, gentle yet so threatening it feels like a dagger gutting me open like a fish.

"It's a very long game, sweet wife." He pulls away and cups my cheek. "I hope you pick the right side." Turning his back, he uses his magic to till the land, ensuring the seeds are buried. "Now," he grabs my hand and drags me out into the fields. "It's your turn. Give life," he orders.

His eyes are cold, a frigid warning not to deny him in front of his people.

My throat thickens like metal in a fire, and then it all melts and expands. I know the consequences of not pouring my life magic into the fields. Galen would kill more of my people.

He's going to kill them anyway...

This is a game. I have to play.

Stepping forward, I flex my fingers, feeling my magic quiver with excitement. Bending down, I press my palms into the soil, feeling its coolness as I dig my fingertips deep into the earth.

Whoosh! I let my magic free, pouring everything I have into the dirt. I listen as the seeds shake and then crack under the soil, so many seeds, the ground lets loose a small tremor. Then, little stems break free as their roots dig deeper.

Life. More and more life magic I pour into the land. My spine hunches as my magic depletes. Stems grow buds, then flowers. In the distance, the small group that Galen brought cheers. Galen remains silent as he stands over me, a hammer pounding a nail into its place.

A heavy gasp shoves free from my lungs. I don't allow myself to fall. It takes all my energy to stand. Slowly, I face Galen. His eyes are smiling wider than his mouth. He looks at the new farm that will feed his human army.

"I expected more of a fight from you," he comments.

"Who says you didn't get one?"

His eyes slide off his riches, then he looks down at me questioningly. I press my palm against his chest, then push up on my toes. My lips feather over his. My smile feels like it's splitting my head in half. "It's a long game, isn't that right, husband?" I mock.

"Whatever moves you make, remember this, sweet wife. You. Are. Mine. I own you, and nothing will change that." He wears a victor's smile.

I play the role of a mirror and grin back. Fuck him!

Own me? No, Galen, you don't own me. You owe a paper with words stating I am your wife, but this woman has a mind of her own.

I know how to break the marriage contract. Titus is right. We have a mate bond. Within the next few days or weeks, it will show. But the consequences of giving in and admitting are something I can't accept yet, perhaps not ever.

It's not just my life. It's my people, and Titus's.

I'm stuck underwater. My lungs burn as I peer up with blurry eyes; freedom from Galen lies just beyond the surface.

Life.

I want to swim and breathe. I want to feel the warmth of Titus's fire.

My shoulders tremble as Everett's words shout in my mind.

Another flashback. Another warning.

"Come, you need to rest," Everett gently touches my shoulder.

"I can sleep for a week and still not have the magic to save them all." I lost two dozen today. Their injuries were too severe for me to heal.

"You don't have to save them all," he says gently.

"Then what is my purpose?" My cheeks are raw and tight from having sat next to the blaze for so long. I hoped the blaze would chase away the icy shadows of death.

"Perhaps you are meant to save just one life." Stooping, he takes my hand and drags me away from the campfire. "Fire warms, but it can also burn, Selene. Be careful not to sit beside it for too long. You and I don't have a life of freedom. We have a debt that is owed, and duty comes to collect. It's time to rest for the night. Remember, it's okay to sit by the fire, to love it, but eventually you have to stand up and continue on your journey. You must bid the fire goodbye and venture into the cold."

I say nothing, allowing him to pull me towards my tent. But for some reason, I look over my shoulder at the fire one last time.

TWENTY-NINE

SELENE

The portal's closure behind us makes the hair on the back of my neck stand. Why are we here and not inside the castle?

Don't let Galen see your confusion. *That's it. Relax your shoulders, squeeze your abs, stand still and don't let the rush of adrenaline sway you.* All I dare move is my eyes as I scan my surroundings. Blackthorn Castle appears as a mountain.

I'm trapped at its base, unsure whether I'll make the climb up. I don't like being this weak and magicless around my husband.

Galen's smirk presses into me. Did he bring us here so he'd have to carry me?

I'd look so weak and fragile. But perhaps that's what he wants.

I fix the mage with a stare, but he looks toward the entrance gates. Black stones larger than houses pile high, forging the outer wall of Blackthorn's entrance markets. The stone is so thick it swallows the clamor of the merchant stands. Rose bushes soar along the walls. The image is hauntingly beautiful until you look deeper and see the massive, thick thorns waiting to slice into an enemy's greedy hands.

Dozens of guards form a protective path for us to walk. Their slight sway creates an aching echo of tight leather and armor stretching. My eyes drag further; the soldiers line the path all the way up to the castle. Proof Galen is worried about his perception.

If he were loved, he'd walk his kingdom freely.

"Fancy a walk?" I bark at Galen.

He chuckles to himself.

Something is up. He's got a double-edged dagger to poke me with today. Not just the farm. Here comes the next blow.

Movement catches my eye; a woman emerges from the line of guards. Gold thread embellishes the seams of her rich velvet cloak. That's a ridiculous number of amethyst necklaces on her neck. Only a mage would be caught dead wearing the entire jewelry store. They have no sense of fashion editing.

I know her; she and Sable fancy themselves friends. Therefore, I consider her my enemy.

She smiles at Galen. That's an 'I fucked you recently' smile.

I don't care. This marriage is over. I'm just playing my part until the show ends.

Magic begins to dance between her fingers. Seriously, how does she move her hands with that many rings?

She stops in front of us and bows. Before I can speak, I spot the most dangerous predator in the castle. Sable.

Great. She's all I need. My twin has been hiding since Titus threw her out of my chambers. It's not unusual. She doesn't strike fast. She's methodical.

Unbeknownst to her, she was giving me the time I needed to help Titus, before I needed to decipher what her plans of attack were.

Instead of wearing the latest vampire fashion, which she loves, she's dressed in her royal fae garb. A long yellow dress made of silk, with a matching silk cloak that covers her shoulders. The dress is simple. The embellishment is evident in the belt around her hips, adorned with gold and gems.

I don't miss the dagger strapped to her side. The hilt is adorned with emeralds set in white-gold. Yellow gold is generally preferred by Fae. My gaze drifts to Galen's crown, which is the same white.

What did she do to earn a gift from him?

Her hair hangs long, with braids holding half of it back, covered with golden cuffs and clips.

I hate that she wears my face. I've thought about changing it.

My face, not hers.

I almost did once, but Everett stopped me from inflicting the scar. He needed us to remain alike.

I sacrificed a great deal for my brother. He did the same for me, but I have these moments of grief so deep, I free fall into them. I hit bottom and feel so much resentment towards everyone—mostly myself.

"King Galen," Sable's smiles is all mischief. Two fae guards join her. I know them, Erik and Victor. They were tasked with protecting the nobles.

Wait... I understand now. My toes curl. Erik and Victor work for Galen. They must be if they didn't die defending the nobles.

"Sister," Sable flashes me a smug grin.

"Is there a tea party I was unaware of?" I jeer at Galen, growing more suspicious by the second.

"Oh," Sable snickers, "there is much tea to spill, sister. Be careful; it burns."

I have no choice but to ask, "What is the meaning of this?" I study Galen.

"Sable is returning home." Galen steps closer and touches my shoulder. That news would have brought me great joy months ago. I hated that Sable was sent here when I was married.

When the war finished, Father realized he couldn't control Sable. She was too unpredictable to keep close, so he marketed her as my companion to help me adjust to married life, a lady-in-waiting. Bullshit Galen allowed.

Would you like to know the true story behind Sable's banishment by my father? Ego, power, and most of all, father's insecurity. No man, particularly a king, would ever admit to feeling threatened by a woman. After Everett's death, Sable was no longer a hazard; she was an arrow shot free, hunting for her target: the crown. She just required support.

Sable sinks her teeth into her smirk as she studies my reaction.

"What joyous news," I scoff.

"Father was quite upset about the nobles. He demanded King Galen return their bodies. Galen thought if I delivered them, it might help smooth things over." Sable's smirk curls up too sharply to be kind.

"You make ripples, not smooth water," I voice. All I can smell is the floral scent of the roses covering the kingdom. It's a deception to mask the shit hidden within Galen's walls.

Sable's presence back home will only heighten the tension between Galen and my father.

A frown pulls at my lips. But of course, that's why he's doing it. Galen told me himself he never wanted peace. He wanted me. He's got me.

This is his silent declaration of war.

I don't move when Galen slides his hand into the dip in my lower back. He looks at the mage. "Are you ready?" he asks.

She's going to open a portal for Sable to use. Of course, Galen wouldn't allow Sable to travel by horse; that would give me time to send a secret message back to my father.

"King Galen," Sable speaks in a saccharine tone. My teeth are about to fall out from rot. "May I have a word with my twin before I depart?"

Galen makes her wait before he replies. "Quickly," he agrees, bends down, and kisses my cheek. "This is the price for denying me, my love," he whispers and then joins the mage.

The sun slips behind a cloud as Sable joins me, a mirror of my own image cast in shadows.

"I've waited so long for this day," she beams as she clasps her hands behind her back.

"I didn't think you missed home so badly," I retort, biting the inside of my cheek and watching her like a hawk.

Weeks ago, Titus asked me what Sable would do after he chose me and kicked her out of my room. I told him she'd attack me. This is her attack. I also promised him I would warn him, so he could protect me as he demanded.

This is me breaking my promise.

Titus was wrong; I am not the most important thing. He is. I am nothing but a bridge to help him. Some bridges don't stand the test of time. It's okay.

Breathe in and get rid of the awful pain in your heart! As long as I collapse knowing he's on the other side. Away from Sable.

"Home," she echoes in an ominous tone. "I hope your memories of it are strong."

What's that supposed to mean? I tilt my head to rebuke her chuckle.

Sable kicks my shoe.

"You're a child." There, I gave you a reply. Not what you wanted? Too bad.

A sprinkle of her spit rains over my face as she says, "You always thought you were better than me." Her balled fist swings like a pendulum at her side.

"I never wanted to be better." I wipe the moisture off my cheek. "I wanted to be nothing like you, Sable," I coldly state. "Different. Opposite. You forced me to be good because your heart is so evil." I smirk as I pretend to inspect my nails.

This conversation is making me filthier than growing the farm did.

"You think you are so wise and sly?" I press my palm to my heart. "You made me, Sable. This is all your doing. There is no one else to blame." I grin. "You made your own worst enemy. The question is why? But you're not strong enough to answer that."

Oh yes, you're seething. All your weapons are aimed at me. Good. That's what I want. Attack me and not Titus.

"You always had everyone's love. Father's. Everett's," she sneers.

That's not why you hate me. That's your cover. I'll bite.

"And you chose their hate and distrust. We each made our beds.

Mine is warm with their affections; yours is cold with their apprehensions. It was your doing."

This will be the longest day of my life. I know it. I'm so exhausted I don't even know how I'm standing, but I numbly am, as I try to get to the bottom of what is happening.

"You made your path." I step to the side. "You carved the way out as a child when you tried to kill me. You chose your fate. No one else is to blame."

"And you made yours!" She looks over her shoulder at the castle. "A queen without a voice. You always chose to hide."

"Your mistake is thinking that is a weakness. A child kicks and screams. An adult weighs their options."

"Do you feel strong, sister?" she cackles. "You have nothing but the crown on your head. Your dear brother is dead. Your husband might warm your bed, but he chooses to set fire to others."

I tuck my hair behind my ear, remaining poised to irk her. "That's a mercy, not a misfortune. I want nothing from Galen."

"Nothing?" She raises a brow and steps in my path again. "You love him."

"Love?" What's she playing at? "I love Galen in the same sense I love you." I roll my shoulders back, preparing for this battle that will end with one of us hurt or defiled.

Her eyes narrow. Here it comes.

I slip on the shield I was forced to build as a child. Unmoving.

"All those times you fucked each other, it was in your bed. Not his," she states.

That's... true.

"Do you ever wonder why?" Her eyes are wide as nets cast into the sea, ready to catch me by surprise because, like most prey, I never suspect the predator will strike from above. We always think the chase is behind us.

It's in front. Like Everett's plans have been.

"I'll tell you, so we don't keep the mage waiting." She glances down and smiles at her body. "It was because I was in Galen's bed waiting for him."

My eyes snap to Galen. He's still talking to the mage, grinning and laughing, no doubt seducing.

He slept with my twin. Why am I not shocked?

I knew the beast he was when I first welcomed him into my bed.

We women always think we can change a man. Men like Galen don't change, and they're too clever to try to change women like me, so they cage us instead. It's slow. They know if they do it in haste, we'll fight back. So they gradually strip us, then seduce us. They wait until they have layers peeled back so they can steal our hearts.

Do I feel dirty? Yes. I chose to fuck him. I tried to make the marriage work. I was bored and had the audacity to think I could behave like a man—that I could sleep around for fun—without developing feelings.

I was wrong.

I do feel. Appalled, furious, vengeful, regretful. A little relieved I never fell in love with him now that I know he fucked Sable.

Galen doesn't feel this way. Men move on; they don't argue. They settle for higher ground while we women kick and scream and claw away at our mistakes.

Women think back; men think forward.

I force down a gulp and smack a smirk on my face. It doesn't reach my eyes. Sable sees that.

"You say that with pride," I respond. "If that is the truth, then you were scraps. Leftovers. People make the mistake of boasting about spoils of war, Sable. The true merit is in winning the trophy before it is passed around and soiled. I was the trophy, Sable. You were the spoils, passed around from Galen's bed and to his men's, no doubt."

My tongue tingles. I feel bad this is what has become of my twin, but I remember how dreadful and evil she is, and I'm not surprised. She is me in another reality if I had made all the wrong choices.

Sable closes the distance; her silken dress flows in the air like a wave of terror. The tip of her nose nudges mine. I don't move. I can endure the dirty, evil version of myself.

She can't.

"I fucked him," she hisses. "He slept with me more often than he fucked you. *Me*. I warmed his bed."

"Thank you," I reply. *Smile wider. There, she believes you.*

My happiness is a trick, a rainbow. Just a reflection. Not real and concrete like the sun, like my inner feelings, which are the furthest from a smirking glow.

The angry vibrations in her chest cause mine to solidify. Did she think I'd snap and attack her? Give Galen a reason to lock me in my room and allow his court to gossip that I've gone feral?

Reaching up, I cup her cheek. "Did you think I would cry, Sable?" I playfully tap her nose, making her feel smaller.

She jerks back. Her hand reaches for her dagger.

I arch a brow. "Do it. Come on, you know you want to, and now you know how much I want it all to end. Grant me the mercy of not having to see your face again," I snicker. I've trapped her. She knows it. If she kills me, I win. If she doesn't, I still win.

She looks at all the people watching and tries to compose herself by pretending to adjust her belt.

"You have always wanted what I had. It's not the first time you've had my scraps. What was his name..." I pretend to forget for a moment. "Oh yes, Claude. You slept with him after I did. He told you it was over; he wanted me back. You killed him, but his family was rather influential." I raise my hand to rub my jaw.

She flinches, but I'm nowhere near finished.

"They tried to start an uprising. Father killed them all; well, he ordered *you* to. He wanted to train your death magic. Father had hoped you could kill them within minutes, but you failed. It took you five days because you were weak. Five days of rotting, decaying flesh. That dungeon smelled so dreadful that Father didn't venture down there to see your final masterpiece. How does it feel to know you were commissioned to make art, but then it was never gazed upon, never hung on the wall to be praised? That's got to be worse than never selling a piece of art at all." I let my attack sink in before I continue.

"You know what I learned from your failures? You think your magic is death. Death doesn't slumber like your magic needs to. You're just rot."

She shakes her head, lost in a red-faced fury. "Death comes in many shapes and forms. I am death!"

"No," I reply calmly. "You're just rot, and that doesn't sound so scary." I continue, "Did Father tell you he forced me to try to bring them back, but it didn't work?"

Suspicion marks her brow. She's wondering why I'm admitting my failure.

I remember that night. I tried so hard to bring them back. I almost killed myself in the process. Everett stormed in and pulled me away. He and my father fought. Everett walked away with a physical scar and I with a mental one.

The truth is, my twin *is* stronger than I am. Death and rot are more powerful than life. Life is wind. It wrestles, roars, and tries to erode what stands in its way. Eventually, it must bow down to the other elements.

Death, oh that terrible, unstoppable beast, is water; it can rise up and rip through towns like a plague. It can seduce men, who are lost in the hot sands; it can also be calm and content as it waits to claim you —to rot you.

I've been as angry as a howling wind at times, knowing that Sable could kill another with her magic. She just needed to make contact with them long enough.

No matter how hard I try, I can't bring someone back from death.

I heal. Those seeds weren't dead; they were sleeping, so it was easy to shake them awake again.

My magic has limits.

Sable's does not.

Sable slinks back, a snake ready to strike. The ground under her feet turns shades of sickly green as she pours her savage rot into the soil. "I'm going to take everything from you."

"You said I had nothing," I rebuttal. "Looks like you need to make new goals." Chills run up my spine. Wind dances over the sweat on my brow, trying to cool me.

"You have no idea what goals I have. Everett was always a step ahead, halting me." Sable brushes invisible dirt off her shoulder. "Now I'm free, and there is nothing you can do to stop me." She aims her nose, like the tip of an arrow at my heart. "I will watch you take your last breath with a smile on my lips, Selene. The world you love, the people you adore, our home, these stupid kingdoms—those are what I will take from you. From everyone who doubted me."

"You'd need an army to take so much," I reply.

"And I shall have one."

"Your loins will be very chafed with the amount of fucking you're going to have to do, Sable. Even then, you will fail because there is no army big enough to take every kingdom."

"You're right." She turns her back to me, then she looks over her shoulder and whispers, "That's why I will make one."

I watch as she strolls over to my husband. Erik and Victor follow her like hounds, chomping at the bit to please their master.

Make an army?

That's impossible... unless you had a rune that could force control over people.

Snap! Swoosh! Bang!

The mage opens the portal; Galen glances my way. Sable slips on a matching pair of silk gloves. A vampire soldier hands Erik a large crate made of old wood crudely nailed together.

"What's that?" I shouldn't show interest, but what does it matter now?

"King Galen told you!" Sable shouts. "Father wants the bodies of his nobles back." She taps the crate.

Horror has me staggering back.

Sable wins this round.

Galen actually looks remorseful as he lowers his eyes to me and takes three steps forward.

"You..." I know what's in the box. "You burned them!" Sable is bringing back their ashes.

Fae bury their dead. It's an atrocious crime to desecrate a dead body. To burn the skin from the bones, to watch the vessel of the person become absolutely nothing. Ash that will soon be watered down and mixed with the dirt. Dirt!

Galen steps closer. "It was Sable's suggestion," he acknowledges.

"Sable..." A cold laugh escapes my lips. "Does Sable have a dick she wields as her scepter? Does she wear Blackthorn's crown on her wicked head? You are the king!" I roar as I belittle him in front of his guards. I glare at him through hooded, spiteful eyes. "Or did you forget that when you fucked her? Was she the one bending you over because it sure looks like it!"

His face pales, then reddens as he glares at her. Whispers start to spread among his men.

"Yes." I nod. "She told me," I state. "You're not the first king she fucked, Galen, but you are the first one foolish enough to hand her an army."

He flashes his fangs. "I gave her nothing but my cock, Selene, enough of the dramatics." He bats his lashes. "Things could have been different had you just bent a knee."

"Oh yes, it's always the woman's fault. That case might be true when I am the one hovering over your dead body, my dear, sweet husband."

"Good," he runs his tongue over his fangs. "We are back to our typical banter."

You stupid fool! "I did bend a knee to you. I was foolish enough to suck your cock, too." I step closer and allow my lips to glide over his earlobe. "Do you know what I noticed when I looked up at you? Weak men only feel strong when others bow down. An intelligent man knows his true strength comes from those he allows to stand by his side. A crown does not make a king. Remember that when someone knocks the precious metal from your head!

"Mark my words, Sable does not need to steal your crown; you're handing it to her by allowing her to leave."

For a moment, he glances at Sable as she approaches the portal. Galen can stop this. Order Sable to remain here. Instead, he shouts, "Leave, Sable." He waves her off.

She hesitates, then smirks at me again before she disappears with the ashes of our nobles.

I close my eyes and rest my head in my hands. Father won't forgive this.

That's why Galen agreed.

He's so fucking thirsty for another war. A war to end all wars, because it won't stop with my people. It will spread over these lands like a disease. As Galen and my father fight, Sable will be hunting down the runes; it all makes sense.

Sable coaxed this, planted the seeds as she fucked Galen.

She needed them distracted so she could figure out how to bring the runes back into the world and make her army!

That's not all. Sable knows I'll hunt her down and try to stop her. So she needs protection, distance, but also an army! She'd never find one here, so she had to return home so she could... take my father's.

She's going to kill him!

I rush forward and grab Galen's collar. "What have you done?" I scream as I shake him.

He grabs my hands with an iron grip. "They're just dead bodies."

"Think beyond the bodies, you fool! There is a reason my father sent Sable here, away from him! He knew how deadly she was, how conniving and evil! If he killed her, his people would think he's mad. And no man of merit would wed her! He knew it was a matter of time before she tried to grab his crown, so he sent her away so he could look for a new heir. But you just sent her back! You just handed her an empire that will tear yours down."

His smile is deliberately slow, like the sails of a massive fleet encroaching upon a land—a kingdom about to be thrown into the passions of death and war.

"I know," he answers.

CHAPTER
THIRTY

SELENE

Have you ever heard news that was so disturbing it made you fall into chaos? Following Everett's passing, I did. I feel the ground stolen from under my feet again as Galen looks into my eyes. This time, I can't fall. Titus needs me.

"I know exactly what Sable seeks," Galen purrs, his cool breath fans over my clammy cheek as he cups it.

His admission is startling, and if I were not in such a state of shock, I'd commend him for his deception. It wasn't just his handsome face that attracted me. I knew he was conniving, and in my sick and twisted mind, that equaled strength and shelter to me.

An honest man might love your heart, but he can't protect it. A man like Galen, one who is always ten steps ahead, steals your heart and locks it away.

I thought that meant I'd be safe. So I gave in, kissed him, and welcomed him into my bed. I never loved him, but I gave him my heart, allowed him to wrap it in steel walls. Cold walls. I welcomed the numbness because it kept me blind, deaf, and dumb to all his affairs. To the man he truly was.

If I had a daughter, would I raise her the same way I was raised?

Like any parent who wants to see their child grow old, I suppose I'd tell her to be numb because that is better than feeling.

Galen glides his thumb along my jawline. "Sable wanted a crown and an army. Mine is spoken for, but your father's... let's face it, Selene," he laughs, "without your brother, your father has no heir. It's only a matter of time before one of his nobles kills him. So I thought, why not send Sable back to get his crown for me?"

I feel like a branch on a tree whose trunk is riddled with a fungus that is slowly slithering up it, chomping away at the bark and slowly exposing it to the treacherous winds and rains of the world. With each truth Galen speaks, more of my bark—my shields—decay. Soon, I'll be exposed, soft and easy for him to carve into whatever trinket he wants, just as a woodcarver molds wood.

"Sable will never hand over my father's crown, army, or lands. The fae will never be pawns under a vampire king."

"I know," he tugs on my bottom lip before he finally drops his hand. "They will be pawns under *my* puppet."

I blink, freeing myself from the confusion. "You think you can use Sable? You're a bigger fool than I thought," I sneer as I lash out and grab his jaw. He lets me touch him, but he stiffens as I lean closer. "She's. Using. You." I push my words into his mouth as I hover over it. "Your crown, your castle, your lands, your army! She will take it all from you."

The corner of his eyes wrinkles.

"It's going to be so easy." I shove him away from me as I step back. "It's all about the long game, isn't that right, Galen? Sable has played you." I exhale a grin. "She's about to shove what you thought was your medicine down your throat, but instead of healing you, she tricked you. It's not your own medicine. It's poison."

I shake my head, look him up and down. "You won't survive this."

Before I turn, I watch my words hit home. Every step Galen has taken is now in question, every future move uncertain.

I turn and begin to walk away. I expect Galen to grab me, to rebuke what I spoke.

He doesn't.

No footsteps close in.

That means he's worried, truly worried he fucked up.

Good. When he's plotting how to take down Sable, I will be working on this mission Everett died for.

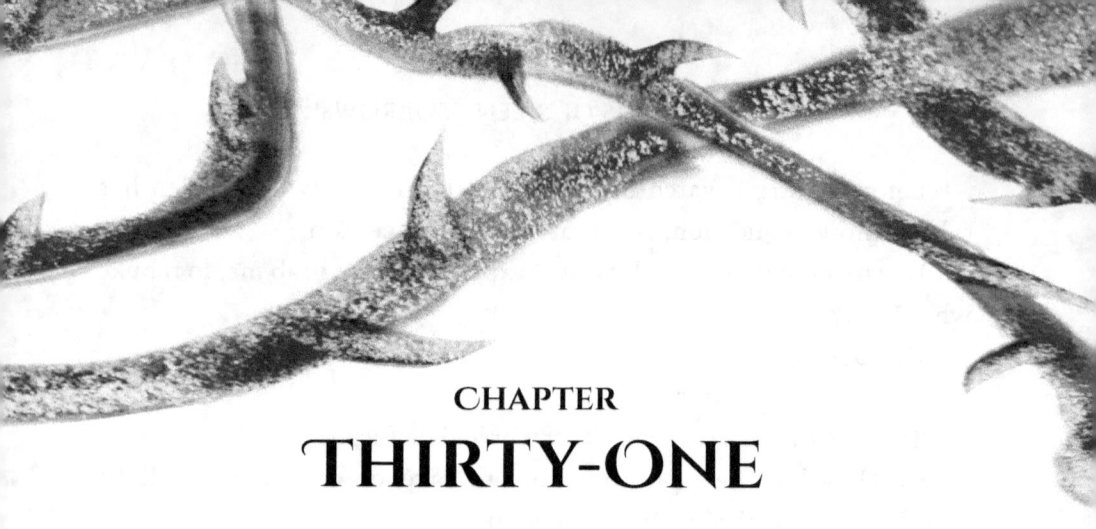

CHAPTER
THIRTY-ONE

TITUS

No, that looks like shit! A groan escapes me as I sweep my hair to the side. Do I look mangy with hair this long? It's been long since my last pre-battle shave.

What the fuck am I doing? When did I start caring about how my hair looked?

Before I turn, I push my hair back to the other side; then I grab my sword—the sword Galen gifted me—and strap it onto my hip. I hate the feeling of its weight.

I like *my* sword. I trust my sword.

I don't want a gift for killing. I want freedom.

I want his *wife*.

"Holy fuck!" I seal my eyes shut, thankful Galen can't read minds. I'd be killed slowly, flayed alive, and kept breathing so I could feel the birds picking me apart.

Where the fuck is Tristen?

He didn't come home after he went to search the library. He either found a hot librarian, or he picked up a book and tried to read it, then he remembered how he struggled to read as a kid, so he went drinking.

Fresh air washes over my forehead as I approach the window, peering outside. Shit, it's a nice view from the queen's tower. Gardens and the village outskirts are visible. Galen's tower has a view of the front gates and the barracks. He's always got his eye on his men and their abilities.

I roll my shoulders and tip my head back. This is my favorite time, when the moon yields to the rising sun, and darkness and light coexist, each submissive so they can look upon each other.

Peace.

My days start like this now. Tristen and I wake up early. We eat breakfast with the other guards, report for duty, Selene and I train, but unlike the sun and moon sharing the sky, my time with Selene is a constant battle of denial.

Our survival depends on following the example set by the sun and moon.

They must keep a far distance, for if they collide, it would be the end of so many things.

Clunk! I jerk as the door swings open. My hands slip free from the window ledge. Tristen walks in with tired and messy hair. I scan his neck for signs of his hookup, but instead I find clean, unmarked skin and no blood staining his collar.

"Where have you been?" I grunt. Being part of the queen's guard means he can't spend all night fucking around.

Instead of Tristen's usual swagger and goofy grin, he's pale, and... is that what his serious face looks like?

"What happened?" I take a cautious step forward. My worn-out boots feel different, unused, like they need to be broken in. Each day feels like this.

Tristen kicks the door behind him and licks his lips. He closes the distance and hugs me. My breath is knocked out of my lungs in a whoosh. He presses his lips to my ear and whispers, "I found someone in the library."

I exhale, pulling back slightly so I can look him in the eyes.

He hurries to add, "It's not what you think. I wasn't hooking up with a hot librarian." He pulls me back in for a hug. I stiffen and float in his arms like a wooden log tossed into an ocean. I allow him to cling to me.

Reaching up, I hug him back, pressing the tips of my fingers into his muscles so I can feel every inch of my little brother. We hug before battle, so I know what this means.

He thinks we're about to go to war. He fears a final goodbye, just as I do.

I smell his hair, catching the scent of soap. Little curls start to twist at the ends of his strands. I look at the color, shades of black, ink spilled onto a white page; some parts are drier and darker, while others are a shade less saturated.

I try to remember what the muscles on his back feel like.

He's strong. He won't be killed today.

I won't allow it.

That's a lie I tell myself before we separate. We try to stay together on the battlefield, but sometimes it's impossible. It's like trying to spot a droplet of water in a vast lake. It's all the same.

Enemies and friends blur into one giant body. You can't select a specific droplet; you just drink it all down. Chug and pray you survive and don't choke. You keep drinking even when your thirst has been quenched. You keep fighting and killing because if you stop, if you resist swallowing, you're dead.

You feel everything yet nothing at all, because you're drowning.

I squeeze him tighter. I miss the days when I was taller and he was the size of a child I could pick up and hold in my arms. I miss tackling him as Nero and Ryker helped me. I miss how Ember would giggle, along with Cyrus as we played childish games that children never should have played. Games of chase that were secretly teaching us how to hunt a target.

Now, we stand as men, trying to hold each other without showing it weakness.

His hand slips up to my neck, feeling my details as I did his.

"Let's go get Selene," I whisper in his ear.

I step back, but he grabs my wrist. "Are you sure you trust her?" He speaks in a fast whisper that sounds like a river overflowing from its banks, pushing and carving out new paths that it shouldn't venture down. "It's not too late to run, Titus. Before bonds set in."

His eyes sweep over me like a baker rubbing flour onto a wooden block so the dough doesn't stick.

My mouth dries. "I can't run from this."

He tugs me closer. "You can! I know what we need, where to look." His eyes widen with a restless excitement. "You and I can go. We don't need Selene. Fuck! You don't have to find the Vitalis; you can master Everett's magic, live with it. You don't have to save the world, Titus." He shakes my shoulders.

My eyes narrow with caution. "What did you find in the library?"

He leans closer so the tips of our noses almost touch. "Everything."

His magic radiates, wrapping us in shadows—shades of grey so dark I can only see the whites of his eyes—eyes that are anxious and terrified for me. His shadows swirl, pushing and rubbing over my exposed skin, eliciting a panicked sensation. "I hope love is worth all the sacrifices."

"I'm doing this because I love you!" I reply. "If I have the chance to make the future safe for you and our family, I'll give my life to make it happen."

My body flinches at the rapid peeling back of his magic. He's pissed, but loyal to me. He walks to the door and opens it. "Queen Selene isn't in her room. King Galen just left with her."

My heart falls to the floor. I rush forward and grab him. "How do you know? Where did they go?" Selene should still be sleeping for another hour.

Tristen shrugs as he looks down the hallway that exposes us. "I went to her room first to beg her to force you away from this path. To save you. And as for where Galen took her, I have no idea. He's her husband. He can take her wherever he wants."

His eyes hit me like a shovel pressing into soft soil. The impact is felt as he heaves layers of me away, making sure the facts sink in.

Tristen grabs my shoulder. "I will fight by your side, brother, but you and I both know it's a battle that will kill someone. Are you ready or that?" He steps back. "Think about it. I'm going to get breakfast. Something tells me we're both going to need extra blood rations today."

I want to race after him. I need to know what happened in the library, but we can't speak safely until we're in a spelled room. Instead, I rush toward Selene's room.

I open the door to find her bed empty. My nose flares as I catch a fresh scent of Galen's magic. Flames come forth, trying to replace the impression he made in the air. I find a pathway of roses he left from the door to her bed.

Flick! I shoot out flames one by one, burning the flowers, not caring about my actions.

Tristen is right. I'm losing control of my reactions.

I fall to my knees and close my eyes.

Where did Galen take Selene?

My chest feels raw and tight as I clean up the mess. I grab a bucket of water and toss it over the floor, ensuring the scent of fire can't be smelt. Then, I open the window and allow fresh air inside. I walk to her bed and find myself slowly lowering my face to her pillow as I inhale her scent.

My skin starts to burn as my magic pulses again.

Tristen is right. I'm playing with fire, but that's my magic. I can control the flames.

That's the lie I tell myself.

I am sure a mating mark will appear any day now, and when that happens... gods help us all.

~

Breakfast meats, fresh bread, soft-churned butter, and of course, pitchers of fresh blood from the donation banks are piled down the center of the dining tables. The aroma in the air makes my fangs tingle. The answers I seek are interwoven into morning gossip.

I spot Tristen as he raises a cup and drinks. His eyes lock on mine as I approach.

"Morning, Thomas," I say as I join Tristen and some of the other men.

Thomas served under me; he was smitten with Ember but lacked the courage to pursue her. He's proficient with a bow, preferring it over his sword, which is why he is usually stationed as an archer.

"General." Thomas and the others dip their chins as I join them. Leaning forward, he confides, "You finally got a day off." He grabs the closest pitcher of blood and pours me a cup.

"Day off?" I question, raising a brow.

"Don't tell us you've gotten lazy since you follow a fae around all day," Roy jokes bitterly. He replaced me as Commander, and I can't stand him. He thinks the louder her shouts, the more powerful he looks. "What's it like guarding her? Do fae women gossip, drink tea, and eat cake all day long, too? Must be nice to have a laid-back position now."

"She is not a woman; she is your queen."

"She's a fae," he spits under his breath.

I press my tongue against my fangs. "Jealousy makes you see red, Roy, and in battle, you need to see every color. The most dangerous enemy is usually lurking in the spectrum, not just one shade."

The air shifts as Roy and I lock eyes.

Tristen clears his throat. "Thomas was telling me King Galen and Queen Selene are just returning. A mage portaled them in and out of the kingdom this morning," he adds as he stabs a pork sausage and slaps it onto his plate.

"Where?"

"Shouldn't you be there as her guard?" Roy counters.

"I'm sure the king can handle his wife, Roy."

"I wonder if he handles them both in his bed? Imagine twins! Fuck, that's hot," Carter joins the conversation. He chews his eggs so loudly you'd think he was grinding down a leathery steak.

"They're fae," Roy grunts in revulsion.

Carter shrugs. "I see a woman with legs that can open."

Thomas rolls his eyes as he adds, "As if either one of you had a chance with Princess Sable."

"Please," Carter spits. "Sable fucks like a man. I've heard the gossip."

"She fucks men who can give her something in return," Roy barks. Sounds like Sable turned him down. "All you can give her is a limp dick and a headache."

Carter smacks Roy, who gets the last laugh.

Tristen's knee nudges mine. "Princess Sable is returning home with the ashes of the nobles who tried to kill you."

My blinks are rapid as I decode his words. Sable being gone is a great thing. One less snake. "Ashes?" I repeat.

"Burned them to a crisp." Roy laughs as he licks the blood off his lips.

"I'm sorry, I don't understand."

Tristen kicks me from under the table.

"Ashes are easier to transport." Thomas scrapes butter over his toast; the sound is like a tormentor's violin, a prelude to pain.

"Galen burned the nobles," I murmur. The facts are like thunder clouds on a day you wished for sun. It takes my mind time to allow them to penetrate.

Selene will be furious. Devastated.

It's another punishment.

"They tried to kill you," Roy adds as he lifts a brow.

"They are fae," I whisper as I grab my cup. "If we lose our ability to respect the traditions of death, then how do you expect us to value life? He should have returned the bodies, not burned them."

The table grows silent. Good, let them think.

"King's orders." Roy's lips form a thin line.

I hold his stare. I feel Tristen's hand slide down his side and rest on his dagger.

I want to rip out my tongue, but instead I say, "The king knows best."

Roy continues to look at me, then he moves. Thomas jerks, having sensed the tension. Roy lifts his cup in the air and toasts, "To the king!"

"To the king!" the room yells back.

I raise my cup, having no choice. Blood fills my mouth. It takes a moment for me to realize that the taste of it isn't normal. Instead of energizing and relaxing me, it's bitter, salty, and metallic.

Spew! I spit it out, covering Roy's face in the blood.

Tristen lurches as he stands, his dagger half pulled out.

I cough and gag as everyone grows silent. A room full of fellow soldiers watching and waiting for me to tell them why the fuck I just spit out a cheer to the king. I stand and try to catch my breath.

Why did it taste like that?

Glancing to the side, I see the truth in Tristen's eyes.

Fuck! It's happening.

Lying quickly to save my throat, I yell, "Poison."

Soldiers stand, and conversations erupt.

"They tried to kill him again!"

"The fae will never stop!"

"Spit it out! Don't drink it!"

Great, now they think this was another attempt by the Fae. That's not what I wanted. The panic spreads like wildfire.

"Poison! They poisoned our blood!"

"I don't feel good. Help!"

"Mine tasted fine. It's from the same pitcher," Roy grunts loudly as he stares into his cup.

Thomas grabs the pitcher and lifts it to his nose. *Sniff, sniff!* His eyes shift slowly towards mine, resembling a nail that might hit my coffin or miss and land on the side.

"Smells odd to me, too!" he shouts. His eyes soften as he lowers his chin the smallest amount, a silent gesture he's on my side.

I wonder how many other needles in this haystack share my thoughts and feelings. How many men and women are getting tired of Galen's disrespect towards the living and the dead?

Clang!

Pitchers are tipped over; soldiers try to gag themselves in fear they have been drinking poison. The lie spreads like salt, drying up the truth and making every thought tainted and vengeful.

News of this will spread to the king, but with so many soldiers claiming the blood tasted off, I should be safe. For now...

CHAPTER
THIRTY-TWO

SELENE

I don't know how I got here, but broken things tend to scatter as they crumble.

I left a part of me at the entrance to Blackthorn, a few more pieces as I forced my legs to walk up the long entrance, through the markets, and then the houses until I reached the castle itself.

More of me was left behind as I walked to my training field; some parts I didn't need, others I don't know how I would survive without.

The sun hits my face like a mother's hand cupping my cheek, forcing my eyes up to look upon it. My knees sink into the fresh grass. The scent of soil and wildflowers fills my nose. It brings no peace. This feels like the end, a final goodbye to everything I once knew.

I fear I will soon know the true meaning of sacrifice; Everett always hinted he and I would find out. He paid with his life.

What shall I pay with?

"Selene!" Titus shouts as he sprints through the path that leads to my field.

"Slow down!" Tristen barks.

"Selene." His voice is calmer now that he's spotted me. His relief is a gust of wind onto a flame; at first, you think it silences the fire that is burning you. Then you realize relief is a trick. The wind actually provided the fire fuel.

Titus, Tristen, and I are trapped like lambs sentenced to slaughter.

I sink into the ground, finally shattering. Now I can pretend.

Pretending is an ability that has helped women survive their lives. Pretending to be somewhere else, with someone else. The world can take everything from us: our freedom, youth, material items, even those we love, but our ability to daydream is the most precious.

Pretending allows us to see those we lost, live a life that we will never be born into, plot out escapes that will never happen.

Dreams.

When we lose that, all hope turns white, not black. You see, darkness is consuming, but in those shaded layers, you still have your senses. As a matter of fact, everything is heightened; you hear more and sense greater depths. You still have hope you will find your way out.

Light is blinding, deafening. It doesn't consume; it eradicates and strips every sense. In light, you see and sense no depths, only more light.

You are its prey.

You hear nothing, because light is faster. It's the enemy that will always outrun you. It travels faster than darkness, faster than everything. Therefore, it will always arrive first, and those who stake their claim first have the higher ground.

Light is a warrior we can not best.

So, yes, in the darkness of my life, I can still daydream, but I fear that soon there will be no more questions, no darkness, only answers and light. No more dreams, just reality about what Galen and Sable have done.

And yes, what Everett has done, too.

"Selene! What's happened?" Titus shadows me like a cloud, his face etched with a worry that feels like thunder. "Tristen, go get a healer," he orders. His jaw sets into a state of firmness that rivals a diamond's strength.

"If you find a healer who can repair time, then so be it, but if not, then stay," I reply in a tone that resembles bones. Nothingness.

Titus drops to his knees. His brown eyes push into my green ones, like the earth trying to tell a dying tree, 'It's okay; I'm here to cradle you until you find your roots again.'

Yet every part of me has been sawed off, branches slowly ripped away, used as someone else's wood to warm them as they survive.

But what about me, the tree with no limbs left?

I can spread my roots, but I have nothing left to nourish, no branches. Just hollowed out memories and hopes.

What's the point?

That's why trees fall. Sometimes there is just no more point in weathering this world.

"Selene," Titus whispers life into my name. I can't grasp it. The brown of his earthy eyes feels like a steaming cup of chai trying to soothe me as he reaches for me. "You're hurt." He glides his fingertips along my jaw.

That touch is so... dangerous. It can cause wars.

"Titus," Tristen warns as he comes into view.

I close my eyes and push my cheek against the soil. If I had more magic left, I would release it, allowing the grass to grow around us. A small detail of beauty amidst all the terrors.

Tears flee from the corners of my eyes as if those tiny drops can water the dirt and bring forth the life I just dreamed about.

Two hot hands grab my face like a pillow, gently pressing into my comfort.

"I am hurt beyond repair," I whisper. "I have failed." I squeeze my eyes shut.

"No, you haven't," Titus responds. My eyes open as he pulls my upper body onto his lap. My muscles melt like metal thrown into a forge eager to be molded into something beautiful. "Tell me what has happened," he demands. He flashes his fangs like the string of my bow ready to fire.

I sense Tristen sitting down; the sunlight darkens as he covers us in his shadow. Tristen's eyes differ from Titus's; they're a colder brown, like dirt lost in frozen tundras, with streaks fossilized grey—memories he wishes to keep buried.

He scans our surroundings. He can see through his shadows. Interesting.

Titus pushes my hair off my face. "You've used all your magic. You feel fevered. You made yourself sick," he acknowledges.

My lip tugs into a sad smirk. "I'd ask how you know that, but we both know how. It's a bush we have beaten so we can walk over it. We chopped it down to the ground, but we forgot about the roots, so it continues to grow."

"I never forgot, Selene. I allowed the roots to grow deep. I knew the cost of uprooting them was one I could not afford," Titus acknowledges. Misery hugs his face like morning dew clinging to grass.

Another tear slides down my cheek.

Titus catches it with his thumb and brings it to his lip. "You are my mate." He swallows my tears.

I'm a coward who has lost everything, so I close my eyes and nod, unable to speak; if I admit this, that means I can lose him, too.

Titus breathes a sigh of relief that isn't shared by his brother, whose shadows darken.

"We have too many problems," I eventually reply. I allow my dreams to fester behind my closed eyes, in the darkness where they are safe from the light of reality.

"Mating bonds are a gift, not a curse." His intake of breath is sharp.

"Tell my husband that."

"We're not the first couple who have had a mate bond destroy vows," Titus gently offers. "If Galen cherished you, I'd feel guilty. I would run and let the two of you try to work things out. That is not our fate. I will fight for you; if I have to steal you away from him, I shall. I will not linger in the shadows for much longer, Selene."

His words make me feel like a vast ocean separates us. I can't risk swimming out for fear I'll drown before I reach him. So, I remain trapped on my island of isolation as other boats sail by.

Tristen clears his throat. "I agree. We have too many enemies at the moment. This has to remain hidden until we can sort it out."

I open my eyes.

"Give us a minute, Tristen," Titus hisses. His eyes quarrel with his brother's.

"We have too much to tell her," Tristen counters. "We can't do this now."

"I need a minute alone with her."

Tristen walks to the edge of his shadows. "One minute can change the course of the future," he whispers his warning as he exits.

Titus cradles me in his chest. We've never been so close, so tightly knitted—like pages bound into a book. We could create such a beautiful story if we were born as different people. Instead, our book shall be short-lived, never given a happily ever after.

"You're my mate," Titus voices with a pride that has me sitting up, still cradled in his lap. My eyes peer at his hands; hands that killed my brother, hands that are trying too hard to save me.

"I felt the bond the moment we locked eyes," I admit. "I thought the pull was my thirst for vengeance, but that quickly turned into a need for something else."

"Why didn't you say anything? Gods, Selene, you didn't even react to the bond. I thought I was going mad."

I bite down on my lip to stop it from trembling. "Some mate bonds are instantaneous, like a burst of energy. Others are seeds that must be planted and nourished. I tried not to water it; I tried to find the seed and uproot it. We can never be, Titus. I picked one thing to focus on— one thing to water and nourish—which was helping you, not loving you. We have a mission, Titus."

The leather covering his biceps flexes like an animal that instinctively jerks back from a deadly blow.

"I never said we didn't, but we're also mates." His fingers press into me. If there were ever a claiming hold, this would be it. "If we suppress love, then what is the point of saving our world? I know you want the world to think you're cold, but you forget that hidden underneath all the frozen layers can lie a volcano. Show me your fire. Stop worrying about burning me; I know how to control the flames or fan them."

My exhale sounds like a bruised laugh. "Our flame is on the verge of being extinguished. I'm suppressing them to save them, to save us, Titus. The world is crumbling." I grab his biceps and shake him. "Galen and Sable are winning. I don't know if that's how Everett intended it to play out. I don't know anything. I am merely a spectator watching a game that will affect me.

"I am rooting for players who carry my future on their backs. I have no choices or options because they have been made for me deceptively, just as Everett planned."

Titus's eyes darken, but my next words offer no light.

"I wish my brother sent you here to steal me away, so we could live happily ever after. Everett was selfless. His interests didn't bend so true love could bloom. We are trapped like dead bones long buried in the sands of time. Layers and layers of Everett's decisions continue to bear down upon us, like slabs of this forsaken land, shoving and trapping us deeper and deeper. We're nothing but creatures meant to play a specific role, so the future can evolve. Maybe one day someone will find our bones, uncover our story, and retell it."

Titus and I are cornerstones; we hold up everything.

If we remove ourselves and run away, then everything around us will crumble.

"A love like ours is worth fighting for," he confesses. He's never backing down. Titus is the type of man who runs into battle, chin high, sword outstretched, feet proud, spine stiff, ready to rebuke the impact; he fears not death but life without purpose.

I press my fingers over his mouth. "In my world, love is an hour-glass. Eventually, the sand will hit the bottom."

"Hourglasses can be turned back over. It can start again." He takes my hand and presses his lips to my palm. My thighs clench as my body purrs. The mating mark will appear in a matter of days or hours. It should be a thing of beauty, like a child. Something you protect and stand in awe of.

But this is life, and the world corrupts children; it takes something beautiful and precious and molds it into a shell of cruelty, a vessel into which it pours more ugly lies.

A mating mark would be a sure sign of Titus's death.

"This will all end." Titus's smile grows like the petals of a flower growing in a thunderstorm.

Does he know hail is about to batter him?

He continues, "I have so many answers to tell you. One day, I will turn our hourglass over, and we will start a new one. We will be free to love each other." He pulls me closer and then forces my chin up. "Let me kiss you."

My eyes drop to his lips. How badly I long to taste them, to have them touch my skin, kissing away all the invisible scars no one sees.

I shake my head. "How will we hide the mate mark?" They appear over each other's hearts. "I am married."

"You are not married. You are chained to a man who cheats and seeks to kill everything you love. Our bond is the key that unlocks you. Once the people see the mark, you'll be free of Galen. The laws permit it."

"You know he is a king who yields to no laws." I feel the blood drain from my cheeks as realization settles into my core. "It makes sense. Everett said you should be king, and now I know what he meant. He intended for you to kill Galen."

How do we kill a king and then unite the people so they trust us? How do we bring runes back into this world and have the strength to keep them safe from my twin?

How?

"I'll do what I must protect my mate. Hey," His hand slips behind my neck as he guides my face closer. "Right now, you're looking at a field that is covered in weeds. It's hard to envision where a garden will grow; we have to take it one patch at a time. One problem at a time.

Tristen is correct. We will sort everything out, and then lastly we will tackle this bond and Galen. Because I know what a mate bond means." He grins widely as he runs his nose along my jaw. "It means I have forever with you, so if I have to wait to kiss you, to make love to you, that's okay because, in the end, I will have you. Forever."

His lips brush over mine like a whisper.

"You make it sound so easy. You make victory certain," I breathe into him.

"It's not easy. I need you to know how hard it will be for me. Asking me not to kiss you is like telling a drowning man who sees shore not to kick and swim. It's forcing me to suffer, a burning cold suffocating death that fills my lungs; begging me to allow the water to replace the feelings I have for you." He shakes his head. "As if water could wash away what I feel."

He moves. Our first kiss burns into my cheek. I want to turn my face. I want his lips on mine, where they belong, not on the side, disguised as a friendship.

"Sometimes life is more peaceful under the surface, Titus. At least you can survive."

He presses our foreheads together. "Survive? You think denying what my heart wants is surviving? You think watching you shine in the light as I am trapped under the currents of our problems is surviving?"

He glides his fingers down my neck, finding my pulse point so he can cradle it.

"Don't you understand? I can't survive because I haven't begun living yet. Now that I have found you, everything is altered. Everything I thought I loved has shifted; everything that brought me joy is empty. Absolutely nothing compares to you, Selene. When I can openly admit you are my mate, that is the day I am born, and then I will fight to survive."

He leans close, teasing my lips as he presses his over mine again. "When I kiss you," his nostrils flare as he pulls away, "you will no longer be Galen's queen. You will be mine."

CHAPTER
THIRTY-THREE

SELENE

Shadows move like smoke over our skin as Tristen steps back into the protective cloud he made for us. I ought to distance myself from Titus, but I lean closer to my mate. It's so natural, like a branch arching to feel the sun so it can be nourished, grow, and thrive. But I can't flourish until I replant us, take us far away from this toxic soil, from Galen. We have to wait, be like Everett was, and think of the future of everyone and not just ourselves.

"Time's up." Tristen's eyes look at me accusingly before they turn to sorrow. He thinks I could have prevented this bond.

My eyes trace his shadows as they cling to him, curling around his limbs like cats purring in glee. I've only seen him use his shadows as a shield. I wonder how he uses them as weapons.

"We need to coordinate and plan the next step. Everything's moving too fast." Tristen rubs his neck. "All this crap—Sable leaving, Galen, and now this." He looks at Titus and me. "No offense, Selene," he pauses, "Actually, I'm glad to offend. Your brother's an asshole!"

"Tristen." Titus's grip on me tightens.

"He is. He was!" Tristen snaps as he corrects himself. "Why couldn't we have gotten a heads up like oh, sparks are going to fly, oh, and everywhere you turn is a spy I planted! I'm gonna kick you down, shove your face in the dirt. But don't worry because one of my spies will help you up!"

My ribs press into my lungs. Tristen speaks the truth. Everett's path both feeds and slaps you as you chew.

I look down at my hands, grasping Titus. As soon as Tristen lowers his shadows, we must let go. It should be easy to step back from Titus, like a drop of water leaving a glass. I know there is more of him. I will be with him all day, as he is my guard.

But over time, drop after drop, it gets harder. Soon, nothing will be left. I won't be able to let go of my mate.

"He's right. I don't know how long Galen will allow me to be here. I'm sure he suspects I'm in my room resting; when he hears I'm at my training field, he will force me back inside."

Tristen saunters forward and sits next to Titus. A cloud of his shadows remains, hugging his legs like a thin veil of protection. "King Galen has his hands full for a while. All his soldiers think their morning blood was poisoned." He glances at Titus, and if the shadows could growl in warning, his did.

"What?" My spine stiffens. Did Sable make her first attack against Galen?

Tristen juts his chin forward. "You gonna tell her or me?"

Titus scratches his sculpted jaw and replies, "I drank my morning blood, but... I accidentally spat it out."

I hold his hand tightly. "Why?" Is it the time-weaving magic? He's been doing well, finding ways to soothe it so it doesn't overtake him.

Has he mastered it? No, but he's getting better. We upped his blood intake to half the normal amount. We had been planning to start a new lesson this week. Instead of him soothing it, I wanted him to try to activate it. Learn to work alongside it.

"Because now that the mate bond is setting in, he can't drink blood." Tristen pushes his shadow towards me. Titus starts to wave them away, but I shock him when I reach a hand out, as one would toward a stray cat. Shadows curl around my fingers like velvet fur.

That's it. Learn to trust me.

Just when I think things are going well, Tristen blinks, the shadows press in and suddenly feel like hands. How did he do that?

Titus grabs my hand and puts it on his thigh. The shadows slither back. As Titus holds my hand, warmth surges up my arm and into my chest. My mouth dries, but other parts of me react oppositely.

"I can drink," Titus counters. "It's just that the taste is awful. Don't worry, I can get by. I'm not picky when it comes to food." He nods, but doesn't look me in the eye.

I glance at Tristen. "Is he telling me the truth?"

"Yes and no. Once mated, we can drink blood that isn't our mate, but most vampires can't swallow the taste. Why would they? Mated blood makes you much more powerful."

"But I am fae."

"Bonds change everything." Titus reaches out and tucks my hair behind my ear, allowing his fingertip to trace the curve of my pointed ear. His face takes on a glow of pride that makes me feel too much. "You're no longer toxic to me, Selene."

I wish you were right. I fear I'm still a poison, just in a different form.

"So you'll need to drink from me." My thighs press tightly together. "I've never been bitten," I whisper.

Titus's magic roars and purrs, and flames engulf our joined hands. I don't flinch; my mind fully trusts my mate. I am aroused by the notion of him biting me and feeding from me. It's like running down a hill at full speed. Exhilarating, a little scary because one off-balance step and you'll tumble down.

I don't want him to drink human blood. I want him to drink from me! He's mine. Mine.

Oh no... that chant will lock me in the holds of insanity until I give in.

I thrust my wrist out as if it were a tray of cookies. "Drink. We're hidden. Now is your chance to charge your magic."

Titus stares at my pulse, his pupils widening as his throat moves.

Tristen recoils. "Absolutely not!" He shoves my wrist away.

Titus bares his fangs at his brother. "Do not touch her." His voice reaches deeper depths as he peers at my pulse.

"You need to drink," I encourage.

"You're playing with a fire that will burn you, Selene," Tristen rumbles. "If he drinks from you, a mark will surely appear."

Titus's fangs sink into his lower lip. "He's right." He lowers my wrist, but this time, he places it on my lap.

I want your mark. I want your lips sucking my neck. I want you. "You need your magic in this den of vipers." I shake my wrist like it's a bone willing to risk the mark. Galen knows better than to try to seduce me now.

"Neither of you is thinking clearly. Stop touching!" Tristen moves quickly, trying to push us away from each other.

Clarity once again enters my mind. I lower my eyes in shame. Tristen is going to think I'm like my twin, ready to sleep around no matter the results. "It was the bond talking," I admit.

A strong, tender hand lifts my chin. "There's nothing to be ashamed of." Titus's eyes follow his hand, filled with longing. "I can drink the others' blood until we are free from this palace." He drops his hand and keeps a small space between us so the bond doesn't take over. "Bonded mates are feared for a reason. Our magic will be enhanced, which means Everett's magic will be stronger. I still need to understand it."

More magic sounds like a good thing. Why didn't Everett want us to be stronger at the start? Why must we wait until everything crumbles? What am I not seeing?

"I don't want you to worry. I'll tolerate the other blood for as long as I can. Then," his eyes float from my lips, to my neck, down my chest till my nipples harden, my abs tighten and my core throbs. "I shall drink from you. I'll make you mine."

Darkness mixes with the lust in his eyes. Titus wouldn't just sink his teeth into me; he'd spread me open wide, claim and mark every inch of me. I'd take it, wear it with pride, as one does a crown. I'd show the world my mate mark.

But I'm a fighter too. I'd claim a piece of him, and unlike an insecure man, Titus would let me take that piece and wear it proudly. No dress could hide the glow of having a mate. Galen would sense it right away.

My stomach plummets and then churns. Acid thickens my throat. I look at Tristen. "I know why Everett didn't warn us about the bond."

Tristan's gaze intensifies, and his shadows grow darker.

Titus would have devised a way to get me out, and I would have fled to my mate. "I was never meant to leave Blackthorn," I declare.

Titus's jaw clenches, his face becoming rigid. I hold my palm to his cheek until he relaxes.

Now, it's all clear to me. "Everett needed us to grow frustrated. He needed to turn you—a loyal warrior—against Galen. Scorned men flee, vengeful men plot. Everett said you'd be king because he needed you to steal Galen's crown. Drinking from me will make you strong enough to kill a king who has indulged in bloodlust. The only way to win the war for the runes is if we remove Galen from the picture."

Titus looks down, his gaze sweeping the floor, absorbing my words. He flips his palm over and studies his hand. He knows they will be soaked in blood again.

But there's more. It's not just about stealing a crown. "Everett's helping you get an army, because we will need one to keep the runes safe. Oh gods, the humans, the farm. It's all planned to give us an army bigger than my father's. So Sable can't win." I cover my mouth.

"Hey, hey, slow down," Titus grabs my shoulders and hugs me. The mate bond's purr quiets all my fear.

"What humans and farms?" Tristen leans closer.

I take a deep breath, then I tell them about the farm I helped build this morning, a guise for building a human army. I tell them of Sable and her plan to kill my father, how Galen knew and is plotting with her.

Titus listens quietly, taking it all in. Tristen suddenly slaps his thigh; his shadows swirl with excitement. "That's why Galen sent Ember, Ryker, Nero, and Cyrus to Lunestra! Think about it, Titus. Galen knew Sable would have opposition when she takes over, so he planted half his army near the border so they'd be close enough to aid her, but far enough away not to cause concern until the perfect moment."

"Wait, back up." I blink rapidly. "Who are Ember, Ryker, Nero, and Cyrus?"

"They are our family," Tristen replies defensively.

Titus nods.

Why didn't he tell me about his family? He didn't trust me. He thought I'd hurt them. "I'd never use them against you," I whisper.

"I know that now, but when we first met, I didn't. You told me to get Tristen out of here, but then we roped him in. I didn't want my other siblings to be caught in the crossfire. Especially with Sable lurking around."

My tongue scrapes my inner cheek, desperate for moisture, but nothing comes. I can't gulp, so I just nod. "I understand. Really, I do. You have to protect your family."

"You are part of my family now," Titus presses, his voice dropping, commanding me to listen.

Titus offers me more details, "They were raised with us. We've always been together; however, Galen sent a lot of his troops to Lunestra when the war ended. Following the instructions, our family went there, and Tristen and I went to Blackthorn. We couldn't understand why Galen sent them to Lunestra. If the war ended, why send your army to conquer more fae lands?"

"Galen would be a fool to provoke the night court."

"Court or kingdom?" Tristen's brows arch in honest curiosity.

I lower my voice, fearing that just speaking the Night Court's name will bring a bad omen upon us. I look over my shoulder, ensuring Tristen's shadows conceal us. "Those beyond our borders refer to our lands as the two kingdoms of the fae. You have my father's kingdom of Solaria and the kingdom of Lunestra, whose king or queen isn't known. But before we started adopting your titles of kingdoms and crowns, the fae lands were divided into two courts.

"Solaria is the Day Court. Lunestra, the Night Court, is sheltered by the mountains, The Cradle of Darkness. Their peaks are tall enough to block out the clouds. Beyond the mountains lies a magical veil. For none can enter and those inside rarely leave. If they do they can never return home. The veil stops everything."

"What are they hiding?" Titus inquires, furrowing his brow in thought.

I tilt my head. "Many things. Or so I was told as a child. I heard they protect the gifts and tools the gods left. Their land is one of peculiar, magical beauty. I heard their trees make music; they communicate. Their flowers glow at night. The fae there are thought to have different origins of magic, strange powers, because they eat from the lands rich with god magic. But these are stories; I do not know what truly is held there. All I know is there is no way inside that veil."

"Dragon eggs?" Tristen offers. You can practically see the money in his eyes. If a dragon egg were found, he would be richer than most kings.

I shrug. "That is one rumor since many of the fae and dragon riders had relations. However, that rumor is centuries old; who knows if dragons existed? There are no dragon bones."

"That's because dragon bones disintegrate once the dragon dies," Tristen argues. He sounds like an excited boy who wishes to go on an adventure.

"Or clever words spun to hide the fact there were never dragons," I argue.

"I'm going to assume everything we thought was a fairytale was once true," Tristen responds with a gleam in his eyes.

"I... I would agree," I answer. "It's hard to change how we think."

"Did Galen ever mention Lunestra to you?" Titus asks.

I shake my head. "I think it is safe to assume Tristen's idea is correct. Galen placed his army there as a precaution to help Sable.

Above all, Galen always expects something in return. He's warning her that he's close enough to strike if she betrays him."

"I've told you what I know." I look at Tristen. "Now tell me what you found in the library," I demand. With all the puzzle pieces, we can plan to seize Galen's kingdom and prevent Sable from obtaining the runes.

Tristen runs a hand through his hair, paints on a handsome grin, and then performs as he retells. I don't know what is longer, the facts or his comments about this old vampire's aged appearance. A few weeks ago I would have pulled out my dagger and told him to cut to the chase. The new mated me, however, looks at her mate's brother and smiles, even laughs at times.

But then, as Tristen reveals more, my amusement is doused out.

Titus holds me as I endure all the hidden facts that the world has forgotten. I absorb everything about Torin and the Vitalis, including how a new rune can be created, as well as the God's Sword.

I've been here in Caldara all along. I just need to find the old castle hidden under the mountain.

The truth—how the dots have connected—is so astoundingly beautiful and complicated. I wonder how Everett managed it. To plant so many seeds, knowing some would perish and others would flourish. How many outcomes did he have to sew in order to protect the final vision for which he died?

"But now we have one huge problem," I blurt out.

"Only one?" Titus answers, a smirk playing on his lips. I want to see his smile when it's free of stress.

"We need Sable. Only death magic can get the book out of Torin's cage. Sable's rot can choke Torin's power." My head drops in defeat. "Sable just slipped free. Even if we find this old entrance into Caldara's castle and we find the book, we can't touch it."

My eyes meet Titus's. It's the same grief and frustration as locating my mate, but I cannot have him.

"Maybe Sable doesn't know about the location yet," Tristen offers.

My stomach rumbles. "She knows. She's been sneaky since we

arrived in Blackthorn. Building relationships and searching for facts. She was looking for the entrance," I state with confidence. "She's coming back, and she'll have an army when she arrives to get the book."

"Then it's easy." Tristen claps his hands. His shadows vibrate with excitement. "We play the waiting game. Wait for Sable to come, lead us straight to the book, and then we steal it from her."

"That's what you consider easy?" I snort, leaning into a shadow. We're going to need a lot of magic for this. We'll need a god on our side, but the gods abandoned us long ago.

Tristen and Titus both share a long look. "It's the three of us versus two armies," Titus states. He turns, trying to hide his eyes from me, to mask any doubt.

Pressing elbows to knees, I lean in. "Soon you'll have an army."

"Killing Galen will be easy compared to trying to convince his kingdom to follow me," Titus murmurs. His words are nearly lost in Tristen's shadows.

"They see you as a hero," I remind him, my voice firm and resolute. *Why can't you see yourself as one, Titus?*

"Because I ended a war. Now I must start a new one."

"I have to have faith that Everett knew this and planted seeds."

"Let's hope flowers grow instead of weeds," Tristen grunts. "Okay, we have a semi-formed plan." Tristen nods with a showman's grin. "There is one other problem we will have to solve. Titus has a big head, all the men in my family do," he winks at me, barely containing his chuckle.

"Why is that a problem?" I ask, playing into his banter.

"We're gonna need to resize the crown."

"I'm not wearing a crown, idiot." Titus shoves his brother. "If you have such a big head, why don't you think before you speak?"

"Never gotten complaints. Just more requests for my large unfiltered charm," Tristen laughs.

"Shut it." Titus ruffles Tristen's hair.

"So we steal a book, master runes, keep it safe, and save the world,"

Tristen grins. "Then you both live happily ever after—stuck with me and the rest of the fam, of course."

I wish I could smile at the picture Tristen painted. But instead, I hear the fate Everett spoke of.

"How do we steal the Vitalis from Sable?" Titus asks. I sense their eyes on me, awaiting a reply.

We'd need... "Time!" I gasp. Everett, you gave us all the ingredients! Heck, you even gave us the recipe. We just had to figure out how to bake the cake and ensure it didn't burn. The clarity of everything has my feet jolting up.

Titus's reaction is that of a defensive soldier. Tristen's shadows deepen as he stands. He scans through them, then nods at Titus, telling him we are still clear and safe beyond his walls.

"Time," I repeat as I grab Titus's hands. "Once Sable has the book, all you need to do is wrap us in a time bubble and snatch the book from her hands. By the gods! Everett truly thought of everything! That's why he gave you his magic. It was the only way we could get the book out of Sable's hands."

CHAPTER
THIRTY-FOUR

TITUS

S elene's hands were spun with steel, then turned into a one-of-a-kind lace. Delicate yet strong.

I want those hands all over me. I want to claim my mate so fucking bad I can't think straight. My breathing is now in a permanent state of labor. My thoughts are always on her, not the Vitalis, my new magic, my family, or the armies against us.

Her.

My mate.

I don't have to close my eyes to hear her heart. I feel it press into my flesh like a loving, tender hand holding mine.

This is what love feels like... breathless, yet you inhale so deeply because you're terrified something or someone will take it. You hold onto that breath, seal it in your lungs in hopes no one smothers it when you set it free.

My fire magic sizzles under my skin, roaring and raging to burn everything standing in our path. For the first time, Everett's time magic dances with my flames, both agreeing and wanting to protect what is ours.

But how do I cradle the wind?

That's what Selene is. I have to let her slip through my fingers and return to Galen. I have to let her roam free until I can drift away with her.

But... that can never truly happen. Everett has doomed us. Once I get the Vitalis, how can Selene and I be free?

Why does it feel like we were never meant to be?

Everett must have foreseen this. Surely, he has another safety net to catch us so we don't fall to our deaths.

"Titus, did you hear me?" Selene smiles; even surrounded by Tristen's shadows, her grin warms me like the sun. Her skin looks more golden all of a sudden, and the shades of darkness in her hair have their gloss back. The angle of her eyes is no longer dull, but sharper with hope.

"I heard you, mate," I murmur. My smile is stained with a sorrow that can only be washed away once she is free.

Free of Blackthorn, of Galen, of all this madness. If I need runes to do that, so be it!

Tristen's glare is a constant weight I now bench press. It's not out of jealousy or hate; it's out of a deep, sorrow-filled longing that I can't be with my mate. Not yet, anyway.

I cup her cheek. Aww, yes, her blush is more coral-stained than red. Unique and precious. "It seems we have a plan," I reply softly. "I need to learn how to activate my time magic, how to make it listen to me."

Her smirk presses into my palm.

"You're forgetting a huge detail," Tristen barks.

Why does he have to spoil this moment?

"As soon as you get that book, Everetts's time magic is gone. Poof!" Tristen's shadows make snapping sounds to emphasize his point. "That means Sable is going to know because the time bubble will pop. Then what?"

"We use our new army," Selene murmurs. Her green eyes darken as she plots.

"Even if we get Galen's army to support us at the beginning," Tristen replies, "who's to say they will be loyal? Knives will be coming for my brother's back as long as he has that book."

"This old vampire, whose name you never got," Selene arches her brow at Tristen, "take us to him. I have a feeling there is more to his story that hasn't been revealed."

"Is that wise?" Tristen asks. "I thought Galen would grow suspicious if you went to the library."

"Galen will be suspicious of every inhale from now on. I have to take the risk."

Tristen looks my way. I see no other option. "We'll plan to go tomorrow."

"Tomorrow?" Selene snaps, her eyes pin me down.

"You have used every ounce of your magic. You need rest," I remind her.

"I need answers."

"What good are answers if you can't think as you consume them? Rest. Recharge. Tomorrow, we will seek out this vampire."

Tristen's eyes narrow as he scans his shadows in the direction of the castle. "We've got company." He breathes quickly.

I nod and step back from Selene. Her hand squeezes mine before she drops it. Gods, that small gesture just pierced my heart. I want to strip the title of 'soldier' from my name and be called a thief so I can throw Selene over my shoulder and run away with her.

But thieves are hunted down.

I will stay and fight to make the world safe for her.

Tristen drops his shadow. We all look towards the castle. "Tell Galen I wanted you to fight me, and you refused," Selene instructs in haste. "Do it," she presses.

I used to see steel in her eyes: cold, hard emotions. The fear that I'll be taken from her has softened them.

"You can't ask me to stand aside as he touches you. I refuse." I release a pained whisper. I can't do this. I know what's at stake. The future of our world, but she's my mate.

Her throat rolls; she forces down her wants and desires. How many times has she been forced to choke on them so others don't see? "If you want to win me in the end, you must."

My pulse beats through my eyes, shading the world red. "I'll win you now." Yes, the bond likes that. Take her now. "You're mine."

"Tristen," Selene pleads. "Stop him. Titus! Look at your brother. If you fight now, his life is on the line too. A few more days is all I ask." She steps back. "Stop!" she seethes in such a fury it forces my bond to pause and obey.

Just then, Galen comes into view with a dozen soldiers. He strides through the rose-covered walkway with a mounting fury; the sun glints off his crown. He always wears it as if it were a shield that could protect him.

The fool should know it's more target than shield.

I step forward, rage so white-hot it blinds me. I'm going to kill...

"You coward!" Selene shouts, then she rushes forward and starts to attack me. "Fight me!" she screams as she puts on a show, hoping Galen will fall for it. Her hands latch onto my uniform, lips sneaking close to my ear. "Please, for me," she mutters a hushed prayer. "Ignore him."

"I can not ignore chains for long," I bite. I'm angry with her for emasculating me. For begging me to step aside as this fucking prick orders her around.

She makes sure to get the last word before Galen gets too close to hear us. "If you care about this bond, you will endure Galen as I have."

Her words loop around my body like a trap.

Galen pulls at his sleeves, huffing, "Selene,"

All these weeks, not once has he visited her training field, nor checked on her. He's not worthy of the title of husband. He thinks it means owning a trophy. In reality, it means bending a knee, forming an alliance, and showing mutual respect, love, and compassion.

I glare at Galen. If only my eyes were a knife, better yet, my own hands to end him.

Throughout my entire life, I thought I owed Galen everything; he provided a roof over my head, fed me; his men taught me how to survive. But it was never out of love, only fear that the crown on his head would be snatched.

I want to melt that useless symbol made of metal. I want to show the world that a true king does not need a crown or fear to rule.

Punch! Selene's fist blinds me. My head snaps to the side, and then more hits come to my ribs. She punches me in the other eye. *I know you're trying to blind me so I won't attack.*

"Selene, enough!" Galen shouts.

I rub my eyes. If I were human, they'd be swollen shut tomorrow.

"Titus," Galen looks my way, "contain her."

It's the way he says it. Like she's a dog that can be locked away. I don't move towards Selene. With blurry vision, I take a step towards him. There. I can see you now. *Fight me!*

Tristen's shadows drift out from his hands. I can tell by their shade his magic is almost empty. He used too much to conceal us. If I attack Galen, Tristen could take one of the guards, but that leaves Selene to the others.

I can't risk that.

Is the world shaking? No, it's my heart, as my mind forces it into a cage for another day.

Selene acts, turning and rushing toward Galen. "Contain me!" She reels back her fist, aiming towards Galen, but she's sluggish, tapped out. He grabs her wrist, smirks, and kisses her knuckles.

You attack, and you're dead. I tell myself this over and over again, trying to tamper down the mate bond.

Tristen steps in front of me as Galen says, "You hit my guard again, and I will take these hands and bind them to my bed. Do you understand?" Galen stews. To prove his point, his magic curls around her clasped hand; he grabs the other and binds her hands in vines.

That's it. I can't...

Green eyes catch mine. Holding me as Galen holds her. A silent plea.

My lips press firm. This is the only time I will tolerate this. Never again. I will make that clear to Selene tonight. I don't care if my mate is stronger than me. I care that she doesn't respect and protect my weakness: her. She uses it against me.

It must take all Selene's energy to straighten her spine and act relaxed.

Tristen blocks my view again.

"I have enough to deal with!" Galen grunts; he pulls Selene back. "I told you to go to your chambers. It seems you crave my punishments." Galen's eyes slide to me. "Burn it," he orders me. "General," he snaps, "I said burn the field. My wife needs it no more."

Selene tries to act unaffected, but this field, covered in wild grass and weeds that masquerade as flowers, was something she had grown to love. It was a cage, but it felt like freedom.

I lower my chin. My chest is tight as I swing my hands behind my back to hide my fists. "King," the title tastes like ash on my tongue, thick and chalky. "I was not able to have my morning blood; it was poisoned. Therefore, I have no access to my magic."

"I know of the bloody poison! Gods be damned!" Galen shouts. "You," he glares at Tristen, "help him get a torch and burn this. I want the field as black as her heart is."

He jerks Selene and tugs her towards the castle. I know Selene; she would have fought, but she surrendered for me.

I hate it.

I don't want her to sacrifice anything for me. My skin tightens, the sun pours its heat into every exposed pore, yet a chill snakes down my spine. A dark warning that Selene is willing to sacrifice much, much more.

How do I stop her without offending her, without resembling Galen, who commands and cages her?

Galen's two guards follow. I step forward. Tristen's palms land against my stomach. I expect his lecture, his hushed whispers of fury. I almost gave our secret away, killed a king, saved a queen.

Instead, Tristen hugs me. "I am sorry, brother." His breath is riddled with fury.

"I can not endure seeing that again."

"You must." He holds me tighter. "Her life depends on it."

I grab him, curling my fingers into his clothing. I need an anchor to ground me so I can think! "What kind of man am I to have stood by and done nothing, Tristen? This is not who I am. I can not be this version she forces me to be. I'm no better than a mindless killer who leaves bodies on the field to rot. Where is the honor? She's my mate!" I cry. "Mine. Yet you all begged me to let another man take her away from me. I listened. I allowed it. I am not worthy of having a mate. I am not a man."

"Hey! Stop!" Tristen shakes me. "You're the kind that thinks with his head, not his dick." He clasps my face as a father would. "You need blood. *Her* blood. Sure, you could have fought Galen now, but your magic isn't charged because you spat out the morning ration. Galen would have killed you in under a minute, then me."

An image of him and me playing tackle flashes in my mind, only this time when I giggle as I hover over him, his lifeless eyes stare at the sky.

Dead. I can't lose him.

"Selene would be trapped in Galen's bed forever. Then what, Titus? You need to be ten steps ahead to beat Galen. Sure, he's not as skilled with a sword; but he's mastered the use of his vines."

Tristen turns my head to the rose bushes that encircle us. Even from this far distance, I can see how large the thorns are.

"Those vines are like hands. You'll slice some away, burn others. Once your magic is used up, when one vine grabs your sword, and the other your legs, then what?" He slaps my cheek. "Galen is a different enemy; he can kill you from afar and close up. You need to find another way to kill him."

"Another way..." I mutter.

I understand, Everett. I know how to get close enough to Galen to make the kill without him noticing. I also know why you put a time limit on your magic. It's seductive, this thought I have.

Turning, I look at the field, feel the wind as it dances one last tango through the grass. I will burn it; I see all the black roses, which I will turn grey and ashen. I see Blackthorn, the mighty castle made of glossy black stone. I see everything I will burn down.

"Time. Everett's magic is the key again!" My grin spreads so wide it reaches my ears.

Tristen's brows furrow. "Even if you trap Galen in the time bubble, his magic will still work."

"That's why I'll trap myself in the bubble. I'll sneak up behind Galen and end him. He'll never see me coming."

That kind of power is unmatched. That's why Everett didn't want me to have it forever. Eventually, it would taint me. Everett knew I'd have to kill Galen before we found the book. We're on the right track.

Tristen's chin falls, his eyes bounce back and forth as he thinks. His nod is slow. "When?"

I spot a weed with red petals, so I reach down and pluck it, holding it between my fingers. "My heart tells me to do it now."

"But the fallout?"

My fingers snap open. I watch as the weed falls. "I need to find Vice Admiral Adrian again."

"The army will listen to the Admiral." Tristen shoulders relax as he nods. "That's why Everett picked him."

"Exactly," I reply. "How much fire do you think it would take to burn that castle to the ground?" I ask my brother.

He pauses, then whistles. "You'd need a bloody dragon."

"Perhaps we will find one."

"I doubt it, but if we do I call dibs." Tristen steps closer.

I shake my head as a laugh sounds from my lips.

Attacking Galen now would have changed everything. Adrian would name no new king; Tristen would die, Selene would be trapped, and Sable would have the book. I run my hand down my face. I must ignore the bond until it snaps and takes over, at which point I will attack Galen, because Everett would have anticipated it.

Timing is everything.

THIRTY-FIVE

SELENE

A heavy scent of roses engulfs my senses as we enter my tower in the castle. "I think you're losing your touch, Galen. These roses have an old lady smell about them," I jab.

No reply. That's unlike Galen. What's he plotting now? To cage me in my room?

Two of his guards follow us; the rest remain stationed like dolls outside. I'm still holding my breath from when I pleaded with Titus to stand down.

His enraged eyes were directed at me, not just Galen. The clench of his jaw told me that letting me leave with Galen had broken something in his mind. It damaged his confidence. He took it as rejection, my lack of faith that he could not win me in battle.

My footsteps drag. The hallway stretches long and endless, like the wars we continue to wage against one another. "When will it stop, Galen?" I blurt out. I lean against the wall to catch my breath.

Galen turns like a tide, his robes sweeping around him in a measured grace. "What?" he replies. His gaze narrows, spotting all the dirt and stains on my clothes. He lingers on the dirt under my fingernails. "You need rest," he mutters to himself.

I sink into the wall, allowing my cheek to press into the cold, polished stone. I raise my chin higher. *I'll never bow to you again, Galen.* "War." I stagger as I push off the wall. He knows I'll never back down; no state of exhaustion will stop me from throwing a dagger his way. "When will you have enough?"

His gaze stretches for as long as the sun rises and sets before he replies, "War is the purpose of life." His turn is a sword's edge—sharp, deadly. He'll never stop.

I shake my head, "It is the antithesis. All the wars you have fought have been to claim everything." I sway forward, taking a step to balance myself. "The enemy you battle now doesn't care about crowns and castles. Sable fights to end it all. And she will."

His heel digs into the floor, practically burning a hole in the carpet runner. His lack of reply shows his regret in allowing her to return home. We soon reach the staircase. The view of his kingdom forces his eyes to gaze out of the window. The smoothness of his brow crinkles like balled-up paper.

He barks to one of the guards, "Tell Adrian to call in the reserves. I want everyone who can hold a sword here." His hand searches for the sword on his belt, as a child holds a teddy bear.

"That won't save you," I mutter. The hilt is so shiny it would slip from Galen's hand in battle.

He nods to himself as his lips pinch into a smirk before he ascends the staircase.

It's time to push him over the edge. Make the self-doubts whispering in his mind scream so loud he can't think clearly. *I need you weak so I can kill you.*

"I can hold a sword," I mock.

"I'd much rather you held something else."

The gap between us shrinks. "Your heart in my hands?" I snicker. My breath tickles his neck.

That neck is going to be so relieved once your head is freed from it.

363

I continue, "I know you're not referring to your manhood, or lack thereof." I turn my head and shout to Jonas, Galen's trusted bodyguard. He's been a loyal dog whose beady eyes are always watching me. Galen has seen it, but does nothing. Galen likes it when other men drool over me. It makes him think I'm a bigger trophy than I am. "By all means," I halt. "Drop your trousers and hand me a knife. Consider it a two-for-one special; you get to witness my sword skills and see your cock in my hands again."

Galen angles his head; the light from one of the stained-glass windows glints off his crown, casting small rainbows all over the path. "Oh, Selene," he shakes his head slowly, but underneath his banter is genuine fear. My comments about how foolish he was to trust Sable have sunk deep, piled with the rumors of the blood being poisoned.

"Is that gray hair?" I nudge my eyes to his treasured mane. 'Bad hair day' has never left his lips. "I see your fingers itching to pluck it out."

"You'll pay for this."

"Me?" I raise my bound wrist to my heart, feigning innocence. "A queen doesn't pay, Galen, her king does. Or have you lost all chivalry?" I laugh in his face. "You need to choose your queen: the ornament who lets her husband fix her mistakes, or the fighter who points out his faults so he can fix them. Tick tock, Galen. Sable approaches with the army *you* gave her."

"You will pay," he repeats, voice dragging low and dark, thick with threat. Is that meant to scare me? My heart hammers, but I refuse to let him see it.

"Don't you mean Sable? You've been fucking her for so long, don't tell me you can't tell us apart by now. I'll give you a clue; all those times she seduced you were because she was plotting to steal your kingdom, and all the times I seduced you were simply to make you shut up so I could sleep soundly."

"Keep lying to yourself. You wanted me."

"Let me embody an echo." I clear my throat. "Keep lying to yourself. You. Wanted. Me. Galen."

Oh, yes. I won this round.

I need to make him feel less and less, to question every turn in this castle. The news of his paranoia and madness will reach the inner gates by nightfall.

Now it's time to make Jonas start to doubt Galen's control over his kingdom.

Turning, I say, "How do you feel, Jonas? Stomach aching from the poisoned blood? It will start soon."

His worry is a worm that digs lines into his forehead. "You've been guarded. It wasn't you. It..." His eyes glance at Galen. "It was the twin, wasn't it? Sable poisoned us, then left. She planned this."

It's an assumption that works in my favor.

I sell the fear, knowing it will keep Titus's true reason for spitting the blood out secret. "I warned Galen that Sable was conniving. But he was too busy fucking her to listen to me."

Galen's eyes sharpen like fangs ready to tear into my neck.

I continue, "Your king traded your lives for sex. He let a snake in. She poisoned you all, and then he allowed her to slither away." I twist my wrist, still bound by his vines. I refuse to let him see my irritation, so I've been wearing it like bracelets.

"It was a failed attempt." Galen's reply is water on fire. He thinks it quells Jonas's fears, but smoke has a strong scent. It will spread to every nook and cranny of the kingdom.

Galen's hand drifts up like a kite searching for a cloud, only he seeks the comfort of his crown.

"Jonas," he barks, "I want a feast planned for tonight. I want them all to see I am not scared of idle threats."

"Did you hear that, Jonas? The poisoning of his men is *idle*. My father would have considered it a personal attack," I taunt.

The space between Galen and me vanishes. He grazes his lips over mine, allowing the tip of his fang to touch my skin. "Careful, dearest wife. In times of war, morals grow thin. If I have to sew your mouth shut, I will." He attempts to kiss me, but I jerk back.

"You forget how razor-edged my tongue is." I trace my tongue across my bottom lip. "Stitch me shut. I. Dare. You."

His throat bobs as he gulps. The tension in the air is so thick I forgo inhaling and continue till the last drop of air has fled from my lungs.

"I shall free myself," I continue. "Cut free everything you have done. Then what will you do? I'll tell you," I lift my chin higher. "You will stand in a corner with nothing but a needle and no more thread as a pair of sharp scissors comes for you."

My gaze drops to his hands. I shake my head in disappointment. "You forget your hands are those of a child; children shouldn't play with scissors, Galen," I mock. "Did mommy and daddy dearest never tell you that? One might think they wanted you to get hurt."

He pushes back without replying, turning like a door on oiled hinges, then climbs the stairs.

"Your Majesty, if I may," Jonas interrupts the silence of our climb, "word has spread to the nobles about the poison. A feast might not be wise." He states once we reach the third-floor landing.

I spot my door, and the ache in my feet internally screams for my bed.

The rhythm of Galen's footsteps turns into a sharp violin. He reaches for his crown, then turns. Darkness flies past my face. I gasp, jerking back just in time to avoid being caught in the crosshairs. Galen's vines fly forward, grabbing Jonas as a gardener does a weed.

"You forget, Jonas, that you do not deserve an opinion." The vines grow, wrapping, binding, and squeezing until Jonas can't help but yelp in agony.

I twist the vines binding my wrist; each twist is a protest from my throbbing bones. I lean into the pain, using it as fuel until my binds snap free.

Air rushes between my lips when I peer at Galen. A thick vine curls around Jonas's neck, digging into his skin so tight I can see his pulse throbbing, beating against it. That's when Jonas and I realize Galen isn't stopping.

Killing his most trusted guard works in my favor. I won't have to sell Galen's madness; he's doing it himself.

Jonas's magic erupts in an angry explosion of wind. The floor rushes to meet me; a sharp bang sinks into my skull from the impact. Any stars I would have seen are blown away as Jonas continues to fight.

Howling cries echo through the hall as his wind finds no escape, so it swirls in circular currents, churning my balance into tidal waves I can't stand against. A burning sensation spreads over any exposed skin. I curl into myself until I can see a break to fight.

Clatter! Metal hits stones. The winds stop.

Galen's crown, his most prized possession, falls to the ground.

A small symbol of how easily a king can be pushed over.

Roar!

Jonas uses our shock as his opening. The impact sends me rolling down the hall like an apple along a table. Galen remains connected to Jonas by the thick vines. His grunts reach my ears, but he holds firm to his magic like reins of a horse.

The scraping of metal on stone pulls the crown nearer. I peer at the crown, ignoring the burning rawness of the wind as it smacks against my eyes. More vines erupt as Galen roars; they block the wind from assaulting me.

I wish I hadn't looked. I watch in grotesque horror as a vine invades Jonas's nose and mouth, suffocating him.

My palms flatten onto the floor as I prepare to stand. My chin presses painfully into the stone. *Close your eyes; don't watch this.*

I can't look away.

I know precisely when the vines reach Jonas's heart. His complexion turns to porcelain. There is no coming back from that. The heart is the most vital organ, and if it's damaged, you're dead.

Like my brother. Stabbed through the heart.

Now is your chance! Pushing, I stand. A natural reflex has my hand reaching for the dagger at my hip.

No! My hand touches emptiness. My head drops. Galen's sudden arrival this morning left me no time to retrieve it.

I see it; what could have been. A backstab to the heart; that's how I would've taken Galen down. Jonas could have been my scapegoat if necessary.

Thick blackish tendrils coil over one another; a waxy squelch accompanies each movement. Jonas's knees are pulled down, and the vines around his torso keep his back upright. Galen's ragged exhales hit my skull like a hammer.

Jonas who? All I see is a thick bush in my hall.

Galen tries to push more magic, but it runs out. This morning, he fueled and refueled his magic beyond what I had ever seen him do. If he drinks more, bloodlust will take over.

He's at his most valuable now. He knows it. Realization sinks into him. Instead of panicking, he feigns calm.

You can't wiggle free from this.

If Galen cared for me, he'd search for me, but his eyes lock on his crown, which lay at my feet. He closes the distance. "Get it," he sneers.

Beyond him, I spot the door to Titus's room and smirk. "A king without a crown. It's an image you should get used to." I kick the crown, pull my spine back, and allow my adrenaline to pull my feet to my room. The door catches my shoulder, my feet scream for my bed. I walk to the nightstand and grab my dagger. I turn, but Galen is there, holding his crown.

"You want to kill me?" He runs his fingers over the metal as if it were a woman's hips.

Instead of unsheathing my dagger, I lower it to my side. I'm a hypocrite. I begged my mate not to act on his desire, but here I am lusting to kill Galen when I have no magic or fight left in me. I'm only standing because my bones refuse to break. "It would be my dream come true," I acknowledge.

"People like us don't dream." He lifts the crown carefully; his shoulders relax when the weight settles onto his head. His walk to my mirror is quick. His eagerness to check his reflection has coated my tongue with acid. "We see nightmares and make them a reality, Selene. You hate me because you see yourself in me."

"The only thing I see equal in us is a desire to kill."

"That's why I love you," he counters as he styles his hair so it curls around his crown. "You see, Sable seeks to destroy, but you pursue what I find most alluring."

"Killing and destroying are the same."

"You're wrong." The corners of his mouth curl. "If I destroy everything, as Sable seeks to do, then who do I have left to kill? Killing is the long game; destroying is the short."

I move so my bed separates us. "I'd tell you you're insane, but you'd just consider that a compliment."

He tugs his sleeves down, then starts to adjust his outfit, smoothing out the wrinkles. "I do love the unique way you flatter me, dear wife."

I pull out my dagger, raise it and take aim. Air floods my clammy hands. Pride pulls at my tired eyes as I watch the blade soar through the air.

Crack!

Galen ducks to the side. He wasn't my target. The mirror shatters.

"That was risky." Galen pivots; his boots crush the shards of the mirror. His glare is a challenge.

"Taking risks is how you survive the long game, isn't that right, Galen?"

A slow, deliberate darkening of his pupils makes ending our relationship so much more satisfying.

"We're finished." I'll never get over the joy of telling him that. "Your time is coming to an end. Grow some more roses so your grave has fresh flowers."

The twisting of his lips resembles the vines that grow. "We never got started. These games we play have just been the flirting a couple endures before they commit."

"Commit?" My fingers mold the dagger's sheath as a soft chuckle slips past my lips. "Your loyal soldier just attempted to kill you, Galen.

More will follow suit." My legs protest; the tremor takes hold, spreading from my calves to my thighs.

I plop onto my bed, hoping Galen doesn't see that my legs are about to collapse.

I run my hands down my thighs, trying to soothe my muscles. Galen thinks I'm trying to seduce him. "What does it feel like to know the war has finally come to your doorstep?"

I kick off one of my shoes. Dirt from the field falls onto my floor.

"My borders are clear," he defends.

"Is that why you called in your reserve army?" I chuckle. "Unlike before, the battle is here; you have no excuse to hide within your walls and plan. Do you think sprinkling roses over a charging army will stop them? Will you stop and smell the roses before they drive a sword through your heart?"

My brow practically meets my hairline. His face turns the color of the blood he's addicted to.

"Your men will want you to prove your worth. That's why you forced Vice Admiral Adrian and Titus to return," I point out, and the skin around his nose pinches. "Your men were too fond of them on the battlefield. You forced them here to drink wine and act drunk, so your men would see they were not gods, just warriors with good aim."

His clenched fist betrays his temper, but I'm not finished.

"Wars don't topple kings, Galen. Doubt does. It's written all over your handsome face. Apprehension will be what claims your crown. Your men distrust you, and you cannot keep them safe. First, Titus was attacked, then your blood was poisoned, now your bodyguard is murdered." My gaze sweeps over the room. "Your walls are crumbling. Smell that? No more roses, just shit-filled air. Death is coming. Someone as pampered as you will gag at the stench. Me? I'll survive. I'm used to nightmares—I'm married to you."

His left eye twitches. Why did he touch his crown again? Haven't I proved symbols won't save him?

"You could chain it to your head, but they're just cut your neck from your shoulders," I boast.

"Shut up!" he snaps.

I swing my legs up and flex my toes slowly. "Next time you wake up, take a moment to enjoy the sunrise." I peer out the window in my room. "It might be your last."

In a fury, he's at my side; the bed is no longer under me. "You think you can address me in such a tone?" He spits as he holds me firm.

He jerks, caught off guard when my palms frame his face. "It's not the tone that offends you, but rather the truth painted before your eyes. You don't love your people, Galen. You love metal formed into crowns and stones carved into walls. You love material items that will soon be stripped away from you.

"Perhaps if you loved your people, you could have held onto them; better yet, they would have held onto you." I drop my hands, knowing it will be the last time I touch his face. He knows I'll never accept him again.

That is what he craved. My acceptance. The prey lying with the predator.

My body hits the bed with a thud. Galen grabs his collar and tugs it high as he looks down at me. "It's not a king's job to love, but to rule."

"A king's job is to be dutiful. You don't know the definition of duty. It defines both loving and ruling."

Titus knows; that's why he's going to be a good king and not a corrupt one.

"If you were a good king, you would have understood that long ago."

"I'm a great king." He puffs his chest wide.

"Galen," I groan, "kings are not the ones who write history. When they die, everything they built can be torn down and rewritten. Once you perish, you will be known for what you truly are. All the nobles who kiss your ass will be the first to burn your memoirs. The people you stomped on shall raise both feet and hands to topple what you built."

"At least I had memoirs to burn. You have nothing."

Wrong. I have a mate. I have everything.

Galen knows he fucked up by entrusting Sable over me. There is nothing he can do to rectify the situation. He has to fight, but I know his ending thanks to my brother.

He releases a long exhale. "You know why I put up with your tongue, Selene?"

"Because I tell you what your men don't."

"That's right. See, you think you're tearing me down. But it's the opposite. You help motivate me. I will win this war. I will eradicate your home and your people from history. Then, I will use their bones to build a new castle, one that reaches the clouds; I shall place you inside a cage made of their ashes. Forever my pet, who loves to bite the hand that feeds it." His triumphant smirk is so tight it pulls his shoulders back as he strides to the door.

"Bones and ash do not scare me, Galen."

He glances over his shoulder, searching for what does.

I reveal nothing. "You have a mess outside to clean up." I lean over and fluff my pillow. "And something tells me that is what truly scares you."

The door slams so hard my muscles flinch.

He's gone. I survived. I curl my fingers into the pillow, trying to slow the shaking of my lungs.

Titus. Mate. I wish he were here to catch me instead of the mattress. I press my face into the sheets, feeling like a puppet that has been passed around so many times my stitches are barely holding.

"Ouch!" I gasp as a searing pain burns into my flesh.

My back arches from the torture. My heart feels on fire. My hands claw at the fabric of my top, ripping it open. The pain has faded to that of a sharp sting.

Open your eyes. You know what has happened. My trembling fingers hover over the pain, too scared to touch my skin. "Gods!" The mating mark has appeared. My eyes gaze upon it only for a moment, lost in its beauty. It feels like a child, something I want to keep safe and protect, but in my current situation, it is a bastard child, one I must keep hidden so Galen does not kill it.

Tenderly, I press my finger to it. A sharp inhale hits my lungs as a rush of magic jolts from it. Glee, safety, love. Titus. His face, his thick dark hair, trusting brown eyes, and his sharp jaw. He's all I see. His body, his actions, his desire for me. It pulls tears from my eyes.

Then reality slams into me. I rush to my closet, tripping and stumbling into the wall. Lost in my exhaustion and panic, I barely manage to grab a shirt to cover it.

I collapse on the floor like a garment that refuses to cling to a hanger. Stand up. *Don't let anyone see you like this, especially not Titus.* He'd worry, see me as fragile.

Okay, I can't stand, so I'll crawl.

I make it to my bed and then using all my upper body strength, I pull myself into it. Tipping my head back, I look at the window. My world is upside down. Everything has changed.

If Galen had lingered longer, he would have seen the mark. Moisture beads on my forehead. My shirt clings to my damp back and chest, like a vest trying to cover the mark. Titus must have gotten his mark, too. I hope he's still in my field, far away from Galen's eyes and war.

My lids remain open wide, my lashes unmoved despite the desperate call to close them so the stinging stops. I gaze at the upside-down world. The weight of the ground now presses down on the clouds. On me.

The life I know is about to be torn open. I'm not just referring to my failed peace-treaty marriage. Everything I have bottled up inside, Titus will eventually drink down. It will taint him because my scars and memories are too dark for someone as noble and heroic as Titus. The selfishness of his actions will change.

I'll change him, destroy him.

All this time, Titus has looked upon me as his queen, someone he could never afford.

The depressing truth is, it is I who can not afford him. You don't toss an old rusty coin into a shining fountain in hopes that the water will clean it. The rust will spread, and soon the stunning fountain will be covered in grime.

THIRTY-SIX

TITUS

The wild grass brushes my boots, a silent plea not to burn it. Sweat beads on my brow, not cooled by the winds since they have vanished along with Galen and my mate. As an ancient oak, I watch Galen's castle, imagining the black stones reflecting my orange flames.

Tristen's steps ultimately cause me to look away. His hands grip two bottles instead of torches. "What's that?" I ask.

"Blood," he answers. I catch the glass bottle before it hits me. "The prick wants this field burned, so let's burn it. Let's test your swallowing skills." He winks. "Drink up, buttercup."

I can't help but roll my eyes. "You and your sex jokes."

"When I mature, you'll miss them."

"Unlikely."

He uncorks the bottle and takes a long drag. The noise of his swallowing makes me crave a drink. "You need a release, and not the sexual kind," Tristen continues. "When was the last time you let your magic loose? Before Everett died? It's got to be driving you insane, Titus.

Drink! Let go; pour your emotions into your fire magic. Destroy something Galen built."

I push the cork free with my thumb. The smooth glass touches my lips right before I drink. "It smells off now." I grimace. How am I going to stomach this?

"They never mention the side effects of being mated. One, you become psychotic."

I snort. "I'm not psychotic."

"You've got a look in your eye every time you see her. It's like you want to push her up against a wall and claim her, but also tuck her in tenderly into your bed; I'm talking pillow fluffing, blankets pulled up to her chin and all. Then, you kind of have this prideful smirk, like you want to show her off, but anyone who looks at her is guaranteed to be dead by nightfall. Definition of insanity." He nods as he rubs the glass of the bottle. "Grade A clinger, you're lucky she feels the same way."

The gulp of blood floods my throat. Fuck! It's bad, like a spicy tea that leaves a bitter taste.

My fingers are ringed with fire. *Yeah, I missed you, buddy. I miss the simplicity of training you. I didn't have to build a friendship because you wanted me to use you. You wanted attention, and I gave it to you.* Perhaps that's why vampires can be so controlling; our magic enables that behavior.

"Try to command your time magic first," Tristen suggests.

Good idea. I'll never have an opportunity like this where I'm alone and fully charged. *Hey, wake up. That's it.*

I need your help. I need us to work together. Please, I'm asking as a friend who requires your help. I apologize if I upset you. I was frightened, so I panicked and yelled at you. I shouted how much I loathed you because I didn't understand you. Give me another chance to learn. Work with me.

My arms sway like leaves as the wind whispers through me.

So, all this time, I had to respect it and talk to it as if it were human.

It fills my fingers, answering yes.

Tristen parts his lips and begins to speak; I keep my eyes on my hands. "Now," I ask it, mentally visualizing what I want it to do. I feel time push out from me, wrapping me in a bubble. Just me. I glance at Tristen; his mouth is frozen open, mid-lecture. "He's outside the bubble."

Magic dances on my palm as if to say, *"You asked for this, fool."*

I wave my fingers in awe of it. "I thought I had to fight you, control you. I just needed to ask." Everett's memory pulls my lips down. "Do you miss Everett? I've been a lousy host," I mumble. The sensation over my fingers slows; it feels like tiny invisible hands hugging mine. "Does that mean you're happy with me?"

I think that's a yes.

"But we'll leave each other soon. Once I get the Vitalis, you'll be free. Promise me something."

The magic dances over my skin. I look up. Tristen's lips begin to close around his word. He's moving impossibly slow. I walk closer, testing how close I can get.

I keep my eyes cast on Tristen's feet, so I don't pull him into the bubble. Now I'm at his back, a stone's throw away. I can do this, ram my knife into Galen. I circle my brother, standing in front of him. That's how I'll do it. I want Galen to see my face, and then when he's taking his last few breaths, I will reach out and pull him into the bubble, making sure to prolong his suffering as long as I can.

"Did you hear all that?" I ask for the magic. "That's why I need to ask this of you. Please don't find someone else once you are free. You're too dangerous. No, I mean no offense. People will see you as a treasure, but men don't treasure things; they tarnish them. You need to run wild and free. You have a mind of your own. You don't need someone to host you," I tell it.

I hope and pray it considers my words. Magic like this is too dangerous to be controlled again.

It doesn't move over my fingers. I don't know whether that's good or bad.

I finally look Tristen in the eye. "Not yet," I tell the magic. I step closer, closer. "Now," I say. The bubble encasing me stretches over my skin; it reaches out and grabs Tristen. He keeps babbling on, unaware I pulled him into my bubble.

"Okay, that's enough. Thank you," I tell the magic. It bounces over my fingers and then pops. Time recoils and returns to normal.

Tristan's shoulders flinch. "Wait... did you just—"

"Yes. I solved it. All this time, I struggled to dissect the time-weaving so I could understand it. That's what we do when we find something new: we invade, cut it open, and see what we can salvage and use. I never needed to fight it or force it to work with me. All I had to do was ask. I treated it like a foe that needed to be conquered when all along it was a willing friend." A friend I will have to say goodbye to. I'm tired of losing the people I let in.

"Remember, Titus, friends have opinions. The magic might decide if it wants to work. Everett figured out a way to control the friendship."

I nod, "I know, but I think it wants to help me."

Tristan rubs his jaw. "They say women overcomplicate things, but shit, men can too." He drops his hand, showing off a shining smile. "This is fantastic." He slaps my back and raises his blood bottle. "You need more?"

I shake my head, peering out at the green field. "I've had enough."

"You gonna burn that shitty rose fence, too?" he wonders.

It will drain me until my knees collapse to burn an area this wide, but I can do it. Selene will hate to see her field turn to ashes, but it was never a place of freedom.

I'll build her a training field with no walls, just open land.

Fire dances in the reflection of my eyes, its weight forcing my fingers to spread painfully wide as it grows, jumping higher and higher until I release it. Tristen stands behind me as I set it free.

The intense heat causes the grass to curl while staying green before turning into ash. The flames happily move, looking for the shrubs that try to trap them. Leaping over the vine wall, it curls back to attack the bushes. Roses burn, the petals curl then fall like rain.

I glare at Blackthorn Castle. "You're next."

~

It happened just after I burned the field. A gift from the gods that would be magically inked into my flesh like a badge of honor not everyone could earn. My mating mark appeared.

Panic pours out of my skin, sniffling the fresh air. If Selene's mark appeared when she was with Galen...

Why did I listen to her? I should have fought to walk by her side as he led her away.

My eyes no longer see clearly, my feet carry me so swiftly I'd win a race against flood waters.

"She's okay," Tristen whispers as he struggles to keep pace with me. "He wouldn't kill her. You and I know this."

He's right. Galen will hunt down her mate. But that doesn't mean he'd hurt her.

A strong odor of horse shit soon hits my boots, and the soil turns muddy. No amount of sand and hay can harden the soil of the barns. Horses whinny as sounds of boots thrash come running out of the stables.

"Hey," Tristen grabs the back of my shirt, my chest. "That's Galen's horse!"

Galen. The sound of his name halts my feet. *Kill him. He's a threat to your mate. Kill him now.*

A palm slaps my cheek. "Snap out of it!" Tristen grunts. "There will be no honeymoon, Titus. Get control over your actions."

No chisel can chip away the stiffness of my muscles. "Galen is a threat," I hiss.

Tristen kneads his fingers on my shoulders; he's so close that all I can see are the shades of his cool-toned brown eyes. "You're a threat to her if you can't get your bond under control."

Me?

The bond doesn't like that. The bond is like another magic I have to understand. It's like my fire, a puppy yapping for attention, but it's got personality traits like fae magic; it wants respect.

Tristen's hand slips into mine, and he leads me up the chipped stone steps to the guard's scouting wall. Heavy boots, the tapping of weapons gliding against the side of bodies as soldiers walk, echo and create a feeling that relaxes me.

We have to think. If Galen is here, then he wasn't with Selene when the mark appeared. This is good. Yes, calm down. I'll get to her, slowly, so I don't alert anyone. I'll keep her safe. I'll make her mine.

Tristen guides us to the ledge of the maze-like walkway. The soldiers use this area to be Galen's eyes and ears from above. This elevated aisle twists throughout the city like veins that direct all the infection—the gossip— to the heart: the castle.

Tristen leans over the edge. "Look," he whispers.

My stomach arches in as I lean into the ledge. Sure enough, Galen and three dozen guards all mount up and ride for the gates.

"Where are they going?"

"I don't know," I whisper.

"This is good?" he wonders.

"Then why do you sound worried?"

"Selene's alone. We have time to think." He looks over his shoulder. "Walk normally. If we're seen running to her rooms, word will get back to Galen." He pivots wide like a mountain, blocking me from squeezing past him.

The walk to Selene's tower is painfully slow, but by the time I make the final step up her stairs, the bond is shouting again.

I smack into his back. "Why the fuck is there a rose bush in her hall?" Tristen steps back; we both draw our swords. "Why does it smell like a dead body?"

My nostrils flare. I know that scent; I've been bathed with it in battle. The blood of a brother. "Vampire blood." I glance at the floor, almost missing the puddle of blood. The reflection of the roses camouflaged it.

What the fuck happened?

Tristen leans down. My eyes pivot to Selene's room. "Look," Tristen points to the bottom of the bush. A boot is poking out from under the thick foliage. The closer we look, the more parts of the body we find. Jonas's face—what used to be a face— peers back at us from within the vines.

"Well... that's not something you'd want to put in a vase." Tristen exhales; he pokes a vine with his sword. "He's definitely dead."

"Obviously." He's got a bush sprouting from his chest!

The bond pulls my feet down the hall, and I practically fall into the door as I barge in. She's not on her bed, but the sheets are rumpled. Where is she?

My chest feels like yarn being wrapped around knitting needles. There she is, sitting outside on her balcony. Her knees are curled up, but her body looks boneless. Joy and relief dilate my eyes.

"You got it?" she states with confidence. Only her eyelids move as they struggle to look at me.

Each step I take is an iron chain cementing the bond. I expect her to tell me to stop. To remind me that she was given to Galen and that I have a duty forced upon me by her brother.

I wouldn't.

I haven't been myself since I came here. When Everett forced his magic into me, it changed me, shook my confidence, made me step back and observe. I watched my mate with another, forced myself to obey her and not attack, to ignore the bond.

I've become a man I would not call honorable. Weeks of torture that I will not endure any longer.

She will let me claim her, or I will surrender to death willingly.

I was trained to fight, to take, and that's what I'm going to do. All this push and pull she's forced me to endure was out of fear for me, for us. She needs to know what kind of man I am. All her life, she has been accustomed to monsters.

I can be one.

Love is a beast after all. It consumes, drives you wild. It needs more and more, and so I shall feed the monster.

"This is over." I point to the walls. Galen's walls. "You're not his. I will never stand aside and watch him lead you away. Do. You. Understand?"

Her breath quivers as she lifts her head. "I was trying to protect our bond."

"Our bond is different, Selene." My fist close like tongs gripping a crucible, brimming with the molten metal that forms our twisted love and unbreakable bond. "I'm just as possessive as Galen, but I also respect you." My hair sweeps my forehead as I shake my head. "But you haven't shown me the same respect."

Her tongue darts out, trying to lick away the guilt on her lips.

I remove the space between us and crouch down. "He will never touch you again. I will show you how I survived in battle. I will cut him down and toss his fucking hands in that bush in your hallway. And I'll keep it there until the message is clear to you. You're mine. Understood?"

"Yes."

"Very alpha male." I can hear the smile on Tristen's lips, as well as the relief that Selene is safe. In typical fashion, he's going to try to lighten the mood with sex jokes. "Touch-her-and-die. Ember told me that's something ladies like. It's in all the books she reads to me. It's always the most badass women who like to be tossed around in bed."

I'm about to turn on him, but Selene casts her eyes down and blushes.

His hand lands on my shoulder. "I think we all need a deep inhale. Deeper, deeper, yeah baby, that's it, take it."

Selene covers her mouth; her fingers are pale and tremble, but... she giggles.

"Look, she laughed. Brownie points for me. I know we had a rough start. I admit I didn't like you, Selene, but that mark on my brother's chest means you're stuck with me. Congratulations, and word of advice, ignore my shit and admire my giggles."

I roll my eyes, and he sighs.

"Okay, okay." Tristen pulls back. "One more question: why is there a rose bush with a face in your hallway, or parts of a face?"

I study her hands. They have one more second on this land of being alone. One more flexing of her fingers opening wide and meeting air. The next time she uncurls her hand it will meet my touch!

There. I close my fingers around her palm. *You're mine. These hands are mine to kiss and love.*

I flip her fingers over like pages of a book, inspecting them.

"He didn't hurt me. He left. I crawled from the bed to the balcony. I needed air," she whispers.

Night's sharp, crisp sense makes my senses remain heightened. The sunset's pink and yellow hues reflect over her face. Even in a state of utter exhaustion, she is worthy of being a painter's muse.

"What happened?" I ask; I begin to kiss her knuckles, one by one, then her fingertips. *My mate! My mate! My mate!*

It roars like a new heartbeat that possesses every other sense.

I've seen mated couples; there's always something untamed in the man's eyes. I imagined it would rival a dragon—possessive, consuming, touch-her-and-die, as Tristen stated. I feel it claw into my eyes.

I've seen happy couples torn apart by mating bonds. It's awful for all sides. The mates can't help it; it's just fate. But since Galen has been a cruel, abusive, manipulative asshole, it makes our bond more special because it saved her. It set her free from the contracted marriage. The eyes of others won't cast judgment; they all know bonds take precedence over peace treaties. Over everything.

I slide beside her and pull her into my lap. My chest is her pillow, my hands are sheets that cover her. Tristen stands guard halfway between the door and the balcony.

Selene tells us everything. "I missed my chance to kill Galen. I'm sorry. I know how you felt when I begged you not to kill him," she admits in defeat. "I didn't beg you to stand down because I thought you'd fail. I..." Her chest sinks. "I want to keep you safe just as badly as you wish to protect me."

The time is now.

My fingers slide from her hair, and her eyes close in delight. "Galen will never touch you again. Do you understand? The dawn of the rising sun will be his last."

"I don't want his touch. I need yours."

"Let me see your mark."

"I'll... wait outside," Tristen suggests, but I stop him.

"Don't go far. I need you to guard her. I'm leaving." After I have just had a taste. One kiss to settle the bond.

Selene reaches out and grabs my face. "Where are you going?"

"I need to speak to someone; Tristen will stay here as you rest."

"Titus... I..."

"I'm going to speak to Vice Admiral Adrian," I confess.

She understands.

"It's happening."

"Yes." I tell her what Tristen and I discussed. My prediction was that Sable would strike once Galen is dethroned and I learn how to communicate with Everett's magic, everything.

She sucks in a sharp breath. "I love you. Not because you freed me from him, not because you're helping my brother, or because of our bond. I love you because you always do what is best for others, not for your own heart, Titus. You and I could run away, but you know that's not my nature, so you stand and fight by my side, and I love you for that, for not putting me in a cage but setting me free."

Freedom has its own risk; instead of telling her that, I press my lips to hers.

CHAPTER
THIRTY-SEVEN

TITUS

O ur lips clash, two warriors running into battle, side by side, hand in hand. I hold nothing back. Fire, heat, passion —everything I pour into that kiss.

As she sighs, her lips part, accepting all I give. Every suck, bite, and pull of my tongue. She molds to me, melts, and coos. All her walls crumble into the palms of my hands.

I catch and cradle every piece.

Men like me—forged in battle—think burning down an empire is the best feeling. It's not. Getting them to open their gates, handing you the keys willingly, that's the best fucking feeling.

Selene just handed me total control.

I open my eyes, needing to see her. Her black hair frames her sun-kissed skin, and those angled eyes press into me like a butter knife, wanting me to cover my body over hers.

Tristen clears his throat noisily. I completely forgot he was outside. He shouts through the door, "I'm going to go further down the hall and make sure no one comes, because we all know you both will be coming. Pun intended. Okay, it's not the time for sex jokes. For fuck's sake, you're lucky Galen went on his little pony ride. Let's hope he's not back soon."

I hear his shadows slide out to cover him and his sword. The door closes. If anyone enters her hall, Tristen will kill them as he remains camouflaged in the dark corner next to the staircase.

That's right. Galen left. I have her all to myself.

She looks away from the locked door and gives in to her desire. Her fingers dig into my garments, fiddling with my armor's fasteners, while her eyes drop to my erection. "I need you now." She pushes forward and straddles my lap as the bond gives us both the fuel we need.

I cage her wrists. Sex has always been an escape for her. She's always been used, never admired, cherished, or loved. "Sex with me is not your escape, Selene. I'm not rushing. I'm going to take my time. I will spend the rest of my life worshiping your body, protecting your heart, and praising your strength."

Her breath causes her chest to rise and fall like the tide. Her hands abandon my clothing, combing through my hair instead. "I'm not worthy of you."

Another kiss is how I silence her. "Enough with this talk; you are worthy of my love. I will consider it an honor to remind you of this every day."

She gathers my face in her hands. "I'm sorry, so sorry I asked you to deny the bond, to ignore it."

"It's in the past." My eyes drop to her lips.

"Titus..."

I'll never tire of hearing my name on her lips.

"I can't stop," the rasp of my voice scrapes my throat. I unfasten my leather armor.

She grabs the hem of my shirt and pulls it off. Her eyes trace my mark; her fingers drift out to touch it. As soon as she makes contact with it, we moan in unison. Her thighs squeeze me; my hands reach out, guiding her hips back and forth against my core.

"Did that feel as good for you as it did for me?" Her breath is like a delicate thread.

I nod. Words have vanished from my tongue.

"What's this?" She peers at the small scar our family made.

"It's a mark my brothers and sister gave each other. If a battle stole us, we never wanted to forget one another."

I expect her jealousy. Instead, she smiles as she presses her forehead to mine. "I'll keep you safe for them."

"It's my job to keep you safe." My hand glides down her spine. Each inch it descends has her body trembling and leaning closer to me.

She moves her head. "No. Our mark makes us equal. I belong to you, and you belong to me."

"You are my equal, but there is nothing wrong with allowing me to be your shield. You've been holding a sword for so long. It's time to let me bear the weight." I tuck her hair behind her pointed ear and study the angle of her jaw.

Where will I kiss her first? There, I press my lips to her collarbone.

"You don't have to fight me to gain my love and affection." Another kiss. "You have it, all of it." She angles her neck, allowing more of my lips to taste her skin.

Her throat rolls as she swallows. The thumping of her pulse pulls my fangs longer. "You've been mine since I released that arrow aimed at your heart. It was my heart to take." Lowering her face, she kisses our mark.

What feels like an orgasm explodes through my body. My back lies against the stone floor of her balcony. I hold on to her like a blanket, keeping her on top of me. Her plump lips suck my skin as she nips it, then she admires the teeth marks on our bond. She spreads her palms wide, roaming all over my chest, down my abs, touching and studying my strength. "By the gods, you're beautiful, Titus," she murmurs in awe. Taking her time, she traces my body with her fingertips. "And I still want your heart, but this time, I intend to keep it safe instead of driving an arrow through it."

A dark laugh slips from my lips. "You're not like any other." I smirk, then I grab her shirt.

She lifts her arms to help me. Just then, a cloud moves, the sunset vanishes, and moonlight illuminates her body as she lifts her hips and pushes her pants down. Her body is a blend of muscle and soft curves.

She's a warrior who has been forced to remain in the shadows. I'm going to pull her into the light. Let her fight and shine.

Her spirit stumbles, pulling her eyes to look down. "I'm scared," she admits.

"Why?" Does she think I'd hurt her?

"Because you see me," she looks to the side, "and some parts of me should remain hidden."

I catch her jaw in my hand and guide her face back to me. "Share them with me so I can vanquish them from your mind. We all have a past, Selene; it's our choice to let it taint our future."

The pad of my thumb catches her tear.

"What aren't you telling me?" I ask. A knot clots my throat. "Hey, I love you, every part of you. If you could forgive me for what I did to your brother, then I can forgive your past. Let me show you what love is, Selene."

That's the cause of her fear. Nobody has ever treated her this way.

"I don't love myself." Her voice is choked. "And one day I fear you won't love me either. You're going to wish you'd let me shatter."

Her truth is more brutal than the roughness of the balcony floor. "I'd only let you crumble because I know I'll catch you. I'll gather up every piece and help you stand again. Look at me. I won't let your scars cause more pain and destroy this moment. I'm going to heal you by giving you my heart. One day, you will look at yourself and love every inch. It will be my duty, my life's mission to show you how much of a treasure you are."

Her soft, warm breasts fill my palm as I cup them, then I bend down and kiss the swell of each one. Her nipple hardens and presses into my palm. An aching sigh escapes her. She cups my hands with hers, guiding me to show how much pressure she likes.

"You don't have to be gentle with me, Titus. I want your marks all over my body."

I fixate on her mark. I grab her hips and flip her, so I'm on top. Her long hair spreads out like a shadow. Her wide eyes reflect the full moon. I bring my face down and suck her nipple into my mouth, rolling my tongue over it.

Her back arches. "Titus, don't stop," I nip her skin, making sure my fangs don't pierce it. Just enough to ensure my imprint lingers until she's begging.

The bond jolts. A new sense invades my body. One I can't fight, nor would I. Her pleasure starts to feel like mine! Every sharp inhale she takes reverberates to my chest, every pull of my tongue, that has her legs clenching, core aching... I feel it. She's about to break.

"Come for me," I demand with a hard suck. No wonder fated mates are always in bed. This isn't sex; it's transcending.

She wraps her legs around my hips, pulling me down to meet her sex. I glide my fang over her nipple again; her head rolls to the side, night paints its shadows over her parted lips that whisper my name, over and over again. My eyes snap open to see our mating mark rise and fall with the fast pace of her heartbeat. A euphoric high slips over my skin like a tailor-made garment.

"More," she pants. "Don't you dare stop." She rolls her hips like a temptress, grinding them into me.

"We're only kissing. I haven't started yet." I chuckle.

"That felt... Titus..."

"I know. I could feel you coming. I can't explain it."

Her blush deepens; her eyes peer at my belt. "I need you. Now." She grabs my belt, pulling it so fast from the loops that it hisses against my leather trousers. She carelessly tosses it aside.

"You sure?" I tease as I roll my hips against her sex. "You wanted to wait, remember? Slow our bond. I think we should take it slow, so you know how I felt," I tease. Pushing up slightly, I nudge her legs open with my knee. "Look how wet you are for me."

I run my index finger along her inner thigh, slow and deliberate, before I find my target, her swollen clit. Lips parted, eyes wide, she moans my name.

"Does that moan mean to take it slow, or is that permission to taste you before I make you mine?"

"Yes," she makes the word five syllables long. "Yes, yes."

I grin. "What's the third yes permission for?"

"For you to take me any way you want; slow, gentle, rough, as long as you're inside of me, yes, to anything." She blinks deliriously.

"You're waving a red flag in front of a bull." I lift her leg, kissing her inner ankle.

"Because I know how to tame you," she taunts. Her hands cup her breasts as she massages them.

"Is that what you want? To tame me?" I tease.

She bites her lip and playfully nods.

"That means you have to see my wild side first."

"I'm not scared of you, mate." She beams. "Show me what you've got." Her eyes drift to my cock.

I kiss up her inner thigh till I press my lips to her wet, heated core. We lock eyes, and everything just... shatters. I lick her long and slow, then I dip my tongue inside and taste her. Her fingers dive into my hair, holding me in place.

"Greedy." I smirk as her wetness coats my lips.

"Needy. There's a difference." She rolls her hips, urging me on.

"Show me then." I blow air over her sex, delighted as her body trembles. "Show me how needy you are, Selene." I thrust my tongue inside her, swirling and scooping. I palm her breast, molding it to my hand, massaging gently, then squeezing it hard just the way she likes.

She clenches her legs, keeping my face anchored between her thighs.

Her hips begin to thrust as she nears her peak. "Slow," I purr; I remove my tongue, but right before she moans a complaint, I cover her sex with my mouth and suck. Hard.

I cover her mouth as she screams into my palm.

I hover over her, bending down, kissing her neck. "You try so hard to make others think you're all spice, but deep down there, you're nothing but sweetness. See how sweet you taste, Selene?" I thrust my tongue between her lips, taking my time. "Like fucking candy," I whisper over her mouth.

Her eyes flutter open, and her lips have a smiling haze pulling them wide. Her hands slide down, wrapping around my cock, taking in my size. "I have to warn you, I'm selfish. I was raised as a princess after all. I want you."

"You already have me." My gaze drops, studying my cock in her hands. It's a sight I love.

"I want more," she purrs as she starts to stroke me, making me harder. "I want you to bite me. I want my blood inside of you, fueling you."

"Selene," I thrust my hips. She squeezes me tighter and quickens her movements.

"Bite me,"

I close my eyes. Think of a kittens, or some shit that stops you from coming in her hand! "When I bite you, I'll be buried inside of you."

"So what are you waiting for?" she smirks, guiding my cock to her wet entrance.

I no longer have the illusion of slowly making love to my mate. Rawness replaces it.

The kiss isn't slow; it spreads like a rapid sickness, tainting everything. Our hands move in a frenzy. I reach down and push two fingers inside her. I need to get her ready. I don't want to hurt her.. *That's it.* More wetness coats my fingers. I curl my finger up, feeling her swollen spot inside.

"Titus..." She rakes her nails down my back.

Nothing else matters as much as she does. Nothing. Not the Vitalis or my family.

It's a frightening thought. It could dismantle everything we worked so hard to accomplish.

I don't care.

Didn't care if Everett's plan went to shit.

I just want her. Need her in every way.

Mate, mate, mate!

Her eyelashes brush against my face as she looks at me. I align myself with her and caress her clit with my hand as I start thrusting inside. "Gods, Titus." Her fingers claw my back again, this time breaking some of the skin.

"I thought you denounced the gods," I murmur. I give her short pumps as a tease.

Go slow. Don't hurt your mate. I watch as her body slowly takes me, inch by inch.

"A cock this huge made me a believer again."

I shift her hips by sliding my arm beneath her. She swings her leg up, planting her heel in the groove of my spine.

I sink further in. "Am I hurting you?" I pant.

"In the best way possible." She swivels her hips, encouraging me.

I slide my hand over and stroke her while I push as far as I can go. "Selene," I gasp. If she squeezes me any harder, I won't be able to withdraw.

We move together, holding each other tight, but it's still not enough. I hoist her leg over my shoulder, determined to go deeper.

"You trying to stab my heart?" A moan escapes her with a smirk. "Yes, right there, gods," she throws her head back.

I thrust so hard we slide an inch along the floor. "Don't start praising the gods now. It's me buried inside of you. Not the gods."

"Are you sure you're not a god? No man has ever taken me like this,"

"No man will ever take you again. I'm the past, present, and future. The memory, the reality, and the dream. Your mate."

"You did the impossible," Selene coos, "You made me a dreamer. I love you."

My heart races wildly. "I love you too, Selene." I slow my rhythm, moving inside her to savor every hot, velvet inch of her embrace.

She rolls her head to the side, exposing her neck to me. "Do it." Our eyes meet. "Make me yours, Titus. Make me yours in every way possible."

I withdraw and then slide in. Again and again. I feel Selene starting her orgasm. Another slow thrust pushes us past the limit. While her body convulses in pleasure, I lean down and sink my fangs deep into her neck. "*Mine.*"

THIRTY-EIGHT

SELENE.

T*he past.*

The tent quivers as the warrior's boots walk past. Their harsh, loud steps felt as natural as my heartbeat. As their shadows fall, the fabric groans and flaps.

I stand like a cloud ready to thunder down tears as the rows of soldiers march to battle. I scan my tent, spotting my bed. How many cots will remain empty? Without a body, how many blankets won't warm up? How many miles will remain untrodden by the warriors who won't march home?

My teeth sink into my chapped lip. I shut my eyes and turn my head toward the door. Swords running over whetstones, strings being pulled into bows, soldiers doing last-minute war rituals were as common as brushing the knots from my hair.

"I'm tired," I whisper to no one.

I tug on the straps of the helmet I stole. My fingers trace the arch of the longbow. I will not wait for another victim in the healer's tent. I'm going to battle, dammit, and I'm fighting!

I'm done. I'm weary in both body and mind. I'll go out in glory. Better than being bartered away as a pawn to another king.

The weight of the quiver I swing onto my back helps strengthen my spine. I move toward the back of my tent, dagger ready.

"Selene," Everett whispers my name softly as he enters. Even from afar, his shadow reaches and grazes me.

The echo of my gnashing teeth grieves my ears. "Don't stop me."

A faint breeze stirred by his step cools my sweaty neck. "Then don't ask me to."

I knew he'd come. After all, he can see snippets of the future. My turn is lightning—a flash of fury with screaming eyes. His broad shoulders, covered in battle-scarred armor, absorb my stare rather than deflect it.

He can afford a new armor, but he's the type that wears a pair of boots till the soles are riddled with holes.

His golden skin has lost its luster. He's got more dirt than freckles staining his cheeks. Under all this war-stress is still my older brother, the handsome fae prince who should be married, plotting safety in the palace walls with our father, not fighting in battle.

That's why I love him. He risks it all for others.

That's also the part I abhor.

I lost him decades ago. It's my fault. I should have told an elder about his foresight. His sanity might have been preserved if they'd helped.

The inhalation of my lungs may fracture my lower ribs. "You're in love with a nightmare you refuse to wake up from. Stop meddling," I say softly.

"That is my path." His unblinking eyes study me, never letting me go. It pulls at my heart, makes me feel incredibly loved, a rare item on a shelf adored and admired, trapped behind glass.

"Leave it. Walk on a new one." The feathers on my arrows—in my quiver on my back—rest against my shoulder. They blur in the corner of my eye. Ready to be set loose in battle.

"All roads must end, Selene." His chin lifts, not in pride but in resignation. "I'd rather decide the ending."

"You continue to drag me back, making promises, but I wake up alone. Let. Me. Go."

"It's not your time."

"If we can choose paths, I pick this one." I stab my longbow into the ground.

Callused hands cup my face. "You're not listening to me," he murmurs.

"I'm going to fight." I peer at his chin, unable to meet his eyes.

"I know. I've seen it, but today is not that day." Slowly, he unbuckles my helmet and places it back on the stand.

"Why?" My lip trembles.

He holds my jaw, pressing firmly so my lips still. "Do not cry for death. Weep for life; it's far more precious, sister."

"You've taught me how to fight; you've always supported me, told me not to cower, but in the middle of a battle, you force me to remain behind."

"I saw this day, and it changed everything. You snuck out and never returned. You died by friendly fire because you were not in the war room. You didn't know we had archers hidden in the west, directly where you ran to fight the vampires."

I shake off the chill that covers my skin. "Then let me die with honor. Let me fight by your side."

His jaw is stone.

I throw my hands up. "I'm nothing more than a piece Father moves on his chessboard. An item you move."

My words are a blow that turns his face sharp. The sounds beyond the tent are silent. He's trapped us in time. "You and I are going to die," he whispers.

I shove down a gulp. For years, he trusted me. Then it became too much for me to bear. I chose myself over him. At the time, it was the only way I could survive without descending into madness.

I regret it every day. I walk this world blind to his plots.

"Tell me something I don't know. Everyone must die." I brush off this statement. What should I do? Sit and cry? I'm not that type of girl. *"We're standing in the middle of a war camp. Let today be that day. I can't live like this any longer, Everett. Healing fae who are forced to go back out and fight. What are we fighting for?"*

He takes my hands. "When we die, it's going to be purposeful."

"*Oh, thank the gods for that,*" *I scoff as I step back.*

Everett pins me with his stare. "*You stopped believing in the gods, Selene.*"

"*They stopped believing in me, Everett!*" *I throw my longbow at his chest. It clatters at his feet.* "*Look where we are. Surrounded by death, and the cause of it. You and Father have forced me to be friend and foe; I heal so they can fight to the death again. That's not honorable. You have turned me into a monster!*"

"*That's man's fault, not the gods,*" *he retorts, shaking his head as bitterness coats his words.*

"*If we are their children, shouldn't they care about us? Where the fuck are they? Why don't they want the war to end?*"

"*Who says they don't?*" *he sharply replies.* "*Every parent has to let their child go. We must watch them fail or succeed.*"

I shove past him. "*I'm fighting.*"

The time bubble snaps, prickling my skin. "*Guards!*" *he shouts.*

I whirl around. "*Don't you dare.*" *Two guards come to my side, each grabbing my biceps.*

Everett steps closer. "*You can spend the battle in the healer's tent or locked up. It's up to you. Today will not be the day you die.*" *He storms past me, never looking back, which means today he won't die either.*

I've never been scared of dying. How can I be? Everyone must. I came to terms with that early on.

I never imagined I'd die with my mate's cock buried so deep inside me I saw the heavens. An ambush of colors, senses, tastes, and smells I can't define.

And when he bit me, fed from me... it changed everything.

My heart? Erupted.

When he drank that first mouthful of my blood, I was reborn.

Ever since Everett stopped me from dying in battle, I've been waiting for death to claim me. After my brother's death, I hoped my death would be soon. I longed for it, for the pain and grief to stop.

Then Titus showed up, and everything shifted. I sensed he was my mate. I hated it. If I were mated, I would have to endure overcoming the grief of Everett's death. It's a dirty fact I don't want Titus to know.

I stopped thinking about death. I was focused on keeping Titus alive. There is something else I haven't told my mate, a deep knot in my stomach that is so anchored and buried, it can't be freed. So I cut it loose from my ship—my mind—I stopped thinking about what Everett hinted at.

But now I feel it, a huge barrier blocking all the warm fuzzies settling in my belly.

I praised Titus for being brave. Yet here I am, lying under him, floating between consciousness, lost in an orgasmic high. I'm a hypocrite. A part of me wants to convince him to run away, so we both can just find a cave to live in and fuck in till the end of our days.

That's a happy ending Tristen would applaud.

Everything Everett has predicted is coming true. Everything... including my ending.

The problem is, I don't know when it will be.

Titus is with Adrian. Tristen has remained outside my door as I sit, hugging my knees. I'm sore in the best way possible. I wish I could bask in that.

I should sleep more, but the tea I just drank makes closing my eyes impossible.

"Tristen!" I shout. A moment later, the door opens.

"Did you call?" He pokes his head inside. His goofy grin is a defense, buying him time to dissect his prey. Look deep in his eyes, and you'll see the offense he's hiding. He's a lethal weapon, just what I need to protect my mate.

He makes you laugh because you step closer and speak freely. He's waiting to gobble up your secrets and turn them into weapons. He uses his thick lashes to make you think he's a ladies' man looking for his next hookup.

In truth, he's scanning the crowd, spotting the predators that might prove deadly to his family.

"Come," I wave him inside.

He steps into the room and rubs his ears. "Sorry, I wasn't sure if you called. I'm still deaf from all the sex screams. Next time, can you warn me to descend a flight of stairs?" He holds up his hands. "Listen, I'm happy Titus got laid, but... yeah... I don't need to hear it, which is odd because sometimes Nero and I share. I don't mind when he's there, but Titus is too much like a parent."

I wrinkle my nose in distaste. "That's a lot of details I didn't need."

"Oh, you'll need them. We hold shit like this over each other's heads." The edge of my bed dips as he sits.

I know what he's doing, babbling to remove the awkward air, so I'll lower my defenses.

He continues, "Wait till you meet the others. Ryker is a scary fuck. He produces more grunting sounds than words, claiming it's his wind magic talking. He looked at a guy once on the battle field. One look from Ryker and the guy stab himself. True story. One less person to kill. It wasn't a fae, so I mean no insult. Contrary to what you think, we don't kill fae for sport. Oh, and Ryker's eyes are violet. Freaky shit."

I cross my legs, feigning a relaxed position. "Violet?" I'll indulge him.

"It's an odd color, right? Have you ever seen violet eyes?"

"Can't say I have," I respond. "So you and Nero are together?" I thought Nero was like his brother? Maybe I was wrong and they consider Nero family because he's Tristen's partner.

"Together?" He scratches his head, "Not like that. We just share sometimes. He's a copy-paste of me. We like the same thing, a woman sandwiched between our bodies."

"So there are two of you to worry about?" I arch a comical brow.

"Twice the pleasure." Tristen smirks. "Not that you'll ever experience that, nor would you need to. Tell me, is sex with a mate all it's cracked up to be?"

Hiding my blush is impossible, so I answer, "Yeah. It's like having sex for the first time, but it doesn't hurt. Every sensation is new, hard to explain. You want it again, and again."

"You're not bashful. Bonus points."

"What's with this change in attitude towards me?"

"Blame it on mood swings. I'll be honest: when I first realized you were his mate, I wanted to find a way to break the bond. But I realized that either way, I'd lose a part of him. If I broke the bond or kidnapped him, he'd never forgive me. He'd always try to get back to you. I had no choice but to jump on this bandwagon and help two star-crossed lovers."

"That's quite a rendition of the truth." *I think you'd still pull us apart if you could. I don't blame you.*

He shrugs. "What can I say? I like to embellish." He hesitates. "Well, not when it comes to myself. I have no lack of confidence when it comes to my cock and how good at sex I am."

I roll my eyes.

"I should warn you, Ember is not going to like you at first. She's our sister, crazy protective, double standard because when we chase guys away from her, she bitches up a storm." He grins at a memory.

"And what about Cyrus? You don't mention him as much."

Tristen's playful demeanor vanishes. "We're protective of his privacy."

"Why?"

"It's a need-to-know basis." He shifts closer to the edge of the mattress. "Why did you call me in?"

"I can see Cyrus is a button," I murmur.

"Yes. Don't push it."

I throw my hands up. "I won't. But if I'm part of your family, I'll need to know why."

"Family bonds are earned."

"Noted," I reply. "Are you this hot and cold with the ladies?"

"Only one certain one."

"How special."

His eyes darken. Did Titus teach him how to camouflage so seamlessly? "What did you need?"

I bite my lip, feeling the ache in my neck from where Titus fed from me. The wound has healed thanks to him. "You'd do anything for your family. I..." I inhale sharply. "I need you to do something for me."

He leans closer, pressing his elbow on his knee. "Something naughty?"

"You could say that."

He jolts back. "I don't like that tone. Here I was, coming into your room, thinking we were going to have fun and play a joke on Titus, but that tone tells me you want me to keep a secret from him." The mattress squeaks as he stands. "Don't ask me to do that."

I lunge forward and grab his hand. "I just... If I ask you to give him a letter, would you?"

He snatches his hand back. "I was just starting to like you. What do I call you? Sister-in-law sounds insulting to the bond." He hems and haws. "Mate-in-law."

"Tristen."

"Don't!" he snaps with a wicked tongue. "*You* can give him the letter."

"What if I'm not here?"

I hear his teeth grind before he flashes his fangs. He walks to the door and grabs the handle. "Newsflash, mate-in-law, you're not going anywhere." He slams the door shut.

I walk to my desk, light a candle and, with shaking hands, I begin to write Titus a letter. Tears stain the page. Just as I pen the final word, I remember the conversation Titus and I had when we first met. Ironic that it was about final goodbyes.

Titus coughs, but his voice only deepens. "During Everett's final battle, he caged me. Stopped time. My brother was on the outside, moving more slowly.

I witnessed swords sink into flesh; I saw the prolonged confusion that death claimed them. I'd rather die instantly than watch the seconds pass."

The hand of my brother's killer slips into mine before I can stop myself. My actions shock us both. There's a spark that curls up our arms. His fingers hug mine.

"Some say a slow death is more precious; it gives you time to say your goodbyes," I murmur.

"What if I don't want goodbyes?" He studies our held hands much longer than is appropriate.

Titus doesn't want a long goodbye, and that's what a letter would be.

I hang my head. "What am I doing?"

The edge of the paper curls as the candle's flame begins to burn it. I hurry, walk to my balcony, and release it. The wind carries it, up, up, up, then it's gone.

CHAPTER
THIRTY-NINE

TITUS

The scent of freshly sharpened metal surrounds me as I enter Adrian's office. Oil and sparks. Grit and survival. Not a bottle of bloodwine in sight.

He'd make a good king, but Everett saw him better suited as a turncoat.

Adrian's forehead becomes silk on uneven ground. "You look different."

I am. I just drank from my mate.

Adrian's posture turns to that of fingers gripping a page they are hesitant to turn. In the blink of an eye, he's standing, slamming his door shut so the silencing spells protect us. He stands firm as a tree, arms crossing—digging deep like roots for answers.

"Show me your chest." His voice is a branch, snapping in the sudden storm.

The blood drains from my face. "What?"

"Your heart. Show it to me."

He knows. Is it that obvious? My magic covers my arms, and the heat from the flames has him stepping back.

He lifts a hand, tugging down his collar. "I'm bonded." There on his chest is his unique mate mark. "I know what the afterglow of the first time with your mate feels like. It can't be hidden; it forces people to take a step back, to reconsider you in every way. You can always sense a predator, and being mated means you are a step above everyone else." He pulls at his hair. "The gods must be with us. Galen left hours ago. He'd use your mate against you."

"That's why I'm here." Orange flames dance in my eyes.

Adrian's hand slides from his hair to his neck. "Wait a bloody second. You've been with Selene, guarding her. No... no... don't you dare tell me..."

"Then I won't tell you." Everett's magic flares, ready to defend me and my mate. *Relax, let's see how he reacts*, I tell the time magic.

His fingers turn into a cast, keeping his neck from bending. His inhale is a strong gust of wind. "You truly bonded with the queen? Hey, don't look at me like that. I know what it's like to have a mate. I know you're about to snap my neck. But remember, I have put my life, my mate's, and my son's life behind you. All my bets are on you, Titus. The men want you as their leader."

I shape the fire in my palm into a ball. "Why not you?" I ask.

"I never wanted a crown."

"Neither did I, but people keep trying to shove one on my head. First Everett, then you." Now I need to accept that fate in order to keep my mate safe.

"Everett saw my future. I'm a hand for you to use." His eyes drift down. "I'm fine with that."

What's he not telling me? I make a mental note to ask later.

"We all have our roles to play. This is mine. I lead armies, not kingdoms and... runes." Sweat shines off his brow as my flames heat his office.

"You know a lot more than you previously let on."

"As do you." His eyes burn into the fabric covering my mate mark.

"What happened to your comment about not knowing what Everett wanted me to find?"

"It was easy to figure out. Everett told me to keep an eye on Sable, to let her break the laws here. So I did." He walks over to his desk. "I kept all her midnight rendezvous a secret from Galen. But my men are loyal to me. They told me everything. Take a seat." He nods toward the empty chair.

My steps feel like a journey until I sit down, preparing to be slapped with more secrets.

His elbow hits his desk as he presses a finger to his temple. "Sable has an eye for kings. We all know she was fucking Galen," he spits in disgust. "But she also spread her legs for Hector Von Manson."

Sounds like a name suited for an asshole; just Sable's type. I steeple my hands. "Who's that? What kingdom does he rule over?"

"You've been so busy fighting the fae, all my men have, but the world is large. Our war is not the only one raging. Hector Von Manson is a mage from the Valley of Sand and Bones."

"That's so far west of here." I reply. How does this benefit Sable? "Wait, that's where the girl with that shadow creature said she came from."

Adrian nods, "Yes. It means the valley's monsters have come here. I've been there. It's all sand, palm trees, and insects bigger than my foot. Takes more than one sword to kill them. But in those burning lands is Hector's castle. Or maybe I should just call it refuge."

"Refuge for what?"

"Not what. *Who*," Adrian states. "Hector trains mages in unnatural ways."

"Cut to the point."

"Hector was the son of King Ferdinand of Sandia."

"Never heard of Sandia."

"Hector burned Sandia and its people to the ground using metal."

"Metal?"

"One of his talents is causing metal to melt. He took all the army's weapons, melted them, and turned them into a big fucking shiny mirror, which reflected the sun. He aimed it at the villages—made of palm wood, and thatched roofs—and the roads into town.

"It got so hot that the houses caught on fire, and people ran to escape, but they only made it a few steps into the road before the heat took them. Poof!"

"Sounds like a noble gentleman." My tongue tests the point of my fangs. Hector is worse than Galen because he'll willingly tear things down, whereas Galen would never burn a castle down. He'd add it to his pages of titles.

"Yeah," Adrian rasps. "One Galen should be concerned about, but his vendetta with the fae blinds him. An army without weapons won't last long. I don't know the extent of Hector's alchemy magic, but I don't want him getting close to my men and their swords."

There's that look again, one that suggests Everett told him this.

"How did Sable get to the Valley of Sand and Bones?"

"I was wondering when you'd ask that." He scratches his jaw, weighing his next words carefully. "The mage Galen has here, the one that sent Sable back to Solaria, that's Hector's sister. Name is Sofia, favorite color is purple, favorite stone to store her magic in is amethyst. Galen doesn't know Sofia is related to Hector, or else he'd keep her as a bargaining chip. She's powerful; most mages can only open a portal a day, but she can open up three to four portals in a single afternoon. A nasty secret she hasn't revealed to Galen yet. Doubt she will."

I slip my thumb into my fist and crack it. I never heard of a mage that powerful. "So Sable has been escaping to see Hector, plotting and then returning as if she's the picture of grace for dinner."

"More like the picture of whoredom. Listen, I have no qualms if a woman wants to fuck like a man. I do have problems when the woman only does it to break vows," he says dryly. "There is more. I'm told Hector has a lot of skin art, odd tattoos, symbols." His eyes press into mine. "So I started to dig deeper, sent a spy who is good with a pen. He copied down some of Hector's tattoos; I sent those to an old friend of mine at Ishmor."

He stands and pulls out a book from his shelf. It slaps against his desk with a sharp pang.

"Ever heard of runes?"

I stare at the book. *Mastering Techniques of Rune Drawing*. I flip it open. It's a how-to book on drawing runes correctly. It stresses the curves and lines, down to copying the exact thickness. If done wrong, the rune will not work.

Some shapes are simple, others... my hands can never reproduce. My pen has been a sword, the ink is the blood I spill.

"You're tone implies you know what Everett asked me to do." I close the book and place it on my lap.

"Connecting dots didn't make me the Vice Admiral of this army. *Finding* dots to connect did. Runes. It's what Everett has you hunting for. I did my homework. There are countless books on runes, full of dust; no one reads them. But once you clear those cobwebs, you can find chapters about a book called the Vitalis. They claim the Vitalis is a master dictionary of runes, it's a source of power, a lifeline. It seems to be where they originated from.

"Now, I don't know if runes really worked the way my mom read to me as a child, but if they did, I'd be damn sure not to give Hector and Sable the master class on how they operate. At this point, Hector's tattoos are just self-expression, but I think he knows that in the future they can be turned into something else."

Adrian pushes off the bookshelf with the speed a loaded treasure ship leaves the dock. Full of alertness, ready to defend against being plundered.

His desk becomes a crutch he leans into as he continues, "I'm scared, Titus, and I don't admit that easily. I'm not one to panic. I plan. Do you think Sable and Hector have this book? The last thing I want is a metal melting fucker who has runes enhancing his magic."

My tongue moves like the hands of a clock, sweeping across my mouth, desperate to find a trace of moisture each passing second. "No," I fail to swallow; my word stands firm and dry.

"You say that with such confidence."

"They don't have it *yet*," I repeat.

"You know where it is." His shoulders lift. Now I have another person I can't fail. My mate, my family, his family, this entire kingdom, and yeah... the world, it seems. "That's what Everett wanted you to find. That's why he wanted you to have this army, to keep the runes safe."

"There's a lot of grey in that black-and-white statement." I add.

"So paint the picture for me." He leans closer, hanging over me like a torch. "I can not order an army without all the details. I need facts so I know where we stand. I have converted a vast majority of this army on our side. Every single person stationed in Lunestra is with us."

My chest skips a beat. *Every* person?

"Yeah." He smirks. "Your family is on our side. They want a king who has walked in their boots, who will walk in them after he gets the throne."

My family. Ryker, Cyrus, Ember, and Nero all support me. It doesn't reveal my stress, but grows it tenfold.

"Not every guard is on my side here; some will rebel, others will defect. When we take over, it has to be swift, Titus. We can't have the transition of power spill into a civil war. I've been turning soldiers, ensuring this doesn't happen, but I need to know what you do, so when the time comes, we're the ones doing the fucking, and not the ones being bent over and fucked. Understand?"

"How did you keep all this from Galen?"

"Easy," he leans back, giving me room to breathe. "He's the one who grew his rose hedges too tall to see beyond. He's overconfident. I never used your name, in case I got caught. But after you ended the war, my men guessed it was you. They prayed and hoped it was a man of your merit we were fighting for. I worked with only those I trusted, then we branched out.

"Galen's nobles think he's a charmer, but his men know he's a tyrant, one who remains in his castle, as we're out there doing the actual fighting. I know you don't trust me. That's smart. But I trust you. I've got my son; he's... human."

407

A human son, which means, "Your mate is human."

He nods.

The outcome is 50/50 for a child born to two different people. Either human or vampire, in Adrian's case. And having a human son makes his situation as a father extremely tragic.

"I've been on this land for two hundred and sixty years, but my mate is twenty-seven human years," he adds. "I have a lot of time ahead of me, thanks to her resetting me. I'm ready to stand by your side till the day I die."

That's why mates are so coveted. When they bond, it shifts their time clock, resetting them to the younger one's age, and the human's life extends into a supernatural state. It's a science just beginning to be studied. I heard a rumor that one human even gained a small amount of accelerated healing after he was mated to a fae. But so much is still unknown.

One thing is clear, though, that extending life won't extend to Adrian's son. He'll have to watch age transform him.

I know what it's like to have parents more concerned with the sharpness of their swords than their child's memories. I don't blame my parents. That's the cards they were dealt. If I can make Adrian's limited time with his son not be filled with war, then I will.

"I'll tell you what I know, but first, you said Everett saw your future. What did he see?" I ask.

He presses into his chair, leaning on his elbow. "Everett saw my son's future. Two outcomes. One where Sable succeeded." His jaw clenches. "He... he..." Uttering the truth is a battle this warrior can't win.

"You don't have to say it," I relent. If Sable wins, his son dies.

"Everett said if I helped make you king and remained loyal, then my son would live."

I place the book on his desk, stand, and fill my fingers with small dancing flames. "Don't seal away all the facts. Tell me what made you hesitate just now. What unspoken truth had your eyes looking down?"

He bites his inner cheek. "Everett said Griffen would be a king."

Flames spread to my elbows. Adrian speaks quickly but steadily, "Not of these lands. Not a king that rivals you, Titus, one that is *loyal* to you."

"Kings are not loyal to one another," I remind him.

"You will start as a king, Titus, but perhaps that is just the base before the climb. I think you'll be more once you get the Vitalis. An emperor unites kings."

"Don't inflate my ego; I'm riddled with holes, and your puffs of air won't remain."

"Food for thought. Everett said you'd be a king, but he told me to push you. And here is my shove." He slaps his desk.

He never told me that because I would have run.

"Explain. Fast." My flames wrap around my neck, warming and soothing my tense muscles.

"Everett said Griffen would... it sounds crazy, but Everett claimed Griffen would become a rider, and he'd get a dragon; he'd be the first, then the others would follow him."

"Dragons do not exist," I scoff, even as I doubt my own words.

"As runes do not?"

A rider? That's... possible since Griffen is human and not a vampire. Fairytales claim that riders were humans who were rune-marked to bond with their dragons. That's why Adrian is fighting for this, risking everything. "If your son can be turned into a rider, he'll no longer be as vulnerable. It's a layer of protection any parent would die for."

"Now you know why I'm doing all this. I do not desire a crown for Griffen's head, for I know the weight it will bear down on him. But I'd do anything to see him not be as fragile as glass in a hail storm. Our world is harsh, Titus."

"Riders do not live as long as vampires do. Their lifespan remains human."

His lip tugs down. "That is a fate I must bear. We can not have everything," he whispers.

I fail to meet his eyes, but the weight of his hope and dreams presses into me.

"Everett said my son would bend a knee to you, that all the dragons and riders would follow you. Yeah, that look on your face is why I didn't say anything. Runes bring peace, but peace awakens monsters. Magic always seeks balance. Dragons and other creatures will wake from slumber."

"You're betting everything on fables," I voice. The book catches my eye: its cover is old and torn, with stained pages. We've been dying for men with crowns; perhaps dying for words is a more poetic way to go.

"Now who is lying?"

"You can understand why this is hard to chew. Everett placed us at the bottom of a treacherous path, quaking the land under our feet, forcing us to proceed without any tools, or fall into a chasm. I'm trying to climb, but every summit I reach, I barely survive, Adrian."

"We have clues, and those are tools enough. You and I both know if the climb doesn't kill us, the descent can. We need to be ready to get down the other side. I need to make sure you succeed, Titus, because my son's fate is on that other side."

"Griffen's fate might be over a few more peaks and valleys," I mumble.

"Then I'll conquer them. I will keep fighting till the world my son lives in is honorable. If he has to die, let it be for life and not lands or jewels."

Breathe in, out, in. I lean over the desk, and Adrian holds his ground as I extend my hand; flames cover my fingers. He looks at the fire, swallows, and swings his hand in mine.

See, he needed to trust I wouldn't let my fire burn him.

Our fingers intertwine. "Till the death." I voice what soldiers do before we run into battle.

His grip tightens as he smiles. "Till the new dawn, brother."

I tell him everything about how we need Sable to get the Vitalis free of the death cage. Hector is a new problem, one we add to the mental list.

"I see two burning items about to singe us." He holds up a finger. "One, Galen. Two, we need to talk to that vampire in the library."

"I'm killing Galen as soon as he returns. Problem solved."

"I need a fortnight to get the army from Lunestra."

"I can not wait a fortnight, Adrian. She is my mate, and he is a threat to her."

He curses, hurries to his desk, and pens a note. "I'm sending them the alert. If they rest only every other day, they can shave off four days of travel, but that depletes energy."

"Will Galen know the army near Lunestra moved?"

"No, all the scouts are in my pocket." He pours the mage powder over the paper, sealing it, and then he holds it out of the window. Magic flares as it takes flight, as a bird would. He turns, brows pinched in thought. "We have numbers here, but there will be a fight after you slay Galen. Not every guard will stand with us. Some will fake it until they see an opportunity to strike you down."

"That is a risk I will take."

He pauses, then says, "I suggest we take out the nobles first."

"Only those loyal. I don't want innocents killed."

"I agree," he replies with a nod. "Are you planning to ambush Galen as he returns? We could shut the gates. Meet him at the wall, but those loyal to him inside would start to fight."

If Selene were not on the other side of those gates, I would agree. I know her; she will run into this battle. I need to do it away from her. I can't risk a hair on her head.

"Do you know where Galen rode, what lands he's patrolling?" I ask.

"Of course. He went southeast."

"Of course he did." I shake my head. When Sable marches her army towards this kingdom, they'll be coming from the opposite direction. Galen's ride is a fake show.

"We will ride and ambush him. Now."

His eyes widen in surprise. "This moment?"

I nod.

"We should sleep one more night. Rest."

"I've lain awake far too many nights as my mate was caged down the hall. The next time I close my eyes, she will be in my arms."

Adrian's gaze drops, and he looks to the window, jaw tight. Then he nods and mumbles to himself as he plots. He strides fast to his desk, pulls out a red candle, lights it, and sets it in the window. An odd reddish black flame grows taller than it should. "It's the signal to prepare to secure the castle."

"Instead of killing Galen's noble soldiers, offer them safe passage out of Blackthorn."

Adrian's expression falls. "Pests that are released instead of killed tend to come back, Titus."

"I want to be different. I want to give people a chance to change. We all pick sides; some of those decisions are made in fear, to protect our family members."

A slow grin spreads over his face, the kind a father wears when his child has made him proud.

"The men with Galen are my spies. They will aid when we ambush him."

"You're staying here."

He reels back in disgust. "Absolutely not."

"It's an order. I need you here. Inside the walls where your mate is and mine."

"You list my mate first. You put my happiness over yours," he mutters. "That's why Everett picked you." Steal rasps as he pulls his sword out. His knees hit the floor as he makes a warrior's bow. "I pledge my life to you, Titus."

This isn't right. "Do not bow. We breathe and bleed the same. We're equal. Stand on your feet. Stand as I do."

He does. I grab his hand, shake it again, and my flames cover the grasp.

"You need to know something before you seek Galen out." He says as a crease digs into his forehead. "I remember Galen before he wore that specific crown on his head. He was a decent fighter, even though his father never let him step into a real battle. He made thorny vines that would hurt if you stepped barefoot on them. But once he got that new crown, the vines changed. They grew into walls so thick that multiple swords were needed to chop them down." Adrian taps his head. "It's his crown; it's different. A vampire smith didn't make it, but rather a mage. I think he did something to it. You know mages can store their magic in items. I think his crown works a similar way."

"Vampires can't store magic as mages do."

"I know, but I think his crown helps amplify his magic. It's a conduit. He can make his vines stretch for miles. No earth magic user can do that naturally."

I think about Selene's training field, surrounded by a cage of vines. Did he do that in one day?

"I suggest you knock that crown off his head first, then you tire him out. It's not going to be easy. When the guards see you, they will know it's time. Trust me. It's you and three dozen men against Galen, but it's still going to be a battle."

"Time is on my side."

Adrian begins to smile as he walks to his door. "I thought you could use another weapon." He pulls the door open. "I intended to tell you when he got here. He was due in two days. He got here early, reporting a smooth journey that sped up his trip. I wonder if Everett employed more spies to guard his route. It seems Everett knew you'd be needing him tonight."

I stagger back when I see who is on the other side. "What the fuck?!" I gasp.

CHAPTER
FORTY

TITUS

"What the fuck?!" My smile practically splits my face as I stride forward.

Ryker's arms open like thunder, swallowing all my senses. His hug is iron, never wanting to let me go. He smells of a long journey battered by hail-force winds.

I move back, cupping his face to study him. His short silver-blonde hair is windswept and dirty, suggesting days of travel. Two arms, ten fingers, two legs, and those eyes of such a rare color, blinking with life, narrowing with a hint of anger that I left him out. I hug him again. "You're safe," I breathe. I glance at Adrian and voice my thanks.

"I'm insulted. Did you think I wouldn't survive without you?" Ryker flashes his fangs as he smirks. He steps inside Adrian's office and closes the door.

"What are you doing here? Where are Cyrus, Nero, and Ember?" I press, still feeling the reeling effects of disbelief.

"Still in Lunestra. I did not inform them I left. You know them." His violet eyes shift as they check me for new injuries. "I knew something had happened after you killed Everett. I'm pissed you only trusted Tristen with this secret."

"I didn't want to risk you and the others."

"That's not your decision to weigh. We're a family; we vote." He holds up his hand. "I know you'll tell me everything, but first we have a king to kill."

With his arms crossed, Adrian leans on the wall and says, "I met with your family during their trip to Lunestra," he shrugs.

"It should have been you who told me." Ryker lowers his chin and glares at me. Sometimes his eyes look more like violet thunderclouds than streaks like the rest of us have. "I was never on Galen's side. I fought for our family. On my march to Lunestra, I felt something was off. The other men kept their eyes on us, as if they were waiting for something to occur. Adrian showed up and told us his plan."

When I blink, the room is replaced by a memory. Blood coats Ryker's face, a crimson contrast to his violet eyes. My ears are ringing from my heartbeat; sweat rains down my spine.

For weeks, Ryker's white hair would have a pink tint. Ember tried to wash it with oils, but it was useless; there was always another battle. More blood. Stings puncture my palms as I dig my nails deep. Metal clashing, shouts of dying men, and crying mothers. The horrors of war grip me sometimes.

A vigorous smack on my back rouses me. "Hey," Ryker says. Oh, I'm back in the office. "Let's make you a king."

Our eyes meet, his searching mine longer than I like. "I never wanted a crown," I protest.

"I know, but I'm going to shove one on your pretty head. That look on your face tells me I'd better sit down because I have a lot to catch up on."

"You'll have to play catch-up later," Adrian announces. "Galen planned to return by sunrise. He was going to parade through the streets. Little do his people know he took the leisurely route." He walks over to a cabinet and grabs a flask. "It's a few hours old, but it will work. Fill up; the night will be long, but the morning will be joyful."

Ryker and I take the blood. "I will tell you everything once Galen's blood is on my hands."

I raise my glass, but I don't drink. Selene's blood still fuels me. "I have a mate," I blurt, slipping the flask in my pocket.

Ryker almost chokes, his eyes piercing mine. "Who?"

I pause, weighing my words carefully. "The queen."

Ryker doesn't laugh. He listens, digests, and reads body language. "She's a fae," I add.

He shrugs, "She could have a dick between her legs for all I care. If you're happy, then I am too." He grabs my shoulder. "If anyone has a problem, I'll deal with them. She's your mate. She's family. It's simple."

"But Cyrus," I press. Before he was placed with us, he was enslaved by a fae lord. Slavery is outlawed across all the land, but this lord lived deep in the mountains. No one ventured there; no one saw the horrors that were happening.

Sometimes in battle, I know I've lost him. He blacks out, kills those fae, thinking they are the old master who tortured him.

"Cyrus will accept her," Ryker states firmly, his eyes holding appreciation. "I'll keep an eye on her."

"It's time," Adrian voices after a moment of tense silence.

My gaze quickly shifts to Ryker's chest, where our shared scar is. The crown isn't on my head, but my neck feels the burden. Ryker's hand moves from my shoulder to the back of my neck. Silent support.

I can't thank Everett for everything he's done, but I whisper gratitude for this, the return of my family, and for leading me to my mate.

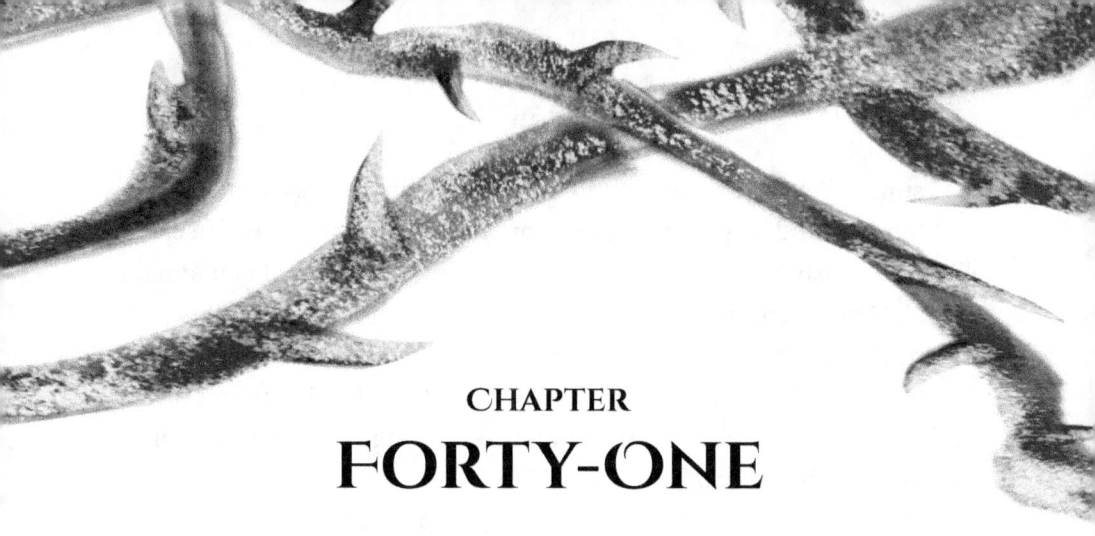

CHAPTER
FORTY-ONE

TITUS

Ryker and I get off our horses, grass brushing our chins, and we creep along in silence. Our destination is the hilltop so we can spot Galen.

Our lungs strain against the unyielding ground. With a small dagger, I cut a hole in the bush to improve our view. Ironically, Galen's rose bushes conceal us. They border the road to Blackthorn Castle, making it appear like a dark, beautiful beast. Ryker alters the wind's direction so we can smell and hear the approaching horse as we look ahead.

I know I can kill Galen, but I have a growing fear. "I didn't tell Tristen I was leaving the castle." I push my fingers into the grass and let out a sigh. "I mean, he knows I'm going to kill Galen." I pluck a blade of grass out and rip it apart.

"Tristen's anger blows away easily. He'll forgive you once he finds a new ass to chase."

"I didn't tell my mate either," I remind him.

"She's got a temper?"

I smirk. "Well, she tried to kill me the first time she saw me."

"Nero would say that makes for good chemistry." He uses his elbows to push up just a little. "Stop thinking about sex. I can smell it on you," Ryker reprimands me.

For the first time in a long fucking time, I'm embarrassed.

"Wow, you're blushing. You know, once Nero finds out you have a mate, he's going to pester you for all the sex details. Fucking a mate is said to be the best sex of your life."

"It's not just fucking or sex," I snap, keeping my eyes ahead so he can't see my fury. I don't like him talking about Selene. For a moment, I felt like hurting my brother. That's the bond making me crazy. "I'm protective of her. Sorry if I snap."

"I get it. I'm protective of our family," he shrugs.

"Having a mate multiplies that feeling," I admit. I force a cough, breaking the swelling in my throat. "There is this noose around my neck, Ryker. I want her by my side so I can see her. At the same time, I need her far away, caged so I know she's safe. I can't win. The rope is pulled tighter."

He cools me down by blowing wind over our backs.

"She'll forgive you." His eyes drift to the sky. The stars can't be seen; soon the sun will break the horizon. I hope Selene slept. She needs to recover and recharge her magic.

"I'm not so sure." My heavy exhale bends the blades of grass into the dirt. "She wanted to kill Galen. In truth, it *should* be her kill."

"Is she that good of a fighter?" he wonders.

"She is but... she's been caged. She trains hard, fights strong, but—"

"Battle is different," Ryker grunts.

"Yeah." Training to fight is a dance; war is an argument. It's not pretty or justified; sometimes, plans go to shit, and you have one second to figure out how to survive. Thinking like that takes years to master.

"Buy her a pretty ring. Nero says women like that."

"Not the kind of women you and I like," I reply with a wry smile.

Ryker and I are brutes; we don't touch silk, we rip it. Finery has no place in our hands. A part of me wants to be gentle with Selene. I want to take the sword from her hand and replace it with a child. I want her to know I will defend her, that she doesn't have to build walls now.

But she'd never let me. She'd find dishonor in that, the same way I find dishonor in allowing her to risk her life for mine.

"Don't think about your mate right now. It's a bonded pair's weakness. Focus on the battle." Ryker widens his elbows, nudging one closer to me.

I'm surveying the area below. "I need to tell you something."

"Is it a plan of attack? Or are you just gonna ride and start fighting? You're my king now, so I was waiting for orders, but shit, you're leaving it all to the last minute. Before you start, Adrian warned me about Galen's crown. I was thinking I would use my wind to knock it off. You hit him with fire, aiming for his hands so he can't aim his vines our way.

"I'll watch your back in case the men with him are not as loyal as Adrian thinks, although from what I've seen, Adrian has poisoned Galen's waters for years. Galen never drank water; he was drunk on wine."

Ryker mentioned only my fire. I still have to confess I have fae magic.

He rolls to his side and watches me. "I know you didn't want this, but I think you need it."

I glance at him quickly, making sure to keep my ears toward the road. "What do you mean?"

"Soldiers can lose purpose when war is endless. With you as king, that will change." His eyes glance to where our family mark is under my armor. "If I die under your rule, no, don't stop me, listen. I want you to know it's my choice. Cry for me, but then make sure you smile, and live for me. You took me into your group, called me brother without an ounce of judgement. You gave me your food rations, shared your blanket, and knocked out Declan because he bullied me about my eyes and hair color. The memories you gave me make death a small price to pay."

Turning my face to the road again, I blink away the tears. My voice is trapped; I can't find words. We observe the grass turning yellow as the sun paints it with light.

"Promise me you'll keep my mate and our family safe," I whisper.

"No. If I promise you that, it permits you to die. Keep them safe yourself." His wind magic blows harshly, shoving off the bead of sweat on my neck. "Galen should arrive soon."

The earthy scent of dirt fills my nose. I flex my toes, roll my ankles, and begin to pump blood into my muscles. "This fight is going to be different."

"You killed a prince. A king is no different. We will stick to my plan," Ryker whispers, though his lips barely move. He wants no arguments.

I trace a circle in the dirt. "It's a good plan, but I have a better one." My eyes fill with mischief. "Did Adrian tell you I have fae magic now?"

Ryker peels his eyes off the valley below. "What did you say?" he breathes.

"When Everett died, he gave me one of his powers."

"*One* of?" His foot flinches against the soil.

My eyes look to the road and scan it. "I'll tell you everything later. I just need you to know I have the magic to time-weave. I'm going to freeze time, so don't be caught off guard when it happens."

"You have fae magic?!" His wind pushes into me, as if disbelieving.

"For a time."

"What's that mean?"

"I'll explain more—"

A faint drumming carries on the wind. Horses. "It's time." Ryker and I stand. "We get as close as we can, knock that crown off his head, and you let me do the rest."

I offer one last glance over my shoulder, down at the valley, where a king will soon lie dead. It brings me one step closer to fulfilling what

Everett wanted. One step closer to losing my old life. I'll be a king, and good kings can't run from their troubles; they embrace them.

SELENE

I dig my heels into the mattress. "There's no way I can sleep," I grunt as I pull my knees up.

A smile appears as I assess my body, then gaze at the balcony. My thighs clench at the memory. Warm breath moves across my open lips. Titus's body and mine had moved as one. Sex had never been about coming together before.

Sex with Titus was like rain caressing your face after months-long battles. Slow, deliberate in cleansing you. Each droplet that hugged my body—each press of his fingers into my soft skin—wanted to remind me I survived, and now there will be peace and admiration. His fingers were rivers rolling over every inch of me, pushing away any memory of another's touch. His lips were as warm as the sun as it slipped through the rain cloud, reminding me that hope was always in sight.

Sex with Titus was a new destination, a new sense, an unimaginable level of pleasure. My fingers brush over where he bit me. He fed from me, his mate... I've never felt so powerful.

I gave him what no other could. There was a sharp sting when his fangs broke my skin, but before the pain could reach my fingertips, it changed as fast as the northern winds. Pleasure seems a word too lacking. I came as water over a fall does—it ramps up, closer and closer to the edge. Faster! Faster! Then I dove, jumped, flew. Leaping to a new destination.

Then we landed, and all those feelings and emotions merged into a calm body of water. I wanted to relax on the banks and study it for its beauty.

I tentatively climb out of bed. I'm so exhausted, but I somehow have energy. Oh... that ache between my legs. I like it. Flaring open my fingers, I feel some of my life magic. I need more sleep to recharge fully.

Titus's scent fills my lungs. Masculine but whimsical—an uncontrollable ocean tide. It makes me want to jump off the boat that has trapped me so I can swim beside him.

Sunlight pouring in from my window causes me to blink. Titus left last night. He should have returned by now. My fingers touch our mark. I can feel he's safe, but there is an anxiousness playing on the cord. Is it Titus or me? Probably me.

"Tristen!" I shout as I swing open the door, spotting him leaning on the wall, one foot crossed over his ankle, just smirking at me with tired eyes. He stayed awake all night guarding me.

"Yes, mate-in-law," he yawns.

"Stop calling me that." I stomp forward. "I need Titus. Now."

"Need him how?" Tristen's eyes swirl with sardonic delight. "Because I don't think the palace can survive another sexual screaming fest."

I can't help but cringe. "Stop!"

"That's exactly what I said when you first started shouting. I mean, the moans were fine, but the shouts?"

I slap his chest, mortified. "I did not scream."

"You're right. You roared." He tips his head back and laughs.

"Oh, gods." I cover my face in horror.

"Hey, some guys like that. Don't be ashamed. Screams are sexy; if I had a chick here to hook up with, I'd be all for it, but I've got blue balls and no time to rub one out."

"Ew!"

"What, you had a brother?"

"My brother was... not like most men. He never mentioned his sex life."

Tristen frowns. "Well, the guys talk about sex. All the time. So get used to it."

I bite my cheek. "Titus does?" Jealousy makes my stomach swell. *Stop. You hooked up; you each have a past.*

Tristen rubs his jaw. "He... was discreet. Always has been. It's more me, Nero, and Ember."

"Oh," I reply with less confidence than I had a minute ago. "Let's go get Titus. You and I should be in on these plans."

"It's about time." Tristen pushes off the wall with a Cheshire grin. "I thought you had become dick-whipped."

"Hey!" I slap his arm, but he laughs.

"I know you, Selene. You don't do as you're told, so I've been eagerly waiting for you to tell me to cause trouble. Fuck Titus for ordering us both here! You can fuck him; I'll just annoy him." He winks. "Let's go see what he and Adrian have planned."

"So now you're going to do as I say?" I cross my arms.

"When it benefits me, yes. Make no mistake, you're not leaving my side. But first," he looks me up and down, "I think you should change."

Shit. I'm still in my sleeping dress. I hurry back inside, grabbing my leather training uniform, but silk catches my eye. Racks of dresses women crave and men adore fill my closet.

Does Titus like silk?

Reaching, I run my fingers down the smooth material. I want to look pretty for Titus, but I also don't want to appear weak. He's witnessed me only in training attire for weeks.

I grab silk pants and put them on. The material is cool and soft. I find a matching top; the high collar rests against my collarbone, keeping my mate mark tucked carefully away. I put my leather belt around my hips, with the dagger on my side warming the silk against my outer thigh.

There's not enough time to brush out the knots in my hair, so I quickly twist it into a bun. I find a mirror. Ugh! I slap my cheeks to add a blush. I step back and nod approvingly at my image.

Tristen raises himself onto his elbows. He made himself at home on my bed, closing his eyes for all of five minutes. "Silk and daggers," Tristen comments as he combs his hair with his fingers. "I like it."

"Ready?"

"Whips and chains?" He bounces off the mattress like a child.

I halt. "What?"

"That's a no, then."

"You seriously think about sex all the time, don't you?"

"Not all the time. I think about blood, guts, and glory, then having sex after."

"So all the time, since sex is the end goal," I say flatly.

Tristen's face lights up. "I have a healthy sex imagination, but life is lacking," he groans. "We're always fighting. We never stay in towns long, so I have no chance of a relationship." He pauses and searches the hall before we enter it.

"You want one?" I guess.

"I don't know," he sighs. "Sometimes it looks nice; other times, I think freedom is better." He slips his hand onto his sword and then opens the door to the courtyard. Once he determines we're safe, we proceed. His eyes take a moment and look up at the sky with a deep, painful longing.

"Maybe you'll find a mate."

"Unlikely." His stare plummets back down. "I can only commit to a target on the battlefield."

"Dating is a battle with different weapons."

A smile escapes him with a snort.

We dash through the gardens to the guard building. Adrian's office is on the top floor. I can't wait to pluck all these black roses out and toss them into a fire.

Once we exit the safety of the inner walls, Tristen's walk changes; he's quick-footed like a cat jumping from window to dresser, eyes scanning every inch before he allows us to take a step. Some guards observe us, but they don't impede. They just nod, then cast their eyes down, avoiding mine.

How are Titus and I going to unite these men? They hate me.

We enter the causeway that the warriors use, so they won't muddy the streets. Black arched stones tower above, creating the ominous look the architect intended. My exhales become a whisper. "Tristen." I grab his biceps and peer at the stars. Their light is so far away it can't guide us towards hope. "There's shouting."

He takes a hand and holds it tight. "Yeah." He nods, and his sword is out before I can blink.

My hand swings to my hip for my dagger, and shadows blind me. I reach for Tristen's back so I don't trip.

"I can't see," I panic. His shadows thicken. Unlike before, where his shadows formed a shield, they now allow me no room to see him.

His arm slips around my waist, and my hips press into his side. "Trust me," he guides me along the way as more shouts sound.

"That's coming from the nobles' houses," I state. *Titus, where are you?* I try to pull on that bond, but it's a new muscle I have to train. I search it again. "I can't feel the bond."

Tristen hisses. "I knew it!"

"What?"

"He left! That's why you can't feel the bond. He's going to kill Galen."

My toes tingle as all the blood rushes to my aching heart. "No, he wouldn't do that without me."

"That bond on your chest tells me he would. He left me behind! I'm the only one he'd trust to protect you. I'm not honored; I'm angry.

We always go into battle together. We have a ritual. This isn't good. Fuck!"

My inhales are half as deep and twice as hard. "I'm going to kill him again," I whisper.

"I call dibs." Tristen snorts, but his hand turns tender as it rubs my back, trying to calm me.

I completely trust him as he blindly guides me. Our walk feels longer than night, and I lose myself in worry. My back hits the hard stone.

"Shhh," he whispers.

"Where are we?"

"Just outside the armory. I knew it!"

"What's happening? Lower the shadows so I can see."

"Shhh," he pushes me against the wall, using his own body as a shield. "Shadows are useless if you keep yapping."

I swing my hand out, hitting something.

"Ouch! What was that for?" I can hear his smirk.

"Don't condescend me! I'll yap when I want!" I burst through his shadow like hot rays of the sun. I almost fall into a rose bush. Shadows wrap around my hips, and hands tug me back. "Let me see!"

"Fine." The shadows float to my feet as Tristen takes a step in front of me.

Hurried steps alert my eyes to the direction the guards with weapons in hand are running. A heavy scent of roses coats my tongue. Fallen petals, torn open by the soles of boots, dirty the cobblestone streets.

Gods be with you, Titus.

A guard glances my way, jerking as if he's a bug hitting a window, caught off guard by my sudden appearance. Tristen raises his blade. The guard steps back, dips his chin, and then continues on his way.

"They're..."

"On our side. Shit!" Tristen chortles with mirth. "Adrian was telling the truth." His glee warms some of my frigid ire over having been left behind.

"All this time, I was surrounded by men who hated Galen. I wasn't the only one trapped living a lie, trying to find an ounce of joy in this cage," I admit.

"I'm sorry," Tristen's hug wraps around me, a quiet canopy shading me from the heat of the truth. "We all escape differently. Some buy silk dresses; others plot murder."

"That's in the past." The night I shot that arrow feels like a lifetime ago. So much has changed since then.

"I am sorry you had to endure the grief of Everett's passing alone."

"It's not your fault." I distanced myself from Everett, dooming us to die without saying farewell.

"In a way, it is. I fought for Galen. I supported him."

I hold his hand gently in mine. "Tristen, you fought because you were a child who was taught to. You killed to eat and survive. I do not blame you. One day, let's make a world where people like you and me have a choice."

"I'd like that." His eyes linger on me longer, showing admiration.

My face softens. "Me, too."

A shadow eclipses us. This time it isn't Tristen's. "Vice Admiral Airendale," I announce when his face comes into view.

He bows. "Queen. Please call me Adrian." He studies Tristen. "I know you're pissed. Titus warned me."

Wind rushes past my brow, metal glints off the sunlight sky, slicing through the air. Tristen presses his blade to Adrian's neck. I stumble back; Adrian stands still as a boulder, unafraid of lightning, just allowing the fury to pass through him.

I yank Tristen back by his shoulders. "What did you do?" Tristen shouts.

Several men paused to observe. "Resume your roles!" Adrian bellows. My breath shakes. I've heard of Adrian and dined with him many nights. Silent and watchful, he waits like a predator in the bush.

"I did as my new king demanded. I kept you inside these walls," he says smoothly.

"You let him go alone." Tristen moves his sword again, but I grab it from his hand. He lets me; maybe he's hoping I'll kill the Admiral instead.

"No." Adrian tilts his head. "I let Ryker go with him."

Tristen's heels stumble on my toes. "What—"

"I've been planning this for a very long time, Tristen. I knew family meant everything to Titus, so I made sure to have them placed in Lunesta with the part of the army I controlled. I kept them safe and made sure to bring them into the fold. Take Selene back to her room. The fight is just starting. Not all the men here follow me. Blood will spill, and I'd hate to stain the Queen's shoes."

"I do not fear blood," I defend, my lips curling.

Respect is evident in Adrian's eyes. "I know. But you're his mate, and you need to be kept safe. I know you, Queen Selene, you would run into battle, but as his mate, your actions create a pull. He needs to focus in order to kill Galen. You and Tristen would be thorns that make him stumble. Stay. Here."

My gulp sticks. "He told you we're mated." Then that means Titus fully trusts Adrian.

Adrian nods. "Titus is ambushing Galen on the road; he'll return a king, I am sure. My orders are to secure the castle." He looks at Tristen. "Your orders are to keep her safe."

Swords slam together as men shout in the distance.

"Now, hurry." Adrian nods, turns, and pulls out two massive swords. If I held them, they would drag behind my feet.

Tristen blankets us in shadows, and his sword is plucked from my hand. Unthinkingly, I let Tristen guide me, lost in a flood of emotions. Everything I wanted is happening this very moment. My mate is claiming me, Galen will be dethroned, and I'll be free. I should smile.

Light overwhelms my vision, causing a blur. "Why are we here?" Blinking helps me see clearly.

Tristen throws open the library doors with the force of a warrior. "Because no one would expect us to be here. It's a fail-safe. If Adrian fails, Galen will look for you in your chambers. They won't look in the library."

He pulls me inside. The slamming of the door launches the air out of my lungs. No one sees us; breakfast hasn't been served yet; the librarians are likely still in bed.

"We're going to find Old Crusty and make him talk," Tristen announces. He walks, and a hand clenches around mine as he continues to drag me. I know he's as hurt as I am, so I don't snap, but I do yank my arm free. His eyes find the red handprint on my wrist. "Sorry. I didn't mean…"

"You're just trying to keep me safe. It's fine," I reply.

"Heads up, he's so old, we might discover a dead body." Tristen speed-walks through the rows of books until we reach a door. He kicks it open and races down the stairs.

The steps are so narrow that I have to pivot my feet to find balance. The light from upstairs barely reaches the bottom, but Tristen is used to seeing in the dark. Flesh hitting stone echoes up the stairs. He continues to pound the stone wall.

"Grumps! Crusty old goat! Open up. Come on. Rise and shine." He begins to kick the wall.

"Tristen." I step forward. Has he gone mad?

"Open! Up!" He slams the wall so hard I know he's injured his wrist.

"Stop!" I grab his hand and pour some of my healing magic into it. He pulls his hand back. "I can heal myself. You need to save your magic. You barely slept."

"I'm fine." Do I need more sleep? Yeah, but I'm not useless.

Tristen kicks the wall again. Nothing happens. He flattens his palms and presses his forehead to it. "Please," he sighs.

Creek! A door emerges and opens as magic illuminates a fissure in the stone.

"See?" an old voice grunts. "All you needed were some manners. Please and thank you."

The scent of mold and wet stone invades my nose. The old man on the side of the door opens his arms in welcome, but his worn robes rain dust in the stale air.

Shit. Tristen wasn't exaggerating. I've never seen a vampire older than this one. His hair is so white it appears almost transparent. His lids are so sagged it's hard to see the shape or color of his eyes.

"I brought a guest." Tristen steps into the small room. I press a firm footstep inside, feeling the old man look me up and down.

"Seems you brought a queen." He steps to the side. "Make yourself at home. I swept the floor."

I ignore his barbed reply. Tristen sits on the edge of the bed. The old man rolls his eyes and walks to the only chair in the room. I stand firm as he studies me.

"What did you need?" His spine bends like soft wood. His belongings are as worn as the books on the shelves up stairs, passed down and reused. And his fingers... I curl my own to ensure I still can. His knuckles are swollen with the suffering of aging.

"Answers," Tristen barks. Can he try to ask politely?

"I gave you many already."

I continue to look at the man's aging face. My lips part to ask him about his time with Everett, but wait, what is that? "I'm sorry—" I interrupt them and look at Tristen, confused. "This is the man who told you about Caldara?"

"I told him a lot more than that," the old man huffs bitterly.

"Yeah," Tristen deadpans. "Old? Check. Grumpy? Check. Terrible manners? Double check."

The old man mumbles as he rubs his temples.

"Tristen..." Dryness stings my eyes from how wide they are pulled. "You said he was a vampire."

Tristen looks at me, confused. "He is. I know we look sexy now, but we do age, Selene. So enjoy Titus when he's hard and smooth because one day," Tristen grimaces, "he and I will be raisins. No offense."

"Much taken." A raspy sigh bursts from the man's thin lips.

My fingertips twitch when he pivots his eyes towards me. They turn up with mischief. The dagger on my belt starts to warm through my silk, shouting at me to grab it. It's in my hand before Tristen can stop me. I aim it at the old man.

431

"Hey!" Tristen stands. "What are you—"

"Who are you?" I bark.

"He's the old man!" Tristen shouts. He comes to my side, his palms filled with shadows.

"Tristen," I begin; the old man smiles, and suddenly, something about him looks younger.

"That man is *not* a vampire. He's a fae!"

CHAPTER

FORTY-THREE

SELENE

The door seals shut, as does the air in my lungs. Tristen advances, diving to tackle the old man. Arms out wide, he curls them in, but he only hugs air. His head smacks against the stone wall. His magic flares out to protect him. The entire room is blanketed in shadows, hindering my sight.

"Fuck!" Tristen grunts.

"Tristen, let me see so I can help!" I plead.

He lowers his shadows, appearing by my side, sword in hand.

"Where did he go?" I whisper, as my eyes fix on the two candles on the dresser. If he were near them, his breath would surely shake the flames.

We form a defensive circle, our backs touching. "Titus is gonna kill me," he mutters.

"We'll be fine," I try to assure him. The door is gone! This is a stone cage. "He was a fae."

"Selene, that guy is a vampire. I saw his fangs."

"No," I argue. We both take small steps, scanning the room. "He was fae; his ears were tipped."

"Tipped? He's a wrinkled ball; you're confused. I'm more worried about how he vanished."

"I'm not a fae." The old man's voice rumbles as deep as a dozen warriors singing before a battle. "Not that I find insult in being compared to your kind."

"Start swinging!" Tristen shouts. He lunges and begins stabbing thin air. His movements snuff out one of the candles.

"Stop!" I hiss. If those lights go out, we're blind.

"I warned him about being pompous and impulsive," the man sighs.

My words get trapped behind my beating heart.

"You're scaring the queen," the old man mocks Tristen.

"I am not scared." I lick my lips. "What *are* you?"

"That's a loaded question." There is a smile in his words. "I have never been able to fully solve it."

"Maybe I can help," I offer. Dust and mold fill my thirsty lungs.

His laugh is so deep it shakes the air.

I step back, trying to grab Tristen. "Tristen! Stop stabbing blindly."

"I prefer to kill, not be killed, but so be it, mate-in-law." His eyes widen at his slip of words.

"Mated," the man purrs. "Congratulations."

"Would you like to shake hands?" I counter. Come out, come out, wherever you are?

I sense magic, smell it in the air like marshmallows melting under a campfire. Yet I see none. A ripple of light and shadows flashes. He's back in the chair, sitting cross-legged, smirking as he fans his robes out.

Tristen dives forward. *Blink!* He's gone, reappearing on his bed, cross-legged and relaxed. "Tristen, stop." I step between them. The silk fabric covering my body feels like a cast, restricting my movements.

The old man stands slowly, offering me his hand. "If I wanted you dead, you would be," he states honestly, eyeing his hand for me to shake.

"Greetings like that do not promote peace," I say sourly.

"I seek something more important than peace." He turns his palm, waiting for me to grasp it.

"What is that?" Slowly, I raise my hand.

"Don't be a fool," Tristen grunts under his breath. I appreciate him letting me make the decision. Titus would have done the same before we were mated. Now he'd pull me back.

"I seek..." He guides his hand into mine, palm to palm, but I keep my fingers open. "Survival for my children and their children. Family is the only thing that makes my existence less painful."

My warm palm meets cool, wrinkled skin as we shake hands.

"Congratulations on being bonded. It's an honor and a rare gift that should be cherished every second you have it." His eyes press into me like a warning fire. He opens his fingers, waiting for my release.

Gradually, I peel each finger back. He swings his hands comfortably behind his back.

He moves his ancient, weary eyes onto Tristen. "It was to be Titus who came to see me, but," he looks Tristen up and down, "You will have to do. Your brother has endured enough, accepted more than one should bear. It's time you pull your weight."

In a flash, I press my dagger to his neck, digging it into old, wrinkled skin. "I will kill you if you touch him," I sneer.

He remains unfazed. "You would try, I have no doubt. If that blade could kill me, I'd welcome it. Now," he swings his hand up and presses his fingers to the blade, attempting to lower it. Not one inch of his skin is sliced.

How is that possible?

"Are you going to let me talk, or is this a pissing contest?"

"I'm comfortable." I keep my dagger high, eyeing the sharp edge that should have cut him. "Talk."

His chest falls. *Snap!* He's gone. Weight hits the chair. Tristen and I turn around to see him sitting there again. "I'm more comfortable like this. I've had enough of the dramatics. Do not dare me to reveal my true nature."

I tip my chin up. "What are you?" I demand.

"I am none yet spoken, merely fantasized about. I am here nor there, which makes me everywhere." He releases an old laugh. "Yet nowhere at all. I am not day or night; I am the in-between. I am lost and forgotten, yet comfortably content. I am the mystery on the horizon that is endless. I am hope, for it is the spring of all life."

I lower my blade, much to Tristen's dissatisfaction. "I am just a queen, whom you can call Selene. What may I call you?"

He rubs his jaw with intrigue. "I am... one with many names. None that matter; I still have not found one that satisfies me."

"You prefer to be nameless?" I press.

"At times, yes. It's tranquil. If they call, I do not have to answer." He crosses his legs.

"That doesn't sound like hope." I assert.

"Hope is not always seen and felt, Selene. Hope is a dream and a nightmare. It is the unknown. Hope is an arrow that guides you, but leads us down a path of more questions."

Tristen warned us he spoke strangely. I think he spins the truth, but tries to make it appear pleasantly alluring so he doesn't frighten people away. He's not rude because we're bothering him; he's angry we don't seek out his company.

"But at this moment, I'd like you to know me by a name." He thinks long and hard, as if pondering which he'd prefer.

"So if I call, you'll answer?" I arch a brow.

His unsettling smile is his response. Such sorrow is evoked by its melancholic angle. Sometimes Everett would look at me like that. "No, Selene. This will be the only time you see me." He glances at Tristen.

"I told you, talking with him is like pulling teeth," Tristen groans. He keeps his footing and blade aimed at the old man.

The old man chuckles. "Perhaps I am teaching you patience. You will need it in the days to come. But you may call me Elderan."

"Elderan," I repeat. "Why do I see you as a fae?"

"Does it not make you more comfortable?"

"I'd rather face the truth."

His grin pulls unevenly. "Are you sure? It will hurt us both."

Tristen moves closer. "Are we sure?"

"Yes."

Elderan's hooded eyes meet mine. "Very well."

Tristen shields me with his body as light bursts all around us. I anticipate pain. Death. I feel nothing, just light so bright I can not see or hear. Am I floating?

Tristen's arms hold me tighter as panic sets in. His body is a mountain, shaking; his voice is a distant roar of an avalanche, desperately seeking to clear everything in its way. His shadows fail to protect us. Elderan's light proves to be an unstoppable force.

"Enough," Elderan softly states. The light vanishes, but Tristen and I are so jolted we can't see. "I warned you. I'll stay in this state of time-worn flesh."

My hands move frantically, feeling the stone floor, sensing my surroundings. Tristen's hands move across my body. "It's me," I tell him. His warm breath brushes against the nape of my neck. "I'm fine," I tell him. "Are you?"

"I think so, but I can't see yet," he rasps.

"Me neither," I reply warily.

"While your senses are recovering, you both will sit down and listen," Elderan orders. "I already told Tristen many things."

Tristen snorts, "I don't get the feeling your mother was a fae."

"I like to observe; that was not a lie. She did raise me, but she was not the first nor the last. As I mentioned, I come and go. She did have the power of hindsight. I just happened to know the story, but I respected her, sat down, and played my part of a child so she could mother me."

"So you're a psycho who likes to play mommy fetish." Tristen shifts so he's in front of me. Everything is blurry now; that's good. Soon I'll see clearly.

"No. But if I do not walk in your shoes, how can I understand? So I do. Sometimes, I am a child; other times, an old man. Once, I was a falcon; that visit was ended when an arrow claimed me. I remember when I visited as a dragon. The views were the same, but the falcon was much slower."

"You're a shifter?" I ask. However, I've never heard of shifters changing into forms like that.

"No," he replies. "What I am matters not. My purpose here is to aid in your survival. Evil has flourished in the absence of the runes."

My heart sputters, my fingers inch out, seeking Tristen's hand. "You speak as if you are a god."

"Gods can be killed. I'm different. No matter what happens, you can only trust two things, Selene. There will always be a beginning and an end. Kingdoms can fall; it gives an opportunity for more to rise. Worlds can shatter, but it just creates more energy for others to clash together and form. A beginning and an end. A genesis and a demise," he repeats. His eyes bounce back and forth darkly, like someone quickly turning pages so the reader can't stop and study the details.

I lick my lips, trying to sound more curious than I am petrified. "Just tell us what you are?"

"You seem like you truly care." His lips twitch. "It can't hurt," he mutters to himself. "I am a Genesis."

"So you start things?"

"Things, worlds, creatures. Yes I start," his voice slips into a state of anxiety. "And others seek to end." His inhale is sharp, closing of this subject.

"If your ability is endless, why not just rid the world of evil? Why do the runes matter so much?"

"My ability is not infinite; my existence is. Do you know what happens when you over mix a batter, when you stir it too much because you love it, enjoy it? It ruins it. And ruin is what the Demise seek. I tread carefully so that they do not find my creations. "And if they were not a big enough problem, I also happened to have made an agreement with the creator of this world. I have many limitations when I visit now."

"Who created us?" I whisper in awe.

"My children made you, but Nerina made these lands you call Panthas," he states with pride and affection.

"You announce Nerina as a lover would," I declare. "Is she your enemy or not?"

"Friends bicker and fight all the time. Our game makes no difference. Love and war are the same; you can't have one without the other. Love fuels war, spurs it on."

"And what does war do to love?"

"It tests it. Makes it stronger. If love fails, then it was never truly love." He hums in satisfaction. "Nerina was unsettled when my children came here unannounced and poured their magic into her lands. She tried to rid Panthas of magic by creating a new creature that fed off of it," he expels a heavy sigh. "But Nerina was never as skilled in making creatures as I was. At first, her new creatures were like vampires; they fed off magic but remained civilized. Unfortunately, during their making, Nerina left a part of them vulnerable, and that flaw was exploited, turning them feral." I can hear him lick his lips.

He's not telling us every detail of that story.

I choose not to interrupt him and continue to listen.

"Nerina turned to me for help. She demanded payment for my children's crimes. They altered her world beyond repair. I gave her compensation in the form of the one thing she always wanted from me, a child from my loins."

"That's sexy." Tristen gags. "Haven't your kids done enough damage?"

"This child is different. They are of my body. My other children are of my magic," he explains quickly. "I made the exchange to save you all. I received permission to visit Panthas as a mentor, plus two casting changes to what has been created by my children."

"Why only two amendments?"

"Panthas teeters on an edge. If Nerina and I interfere anymore, our enemy will come and demand retribution. Panthas will be in your hands. A parent's help can only go so far before it becomes harmful." He deadpans, cold as stone. "First, I altered the Vitalis, and then I began to mentor those who could—"

"You little prick!" Tristen spits. His entire body shakes with rage. "If you had the Vitalis, why not just give it to us?"

"I did not have it," he clarifies.

"Then how did you alter it?" I ask sweetly. *Let's catch this bee with honey and not insults, Tristen!*

"The same way I create or change anything. I simply do it. Your small minds can not grasp that, so just accept it."

I elbow Tristen. *Let me do the talking!* "How did you alter it?"

"I made it so only a creature of my choosing could create new runes. Why the glum look? That's a measure of comfort, is it not? Now, only those I select can draw in the book."

"And where is the child you and Nerina had?" I probe.

"I won't answer that." His shoulders shift out of their hunched posture and become a square so sharp that it feels like a wall is between us.

"Why?"

"Careful, Selene. I answer out of kindness, not duty."

"You sound like a lifeboat riddled with leaks," Tristen sneers.

"You don't always need a boat to save you. Sometimes a plank will keep you afloat, boy."

"What about this feral magic-feeding monster Nerina made? Is that the second alteration? You killed it."

"Killed?" He rolls the word on his tongue, trying to eject the sour taste. "I told you, I am a Genesis. I start, I do not end."

A chill runs down my spine. "So this beast is still on Panthas?"

"As are many things here, Selene. Perhaps my new creatures can make a rune to help combat it."

Combat and not kill. His words were chosen carefully. I want to scratch my skin and shake him free.

Tristen lifts his chin a fraction. "If your new creature can make runes, then why was my brother involved?"

A cold look settles on Elderan's face as he states, "That leads to the second amendment I'm allowed to make. I have yet to make the creatures that can create runes. Titus will be one of them." He claps his hands in glee.

In a heartbeat, I'm standing, my dagger aimed at Elderan's heart. "You're not touching my mate!" I growl.

He looks lazily down the blade. "That blade can not splay me open." To prove his point, he leans into the tip. His skin simply bends around it. He chuckles as he stands and tugs at his robes. "I'm giving you the opportunity to save your world, to choose good over evil."

"Your mentorship feels evil!" Disgust drips from my words like venom as I glare at him.

"My creations will safeguard everyone, regardless of whether they are fae, vampire, or otherwise. That doesn't seem evil to me. I can't magically save you, but my guidance hopefully can." He points an arthritic finger at Tristen. "Like I mentioned, Tristen, it's time to pull your weight."

Oh shit! "You... you intend to make Tristen into your new creature," I breathe.

Elderan applauds. "You truly are a marvel, Selene. Galen ought to have heeded your advice. Tristen will be first, but eventually, Titus will need to be changed. You'll need many more if you wish to fight Nerina's creatures, plus the others that have been born here."

"Yeah, no thanks." Tristen seizes me and pulls me back to the door's location. With his eyes trained lethally on Elderan, he begins kicking the wall with his heel. "Please open the door."

"Oh, it's far too late for manners." With a laugh, Elderan begins flexing and cracking his knuckles. "I'm helping you as a grandparent would. I'm ensuring my lineage survives."

I open my arms, trying to cover Tristen. "Change me! Leave Tristen and Titus out of this."

Elderan stills, looking at me as one looks at a sunset. "It is Tristen's fate."

"Fate can change. Everett taught us that," I argue, but my pleas fall on deaf ears.

Tristen kicks the wall with more force. "I'll pass, but thanks," he spits the word in contempt, "for the offer."

Elderan's exhale lands harder than Tristen's fruitless kicking. "It's funny you think you have a choice, Tristen."

CHAPTER
FORTY-FOUR

TRISTEN

If we make it out of this room, Titus will kill me for putting Selene in the line of fire.

"It's funny you think you have a choice, Tristen," Elderan beams. That old, crusty prick snaps his fingers. A force slams into us, trapping us against the stone wall.

"I can't move," Selene whispers. The fear in her voice would break Titus's heart.

I gulp down my apology for dragging her here. This is all my fault. I'm going to be the one to kill my brother's heart.

Elderan steps closer. He looks like an over-cheery hugger ready to smother me. "This is an honor. One I hope you will carry with pride. I like challenges; it makes time not feel like a void. I could have turned my back on your world, and let the new evil that has evolved here take over. It seemed cruel to watch another world fade into nothing. To watch more of my children die. So, I made a truce."

"If you're looking for a 'thank you', you'll find no gratitude from me," I sneer.

"You remind me of the others. So prideful until you hit rock bottom." He sweeps his foot over the floor, and dust stirs. "This is bottom—well, shortly it will be. It'll be interesting to see you stand, or stumble. I can offer my advice, but it's up to you to follow it," he shrugs.

"You said you wanted our survival!" Why can't I feel my shadows?

"I do. I want you all to survive. This new world will be wild and feral at first, but everything can be tamed. My other children learned that the hard way. I had to allow them to watch their siblings fall so they would respect the lesser I created. Humbled men are willing to agree to peace, Tristen. Remember that. It's good advice."

"Fuck you!" I spit.

"My time has come. When I return, you will either all be dead or thriving."

"You're a shitty mentor." I don't want his help! I won't suffer through the absence of losing a parental figure again.

"A mentor is not a constant hand that holds you, Tristen. I will return eventually. If you follow my advice, I will grant you more. Make a new breed of warriors, keep the world safe, and use the runes to defeat the evil that seeks to devour you.

"I'm giving you the power of becoming a marker, Tristen. One day, you will understand how I feel and why I cannot be a constant shadow."

"I'd rather be a fucker who shoves my sword up your ass!" I grind out.

"I've seen your soul. You want others to think it's gray, murky. It's not. There is honor in you that years will sharpen. You're young, you have so many trials yet to come, but you have survived so much already. You'll endure this. Titus will be..." He glances at Selene. I want to cut his eyes out of his body. "In a deep state soon. He has a lot on his plate. It's time he had help."

What the fuck does that mean?

He waves his hand. My body moves like a doll until I'm lying on the floor. Dust clogs my nose. "I thought you swept the floors," I taunt even as fear grips me like a vice.

Elderan flashes a crooked grin. "You're the better person. I see that now." He crouches down next to me.

When I look into his eyes, light shoots forth, like a star in the night sky cutting through darkness; it grips me. Makes me feel small and insignificant.

He continues, "I'll explain how it works. I'm going to give you the power to make a stronger breed of vampires. You will bite them, drain them dry, and right before they pass over, you will feed them your blood."

Bite a vampire?!

"The girl," Selene whispers, grabbing Elderan's attention. "Tristen, that small child with the Shade, Titus said she fed from a vampire."

I press my tongue to my fangs. I don't want them to vanish and appear as Titus described. Ladies love my fangs.

"Oh no, he's not going to be like her, but fast thinking, Selene. Fast thinking will be what..." He snaps his mouth shut and pretends to cough. "Anyway, I am not making you what she is."

"What is she?" Selene presses.

"She is... a creature born of anger, pain and jealousy. She is Nerina's."

"That girl is the monster Nerina made?" I question. My fingers tingle. I can't hunt down children.

"Nerina made many creatures here that went awry, but yes she is the one that feeds off of magic. Evil has taken over her. That child is just a shell now. Perhaps she could have been something else if given a chance. Some wild dogs can be trained if someone were only to take the time to love them. Nerina's creatures feed off magic. I never said it had to be good magic. Consider that suggestion."

I grind my teeth. He speaks of innocent life like it's a deck of cards he can shuffle around. "I'm not a shell you can have, Elderan!" I shout.

"There's that pompous prick." Elderan shakes his head. "So be it. Let's focus on you."

The blood drains from my face. "Never mind. Talk about the girl." Why did I do that? Because I was scared and wanted answers. Now I have more questions.

"Oh no. This is a lesson. You wanted attention, now you will get it."

"I wanted answers!"

"You'll get them," he applauds himself. "As I was saying, you will have the magic to change vampires, bite, feed to the point of death, then offer them your blood. They will change."

I fight to move. I can't. This is happening. I accept it and start asking questions. "Change how?"

He kneels and opens his palms. A small ball of bright white light appears. He hems and haws, looks at me like I'm a cauldron he's going to cook a stew in. "I need warriors to look after the book, to look over the magic of these lands.

"Hmmm. Actually, let's amend this." Elderan shakes his hand like a pepper shaker. *Crack! Spark!* "You can change others, not just vampires. That's more fair." He moves his fingers, causing the magic to dance. "You can change anyone, so pick wisely. Pick those who can be warriors.

"Let's add more, make this fun. We need to strengthen you and those you select. Your magic won't run out. You won't need blood to fuel it either. Yes, I like that."

Change anyone! "Humans don't have magic," I blurt out.

"That's right." He shakes his hands, pushing his fingers into the light like dough. "Let's change that. Give them magic, make all your new creatures equal."

"This is madness," Selene mutters in fear and awe.

"Madness gives way to hope," he rebuts. "There is the problem of your hearts. Hmmm..." His face turns pensive. "Do I do as I did to them?" He claps suddenly, the magic in his palm sparks. "So be it. Only a handful of swords can kill you. Be careful, for they are in this world now."

"What sword?"

He shakes his head with much disapproval. "I answered this when we first spoke."

"The sword in the Vitalis," I acknowledge, recalling the memory.

He raises an eyebrow. "Bravo. You catch on quickly. There is hope yet."

"I don't like the sound of that," I mumble.

"But you liked the other gifts, didn't you? Don't be selfish, don't accept more magic, strength, and life without expecting a balance."

"Don't do this," Selene stresses. "Please. This isn't what my brother wanted."

"Everett," Elderan speaks with longing. "He wanted so many unselfish things. But he saw this. He knew what was coming, Selene. He warned you. We all have sacrifices. This shall be Tristen's."

He looks back at me. "Be careful who you sire. I know the guilt a parent carries. It humbles you. Start with Titus once he can manage it, then make others." The magic floats off his palm and drifts toward me. My chest keeps hitting the invisible grip he's trapped me in, making each rapid inhale shorter.

"Stop!" Selene shouts in a wild fury. "Please stop!"

I want to fight, scream, and kick for my life. Instead, I push my shoulders down. "It's okay, Selene." I swallow down my fear and face death with unblinking eyes.

Elderan's eyes glow with delight as his magic runs down my cheek, caressing it as a lover would. It dances over my jaw, purrs down my neck, and then hums with glee once it hovers over my heart. His magic pierces my chest, cracks a part of me. It's a powerful boot stomping on a snail's shell. I'm defenseless, weak, brittle.

Selene, screaming my name, is the last thing I hear. Gods be damned, I had to die hearing her screaming again. I wish it were screams of pleasure rather than tortured cries.

Bellowing light eradicates my shadow magic, making it cry out, sizzle, fume, flare, and then break under the weight.

You fought hard, my friend. I am the one who failed you.

It whimpers. It's still there, being forced to endure alongside me. Elderan's magic stretches us out as one scrapes honey from the comb.

My heart stops, and then I feel nothing at all.

But I welcome it because if I survive, I know I'll never feel this much peace again.

CHAPTER
FORTY-FIVE

TITUS

The steady sound of my horse's hooves calms my heart; my eyes are narrow, lashes lower. Fingers clench the reins. Dirt flies into the air, mixed with the deep snorts my horse exhales. It all merges into a storm, provoking and preparing me for the battle.

The hardest battle isn't winning the war; it's returning home. Sitting down to eat with your friends and family, those emotions turn on. The smooth motion of your knife slicing into the steak evokes the memory of your sword's deadly precision.

You learn that you have to split your soul in half. There are versions of yourself: a warrior, a man who has to sleep at night, a big brother. They all must coexist to survive.

One hundred feet away, the guards' horses turn their ears. We've been spotted. They presume a defensive stance, then... oh yes, they know who I am, and what hour of the night this is. I watch with sick pleasure as their lips curl up.

It's a warning to the future me. Never trust fully.

449

Adrian plotted all this as Galen sat back and over-drank.

Seventy feet away, they break formation, exposing Galen abruptly. His crown makes him an easy target. He spots me. The look of alarm gives way to annoyance. He must think I'm here because of Selene.

I am.

If it didn't spook the horses, I would cover my body in flames. "Now!" I roar.

I feel Ryker's glee when his arms raise. He's a conductor who commands a loud and powerful orchestra; only his instrument is the wind.

Galen's annoyance turns to suspicion. Yes, he knows. He looks left, then right, but his guards are moving, guiding their horses away like feathers shot off a bird. Scattering until only the barren animal is left for the predator to pick and pull to shreds.

A fierce wind causes a panicked reaction in the horses; mine rears, but I trained my eyes on my target. Wind barrels towards Galen with such force that you can see it. Galen's magic flares, spooking his horse. The dirt boils, cracking open as vines start to shoot forth, but he's too slow. The wind slams into him, snapping the saplings in half.

His horse falls over, scurries wildly before it abandons him. Everyone underestimates wind magic. Fire magic sounds intimidating, but fire takes time to burn defenses; seconds or minutes the enemy can use. Wind tramples you, shakes your legs, and knocks your boots free from the ground. It's sudden, and so stunning.

Ryker leaps from the saddle, swift as thunder breaking from a cloud, to ambush. His hands are lightning-fast, rising and striking with torrential downpours of gusts. Small shrubs rip free from the ground, stirring dirt. The start of a canvas of chaos.

There! Metal falls, smacking into grass. Galen's crown! He lies stomach-down, hands reaching for his hair. His crown-less state causes his eyes to shift to his true predator, crawling free from the narrow slits.

He searches for the crown before his enemy. Adrian was right; that crown is a secret weapon.

Galen snarls, boots digging into the soil as he lunges on hands and knees like an untamed beast. His fingers shoot out, fighting the wind, reaching toward his weapon.

Ryker reels his hand back, preparing to backhand Galen with another blast.

I jump off my horse. "Run!" I order the loyal animal. I won't see it slain in this battle.

Oranges, yellows, and deep ambers cover my vision. My flames consume me. The grass sizzles and catches flame under my boots. I charge towards Galen, my entire body a walking fiery silhouette. Just as Ryker's wind touches the crown, picking it up to throw it further away.

My lips curl, but the smile drops. A vine becomes a lasso, seizing the crown. Galen bellows a war cry as he tugs it back.

Flames crash into it, embers pour down like rain around me. I target that single vine; it can change the outcome of tonight. Closer and closer the vine pulls the weapon back to its master.

More fire! More heat, hatred, and willpower! The vine twists into a tortured braid, curling and knotting. Desperately trying to obey Galen, but my fire is too intense. *Snap!* The vine breaks, and the crown hits the dirt. The wind drags it.

"This will be a fair fight!" I shout.

Galen's raging eyes slice into me. He pushes to stand and has the audacity to wipe the dirt off his clothing. "Traitor!" he howls, eyes searching for his guards. "All of you! I will kill every single one of you. Your families, everyone who shares your blood, will suffer!"

"Those are the last words you choose to be remembered by!" Ryker shouts. "How poetic."

The other soldiers give us a wide berth as they circle us, ensuring Galen can't escape. He notes it, and instead of attacking, he tries to engage in conversation. "Who are you?" the king spits as he looks down his nose at my brother.

Ryker tilts his head; the moonlight makes his odd shade of hair appear ghostly. It's an undying shade caught between life and death. Immortal.

"You don't deserve to know my name." Ryker silences his wind so abruptly that it causes a ringing in my ear. A cool, eerie chill slips through my fire and clings to my skin. "And the last thing I will tell you is that your name," he arches a brow like a dagger, "will never be spoken again." His grin is saccharine, full of malice.

He stomps his boot on the crown. Galen's jaw clenches so tightly I'm almost certain he cracked a tooth. He cares so much about an object; I can see the pain and fear that it's damaged.

"I let snakes into my garden," Galen spits as he widens his stance, eyes quickly searching for an escape. He's delusional.

"*You* were the snake!" I lower my flames so he can see me. "You let birds of prey in. We watched you from above. Judged you. We found you guilty, slippery, and slimy. You tricked so many, Galen; for snakes are feared for their bite—your words were cruel and sweet. You forgot predators with limbs, arms," I cover mine in fire, "legs, hands that are used to holding a sword—more than your daily fuck—those predators are the real ones. Now we will cut your head from your body so you can never strike again."

He raises his two hands, shuddering like he's lifting a mountain. The ground quakes. *Boom!* Dirt and chunks of grass assault me. Ryker tries to use his wind as a shield.

I stumble back as vines erupt from the earth, cracking and splitting it open. Something blocks out the stars. Vines, a wall, no, a cage of them. He's trapping himself; he can't run, so this is the option he picked instead of fighting like a man.

Ryker looks toward me. "This is my fight now," I warn him. He nods and steps back as I approach the cage. "You could have died like a man. You picked the path of a coward. Hiding!" I shout as I step forward, shaping my fire into a sword. Reaching out, I touch a larger branch; it's warm, thick, and waxy. Fresh.

My fire will need time to spread. My exhale coats a branch in fire;

flames search for an opening through which the heat can seep in. *There. Got you!*

"I gave you everything!" Galen shouts from inside.

I circle the cage, inspecting it. "You trapped yourself; you'll die in fire and smoke unless you come out and fight me. Sword to sword, like a man."

He laughs, then, like a predictable snake, he strikes. I see the assault a second too late to form the time shield. It's not just a cage he built; it's a weapon. Thorns erupt, stretching out as far as a limb, reaching for a target. I hiss as one stabs me in the thigh, halting my steps and trapping me.

I grunt as I push myself to the side, freeing my leg. I slap my palm to the wound. It's deep, stabbing me like a dagger. Nostrils flare, lips curl as I push my healing magic into it. The bleeding slows, but the cut remains open.

I step back and roar as flames leave my body, spreading faster and faster until his cage is covered.

Come on, you coward.

He forces us to wait until a large section of it crumbles in and a path is clear. In the center, Galen stands, surrounded by smoke, framed by flames. He smirks, with arrogant eyes, at the black roses he holds in his hands.

That's when I notice it. The ground is covered with black roses.

"Sword to sword," Galen murmurs. He must not have much magic left. I used a lot, but I had my mate's blood to fuel it. I could easily last fifteen more minutes.

Without his crown, he's used every last drop he had.

"I don't obey your orders now, Galen."

"Tell me, Titus," he caresses the rose with more admiration than I thought his eyes could possess. "Did Selene put you up to this, twist your mind, promise you love in exchange for my death? She's just like her sister; you think it's just a fuck, but they don't just take your body, they screw with your mind."

He doesn't let me answer as he begins to pluck off each rose petal. His forehead shines with sweat as the rest of his cage burns down.

"Selene will betray you. In the end, she will pick herself." Galen sounds like a wounded lover who is clinging to life and lost dreams. Broken. Accepting. "And it will kill you. This will all be for nothing."

He holds the stem tightly, eyeing the cluster of seeds once hidden, now free. In a violent gesture, he rips out the seeds, tossing them in the air. If he thinks his memory will survive and grow like those seeds, he's wrong.

I'll find every seed, every flower, and burn it from this world. All for my mate; never again will her eyes look into dark and thorny petals.

"She thinks she won, but I warned her. This is the long game. She has no idea how it's played. In order to survive, you can only care about yourself. It will kill her." He laughs. "But I don't think it will kill you, Titus. I think you'll survive and be forced to suffer."

I pull my blade free and close the distance. Galen knows he's cornered. A raise of my hand would cover him in flames. But that's too easy. "Take your sword out and fight me," I demand. Burnt vines crunch under my boots.

He smirks at the floor of his roses. The petals are thick and saturated with fragrance; they'll take time to burn. He levels me with a cold winner's stare. "No."

His reply feels like a hidden attack I didn't anticipate.

"Burn me. Burn my body with honor. That's what you do, isn't it, Titus, the honorable soldier who won my war? You burn and bury. I heard that the men found it noble. I found it lacking. I hoped you'd die in battle. I never dreamed you'd win it all for me."

His chest widens with a lungful of smoky air, and my eyes narrow.

"You won," he admits as he nods. "You took my crown, depleted my magic. I could draw my sword and fight you, or I could stand down, not rewarding you with the drenching of my blood upon your blade. A weapon I gifted you. I might die, but in the end, I won this battle." He leans closer without fear. "I denied your predator a kill it craved. Hungered for!"

He tips his head back and laughs in my face.

Each exhale fans my flames, but deep inside, water is poured on my vengeance.

"Some battles are fought with swords; others are won with words." He opens his arms and mockingly bows.

He's right.

I hate it. I want to lash out, cover Galen in flames, so his wicked tongue curls and withers away. How did this happen? How did Galen beat me?

"Your mistake was fishing with no bait," Galen continues. "I see your wants, a need to slay me in battle so you can wear that badge when you return to Selene. I refuse to bite. You may take my throne, wield my crown, but you will not have my honor."

"Honor?" Now I laugh. "All your life, you have given orders. It's time you tried on a different pair of shoes, a soldier whom you so carelessly place into battle."

He kicks his foot out, rolling his ankle; his eyes reveal the truth as they gaze at his burnt roses; his smile isn't genuine. "I rather like my shoes and prefer to die in them."

Talking is granting him more time in this world. It's done. "And so you shall."

Flames seep out from my feet, racing over the brown, crispy grass, closer and closer to him.

Wait, I'm giving him the death he wants. It's an order that I'm obeying.

I raise my sword. Molten shades of citrine encompass Galen, reflecting off the sharp edge of my blade. His smile is ice that slips out of a cup. Left alone to melt and die slowly.

Galen's pride jolts. The admittance he's not getting the last order granted slips free like a balloon, before he recovers and realizes it's attached to a string. There is no escape.

I glide like wind, sailing forward, the tip of my blade pressing into his leather cuirass. He didn't wear his metal breastplates; riding southeast meant no foes would confront him. His eyes drift down, looking at the sword. I press my torso into the hilt, and a slight pinching snap signals that the leather cuirass has been sliced.

I watch for his attack, but he's got no magic, and his sword remains sheathed.

"You're a coward," I spit in his face. Crackling snaps of my flames egg me on.

"Yet I stand still, accepting death." His eyes trace up my sword until our eyes join. His smile will torment me.

I failed. Sure, I'm going to kill him, but his words were an enemy I can not slay. His lack of reaction to death was a foe I did not anticipate.

My toes curl as I lean all my force into my right foot. My blade is sharp; it cuts flesh like butter, but once you're deeper, you need more force. Muscles, tendons, and ribs. It's all much harder. Slower.

Galen growls as my sword becomes a part of him. His body sways, not from pain but from determination to not give me an ounce of glory.

He leans into my blade, attempting to drive it deeper. I steer him back, refusing to allow him to kill himself. A grunt has my blade chipping his ribs, slicing through his lungs, and finally his heart.

Blood weeps from the wound, so much that it turns into a pool reflecting my fire, and his crumbling vines.

Your mission was to kill him; your goal was to make him suffer. You thought you lost, but in the end, you achieved what you needed to. The noble soldier in me tries to find reason.

Shut up!

I wanted his pain to be transformed into badges of honor that I could decorate myself with, so Selene could see.

His knees shake as mine do, but for a different emotion. His hands grab my wrist. Using my sword, I steer him down like a fork guiding meat. Controlled, deliberate, ready to be cut up, then devoured. He's skewered against the smoldering floor, surrounded by his burning petals.

I drive that blade deeper and deeper, piercing the earth. Cursing it for birthing such a man.

I cover my body in flames, giving him a horror-filled image, before I allow the fire to consume him. The sound of a gargled laugh bubbles from his lips.

"I see it... in your... eyes. Failure. I... won..." His lips curl up, and his head tilts to the side.

All his roses fill his view. I lash out, burning them. I dig my fingers into his jaw, burning his flesh, forcing his eyes back on me. His life is fading, but his heart still beats, and each thump has more blood oozing from the wound.

"You think you've won," I hiss. I unbuckle my cuirass, toss it into the flames, and rip open the collar of my undershirt. Through blurry vision, he spots my mate's mark. "I won, Galen. I have what you never did. Selene is my mate. Mine."

He tries to speak, urging death one moment of hesitation so that he can taint my victory again. I shove my fingers into his mouth, discharging the heat of my fire. A tortured wail rumbles through his body. There, his eyes shift into a beggar's, calling for death to take him.

"Never again will you speak." I stand and spit embers onto him. I step back. "Never again will I allow a man like you to rule these lands."

I glance at the fire as it jumps and picks him apart like a bird of prey.

"Have your way with him," I tell my flames. They sizzle with glee as they cover his body, boiling and blistering his skin. I watch as he takes two more breaths, and then his chest rises no more.

Fire and salt coat my tongue. Bitterness. His death was too simple.

"It's done," Ryker's deep voice presses into me from a distance. He gently pushes the wind over the nape of my neck.

"He refused to fight me." I glare at Galen's body as it begins to melt away. I have only a few more minutes of magic left.

"In the end, the only thing that mattered was his death, Titus." Ryker comes to my side, waiting for me to lower the flames on my body so he can come closer.

"You and I know that is a lie. It mattered. Greatly." I bitterly keep my fire up. "I want to be alone."

"That is why I will remain by your side." He dares to step closer.

I'm not controlling the heat. It pains him as he risks his flesh reaching out to grab me. For one second, the heat touches his fingertips. He's a stubborn ass. He doesn't flinch.

"Don't let Galen win. You have the castle, the army, the queen, and this." He grabs my hand. Galen's crown fills my palm as Ryker forces my fingers closed. He steps back.

I despise this putrid lump of metal. Raising my hand, I pour every ounce of fire I have left into it. Watching as the metal gives way. I stride closer, hovering over Galen's body, holding his melting crown out as it drips into useless nothing.

That is what his memory will be. Nothing.

I am a grain of sand, unsure whether I should scatter and seek solace or settle into a dune, pressing into the arms of my family who wish to make me into something solid.

This victory is lemonade made with rotten fruit and no sugar. I don't want to gulp it down. "This is what you wanted, Everett. I'm king, but Adrian was right. I crave something else. No crown on my head, just the merit of my worth and actions. Kings do not bend knees to other kings."

I cannot strip this world of titles; that will only cause more wars. "How do I stop an endless cycle, Everett?" I rasp.

Make them fight for the same cause. Make the protection of runes more important than castles and titles.

Is that the trick? What leashes them will also give them more magical freedom?

"Titus," Ryker's voice presses into my neck. The sun has settled into its morning position. Morning breakfast will be served with the news of my actions.

Oh, when did the fire turn to ash? Where are Galen's bones? I step closer. No more. I've lingered too long. My magic is used up; consequently, my flames have vanished.

"That burden of uncertainty on your shoulders can be shared, brother. Everett made sure you had a net to catch you. I'm here." His hand gently touches my shoulder. "We do not have to solve every question; we need only answer the more pressing ones. We need to return and make sure the castle is secure."

"How do I deliver victory when it's served on a rusty platter?"

"You garnish it," Ryker claps my back. "Focus on your next task and how it will change the world."

I know my mate. She doesn't like cherries on top; she likes the truth. I don't know if Selene will forgive me for taking this kill from her.

SELENE

Elderan steps back, tugging the light magic he used to change Tristan into one of his new creations back into his eyes. His robes are as stiff as the walls of the small room. For one blink of an eye, nothing moves, not my heart, not Tristan's body, nor the dust particles drifting in the air.

Static prickles along my skin, and then Tristen's body collapses. "No!" I cry.

I shove forward, expecting a push back, but I'm free too! I blanket Tristen with my body, then shake him. Is he dead?

I slap his face. "Open your eyes!" I plead. He looks... dead. He bears such a resemblance to Titus, it's haunting. "No!" My inhale burns. "Tristen, wake up!"

Why do I feel like this is a warning of what could happen? My mate, dead in my arms.

Sealing my eyes shut, I blast my healing magic into him. But I barely have any left. I've been treating sleep like an option when I should've made it a necessity.

"Do not waste your last dredges of magic. You will need it soon," Elderan says flatly.

A faint exhale warms my palm. "Tristen!" He's alive. I rub his cheeks, trying to bring color into them. "What did you do?" I scream, cradling Tristen to my chest and rocking him.

"I told you already," Elderan bites with exasperation. "I changed him. I did my part; I played my last hand. The rest is up to you. Your fate is in your own hands. Let's see how this plays out."

I whirl around, arms and legs spread wide, covering Tristen. "We are not games! Not pawns for you to move!" I snarl.

Elderan angles his head; his appearance shifts, as does my breath. He stands taller, younger, with a body of brutish strength. His eyes gleam intensely, like stars against the dark. If they're supposed to inspire hope, I feel diminished. He begins to glow a faint shade of colors, like the night sky exposing its dark depths.

My toes curl. His jaw makes Titus's look like a child, but what scares me are his haunting eyes, not of light but dark heavens, vacuums that pull at my chest, trying to drag me closer.

He's seen life, death, and the in-between. Traveled the heavens, moved the lands all with his exhale.

Don't ask how I know this. I sense it as one senses a pebble in their shoe.

Thick-cored arms crossed like chains, an exposed scarless torso, nothing but leather pants covering his legs. No weapons. He needs nothing, only his blinking eyes and dancing fingers.

My chin and shoulders inch in. "Are you a god?" I sound so weak. I know he said he was endless, but isn't that the true definition of a god?

"I already answered that."

"You said those we called gods could die. Maybe we labeled them wrong. Maybe *you* deserve that title."

Amusement lights his face. "If I were, shouldn't you be bowing?"

I am no coward. I raise my chin. "Not all gods deserve to be praised."

His eyes turn from hot granite to soft silk as he tips his head back and laughs. The sound is a drum so deep it changes my heartbeat for a moment. "Oh, Selene. I know what men see in you. I dare say you intrigue me."

I growl, feeling my mate mark burn.

He holds up his hand. "I would never touch you." He rolls his eyes. "If only others felt the same."

Tristen is right; speaking with Elderan is running in circles. I jab a finger towards Tristen. "Undo what you did to him."

"It's too late for that." He glances at Tristen as if he were picking an item from a wardrobe. "The change has started. You can't remove spice from a mixing bowl; it's best to accept the new taste."

"You sicken me!" My finger curls in. "This was not what my brother wanted."

Elderan steps forward, and I almost stumble. It feels like the land quakes beneath my feet. "Your brother was the catalyst that saved you all." His words hold no bitter notes, but his eyes find me lacking favor now. "I tried to guide others, but they turned out like Torin. They molded my advice to their own agendas. Everett was the first one to listen. I came here in another form, spotted Everett, and talked with him.

"I was so accustomed to seeing men want objects, but your brother wanted something else, and that intrigued me. It was Everett who saved you all; he deserves your bowed heads. Now, it's up to you not to dilute his end goal."

I crumple, sinking to my knees. I pull Tristen's torso onto my lap and push his hair off his head. He's hot now. Is that good? No, wait... that's a fever.

"I did not cause your suffering, Selene. Don't bite the hand that feeds you."

"You aided it!" I cry.

His shadow looms over Tristen and me, but inside the darkness, it's bathing us in light. "Bandages can hurt when applied, but their purpose is to heal, as is mine." He waves his hand, and the door appears.

A faint draft of air from the stairways touches my cheek, but I feel sick.

His light builds. I know if I turn to look, it will blind me again. I press Tristen's face closer to my chest.

"Tell Titus not to be fooled by peace. It is a prelude to turbulence, just as the ocean stirs slowly before a storm." His hand on my shoulder shocks me; his light illuminates my body. "Sometimes fighting—sailing against the current of fate—is what batters the ship the most; allow the tide to sweep you to a new destination, Selene."

Light fills every nook and crevice of the small room, climbing up the stairs until it fills the entire library. I gasp, curling inward as I squeeze Tristen to me. By the time I control my breathing, the light vanishes, creating a loud snapping boom that shakes the land.

The castle trembles, and dust seeps out from the cracks in the stones, raining down on me.

We're alone.

Everett never warned me about this. Does that mean we altered the future Everett saw?

"It's okay," I tell Tristen. "You'll be okay."

I'm happy he's unconscious; I'd hate to lie to his face.

The land shook for miles when Elderan vanished. Adrian saw a flash of blinding light and rushed to the library. I ordered him to bring Tristen to my bed; the location was private and secure, rather than the medical wing.

Adrian's questions were a relentless whip, digging into my spine. I had no answer that made sense.

No treatment has helped alleviate Tristen's fever. They started an IV with human blood in hopes that his magic would help keep him strong. A second IV has vampire blood to help heal the unseen damage.

I pace the room, too scared to stop, and sit by Tristen's side. Adrian hasn't received word from Titus, but his men come and go with updates on securing the castle.

"Where?" Titus shouts.

I've been in such a numb state that I didn't feel the bond tug me until now. I halt, stomach plummeting as I look at Tristen; chest bare, only a thin sheet and his boxers cover him as his body sweats with fever.

How do I explain this? I failed to keep your brother safe.

Will Tristen even be the same person when he wakes?

Reaching out, I touch the wall as the room spins. A pull jerks my eyes to the door. Titus rushes inside, eyes wide as chasms. They lock onto me like a hook in my cheek, breath flees from my lungs, needing his to replace it.

I sway, stumbling forward, rushing to him. A cry of relief fills the room as his hot exhale stirs my hair.

"Mate," he murmurs. His hands hold me as tightly as skin clings to my bones, but it doesn't feel close enough. There in each other's arms we linger, forgetting time, our problems, and tomorrow. Everything feels whole. Secure.

"I love you." He presses a kiss to my head.

I sniffle, pressing my ear to his heart. "I love you, too." *Thump, thump*; perfect and steady. He's alive!

"I'm sorry," he confesses.

Time breaks. We're forced to confess our sins. I look into his eyes, swirls of brown, like wood split open by smoldering embers. His face is covered in smoke and dirt.

He raises his blood-covered hands to cradle my face, then lowers them upon seeing the grime.

I grab his hands. "You killed Galen." All those nights I slept with Galen, put up with him, tried to make this sham of a marriage work, it's all for naught.

I'm disillusioned with myself, with life, and with a woman's role in general. I want a world where my daughter is not a coin to be bartered.

How did females who can make a child and ensure the survival of our kind become so powerless?

Galen's rule is truly over. Repeating it doesn't make it feel real. I need to etch it in stone, burn his throne. Better yet, I'll parade it through the street so the people he never viewed as worthy can take a seat in it.

But Galen is one king, and if the future Everett foretold must unfold, it means Titus and I need to dethrone many kings. I want to relish the sweet taste of victory, but the sour tang of reality overpowers it.

"I had to," he replies with a mixture of pride and remorse. "I know you lusted to be there, but I had to do this, Selene. I couldn't think with you at my side. I needed you here with Tristen, safe as the world crumbled."

I swipe my thumb over a deep indent in his palm, thick with Galen's blood. "I should have been by your side, helping you find purchase to stand. With *you*, Titus, not your brother. Do not betray me again. If your feet are not on firm ground, then mine are not. Distance does not create an illusion." I swallow my resentment. "I am not a bird to be caged. I am a creature that longs to fly with my mate by my side."

"I can not make a promise like that. You are my heart; I cannot expose it to death." He presses his forehead to mine. My lips press into a flat line. He's smart enough not to kiss away our problems. "Hate me for this. I can bear it. I cannot endure a life without you."

I want to fight, but it would be like shattering a mirror. I would do the same if his life were on the line. I'd lie, escape, and slay any beast who tried to harm him. I'd give my life if it meant he was tucked safely away.

Words stick in my throat. Great effort shoves them free. He needs to hear it. "I understand."

Like a fish jumping upstream, escaping the claws of a bear, the grief swims out of his eyes. I cup his face and guide his lips to mine. Love forgives. Hate does not.

I show him the meaning of this as my lips glide over his, exchanging our sighs of relief before I seal our mouths together. A heat of desire rushes down me. My hands slide down his neck, trying to anchor him to me.

His lips chase mine, but I run my nose along his jaw, till I press my lips to his ear. "But do not cast judgment on me when I do the same," I warn him, pressing my feet flat and standing firm. Fighting for control when it comes to our safety will be our biggest obstacle.

He wraps a hand behind my back, jerking my hips to his, kissing me with brutal force only a warrior can wield. I melt—flesh and bone —I am no more.

Only in his hold do I resemble something again. A newer, stronger version of myself.

Longing and desire drift down my throat. My hands reach up, clawing Titus's chest. Wait, why do I feel skin where his armor should be? Was he hurt?

My eyes open. Titus's lips trail down my jaw, a seamstress to the tears my doubts tore open.

I smile when I spot the mate mark exposed. Galen died knowing I was never his.

"Later," Titus promises as he nips at my neck. His sharp fangs tease my sensitive skin, but do not pierce it.

Adrian enters the room, arms crossed, eyes sharp as daggers, glaring at me. Tristen whimpers, and embarrassment burns my cheeks. We got lost in each other. I wish we could have stayed, but that is not our path.

Titus rushes to Tristen's side but keeps hold of my hand. His thigh is covered in blood. Gently, I search for a wound. "It's healed," he clarifies.

Was that the only wound Galen inflicted? I know Galen; his specialty was his mouth.

"What happened?" Titus spots the IVs filled with blood, and his eyes narrow with worry.

I tell him everything, how Elderan altered the Vitalis, appeared to be a god but claimed he was something more. Elderan was able to make one last alteration, selecting Tristen to become a new creature, capable of defending the people against the world's evils and wielding new magic, like rune drawing, siring others, and having a long life.

Titus's hand trembles as he pushes back Tristen's hair. "A new creature," he repeats. He hugs Tristen's hand to his chest and shakes his head.

I step forward. What do I say? My feet dance back as I pull at the silk sleeves of my shirt.

"The blade in the Vitalis." Titus glances back at me. Fear dilates his eyes. Knowing a single weapon we must encounter can kill his brother. "And he wanted me to be... made into... what Tris will be?" Titus asks.

"That is what he said." I stay back, weighed down with guilt. "I don't want you to change," I selfishly whisper.

Adrian's eyes dig into me. "You should have obeyed my orders and gone to your room," he hisses under his breath.

"I..." I lick my lips. Where has my voice gone? "I fucked up. I should have demanded that Tristen take me to my room. I... we both were pissed you lied."

"That does not give you an excuse to disobey orders," Adrian bellows.

Titus presses on his temple in exasperation. "There is nothing to forgive. This castle is not your cage. You can roam as you wish. We need to focus on what we have gained."

He looks utterly depleted. I want to rush forward and alleviate his aches.

But I don't. I'm a hypocrite. I haven't forgiven him for lying to me. That's going to take time.

Darkness eclipses me. Looking over my shoulder, I see a man who wears a mask of beauty and fury. Silver-blond hair, eyes as intense and consuming as a cave of amethyst. His lips remain pressed together, feet unmoving. "I'm Ryker," he announces.

Ryker observes me, says nothing more, and then joins Titus but positions himself on the other side so I'm in his sights.

I continue stepping away towards the balcony, taking in the fresh air. I feel like I'm intruding upon a moment meant for brothers.

"Hey, I'm here," Ryker whispers into Tristen's ear. He looks at Adrian. "The castle is secure. Only two nobles left of their own accord; a dozen were slain, and the rest said they would bend a knee. Your commander has them under surveillance."

He pauses when a new sensation prickles the air. Hitting me first since I'm the closest to it.

We all sense it. I glance to my side as the air on my balcony shifts. My gaze follows the curves of the skeleton frame that surrounds my tower. Galen cultivated it. I stood by his side and watched it grow. It was a wedding present. Then he had a vampire who had the magic of turning things into stone, transforming them into this solid state.

I've scaled those vines many times when I'd sneak out for nocturnal adventures. Galen never looked, nor cared, because he was fucking others.

My eyes narrow as I consider the opposite, that someone might have climbed these walls, so they had the memory of my room, a recollection used to open a portal if needed.

My gaze snaps back to Titus, who is kneeling over his brother a few feet away. It happens so fast, like stubbing a toe. We are seized with the pain of our misstep.

Snap! Magic expands, splitting the air as a portal rips open next to me. The blast tramples me, shoving me down, as the portal opens directly where I stood. Before I can stand, hands grab me, cold and hard. Titus's roar snaps my head up. His eyes darken to cold brown dirt, too hard to be tilled.

The air crackles. Behind Titus, everyone is frozen, but I'm not, nor are the hands holding me, dragging me into the portal. Titus time-weaved, but my captor is safe inside the bubble with me. I dig my heels into the stone, reaching my arms out for Titus.

My feet lift off the ground. *No!* The portal swallows me. My ears pop. The impact of the toss has my ribs slamming into the unknown destination. The side of my head is next to strike.

Darkness. Numbness. My mind screams, *Do not succumb to passing out!*

My first attempts at clearing my vision paint only black, then shades of dark shadows, until I realize stones surround me. The same stone was used to build Blackthorn Castle.

Am I still in the castle?

My teeth clench as I roll over. Over me is a firm, arched tunnel. That's odd. Blackthorn consists of high stacks of cut stone. This tunnel goes *through* stone.

"Selene!" Titus barrels through the portal right before it closes. A solid mass of muscle painfully pins me as he lands. I can't breathe from the weight, but instead of trying to roll him off, I hug him closer.

Why did you come for me and risk everything again?

This, whatever this is, is my turn. You slayed Galen. I must win the next round of this sinister game.

Footsteps reverberate within the tunnel. "Look what we have here. A two-for-one special," a dreadfully familiar voice purrs.

Titus pushes up, looming close. Our eyes meet, lost in a turbulence of emotions.

"Oh, this is perfect!" Hands clap. It sounds like the thread of my fate has been sliced. "Sister. It's about time you proved yourself useful."

Sable crosses her arms and smirks down at us.

CHAPTER
FORTY-SEVEN

TITUS

I'm a violin out of tune. A string deep within my chords splintered and broke.

When that portal opened, I panicked—made a deal with darkness, handing over my heart to save Selene. I used all my magic to kill Galen.

I don't know how I time-weaved. It lasted but a second, but that was all I needed to reach the portal and dive inside. One second was all it took for my mate to be ripped from my arms. One second of using my magic when I had nothing left weakened me in a way I fear is irreparable.

I spring forward, hands reaching for the flesh of Sable's neck. Shock turns to joy when my fingers wrap around her skin. But then joy erodes, crystallizing into a plague of decay.

I'm a wooden ship left in the harbor: salt gnaws at my hull, and my stomach twists with pain. Sable's smirking eyes tear me plank by plank down to the keel, crumbling all my hopes that Selene and I can find safe waters.

Sable's face reddens from lack of air, but her grin punches me as hard as an anchor drags and tears into the ocean floor, forcing me to halt. Magic tears my ribs, breaking, bending, pushing two of them into my lungs.

It's her death magic! If I don't release her, it will spread, taking root.

I let go, coughing up blood. My breath is too short. My subconscious scrambles to heal me, but it's like licking a plate you savored. Nothing is truly left. I need my mate's blood so I can have the power to heal, but feeding from her would alert them to just how strong we are.

I reach out ready to cover Selene, but her abductor presses a dagger to her chest.

Sable rubs her neck. "Titus, ever the noble guard protecting my sister. Galen must love you. Jumping through portals into the unknown to save my twin."

She doesn't know I killed Galen.

Selene swallows and looks at me with eyes that lie. *It's okay; this will be okay. I'm fine.* She silently blinks.

My rapid inhales fill with chalky dust. I need blood to help this wound heal. But how? I check our surroundings. My eyes adjust to the faint light. Darkness clings to the walls as they curve into a carved-out arch. We're in a tunnel. Pressing my toes into my boots, I note the uneven slat of the ground; my eyes follow the pull, stretching down into a slope as black as Sable's heart. The air is stale, devoid of life. Only mage lights, which hover around Sable and her mages, light the way. Even if we run, the path will be blind unless my fire can light it.

"Where are we?" It's a stupid question I can answer myself, but Sable loves to talk. I'll use that weakness to my advantage.

She glides a wicked finger down the stone walls. Only magic could carve stone this smooth.

"It's marvelous, isn't it?" Sable gloats. "I heard the King of Caldera had earth magic; he specialized in liquefying stone. Have you ever picked up a rock from a babbling brook, one that was forced to allow water to tunnel through it? That is what the old books describe

Caldara as, a stone filled with polished tunnels framed within the mountain. The king carved these tunnels himself." She smacks the wall. "It's written that his castle was pulled and shaped from the mountain. He thought he could reinforce the walls, but the rocks were stronger."

The chill that blankets my skin can never be shed. We're where Everett wanted us all to be.

Selene's lips part, ready to beg her twin to free me. A moment later, she snaps them shut. Sable would relish killing me if she knew Selene cared. Selene knows it; she's plotting how to get me out alive.

Me, not her.

I shake my head. *I'm not leaving without you.*

She looks to the floor, her face pale with secrets she hasn't spoken to me.

"How?" I ask. Fighting is useless. I'll let Sable lead us to the book, then find a way to attack.

The man holding Selene nods his head. His partner, a small female mage, places cuffs around my wrist; mage cuffs intended to bind magic. The small female removes my sword, covered in Galen's blood; the weight of it has the tip clumsily hitting the ground.

"You've been busy. Who did you kill, Titus?" Sable dances closer to me, taking her time to spin as if I want to admire her curves. She pushes up so her lips kiss my ear. "That looks fresh," she purrs.

I twist my head away.

The man holding Selene grunts, pressing the knife closer. He sends his magic out. I expect an attack, but it hits my sword, melting the metal.

Hector! I look at him fully. He's my height, leaner, with exposed arms covered in runes. All bark, no bite, since magic isn't linking them. His skin is tanner than Selene's sun-kissed glow; his dark hair is shaved short. Eyes dead and cold.

The woman who cuffed me joins his side. Her dress and jewels are oddly placed, her brown hair pinned into a high bun. She's Sofia,

Hector's sister, the mage who opens portals as easily as one flips the pages of a book.

Mages are limited to opening portals to places they've seen. Sofia must have snuck into Selene's room, preparing for the day she'd ambush Selene, taking her right out from Galen's nose and delivering her to Hector and Sable.

Another mistake Galen made. Other kings do not allow portal-opening mages to wander their lands freely.

But she brought us here, into the tunnel. That means they found it before we did! Sable could have taken the book. Why bring Selene here? Why risk it?

I look at Selene. She's figuring it out, too.

"You know why we're here," Sable grunts at Selene as she finger-combs her hair. My fingers twitch, knowing it feels the same as Selene's. Silken. "I always had a suspicion you knew what Everett was hunting. You were like his notebook." Sable's words are sour and rotten. "A place he jotted down ideas, vented." She whirls and faces me. "But your reaction is odd, Titus."

She comes closer and... fuck! Her eyes widen, narrow, then glow with glee at my exposed mate mark.

"Oh... my..." She tips her head back. Her laugh echoes like a wildcat. She leans over, grasping her stomach. "I always planned on making you suffer, Selene. I planned to have you watch as the world burned, but here I am with your mate." She spins on her toes, grabs Selene's silk shirt, and rips the neckline open, exposing her matching mark. "Mated."

Jealously rolls off her tongue. She looks over her shoulder at the melted sword. "Galen must have loved that. That's his blood, isn't it?" She grins.

She's fast. I'll give her that.

"We're wasting time." Hector shoves Selene down to her knees.

I dive forward; it's my only chance to defend us. Landing on top of her, directly above her heart.

"Do it," she whispers. I bite her, sucking down only a gulp of her blood before magic yanks me off and sends me flying down the tunnel. The mage cuffs prevent me from attacking outward with my magic, so I focus a small dose of the magic into healing my lungs and ribs.

"That was very naughty, Titus," Sable scolds me. "I love to play with bad things. Perhaps you and I should play." She looms over me.

I tug at the cuffs. I need to get them off.

"You like them?" Sable mocks. "I could chain you to my bed, allow my twin to watch. I share her face; I'm sure I could get you hard. Oh, come on, give me a snarky reply." Sable turns. "Nothing from you, Selene? Oh, this is no fun," she pouts.

"Enough, Sable. It smells. Let's move." Sofia's sister lights another mage light and inspects her nails.

"I'm going to say this once." Hector's voice is ice as he looks at me. "I need Selene, not you. Sable, you can do what you want with him, but if he tries to attack, he's dead." He looks down at me. "Understood?"

I grind my teeth.

"Hector." Sable rushes to his side and kisses his lips, but his eyes remain open and on me.

Sable thinks she can wrap every man around her finger, but the higher she climbs, the less they bend and break. Hector stands tall, unmoving. Sable was the one who was bending, not him.

"It's a straight path down." Hector steps back, flexing his fingers; even his knuckles are tattooed. "You will go first." He glares at me. Slowly, I stand, pressing my hand to my ribs so he thinks they still pain me. "Then Sable, then Selene, and my sister and I will be last."

Sable pouts. "But I want to have fun with them."

"You can have fun." Hector grabs her chin. "Once I get our book." He kisses Sable with a lover's fury.

Sable grinds her hips into him as she moans. I'm about to look away when Hector opens his eyes and glares at me again, like a knife ready to peel flesh from bone.

He fists Sable's hair, pulling her away. "Go," he orders me.

I take a hesitant step, eyes searching the darkness. The weight of

Selene's stare has me faking confidence. My exhale fans out like heat over sand, stretching far and wide.

"Our brother's killer is your mate," Sable taunts, her breath heating my neck.

"It could be worse," Selene snaps, trying to make Sable think she doesn't love me.

"Nothing is better," Sable sings. She traces her fingers down my neck as I walk. "Titus, how much do you know?" she persists. I want to walk slowly, but hearing Sable gloat has me quickening my pace. An expert made the path, and not a single stone is uneven, allowing me to catch my breath.

"I'm more curious," Selene replies, "why do you need me?"

"You must know a lot, sister. Everett was so detailed, but he had no idea I had someone on my side helping me." Sable spills like water. Hector's exhale is a hiss of irritation. Having such a blabbering weakness clinging to his side doesn't sit well, but he doesn't stop Sable... because he needs her to get that book for him.

Has Sable considered what comes after? Once she frees the Vitalis, I doubt Hector will be so tolerant.

"For years, Everett was ahead. Then I met Hector, and he gave me all the tools I needed. Told me where to turn." Sable blows Hector an air kiss.

"And what did that cost you?" Selene retorts.

Sable hesitates, looks over her shoulder at Hector, and smirks. "Nothing."

Selene laughs. I close my eyes. I want to hear that sound again.

"You're just jealous someone loves me. Me. Not you."

"You're just his pawn," Selene sneers.

"Enough!" Hector snaps.

"Do you see what I mean, Hector? This has been my life, tolerating her, enduring her!"

"Endurance builds strength. You should be thanking me, not bitching to your boyfriend," my mate quips back.

That's my girl. I smirk.

"I'm going to end you slowly."

"A slow death will seem fast compared to the years I've had to look upon your face," Selene replies.

I love seeing Selene fight because I know she can hold her ground, but I need to cool this down. "Where am I going?" I ask.

"We're going to the Vitalis," Sofia replies, then she floats another mage light over me, helping me see my next step.

"Why did you tell him?" Sable hisses.

"So you'd all shut up. Tell him the rest, or I will," Sofia responds. Why do I sense her eyes on my back?

"You're no fun," Sable grunts. She can't stand someone else stealing her thunder, so she spills everything like a rainstorm. "The Vitalis is the book of runes, the book Everett was after. I found all the little details Everett thought he hid from me."

"If you found them, it's only because he wanted you to." Selene sours Sable's glory. "Did you pause to ponder the reason, or did you simply embrace your customary ignorant role?"

"He *didn't* want me to find them!" Sable rebuttals. "Everett killed so many, Selene, all for the runes. The brother you thought was selfless was, in fact, the most selfish man alive. He wanted the runes so he could rule."

"And your noble hearts want them to what?" Selene counters.

Stale air dances over my forehead; we're getting deeper into the heart of the fallen mountain. So deep, this tunnel survived the impact. Reaching up, I touch my heart. Everett's magic will leave me soon. I never mourned his sacrifice; I had a piece of him inside of me, still living. Soon I won't.

When will it happen? As soon as I see the Vitalis, or after I touch it? When do I prepare to bid farewell?

"I never cared about ruling, Selene." Sable savors this moment like one sucks a spoonful of sweets. "I cared about endings."

"So your dream is to find the runes and set the world on fire, to sit on a throne of embers and ashes."

"Every throne is built on ash, Selene! You're still blind. I don't want a throne. I want everything and nothing at all. I want suffering, misery and demise. It's my purpose, like my magic."

"You're mad. You always have been." Selene's words are held together with pity. Selene paints a picture in which she hates her twin. But deep inside her is a seed her magic keeps alive, a small flower of hope that her twin can change. I wish I could tell Selene that the flower she is protecting is a weed that will spread and harm her. There is no saving Sable. No one wants a shell with holes.

"What is madness, but another way of thinking? Why is your way right and mine wrong?"

"Because massacre isn't right, Sable. We're not beasts. We have minds, subconsciousnesses that think and feel."

Sable lowers her voice, as though she's sharing a secret. The words that emerge are a steadfast force, an avalanche grabbing my ankles. "My subconscious was stolen long ago."

"It was never stolen. You just locked it away."

"That's how I survived."

"You could have turned to me, your twin."

"A twin is not a gift, Selene. It is a mirror that points out all your flaws, as father often reminded me. You don't break something beautiful; people would notice. You grab something ugly, this way no one realizes what you have done, because the person was already overlooked, Selene."

Selene snorts, "Finally, we can agree. I saw every stain within you and made sure it did not mar me."

"Don't listen to her," Hector chides, his feet moving to Sable's side. I can't help but look over my shoulder. His words are soft, but his eyes are stone.

Oh, Sable, you have no idea what's coming. He's going to flay you alive, and I'm going to watch. I just need to slip these cuffs off, kill Sofia and Hector, get the Vitalis, and save my mate.

"Sofia has been more of a sister than you ever were," Sable adds.

"Poor Sofia," Selene acknowledges. "If Sable considers you a sister, be prepared for a knife in your back."

I smirk when I hear Sofia's steps falter. The truth can be so utterly bitter.

A smack sounds. I turn, spotting Selene's face angled from Sable's hit. I lift a foot, ready to kill Sable. I see red, but in that haze, I spot Hector's brow arched in my direction. I've gained no ground since killing Galen, forced to watch my mate being attacked.

Selene doesn't bother touching her cheek, blinking the attack off like it was nothing. "I thought you had a better hand, Sable. Pride has weakened you." Selene's smirk is a stable flame piercing through the dim light.

Sable stops, standing like a pillar blocking Selene from me. "Do you know how you sharpen a knife, sister? You glide it over softer stone. I turned my weaknesses into strengths. Used them to sharpen all my dull edges, every aspect of me that resembled you, I removed."

"Must be hard to look in the mirror then." Selene rolls her shoulders back.

For a moment, nothing ripples. I spot Hector's eyes glaring into Selene's back. Sofia steps in front of her brother, shifting my view off him. Her eyes narrow, shoving into me like hands trying to... warn me.

She moves her hand and throws another mage light into the air. It floats ahead of me. Helping me. Selene's eyes hold steady like a fishing line trying to lure in its prey. Sable holds her tongue, then slowly turns to face me.

"Maybe I should kill you now?" She runs her hands down my chest, over my mark, digging her nails into the skin, clawing at it.

"Enough!" Hector snaps. "If one more of you speaks, I will cut your tongues out."

His true colors showed quickly.

Sable leans to the side, pushing her hips out. "You would miss my tongue too much."

Hector breaks the formation and grabs Sable by the neck, dagger in hand, and pushes it to her stomach.

"You need me," she smirks.

Selene and I share a glance. We need her, too. Selene nods, even smiles. *'I'm fine, let this play out; we will escape somehow,'* her eyes say.

Hector glides the dagger up her body before withdrawing his hand. "Enough chatter. Fools delight in useless bragging. Wise men know the power of holding their tongues."

Just like that, Sable curls around Hector's finger and listens.

I recognize that expression. Vengeance mixed with embarrassment has deadly outcomes.

Who will betray whom first?

CHAPTER
FORTY-EIGHT

SELENE

S able is winning.

Could I fall to my knees and beg? Sure.

It would do no good.

Could I ball my fists and fight? Absolutely, but it would be short-lived.

Instead, I wear the shoes Titus has had to endure. I watch his fate dangle on a rope, in the hands of others. Effortless to stop it.

Down here, Sable and Hector hold the power. I must wait for the perfect moment to strike.

Watching Titus grind his teeth, mentally bend a knee so I'm not hurt. It guts me, scars so deep I'll never walk the same. I deserve it. I asked him to bear this pain when I denied the bond, after all.

Sweat beads down my spine, causing the silk of my shirt to cling like an itchy rash. It's poetic that we're now trapped in a tunnel, forced not to run away. This is the end of the journey, and endings create new beginnings.

One person will walk out of here with the Vitalis.

I must make sure it's Titus.

My eyes roam over his broad shoulders as he leads the way deeper and deeper into Caldara. He's always been a guiding light, even when he's mere embers and smoke. A born leader who will make Everett proud.

I glance at Sable as she hisses and grunts, biting her tongue as she follows silently. I feel Sofia's eyes on my back, as well as Hector's.

"Elderan," I whisper in desperation. Nothing happens. He said I'd never see him again.

Setbacks are not failures; they give you a different perspective. Everyone says sink or swim, but what if we do both? What if, when we desperately swim, we accidentally swallow too much water, allowing the weight of our mistakes to pull us down?

What then?

Why is it sink or swim? Why not both? Why can't I sink, but then choose to swim, to kick and scream out all that water and fight, swim again, and again?

Death can't stop me. It didn't stop my brother.

That's what it's going to take. Failure to succeed. Sacrifices, as Everett always alluded to.

Hector's exhale signals relief. His steps heighten to eager stomps. "Hurry up!" he shouts at Titus.

"Are we close?" Sofia whispers. She's brave. I believe Hector would cut out all of our tongues.

"I sense the metal... it's different," he mutters more to himself. A mage light floats out like a buoy into the darkness, bobbing in the stale air. "More light, Sofia!"

Sofia throws out half a dozen more mage lights that sink into the larger room. A few gemstones on her necklace lose their sparkle as she uses the magic she stored in them.

Titus looks over his shoulder at me, masking his worry with a warrior's stare. I force a smile, one I wish he'd grab and own. *I'm fine; please believe me. I'll get you out of this mess.* I will myself to believe it, as well.

His feet halt, and Sable runs into his back. It's like an IV has been infused into us all. A jolt runs down my spine. Magic is ahead, but it's different.

Titus holds up his hand, warning Hector to stop. Hector does because what we hear makes us all pause.

Ba-dum, ba-dum, ba-dum!

The sound is as deep as thunder and static-like lightning. Pulsing in warning. Repetitive, scarring yet calming because we all know that sound, for it resides within all of us.

"That's a heartbeat," I whisper through hesitant lips.

The mage lights that entered the room pulse from each loud thump. Light travels, showing us a glimpse of the room ahead: carved stone hollows out a large cavern. Directly across the space is another tunnel entrance, the slope leading up, but the roof has caved in.

Does that lead to Caldera's castle?

I peer over my shoulder at our exit, which must lead outside. No one but Torin used this passage, and now us.

"Why is there a beating heart?" Sofia bends down, picks up the ends of her dress, and steps back.

Metal flashes in front of me. Hector comes to my side, his sword raised high. He's the only one with a weapon. Glaring down, I look at my outfit. All silk. I look at Titus. Buckles. Can Hector fashion them into deadly weapons?

Then there's Sofia, but she's scared. She's used to running through her portals rather than fighting. I can take her down. Hector and Sable are the biggest threats.

It's okay. I'll think of something. If I can get Hector away from his sword, we might have a fighting chance.

"My twin is going to betray you," I whisper to Hector. Our eyes clash, and I widen my stance.

Is that a smile or a snarl?

Sweat drips down his temple, over his tattooed skin. So many runes... where did he find them?

"You helped the wrong person," I add.

He leans closer. "Sable helped me," he hisses.

Why did he admit that?

He pulls away with a grin that stretches wider than the known lands. "Enter," Hector orders Titus.

Titus holds up his hands. The mage cuffs slide down an inch. "Take these off. I give you my word I will not attack."

If the Vitalis is in that room, it means I'm about to lose all aspects of my brother truly. His magic will flee soon. This is not the final farewell I wanted.

Hector's finger twitches, and Titus's chest recoils as a buckle starts to melt. "Enter. Now." Hector warns him. "If not, I will sink this into your heart, and your mate can watch you die."

Titus and I share a lover's panicked glance. If Everett's magic vanishes, we lose the shock of a surprise. Fate cannot be that cruel— my brother can't. Everett's magic will wait until Titus has the book in hand, surely.

"I'll," I try to offer myself, but Titus steps forward, chest wide, ready to be my shield.

I follow his steps, but Hector grabs me, "Not so fast."

The heartbeat quickens, and the room glows with a grayish-blue light that exhales over Titus, illuminating him. Titus's eyes widen, his jaw slackens, and his chest caves in as a father's does when he cradles something precious.

I sense his wonder, relief, and worry. I know what he sees before anyone else does.

The book Everett gave his life for. The Vitalis.

"You were right," Titus's whisper echoes into the tunnel. Memories of my brother pull tears from my eyes. We did it! We found it! But what cruelty has been bestowed upon us, to see, yet not touch.

Titus starts to turn his head, searching for my eyes.

"Titus!" I scream when his back arches. He yells in pain, falling forward, knees and palms smacking against the hard stone, the mage cuffs digging into his wrists.

Sable and Sofia scramble back. I dive forward, hands reaching like ropes, feet springing forward—an undying insect that fears nothing, no human boot squashing me, no lethal poison sprayed upon me, only the loss of her mate.

Hector jerks me back, curving his body over me... shielding me. Why is he doing that?

I twist around his torso and spot my mate. Titus's black hair hangs wet over his forehead; his nails dig into the stone. His lungs hammer louder than the eerie heartbeat. Light bursts from his spine, jumping out like a predator, but instead of attacking us, it disintegrates.

I'm a deadweight, watching as Everett's magic tears itself free from my mate, just as Everett ordered it to do. The air smells like a floral candle has been blown out.

Drip, drip, drip. A few lone tears fall from Titus's eyes. He peers at me, on his hands and knees; he resembles fire that was smothered by water. Smoking, hissing, exhausted. He flattens his palms awkwardly with the cuffs binding him, preparing to stand.

"I'm fine," he gasps out lies.

"Is there a creature?" Hector pushes me into the wall, covering my back. He swings his sword out, blocking Sofia and Sable from venturing further.

"No," Titus replies truthfully. No creature inside hurt him. He stumbled because Everett's promise had come true. Time-weaving departs when Titus *finds* the Vitalis.

Why, Everett? Why not allow him time-weaving forever? What future is so terrible that you did not give foresight to Titus? What tragedy is so horrendous that it would have made Titus stop his search, allowing Sable to get the Vitalis?

"What is the cause of the heartbeat?" Hector hisses, and Sable shoves closer, her eyes sour at Hector's hold of me.

"Come and see for yourself." Titus stands, locking his knees so he doesn't sway.

"I'll go," Sable replies. She glances at Hector, and he doesn't stop her. That pains Sable. She pushes his sword down and enters the room, stepping a few feet above Titus.

"What do you see?" Hector shouts.

Sable covers her smile with her hand, speechless for the first time. Her eyes widen in wonder; her black hair taking on the same grayish-blue shine that covers the room. "Marvelous. It's... real." She waves her hand. "Hector! Come!" She giggles.

He looks at Sofia before pressing his sword to my back, steering me into the room first.

Ba-dum, ba-dum, ba-dum.

My chin enters first. The sight makes me stumble into Titus's side. Hector is so awestruck that he strides ahead with Sable. He doesn't see what's happened—that I've touched my mate. Titus slowly grabs my wrist, guiding it to his fangs.

Ba-dum, ba-dum, ba-dum!

Is that my heart or the one the room possesses?

Drink! Hurry! Titus is our only hope of surviving. He needs his fire! His gaze shifts to the tunnel, where Sofia stands, too scared to enter, her eyes fixed on us. *Shit!*

Instead of dropping my wrist, he kisses it. He was born a lover, forced to be a fighter. Sharp fangs cut me. I gasp with pleasure, but Hector and Sable think I'm still awestruck.

Sofia watches as Titus swallows gulp after gulp, fueling his fire. Why isn't she saying anything? Her pretty face, which seduced Galen, turns apologetic. All the jewels on her neck look more like weights.

Ba-dum! Titus pulls another mouthful. *Ba-dum!* He gulps it down. *Ba-dum!* He's about to stop, more worried about my current state. I press my wrist deeper into his fangs. Another swallow, he licks the wound, stopping the bleeding before the others see. He kisses my fingertips, then lowers my hand.

"I've never seen anything so stunning," Sable coos.

Titus looks me dead in the eyes and whispers, "Neither have I."

I'm scared to peel my eyes off him. "I love you," I declare, then I look ahead. Grey-blue light fills the large space. Now that I'm inside, I see four more entrances, all caved in.

Rubble and debris are scattered on the floor. But like the tunnel we used, this room withstood the collapse. Three dozen men could easily occupy the space. This must have been a safe shelter if the castle was invaded. They planned to run down here, regroup, or flee.

There in the corner is the source of the heartbeat. A grey-blue shield of magic, with glowing veins thumping with life. Torin's sacrifice, his death magic he forced into a cage over, "The Vitalis," I murmur in awe.

I don't know what I expected. Something small, held in your hand like a normal book. It's not small. It's large, giving the user enough space to draw intricate details, making runes hard to duplicate.

The pages are an odd shade of metallic, like gold and platinum threads were woven or melted together so tightly that they became smooth, like a fingerprint, still flexible to push a pen against. The front and back covers of the book are pulled back, exposing the inner pages —the guts and heart.

Deep in my chest, I know the book is in agony. With each beat of Torin's death cage, the pages flap, but there in the center, the movement stills, pinned down.

The most magnificent sword I have ever laid eyes on skewers it like a piece of meat.

To cement everything Everett and Elderan told me, the skeleton lying on the floor is proof. It's Torin's bones. Hector spots it as I do. Sable steps closer, bends down and grabs a bone. Chin held high, she looks at the cage of death, pulls her elbow back and tosses the bone at it. As soon as the bone comes into contact with the cage, it disintegrates. "Everyone coos over the birth of life, but there is nothing like the awe struck silence death can produce. It's magnificent," sable mumbles to herself. "It's what I want. Silence."

If silence is what you seek, why do you conceive such resounding chaos, Sable?

Titus begins to raise his hands, trying to slide the mage cuffs off. Sofia strides forward, desperately shaking her head. Pleading for us to wait. Her movements cause Hector and Sable to spin around.

"Don't let them touch, Sofia!" Sable scorns. Her long hair flows with the freedom I long for.

"I'm separating them." Sofia dips her chin, grabs my hand, and tugs me away.

Sable rolls her eyes, then looks at Hector. "Melt it." She runs her fingers down his back.

Ignoring her smirk, I examine the blade; its intricate design suggests a master smith. Set within the pommel is a glowing gem not of this land. It appears to be a source of magic, transforming into rainbows of color that captivate us all.

The grip shines, as if a star's inner light, twisted and melted into a cable pattern, powered it. Etchings cover the blade that suggest a language, a narrative, or both.

"It's happening," Sable gloats as she looks at the book. The first page has a rune, but it's faint, as if the ink wept from the pain of the sword stabbing it. "I'm going to start with Solaria. The home you loved."

Hector's hands raise; his magic slithers out, hissing like sand, seeping through the beating death cage. His body reacts as the magic encircles the sword, but nothing results. His neck muscles throb as he makes another attempt.

The sword does not bend or melt under his touch.

"Sable!" he shouts. "Come. Torin's magic must be blocking mine."

Sable hurries to his side. "We don't need to save the pages. I'm telling you, new pages will regenerate—"

"I told you, I do not have time to learn how to create new runes! I want *those* runes!" Hector jabs a finger at the book. "That is why I did not let you kill your twin. I need her to heal the pages! Do you understand?" Sable tries to nod as her face flushes in shame.

A wave of stillness freezes my frantic heart. *That's* how I fit in.

"You want the runes on your body to work," I surmise. Everett didn't place me in Titus's life because I was his mate. Being mated is our biggest foe in my brother's eyes. It's a distraction.

Everett saw a way to slay this problem—to keep Titus focused.

Everett warned me; I ignored him, and in that bliss, I found love. But ignorant bliss is a cloud. Clouds move, dissipate. They make way for a new horizon.

My true purpose is to heal the book so Titus doesn't have to start from scratch. After that, I am useless.

"That's the plan," Hector replies. He steps back, eyeing the book with a deep longing. "Sable is going to get me the book; you will heal it." He glances at Sable, showing a strange kind of affection. "And then I'm going to help Sable destroy everything.

"Now get me the book, baby." He guides Sable to the cage.

I can practically feel her anxiety churn my stomach. She reaches for Torin's cage, hesitating before plunging her hand inside. The steady beating of the heart skips a beat and then panics, wildly filling the room, invading our ears, trying to change our own hearts.

Sofia slaps her hands over her ears, then looks back at Titus and voices, "Not yet."

She wants Sable to free the book before we attack. Titus struggles, pushing his wrists against the tight cuffs. It's stuck on his thumb. I recoil in discomfort as I witness him breaking his finger so he can slip free.

Sable's fully inside the cage now, hovering over the book, her death magic spreading out from her feet, crawling up Torin's wall, spreading her rot.

How long will it take until Torin's cage crumbles?

"Pull the sword out," Hector orders her. She obeys, wrapping her fingers around the sword. But there's no way she can pull it free; it's dug deep into the rock.

Her spine tenses, her shoulder rolls back. "I feel..." she tugs the sword. Metal lacerates rock. The sword begins to move! "Powerful." With a tilted head, her gaze lingers on the sword, more so than on the Vitalis. Sable pulls it forth with some unknown magic.

How did she do that!

Hector looks back at his sister as if he's falling with no net. Sofia nods as a tear drips down her cheeks.

Sable swings the sword somewhat clumsily. The tip touches Torin's cage; one small touch, and the heartbeat stops. A ripple of energy surges, howling and thundering, then just as Everett's magic vanishes, so too does Torin's death cage. A static charge stings us all.

I breathe in tight, electric air, quickly exhaling it. My lungs scream for deep breaths.

The Vitalis is free. No one dares to move. Titus exhales a million emotions in one breath. His thumb is swollen and broken, but he frees his other hand and then coats his fingers in fire.

I begin to smile. Am I celebrating too soon?

He looks at me with lust, longing, stability, and promises of forever. "I love you," he states. Fire licks up his forearms. He pulls his arm back, and a larger ball of fire fills his palm. The room flickers with orange shades, altering the others.

I step aside. My smile is wide, ready to watch him fight, not only for my honor but for a future where everyone can be free.

Titus twists, ready to throw. Right as he swings, I turn to look at my twin.

What happened?

The certainty of the future Everett died for is in question, tossed like a coin. What side will it land on?

CHAPTER
FORTY-NINE

SELENE

I see myself, wide-eyed and panicked, tear-filled, astonished, unable to grasp what has happened.

Sable can't comprehend it. Neither can Titus or I.

My heels lift. A part of me wants to rush towards Sable, even after everything. Memories have me stepping back.

Hector stands firm, a feather strong enough to fly yet delicate enough to be plucked free. Deep down, he can't understand either.

Was it fate that compelled Hector to do what he just did?

I didn't hear it or see it! The look on Hector's face—falling without a net when Sable brandished the sword—he fixed it. He landed, but in doing so, he shoved my twin over the edge.

"Stop, Titus," Hector shouts. His voice no longer icy. It's paper-thin.

Titus swings his fist to his side. He cradles the fire, unsure what to do.

Sable's fingers uncurl, like water forced to evaporate under intolerable heat. Inch by inch, they open, and the weight of the sword in her hand clatters to the floor. My heart skips a beat as the metal echoes a dreadful melody.

I feel Titus look at me, grab my hand, and force our fingers to knit together so this shock can't separate us.

His fire covers my palm, comforting me as an old chipped teacup filled with tea would. I hug his hand to my chest, just like I would that beloved teacup. A flush of warmth touches my stony heart as he adjusts the temperature.

I shake my head. A ghastly truth trembles on my lips. A premonition of how this is all going to end. Just as Everett told me.

Sacrifices.

My twin and I are the same. We're just used differently. We're pens that sign peace treaties and declare war. Fires that warm and consume; maps that show ways and mislead.

That premature smile is slapped off my face. Reality settles like boulders in my belly.

I look at Titus as one does their favorite tree, knowing winter is about to claim all its lush vibrant leaves. Those thick branches that shaded me are going to be skinned raw, barren, exposed, forced to survive the cold, lonely winter in hope spring will come. "I love you." I whisper. *Spring will come and shine upon your handsome face again. You will live and smile, laugh and love. You are our hope for survival. I am just a ladder that helped you. That's okay, my love. I would mold myself into endless tools to help you get the Vitalis.*

I will.

He keeps his eyes ahead on the ghastly spectacle that has beguiled us. "I love you, too."

I squeeze his fingers covered in fire, and then I face my fate. Only mage lights fill the room, keeping it dim, as if to aid in covering up this sin. Reaching behind her, Sable claws at her spine, desperate to unearth a soul-crushing torment of the dagger in it.

Hector's breaths are waves clashing against one another, trying to drown out the horror of his actions. But when you drown, feeling persists. The pressure bearing down, the weight dragging you under, the burn in your chest. Under the waves, the water magnifies everything.

Hector's arm is still outstretched, and in his fist, I see the dagger he plunged into my twin's back, piercing her heart.

A death blow.

Sable tries to rebuke it. Her fingers touch his, clawing to remove the blade. I knew he'd betray her, but why now? She was his backup against Titus and me.

Sofia runs in front of us. She looks at Titus's fire and gulps. "Let Hector explain," she pleads. Should we accept it?

Hector doesn't remove the dagger. Instead, he slides his hand down her back, over her hips, where he spins her into his arms. He falls to his knees, cradling her to his chest. The Vitalis, the book we all want, sits there, another spectator in this terrible confusion.

"I am sorry," Hector exhales a terrible apology filled with anguish. He pushes her hair back, peering into her eyes.

He does love her.

I wish he didn't. I wish Sable hadn't died, knowing that love kills.

Was his cruelty a lie? Something he forced himself to learn because it was the only thing Sable responded to?

"You were my dark paradise," Hector's lips twitch up. "I wanted to get lost in you, Sable. To build a shelter we could have survived in. Just you and me. No one else." He glares at the Vitalis. "Nothing else." He chokes, "Your lips were poison I gladly swallowed. I thought I could withstand the illness that is a side effect of loving you. I thought little by little, I could render you into an antidote. But some poisons are just too wicked to be reversed."

Sable strikes, grabbing Hector, shoving her magic into him. Her nails scratch into a rune tattoo. Her death magic stings, then soaks into a part of him like a sponge. His tattoo begins to fade, and his tan skin turns a pale greenish hue.

He hisses and slaps his hand over hers. Not removing her, only pushes her hand deeper into him.

"You'll be dead before your magic can kill me," he admits affectionately. "I won't let you die alone, Sable." He holds her tighter.

My hand covers my trembling lips. I compel my blinks to push back my tears.

Who am I crying for? Hector? Sable? Both?

Maybe it's the fact that love betrays its admirer. Love is a master trickster; it restores and ravages.

I glance at my mate, his fire covering our held hands. His muscular chest displays our mark. He stands protectively, like a warrior prepared to give his life for the weak. I'm honored to be his mate, grateful I had one night with him. A night filled with love and passion that was reciprocated. One night surpassed all the others I endured in this harsh land.

Sofia bends down and picks up the mage cuffs; she puts them on, adjusting them to fit snugly. "I'm on your side," she admits. She cuffs herself, proving her point, then drops to her knees, sits, and looks down. It puts my senses on alert.

Titus tries to pull me behind him, but I step one foot ahead, eyes locked on a different version of myself dying.

"I do love you, Sable." Hector's voice is thick and raw, a fresh burn, blistering the skin to protect the tissue underneath. "I tried to change you." A tear catches his bottom lip. He licks it, forcing himself to swallow what he's done.

Even when facing death, Sable remains cold. Blood pours out of her back, covering Hector's lap. "That's... not... love." If she had the power to yell, she would have.

"You once told me you were incapable of love, Sable. You thought that statement connected us. Hate bound us in your eyes." Hector's throat bobs. "It was a lie. You do love," he nods repeatedly.

Reaching out, he dips his finger into her blood.

"You love this." He smears her blood on his fingertips. "You adore your aggression and cruelty above all. Something broke inside you when you were younger. Shh, it's okay. I understand. Instead of clinging to hope like your twin, you clung to detachment. I never lied when I told you we were cut from the same cloth. You see, I used to be detached. People grabbed me. I was given no other option. I was stitched to their unraveling edges. I became a part of a quilt that was oddly shaped, but nonetheless it proved warmth. Love. I was forced to feel, to fight for those who had no voice." He curls his fingers into a fist and then glares at her. "To fight those who intend to steal voices."

My tears pour out faster than her blood does now.

Hector rocks her back and forth. "I tried fighting you with my lips and my hands; I tried to soften you—reshape you. I gave you rough-ness because you rebuked joy. I tried everything to break you down." He stops rocking, like he's been slapped.

He grabs hold of a sharp inhale, forcing it into his lungs.

"Even last night, I tried to alter your mind, tried to carve out a piece of land we might both have, a place we could make a home, but you denied me. You told me homes are knives that plunge into your back. They trick you into thinking you're safe when you're not. That's because your home wasn't safe, isn't that right, Sable?

"I know!" Hector sobs. "I know what your father did to you. You whispered it when you had nightmares."

Wiping away tears, I try to see what eluded me in childhood. Something dark and sinister happened to my twin, something I missed, something much more destructive than the normal lessons my father forced us to endure.

Our home lacked love, but... it was still our home. I found safety within those walls.

What did Sable find?

"You hate the word 'home' because of what your father did to you. You hate your twin because your father picked *you* to hurt. Don't you? Something similar happened to me, and that's why I never gave up hope that I could fix you. I fought until now, until you held that sword like a match you were going to throw into oil."

"Sable!" I stagger forward but stop. What did I miss? What did our father do to her?

Does it excuse her actions or explain the root cause of them? When the victim becomes the aggressor—when their definitions of right and wrong have been erased—how do you judge them?

"You tried so hard to make others think you don't feel, but your motivation to burn down the world shows us all you *do* feel. You do feel the bitterness of dying. It's a relief you welcome. It's not the knife in your back that made you gasp, not my betrayal that made you cry. Pain has become a numb ocean you have mastered sailing."

Sable slides her hand to another tattoo, trying to kill it from his flesh, but unlike the other, this one remains. Her magic is fading.

Hector continues, "I would have pledged my army to you if you had wanted to change the world."

Her hand slips free, slapping in her warm blood. I seal my eyes shut for a second, ashamed to be a voyeur.

"I did... want to... change it," Sable breathes, a faint smirk at her lips.

Hector's shoulders shake. "Destruction is not change, Sable. I wish I could have modified the future. I tried so hard, but in the end, he was right. He warned me it would end this way."

"We all had to make sacrifices, something that alters our souls, but it anchors our destiny, ensuring we can withstand the trials ahead. He told me instinct would thrust my dagger forward, but my heart would fight to hold it back. He said the path I picked would shift everything. One was the future he wanted; the other was no future at all."

My eyes meet Titus's in recognition. "Everett," I rasp. Titus looks back at Hector, then down at Sofia.

"We were never Sable's pawns." Sofia tilts her chin up. The once-beautifully sinister woman now looks like a child who is lost, scared, but in us she finds hope. "Sable's both our pawn and opponent. Everett knew if Sable found the book alone, we'd all lose. So he tricked her, placing Hector in her path, which is why he's covered in runes. Hector was bait. Sable bit the hook and dragged us along. You know your side of our story." She finds her brother's eyes. "We've been waiting to tell you *our* side."

"You..." Sable hisses at Hector, "Didn't win. My twin and her mate will kill you."

Hector's palm cradles her face. "Neither did you. That's all that matters."

Sable gnashes her teeth. As a last resort, she shoves herself off Hector's lap, falling onto the stone floor. I let out a horrified gasp. The dagger twists and plunges deeper into her, curving up as her back settles onto the floor.

She's ending this. It's her last attempt to have control.

Her cry is a twisted braid of mocking laughs. Tilting her head back, she locates me, her expiring gaze piercing me like arrows. All the color vanishes from her face, bleeding out onto the floor. "I order my magic—"

"Don't let her speak!" Titus roars. Flames shoot from his hands, aimed at Sable, but as they near, a smirk plays on her lips.

I feel it instantly. Her departure severs something deep in my gut, something that holds my feet to the ground. Hector scrambles back, suffering burns on his thighs. Titus's magic fills that corner of the room. Hector drops and rolls on the floor. Sofia runs through flames, grabbing her brother with her cuffed hands.

Titus surges forward, a torrent of fire and savagery. Sable's body is unmoving, a dead branch Titus can't shake from his rage-filled mind. The claim of killing her is stolen. Only her silhouette is seen as fire consumes it. Then her shape changes as the flames begin to tear and rip into her.

Burned. Nothing but bones, then ash. It's not our way, but Sable was never a fae at heart. She was something scarred, mutilated, and forced to twist so she could stand and survive.

I plaster my eyes wide, watching her burn away. "Now you're free of that harrowing flesh and broken bones, Sable. I'm sorry I was not your shield. I was forced to be a different kind of weapon," I whisper.

Titus looks back at me. I don't share the relief that courses through him. He doesn't realize what he did—that he burned a fae.

It will haunt him. I wish I could remove it from his mind. I pray someone can.

Titus walks through the fire and grabs the Vitalis and the sword.

"I'm on your side, as is my sister. Everett sent us," Hector shouts, hands held in the air as his mouth twists in anguish from the burns on his legs. The bottom of Sofia's long dress is singed off, but the skin on her legs looks untouched by the flames.

Titus stops, peering at his trophies.

"Everett, he did it." I focus on my struggling heart. "As did I." A lone tear falls on my faint smile. My desires and regrets are irrelevant. As Elderan said, it's about survival and the future of our world.

We're so close-minded, selfish; it's not about Blackthorn, not even about the Vitalis. Kingdoms and runes won't matter if there is no one left alive. This was never about finding my happiness; it was about hope. Without hope, survival is fruitless. In tough times, hope dulls the suffering, and in good times, it intensifies the joy.

The earth sways as promises are fulfilled. I begin to wobble forward, too overwhelmed to remain standing. Biting my tongue, because I know what I must confess next will tarnish everything. I look upon my mate, at his beauty that is about to sicken into heartbreak and cruelty.

His strength will be tested, never fully mended; his hope in happy endings, in victories, is all about to be erased.

"We did it, Selene," Titus laughs. It's a beautiful sound that kisses my heart.

It sends me off, allowing me to let go. To accept what I ignored. The signs were there all along. Everett never lied; he only suppressed the truth, just as he withheld his magic of foresight from Titus.

Because Titus would have seen that Everett's victory, unfortunately, meant Titus and me would lose.

"Selene?" Titus's smile falters.

Oh no. He knows.

I search our bond and do everything in my power to silence it. It's... easy because... should I confess it now, or wait till he realizes what has happened?

I lose my footing and fall forward. My knees hit the stone floor. I don't feel the impact. Only his love for me.

"Selene!" Titus drops the book. Handing over everything we fought for. For me. His mate.

Now I understand, brother. In order to win, you have to lose more than you'd ever imagined.

CHAPTER
FIFTY

TITUS

I refused to let Sable speak. Nothing good would spew forth from her dying lips. I understand better than most the power a fae wields in their final moments. I watch her burning body, the flesh curling like paper, charring, ripping, revealing muscles, tendons, and finally bone.

Soft shields, that's all we are in the end, yet we can cause so much damage.

Sable almost won. The minute she touched that sword, a knot formed in my gut. Hector—the last hidden pawn Everett played—prevented her from winning.

Many questions need to be answered. Now we have time to solve them. To understand the runes, keep them safe and secure.

"I'll show the world love," I declare.

The smile Sable painted on her dying lips doesn't fade. It's a candle wick that carries the fire, rather than allowing it to consume her. It remains until it hits bottom, her skin slides off, and falls into the fire below.

Tristen, Ryker, Adrian... I did it!

Tristen? Shit, he'd better be okay!

Cyrus, Nero, Ember... I'm sorry I didn't tell you my mission, but I did it! We can celebrate as a family!

Turning, I see the Vitalis, covered in flames, but it's immortal to my fire. Reaching down, I grab it and the sword. The minute I lift the blade, a power surges through me. I feel invincible, energetic, deadlier. *I'm* the sword, refined, forged, altered. This is what Sable felt, how she pulled the blade free. If Hector hadn't betrayed her, she would have slain us all.

I'm tempted to drop the blade. Is this what I need to keep the book safe?

This mission Everett forced upon me was like falling into a cactus. At first, your wounds don't look bad, you pull yourself up. But up close, deep within your flesh, there are a million thorns. One step at a time, I have removed them. Made the world safer for my mate.

So many lives were forced to merge so I could get this book, so the future has hope and light, not darkness.

I step through the fire, spotting my mate. "We did it, Selene," I laugh. That sound hasn't emerged from my chest in so long.

I want to make it again as I hold her, as I build a home with her, and start a family. I want to savor her, protect her, cherish her. I want to fight at her side. I want to be a ruler worthy of a queen like her.

The world feels warm for the first time in so long. When we exit this tunnel, will the sun refresh me as others say it does?

Again, I close my eyes and breathe out. We did it. I know there are battles ahead, but shit, I want to jump, climb a mountain, and scream my victory at the top. I want to lay my mate down on that mountain's edge and make love to her, under the sky that still twinkles because we're still alive, as is our world.

My eyes snap open. Selene sways, eyes filled with tears. Her silk clothing is torn and dirty, like my motivation was before I first laid eyes on her. Her complexion is pale, as shallow as our success was. I silence my flames, hoping it brings some life back into her beautiful face.

Oh shit! My fire. I shouldn't have let the fire burn so hot. I just lost control. Fire... I burned her twin! I burned a fae and desecrated their body.

Selene's eyes lower to my feet. Slowly, they rise, measuring every inch of me, as if it's the first time she's spotted me. I expect outrage and disgust. But her lips twist when she looks at our mating mark. It tugs and pulls me... but not in the way I hoped for. It's filled with sorrow, and something deeper I can't decipher yet, because... she's blocking me.

Shit! I know she hated her twin, but she just lost another member of her family, and then I burned the body. That has to affect a person.

I step closer. *It's okay. I'm here. I'm going to keep us safe. I know we still have foes to face, but for just one moment, I want to celebrate.*

I raise the sword and the book. I started this journey to save myself; I ended it to save Selene.

"Selene," *I'm sorry I lost control.*

She sways forward, like jello poured too early from its mold.

"Selene!" She's falling, slipping from my eyes, the ground pulls her lower and lower. I empty my hands, diving forward to catch her. "Selene!" I land on my knees, cradling her to my chest. Her sad eyes look to where Sable burns. A sick feeling tethers me to it, and then she stops blocking her emotions from me.

"I'm sorry," she chokes. Instead of her shock over my actions, or love for me, I feel... a departure. Distance. Things she kept hidden.

"Selene! I...what's happening?" I force her eyes to mine and look at her mate mark. I cover my palm with it. Why does it feel faint? She's in my arms! I'm holding her!

"I don't understand." I declare in sheer panic.

I hold her tighter, but it's like grasping clothing on a hanger. I want to slip those pieces on and claim them as mine!

"It's... okay," her voice is a soothing whisper. Salt that burns but tries to disinfect.

She's not alright!

"What's happening?" Sofia's panic rings in the background.

"I don't know." Hector's worry plagues me more.

I don't know either! Everett never mentioned... suddenly it's not my mate in my arms. It's Everett, dying as he speaks his final words. *"I give my magic of time-weaving to you, Titus, to use until you find the Vitalis; then, I release my magic back into the lands. But my magic of foresight, I release back into the world. If you were to see what you must endure, you would grab the sword from my heart and thrust it into yours."*

I would have plunged that blade through my heart if I had seen this.

"No!" I glare at Selene. I see my future in those green eyes. My destiny!

Our love is what poets preach; it will replace tavern songs. Two enemies forced to love, forced to fight side by side to save the world.

I grab her hand, spreading her fingers wide. Fingers that tried to kill me, shatter my heart with an arrow. Hands that loved my body, mended my fractured mind.

These hands are what carry me now. Why do they feel cold?

"Bend your fingers around mine and hold me! Hold onto me!" I roar.

Nothing. No lover's touch comes from her hand.

Did she know?!

Did she know?

No...

No!

Is that why she fought the bond at first?

I sink my fangs into my wrist and then push my blood into her mouth. She chokes on it, swallowing some. "Drink! It will heal you."

She tries to swallow. "Titus..." All the blood she drinks is coughed up. "This is different. This can't be healed. It has to be set free."

"I don't understand."

Her fingers fall limp over mine. "You do." Blood drips from Selene's nose. Reaching up, I push it back inside. *Stop bleeding! Stop!* More slides out. *Fuck no!* I wipe it away with my sleeve. "Titus..."

I glide my thumb over her cheek. Blush for me! "Come on! Stop looking so pale, Selene," I seethe.

Her lips turn ashen, dry, and cracked. Bending down, I kiss them, breathing life back into my mate.

Come on, kiss me back with more passion!

I add more pressure as I twist my tongue over hers.

Come on!

She tries to kiss me back... tries so hard.

My tears stain her face. "Whatever is happening needs to stop. Do you understand!" I shake her. "You're my gods-damn heart, my life, Selene. Selene! Stop this... it hurts... please stop. What happened? Tell me so I can fix it!" I look over her body for damage, but I see no deadly wound.

But her skin is all wrong; it's too sallow, her eyes are yellowing, her pink lips are blue, her tongue sticks to the roof of her mouth as she tries to reply.

"What happened?" I beg her. I didn't allow Sable to speak! I stopped her. My fire burned her tongue before she could curse Selene.

"It's not your fault," Selene sighs, her voice barely audible. The shine of her hair turns matte. "Fae magic dwells inside of us; it hears our inner thoughts. You did all you could. Your fire burned Sable's words from the air, but she thought them before she spoke. Sable set her magic free. What's done is done, my love."

Sable's magic.

Death. Rot.

Selene barely manages a nod.

"No!" I shake my head, urging my ears not to listen. "Sable didn't win. She did not force her magic to kill you! We can reverse it, just as we did Torin's cage."

"Titus," she tries to swallow but fails. "It's done."

"Fight for me!" I roar. "Fight!" A cavity rips open my chest, revealing my heart. Just as Everett's magic bonded with me, Sable's does with her. I can see death over Selene, grabbing her, claiming her as its mate and not me.

Just as I had no choice, neither does Selene.

"I am fighting. These last few moments are my peace."

"No!" I scream. "I burned Sable!"

"I saw it in her eyes as the flames consumed her. She ordered her death magic to kill me." Instead of slackening, her body starts to stiffen just as bodies on the battlefield do. I know what comes next, after the heart stops.

She'll bloat, then her body will start to disintegrate and decay.

"It's okay, my love," she rasps.

"It's not okay!" My flames erupt from my body, covering us for a moment. I control their heat, keeping her safe. Warming her cold skin. "Sable did not win! You're not dying!"

"I'm not scared; I'm angry, but I always knew this was my path."

I am flesh no more. Solid stone forced to remain unmoving as Selene speaks the truth she kept hidden.

"Titus..." Selene struggles to raise her voice over the fire. I lower my flames. Watch as the green in her eyes turns as leaves do in the fall. "You never wanted a long goodbye, so I will tell you this."

"No! I refuse to let you die. Heal yourself! You have life magic. Healing magic!" My wild eyes find Sofia and Hector. "Heal her! Do something!"

"I have never been able to bring someone back from death, Titus. Sable's magic will live and fight until I am gone." Selene's voice is so faint, it's only the mate bond that alerts me to it. "Do not let this all be for nothing. Do not let my death be in vain."

"You're not dying!" I start to stand with her in my arms. Instead of molding to me as clothing does, she's stiff as a board.

That's when I sense it. A scent I'm used to smelling on the battlefield.

Decay.

Sinking to my knees, I gently place her on the floor. I look at her mate mark; it starts to sink into her grey flesh, withering away. I glance at my mark on my living, healthy skin. It's there, but it's starting to fade.

"I am dying. I knew this was my ending. Everett warned me."

Her admission is a knife in my back. A shock that forces me to cry more. I claw at my throat, trying to thin the thickness choking me. Deep breaths are impossible.

Panic. I'm having a panic attack.

There's an ache in my chest that is killing me. I don't fight it. I allow it to spread because if she dies, then I need to as well.

"You... knew," I gasp between grief-filled breaths. "Yet... you let me... love you." I almost shove away, but I grab her hand, her hard, cold hand.

No! That's impossible. She'd never be this cruel. Never trick me into loving her to fulfill Everett's mission.

"Loving you was my only tranquility. I spent my final days happy."

"And what about me?" My fingers press into her skin, beating it as one would an unmoving heart, demanding it come back and be held accountable for its crimes. "What about my days? What about my future without you?"

"The man I love has... undying hope. Do not let... my death extinguish that. It's what... the world needs to survive. Survival does not mean we all get to live, it means those who survive can retell our stories. Sing our sorrows so they can heal."

"I wish I had never loved you!" It leaps from my lips in a desperate attempt to save what is left of my shattered heart.

It sickens me, kills every emotion, every dream of a future and family, and every connection I ever made is tainted, poisoned.

"It's okay," she nods, eyes humble as if she can see a future where I survived.

She grinds her teeth, fighting to utter her next words. "Sometimes, it's okay to sink, because once you're at the bottom..." Her words are short, quickening, fearing she can't finish them. "You get to watch all your loved ones swim away. Swim, my love, swim for us, find new shores, make the world a better place."

She blinks rapidly. Scared.

She can't see anymore.

I press my lips to hers. A barely-there smile touches her lips.

"I'm here. I won't accept this."

"Don't let... the tide of my death... overtake you. I love you... I want you to love again, for me... for us. Find... happiness. Survive."

"No, no... no, Selene, please. Please!"

She widens her eyes, turning her head to where I dropped the Vitalis, as if she can sense it without her sight. "I order my life magic..."

No, no, no! Gods no! No!

I try to clear my vision so that I can see her. Then, I close my eyes. This is a nightmare. Everett would never force this outcome onto my shoulders. No man who has found his mate could bear this.

This is wrong.

We didn't win.

Selene continues, "To heal the pages of the Vitalis, to restore what has been scarred." She turns, and I open my eyes, sensing her blind eyes gazing upon my dark shadow.

I promised to be her shield, to cover her from outside attacks. The true beast was her; she was her end. Her untold truths, her sweet kisses, and the lying promises of a future. I needed to protect her from herself, from her willingness to accept this fate.

She never wanted a mate; she fought us, ignored us. I should have listened.

Instead, I stood by her side as she played wife to another, sister to a man who cursed me, baited me.

It was all a lie.

Love is a lie.

A lie I would swallow again if I could have just one more day with her. One day... that's all I had with her. Our bodies joined only once. One time... does that make this easier or more unjust?

"Restore all the scars. Mend his heart when it's time."

CHAPTER
FIFTY-ONE

TITUS

Light slams into my chest. For one heartbeat, I'm back on the battlefield, swords clashing, people roaring and screaming. The scent of death surrounds me. My hands are heavy; Everett's dead body weighs them down.

His magic invades me, fusing with me.

I have no choice.

Another heartbeat. I jerk.

Where am I? Is this real?

I'm back in this forsaken mountain, freed from Everett's magic, but wait, what is that warmth in my chest, gripping my heart, forcing it to beat?

I know if it weren't there, I'd be... with my mate. Losing her should have killed me.

"Selene," I rasp. I crawl back to her, no longer a man, more animal on my hands and knees.

I splay her out, close my fist, and demand that her heart beat again. I push and shove, forcing my lips over hers as I breathe. Again and

507

again. She's like a balloon; my breath inflates her, but so quickly she deflates.

Nothing happens.

Her eyes don't open.

Why do I sense an invisible part of her floating up, up, and... away?

Gone. Except for that magic forcing my heart to beat until it's strong enough not to need her magic keeping it alive.

She must have truly loathed me to have placed me in a perpetual state of torture, forced to survive this outcome.

My lips part, but no man's voice comes forth. Agony. Anguish. A beast unlike any the lands have encountered howls. My magic pours from me. Spews like molten fire. Useless tears, unheard pleas.

All I see is fire and lies. It's what this world is built on.

How am I to change that?

Why should I?

I hand over my control to the beast, allowing it to do its worst, stretching far and wide, filling the room, rushing down the tunnel, as I set fire to everything. I don't block out the heat; I feel it coat my skin. I won't burn. Never have.

Maybe if I push it hotter and hotter, I can change that.

Hopefully, I can.

Hope...

I snort. You wanted me to have hope. Here's hoping I don't live to see tomorrow. Here's to hoping I wake up, or hoping that I died on that battlefield when I fought Everett, and this is the afterlife I deserved to suffer in.

Here's to hoping that hope burns.

CHAPTER

FIFTY-TWO

SOFIA

I never want to fall in love. Never want to feel what my brother felt as he drove that dagger into Sable.

He loved Sable. I can't understand how, but he did.

Hector tried so hard to change Sable, but no matter how you chisel stone, in the end, it's made of the same thing. Whether it's fashioned into a boulder, brick, pebble, or dust, it's the same matter.

"Selene's dying!" Hector's panicked whisper pulls tears from my eyes.

Can Titus see it as he begs her to live? She is death. Her skin has already given up.

No, he can't. Titus tries to force his blood into Selene's mouth, desperately hoping it will heal some part of her. Selene's wounds are too catastrophic.

I look at Hector's small patch of skin that Sable rotted. It's green and raw, infected, and in need of a mage elixir to heal it before its roots start to spread deeper into his healthy skin. We can't heal ourselves as fast as vampires can; our inner healing is like a band-aid, good for small cuts and wounds, but it uses all our magic.

"What do we do?" I'm too scared to move, to interrupt Titus and Selene. I look at Hector as he cries; it's like watching Sable perish again. "Brother," I touch his arm.

He grabs my cuffs, melting the edges of them so I can slip my hands free.

Suddenly, light pulses in the room. Magic leaves Selene's body, and a piece of it slams into Titus. Another flare flies to the Vitalis, snapping it open. The pages flip wildly as the wind stirs.

Hector's body jerks, and he yelps as he rolls onto his back. "Hector!" I grab him, careful not to touch his burns.

What in the world... His tattoos begins to glow, shimmering as some invisible pen traces over the pattern. Frantically, I look back at the Vitalis. An open page stares back at me. The faded ink is now deep and permanent. The stab in the middle of the paper slowly knits closed!

"It's... healed! Hector!" Just as Everett told us they would be if Selene chose the right path. "Hector!"

He groans as he rolls closer to me. I grab him. "Are you okay?" *Shit!*

Before I can speak again, Titus roars a sound that will forever haunt me. Heat! All I feel is fire rushing towards us. I cry as I cover my brother. I open the portal, but I'm worried I'm too late. The fire grabs me, covering my back as I push Hector through it. Then myself.

My body arches, recoils, but at first I feel no pain. Just signals to my mind that something is hot!

Screams, shouts, panic. Hector and I hit solid ground. Our kingdom was too far to portal to, so I took us to the closest place I could think of.

Oh no! Now I *feel*.

I scream, trying to roll over, but no! That's where the pain is. I roll onto my stomach; tears cause my face to slip over the stone floor.

"Fire!" Someone yells.

"Adrian! Move Tristen! Get him out of here!"

"Guards!"

A strong gust of wind shoves me with such violence that I slide over the floor.

"Sofia!" Hector yells, but then he groans. He's hurt. "Don't touch her! We're on your side. Everett sent us. Please! Titus needs your help!"

My fingers curl into the cold floor, trying to dig into it, so I can bury myself. End all the espionage and suffering.

My back's so hot. "It stings," I cry, so wracked with pain, I can't move. Boots come closer, a shadow kneels, lowering his face so I can see his eyes.

Violet eyes. "If you try anything, I'll peel the rest of your flesh off."

"Death seems welcomed," I choke.

"Sofia! Fuck! Her back! Stop, I'm not fighting you. Help her!"

"You can't move, can you?" Violet eyes state. I shake my head. "Good. There's no escaping me."

I close my eyes, pushing out more tears.

I must have blacked out; all I feel is torment as my eyes flare open. "Stop!" I scream at the hands pressing into my back.

"It's a healing ointment."

That's not my brother. "Where's Hector?"

"He's not here."

"Where is he?" I groan in agony.

"I'd be more worried about your lovely neck."

I can't stop shaking. I portaled us to Selene's room. This isn't it.

"You're in the dungeons."

That voice... "Violet?" I groan. I'm still face-down on the floor. It's damp and musky, filled with ghostly whispers of tortured souls.

I twist my neck. I'm in a cell. I pivot to see the violet-eyed man. His face assaults me—cold, hard, sharp, emotionless at first glance. His hair is lightning, wicked, and scary, yet enchanting. He's dressed in fighting leather, covered with weapons on his back, hips, and tucked in his boots.

His arms are more muscled than most warriors. His knuckles are covered in scars as he pours out more ointment into his palm. His hands move over my scarred back, applying the ointment.

As if sensing my stare, he stops and flashes me his fangs. "That doesn't scare me," I mutter.

"The chains on your wrist should," he retorts.

Mage cuffs. I huff, "Not all chains are made of iron." I wiggle my wrist. "This is a comfort. Sometimes my magic is so consuming, I find a dark, lonely corner and scream." Oops, did I say that out loud?

Hooded eyes narrow, causing the violet to look more amethyst. My favorite color. "I'll find out what scares you."

His smirk doesn't reach his eyes. I'm not sure eyes like his can smile.

I melt into the cool floor. "I'll save you the time and just tell you."

His mouth twitches, but before I can answer, he asks, "Can you open another portal?"

"What?"

"When I slip these pretty little cuffs off your hands, can you open a portal? Or are you nothing but a deceitful, scarred mage?" Scarred. The ointment helps with the burns, but I'll need another cream within the first hours to erase the scars, or they will be permanent.

How many hours have passed?

He leans closer, "And before you ask, your brother talked; he had an odd story to tell. One I don't buy."

"Stories are not meant to be sold. They are intended to be listened to."

His hand slides under my chin, twisting my neck so I can see him fully. He says nothing, which is more unsettling.

"Why would I portal us here?" I break the tension. "We had the Vitalis. I could have grabbed it and run. Instead, I came here. We've been on your side. We're still on your side."

A cold wind presses my face back down. He lets go and steps back. "Answer me." His tone sounds like a war hammer swinging down.

Closing my eyes, I tug at my magic trapped under the cuffs. I've always been different. Unlike other mages, my magic has much larger reserves. My father found out and tested me brutally. At most, I opened twenty portals in one day.

He pushed and pushed until I almost died. I listened, because I craved death; I wanted his teachings to stop.

But I always woke up. Always. Just as I did now.

Sighing, the man kneels, places his hands on my hips, turning me gently onto my side. Air flows where clothes should cover. My dress is gone!

"You changed my clothes." I gasp. How long was I out? I have on loose pants and that's it. A thin cloth was laid on the floor.

He presses the fabric to my breasts, keeping me covered until I'm stable on my side.

"Changed?" he grunts. "They were burnt away."

"You still covered me." My throat thickens. Terrible memories plague me. I'm not horrified he saw me naked; so many others have.

His right eye narrows, like a pair of tweezers that can see the thorns under my flesh.

I don't want him to see that part of me. "Yes. I can open a portal."

Did I expect a smile, shock, or anger? Violet eyes reveal nothing. He's a wall no one has dared to climb.

"You're lying," I whisper. My throat burns; my cheeks feel tight and dry. I know what eyes like his want. They want to be scaled and conquered; they want to crumble into hands that are capable of love. Looking in the mirror, I saw the same eyes staring back at me not so long ago. Then Everett found me. He loved me in his unusual way. Everett collected broken toys; they made the most loyal of soldiers. Everett knew we'd always feel our cracks, and that we'd admire the glue that filled them now. I will forever fight in Everett's honor. I will continue to recruit in his name.

He sinks onto his knees, his eyes locked on mine. "Excuse me?"

I feel like this man, my captor, needs saving. All he's ever been is an object that other people move. My exhale widens my back, but no pain assaults me. I tell him the same thing I told Hector, the same statement Everett told me.

It saved my brother, turning him into one of Everett's spies.

"Your voice is chalk pressed onto a board. It has one purpose: to deliver a message. Nothing more, nothing less. You're a soldier who does as he's ordered. You don't ask, for fear you'll be killed. What kind of life is that?"

"The kind that kept me alive."

"Are you?" Palms to the floor, I push myself up, making sure to keep hold of the thin material covering my chest.

He doesn't shift back to give me space. "Am I what?" Wind swirls around him in warning, but it also pulls me closer.

"Living?" I question. "My brother and I were like you." I hug the fabric. His eyes trace the curves of my body. "Chalk. Nothing more and a lot less. Everett filled us with hope. He gave us a purpose, turned us into hands that hold chalk, set it free now. I know why you asked me if I can open a portal. You want me to take you back to Titus."

He's unmoving as pages in a book, waiting for me to turn them so he can reveal more of his plot.

"I can," I admit. "But I fear what you'll find when I do. Empty men can not fill others."

He seizes my wrist, hands harder than mage cuffs, dragging me to him. The thin fabric drops between us, leaving only his leather cuirass to cover my breasts. A raw burn kisses my kneecaps from the swift motion. "You're going to take me to my brother, and if he finds you guilty, I will be the one to kill you," he states.

Hector and I feared this. We knew Titus and Selene might not forgive us. If we had to die so the world didn't perish, we would. We saw what the other side was capable of.

Shades.

Terrible creatures that can sicken an entire town. That's why Hector killed our people. Like stars in the night, the Shades emerged from the darkness. A plague began to spread, blackening veins and eyes. It turned some humans and mages into beasts.

Hector had no choice but to burn our lands and those infected, so it would not spread. Only the army that was outside the walls survived.

Boots slap against damp stone. "Ryker!" a man shouts.

"Ryker," I whisper his name, tasting it on my tongue.

His scowl runs over me like flood waters drowning out my fear. He stands and exits the cell, but not before he looks over his shoulder at me.

~

"Lift your arms." Ryker's jaw stiffens as he removes my mage cuffs. His voice echoes off the walls of the dungeon, drowning out the faint drip-drops the walls produce, and weeping from other prisoners.

I do as ordered. "You're angry I didn't fight to keep my privacy," I state. "It doesn't matter to me."

Why did I admit that?

"Dignity should matter."

"I do not define dignity with my vanity," I reply. "You're not the first man to see my flesh," I whisper.

His hands tug the shirt down. "I'll be the last." He locks eyes with mine, fingertips digging into my hips before he grunts and steps back.

Vice Admiral Adrian Airendale stands watch. Adrian was Galen's prized horse. When did Everett turn him into a spy? "What do you define dignity by?" Adrian asks.

Ryker grabs my wrist, his hands replacing the cuffs. "Doing one's duty to the end," I answer.

"Ryker's going to need a large bag to put the Vitalis in, and something to grab the sword with. It had a strange effect on Sable when she grabbed it. I would hesitate to touch it with bare hands."

"We didn't ask for your input. Now," Ryker drops my hands and squares my shoulders, "open the portal."

"If you think Titus is walking out, you're wrong. You will be dragging or carrying him. But, so be it." My magic swirls, the destination visualized in my mind. The portal opens, filling the small cell with light. Ryker's fingers hold me in a vice as he begins to guide me through the portal.

I wrap my heart in a cast, knowing what lies on the other side is bound to break it.

Love is a beautiful thing. We sing praises about it; we go on adventures to hunt it down.

We never talk about life *after* love. We never mention how our palettes go from colorful to nothing; not gray or black, or muddy tones. Just nothing.

We never show the massive wound love leaves behind. We never admit the struggles we endure when we try to fill that gap.

We never talk about the after, because if we did, no one would seek out love to begin with.

CHAPTER
FIFTY-THREE

RYKER

The portal behind us closes. Half a dozen mage lights Sofia sent in first should have lit our way. Smoke grabs hold of them, dimming our vision. Hot cinders burn our lungs.

"Ryker!" Adrian coughs. Our magic ignites, winds stir, pushing the smoke down a long tunnel.

Sofia's cough turns thick and congested. I push fresh wind around her face. Then, I put the mage cuffs back on her. Adrian and I take a tactical position.

Sofia truly brought us to Caldara—a jail for broken things, including my brother. We have men marching to the mountains where Hector told us the hidden escape tunnel still existed. That's how he and Sofia found this place. They never brought Sable here till the final day, just in case she came by herself to steal the book.

Hector spewed his story. As soon as Everett was mentioned, Adrian believed him. I have many reservations. All I care about is making sure Tristen opens his eyes and Titus is back. I don't care what shape either of them is in. We'll fix them. I just need them in my arms to mend.

"Ry... Ryker."

Why is Adrian's voice so anxious? I swing my hand towards him. Wind glides over the tiny grooves of my fingerprints, ready to attack.

Oh, no... the enemy isn't one I can fight. It's mental.

I guide Sofia to Adrian. I don't step forward.

Don't be dead! Please! I swallow. Titus lies on the floor in a fetal position. Black smoke curls around him like a blanket. He's completely naked. Exposed. Everything has been burned away. His flesh shows no new scars. That worries me the most. Invisible scars are the roughest to mend. You can't see the extent of their damage, so how do you know how many bandages to apply? Too many and you suffocate the patient; too little and they bleed out.

It's a guessing game, one that takes decades to play.

There! His chest moved. He's alive.

No, Sofia is right. He's a shell. Shells are neither living nor dead; they are lost in the middle. A home made of calcified walls with no soul to fill it.

My body sways as I step closer. To the left of Titus, a few feet away, something demands my attention. The Vitalis, and there, that's the sword Sofia warned us about.

Selene? I peer back at Titus. It's just him.

I glare at Sofia. "You said Selene died. Where is her body?" I demand. All my fury is aimed at her, the easiest target. Her lips tremble, her finger shakes as she points to Titus. No, under him.

I glance back. No trace of Titus's clothing or armor remain. I inhale. I've learned to smell details on the wind. That's burnt leather, and that's... flesh and bones. I know that smell better than my own scent. My life has been a series of battles; the only highlight is returning to my family.

Titus's skin is red, raw in some spots, but still whole, not burnt off. When his magic first evolved, it used to burn his clothing off; it took him practice until he controlled the flames.

He lost control here. Sofia told the truth. I shake my head, not wanting to accept that his mate died.

"Titus, it's me, Ryker." My next steps don't land on the stone floor. What's that? Sand. My forehead furrows. Realization slaps my mouth open. That's what Sofia pointed at. Ashes.

Titus is lying on a pile of ashes.

I jolt back, unsure where to step. But the only way to reach him is to step on those burnt bones. I freeze, caught off guard. If this were a battle, I'd be dead.

My gaze falls upon Adrian. He's realized it, too. Sofia's eyes meet mine as if they were helping hands. I peer back at Titus, forced to step on his dead mate to reach him. Using my wind magic, I gently try to clear a path for my feet. Crouching down, I touch his back. "Brother,"

Nothing. His eyes are red, swollen, unblinking slits as they look at something I do not see. It takes me two attempts to swallow.

"I'm going to get you out of here." I rub his back.

He's catatonic.

"Adrian, get the book and the sword," I order him. We should have brought a bag, like Sofia said.

Adrian pauses as he hovers over the Vitalis. "One book has changed so many lives," he mutters to himself.

"That's the power of a book," Sofia warns.

I'm scared to move Titus, worried my touch will make him crumble. "Brother, I'm here. Tristen needs you. I need you." I run my hand through his hair. Cinders fly out; it's smoking hot but still shining with life.

A sharp inhale has me grabbing his shoulders, trying to sit him up. The ashes under him hold his impression. He's boneless, limp, but his eyes stay open.

For the first time in my life, I cry. Not tears of sorrow, but fury. I was too late to run through the portal to help him. I stood across the bed so I could watch Selene, but I should have stood by Titus's side. The distance of those few feet changed his life.

I grunt, grabbing him, hugging him. I slap his back. Hard. "Titus!" I shout in his ear.

Talk to me. Fight me. Cry in my arms. Do something. Don't be a shell.

Sofia is right. I'm empty, too. How am I going to fill you?

I use my wind to help give me a boost, deadlifting him as I stand. Crouching down, I press his stomach into my shoulder and roar my fury as I heave him over my shoulder. Adrian returns to Sofia, Vitalis in hand, the sword strapped to his back. He grabs Sofia's wrist, removing her cuffs.

She looks past me with grief. Then she grabs the hem of her shirt and rips off a large section.

"What are you doing?" I hiss. Adrian, dagger in hand, aims at her. My wind helps keep Titus lifted. I was drained after the battle with Galen. Once Titus ran through the portal, I drank more, then I drank again before we came here. I should rest so I don't slip into bloodlust.

Sofia ignores Adrian's dagger. "That's... it's Sel... it's... her ashes."

Sofia takes a step, opening the ripped material in her hand. "This is not a resting place meant for a queen. This is a prison. Let me take her so Titus can spread her ashes."

A chill hollows me. Sofia's affection towards my brother's turmoil fills it. I dip my chin, still shocked at her attempts to heal my brother. Her eyes trace over my face as she passes me. Eyes that are like layers of the earth.

If I keep digging, I'll discover her core, but like she said, empty men can't fill others.

CHAPTER
FIFTY-FOUR

TITUS

You thought I could be a king. Now, I sit in a cell.

Mage cuffs are my crown.

My family put me in here with much reluctance. They feared I'd run. Or worse.

The burden of my eyelids is a battle I succumb to gladly as I seal them shut. Footsteps come and go. All my family has visited, except Tristen. Has it been days, weeks, centuries?

Has the world burned yet? My heart has.

I want this to be a nightmare I wake from.

My mate lied to me. Tricked me into helping her, so her brother could win and I could lose. She was a liar who sought to kill me from the start.

How can I feel nothing, yet everything at once? I'm torn to threads, but threads can be spun just as Selene's true nature was. Selene and Everett's lies have stitched me into savagery.

Click.

Someone enters. Ember and Nero have been relentless, sleeping in my cell, curling up to me as they try to soothe me. Adrian and Ryker come to talk, they tell me of our positioning, and what has happened all over the lands.

Old buildings that have stood the test of time, that had runes etched into the stone, have awakened. The runes are alive, but no one understands how to use them. Why do the runes on stone hold strong, but the runes on Hector work like our magic, igniting then sleeping until they are activated again?

Ryker told me Hector is their test subject.

I guess that means Ryker trusts the mage.

I don't really care.

As soon as I see the Vitalis, I will do what Torin failed to do. Destroy it. I'll make sure Everett doesn't win.

A throat clears, but the visitor doesn't speak. I remain lying on my side. I couldn't move if I tried; my bones have fused this way. Humidity presses into my face. A deliberate action to make me thirsty.

"It's me," Cyrus acknowledges. Another wave of his water magic has my throat aching for a drink.

I hear him walk to the opposite wall and sit down.

"I'm not going to try to fix you," he admits in his deep, soothing accent. "Some days I feel like you. Inside, I'm lying down, unmoving. Dead. It's comfortable to stay that way. Moving, feeling. It hurts."

His boots slide over the stone as he settles.

"I've got a letter in my hand. Hector had it on him. It's from Everett. It's addressed to you."

My eyes snap open. Cyrus's hazel eyes show no glee. His brown hair is freshly shaven, and he's got a tan from marching in the heat of the sun. It makes the visible scars on his forearms an angry red hue. His face is the only part of his body not scarred; his old master wanted to keep it that way.

"I'm not one to pry, but I know if I give you this letter, you'll destroy it."

"So..." My voice is dry, sharp, shattered clay that failed to withstand the kiln. "Let... me."

Ember would have hugged me and cried; Nero would have thrown a party. Cyrus's lips thin, eyes glue to the thick letter in his hand. "If this letter were another knife, I would, but I have a feeling it's glue."

I cough and then curl more into myself. "I thought you weren't here to fix me."

"I'm not. This letter is," he answers. "I'm going to read it." The cracking of the wax seal makes my heart—kept alive by Selene's magic—skip a beat.

Not waiting for a response, Cyrus begins. His knuckles turn white. His skin has lost some of its sun-kissed hue. It makes his saturated hazel eyes more molten against his skin. More eerie. Everyone thinks Cyrus has tan skin, that he's from the East. He's not; he's naturally a pale shadow. That's how he was stolen as a child. Now he's always in the sun, tanning his skin a golden hue so he can't be invisible again.

Why did he let himself sink into the shadows again? Was it due to where he was stationed, just outside Lunestra's dark and gloomy borders?

Titus, I know exactly where you are right now. You're in..." Cyrus's voice tightens, "*a cell in Blackthorn, plotting ways you can destroy the Vitalis.*"

Cyrus hesitates with shock before he starts again.

I warned you of this ending. I need you to know I tried to save my sisters. For decades, I sought to find a different ending. When all hope became lost for Sable, I added new players in hopes that it would save Selene. It always held the same end. We failed.

No words can describe your state; this letter isn't meant to soothe you. It's meant to give you closure. I've seen our world when the enemy wins. I watched Cy...

. . .

Cyrus stops reading. My chest is so tight it's turning into a snare, hoping to catch a breath.

I watched Cyrus die as he failed to locate you. I watched the sands of Nibia chip away at his decaying flesh; I watched the grains hollow him out, as they curled around his exposed body.

Cyrus's voice deepens.

Nero was the first to die. Ryker and Ember met their end together as they tried to save Tristen. Tristen was captured and... experimented on.

Cyrus hisses as his fingers curl around the paper. "I need a second," he admits.

Don't do it. Don't give Everett the reaction he wants. The pain in Cyrus's voice has me struggling to sit up. My aching bones press into the corner of the wall I've made home. The chains on my wrist block out my magic, which is depleted since they haven't given me blood.

"Okay, I'm gonna continue." Cyrus keeps his eyes down.

You... you were one of the last of your kind. Of all vampires. You hid away from the world as it burned; eventually, a fire hot enough to burn your skin claimed you.

I witnessed so many endings, all the same except one. Selene's death was the only way we won. Her death healed the runes, giving you weapons to use against the Shades. Without Selene's death, the Shades would have raised an army as you struggled to learn how to draw runes again.

Selene's sacrifice gives you protection for decades, time to learn and understand how to create new runes. Time needed to help Tristen become what he needs to be, to foster an army of these warriors and other soldiers to keep the runes and society safe.

I've included a map with this letter. It holds the location of two dozen dra...

"Holy shit." Cyrus guides the paper closer to his eyes.

Dragon eggs. Find the rune that makes Dragon riders. Bring Adrian's son to them when he's old enough. Dragon fire and weapons forged with it are the only tools strong enough to slay the Shades and the other evil that will continue to grow.

*I'll give you a head start. The girl Galen killed, who fed from the vampire, **she** controls the lump of shadows. **She** was the Shade. In the next coming months, you will learn that the lands to the west call the shadow beast a Phantom. Shades have the ability to separate us from our shadows. Without our phantom self, we can't be mentally grounded. We go insane. Shades use Phantoms like dogs. But they realize they can do more with them, like build armies. Not every Shade is the same. Some can sire, others go mad, and some are just hungry and scared so they attack.*

The girl Shade Adrian thinks he buried didn't die. She regenerated hours after they buried her. And all those affected by the plague that spread in Hector's land were victims of a Shade who sent their Phantoms in to make more. They went mad because the Shade stole their shadows.

There is a specific protection rune that looks like this.

Cyrus is so entranced, he doesn't turn the page for me to see.

It can prevent the plague that the Shades spread from entering the body. Spread this rune, allow everyone, even your enemies, to have it. It will hinder the Shades from building their army until the dragons are old enough to produce fire.

You're wondering how runes work. From what I have seen, most runes function like magic; they need rest to regenerate. If tattooed, they don't need to be retraced, but the wearer must stay aware of their rune's state. Just like with magic, they can sense when it's running low and needs rest to refuel. Be cautious about how many runes you permanently mark on your body. Overuse can lead to failure of the heart.

The future I see has many preferring runes etched onto jewelry or inked with materials that fade. They choose their runes based on daily needs. These items act as conduits, transferring the rune's magic to the user. I suggest you spread the protection rune this way. Stamp it onto coin pendants, bracelets, rings, anything! Just make sure everyone wears it, from elders to newborns. Don't let the Shades build an army.

Cyrus gulps. "At least he gave us a running start," he mutters as his eyes reread that last section.

"A start?" I quip. My spine cracks as it pulls straight. "He gave me an end."

Cyrus's honeycomb eyes lock onto me tightly. "Endings mark new beginnings. I was you once. I laid down and took it. Crawled so deep inside myself, I told myself I couldn't feel or think. It was a lie. I felt, and my mind was a festering wound of sickly thoughts, Titus. I was turning into the monster I resented. Our family was an antibiotic that saved me. Whether you like it or not, I'm going to shove the medicine down your throat and force you to swallow."

I'm so weak, the only action I can make is a dry snort. "So after every mark he put on your body, you forgave him? Bullshit!" I've seen his night terrors.

"Forgave?" Cyrus lowers the letter, leveling me with a livid glare. He rarely speaks about his past. "No. I'm not telling you to forgive Selene. That's up to you. Our monsters are very different."

"I don't think so. Your monster loved you. Selene loved me. They both destroyed us in the end."

"You loved Selene. She gave her life for you. I never loved him."

"You can go," I mutter as my heart twists bitterly in my chest.

"I'm not done with the letter."

"It doesn't matter. As soon as you free me, I have one mission in mind."

"So, after everything, you're going to let these Shades win? After every battle I have fought, you're going to let dunes be the foe that slays me?"

"Win? There is nothing to claim. I am nothing; these lands are poisoned with greed. Let them have them."

His exhale is a hiss. "You turned your back on us so easily, but when you turn your neck, you will see us fighting to save you."

He raises the letter and begins to read.

I have one more prediction to tell you. Once you're free, one outcome makes everyone's sacrifice useless. You take the sword and cut out the pages healed by Selene. It sets you back a century. During that time, your enemies grow. You all die.

The other outcome is that you listen to me and do as Elderan asked. You help your world become stable, usher the runes back in, and create a governing system that unifies all the broken lands. I promise you, in the end, saving others will be worth it, Titus. You'll find peace. I've seen it.

I am sorry, Titus. I wish I could have made the road you walked paved, but how do we learn if we never fall?

Before Selene left, she wrote a letter to you, but she burned it. In doing so, she pushed you onto the path that kills us all. During one of my visions, I watched as she penned it, and I copied down her words on the following pages. Read them with an open heart.

Cyrus flips the page back. "Do you want me to continue?"

"My choices were robbed from me as a child. Picking a side has been an illusion."

Cyrus understands that more than others.

"I'm gonna read what she wrote," he states solemnly.

Titus, I just had the best night of my entire life. We made love.

I close my eyes, trying to ignore Cyrus, but as he continues, all I hear is Selene. I feel her in my heart, squeezing it, forcing me to listen. My eyes snap open, searching for a dagger on Cyrus. One I can use to stab my chest, but he's come empty-handed.

I know Everett loved me, but he also used me. That's tainted love. Our love is pure.

"Liar," I hiss through my dry teeth.

But something has haunted me. It's taken our pure love and bottled it, capped a limit on how much we can consume. Every one of Everett's spies who has appeared only talks about you and your future. Never us.

I kept something from you, Titus, something I chose to ignore. I buried it deep, but your love eroded it. Everett warned me about sacrifices. He'd look at me with knowing eyes—he saw my ending. He was preparing me.

I turned a blind eye, but as more of the truth comes out, and our road grows narrower, I fear it will only be wide enough for one of us to walk down. If this happens, I need it to be you. The world Everett saw, a world I would gladly be called a mother in, is a world you live and thrive in.

I shake my head, and seal my eyes shut, my anger and grief turn my tears into steam.

. . .

I have never been mentioned in it. I think I know why. It shook me free of all my ignorance.

I just need you to know that if something happens to me, please don't hate my brother. I'll be furious that I never got to spend forever with you. But I'll survive the here and after knowing you're safe, and the world is too.

What good is our love if there is no world to house it?

What good is love at all?

If something happens to me, please don't blacken the lands, please let others love for us, please let them live for the future we never got to have, and... I can't believe I'm writing this, but please find love again, Titus.

I don't want you to; I need you to. You deserve a happy ending. I do too, and having you as my mate was the happiest ending of all.

I've seen men who rule refuse to love and trust. I've been married to one. I don't want that fate for any other.

I hope I'm wrong. I want to spend forever with you. I'll hold on to that hope until I must let it go in order to save you.

I just need you to know everything I did and didn't do was because I loved you. Love has no limits; it refuses to break, so it bends the rules. It allows me to gladly sacrifice myself if it means the love of my life gets to live.

We once spoke about long and short goodbyes. I remember you said you didn't want long goodbyes, so now that I've said my peace. I'm going to bid it farewell and pray I misunderstood Everett's vision. I'm going to pray I have the honor of standing by your side forever. But if I can't, I will die happy, because unlike so many others, I found my fated mate, but more than that, he loved me; he never used me.

I never needed to be freed, Titus; I just needed you to make this world bearable. You can change the future. So change it for the better, my love.

"I'm alive," Tristen states as he enters my cell.

I'm dead inside.

I peel my eyes open and look at my brother. There he stands. He looks the same—tall, strong, muscled, raven hair—but his face lacks his usual playful glow.

Our gazes lock. He licks his lips, and my eyes water. "You want us to hate you. That's why you're doing this. If we hate you, it's easier to let you go. But if we love you, it forces us to walk this road of misery with you." Approaching my corner, he sits beside me, sighing heavily. Extending his hand, he flexes his fingers. "I'm the same, but I'm different. So are you."

Tristen's eyes lock onto the letter Cyrus left in his place. I haven't touched it. Suddenly, Tristen grabs me, covering me in his shadows, blanketing me the only way he knows how. He's crying. And I'm... sobbing.

This scene played out before, only the roles were reversed. It was the day the news of our parents' deaths reached us.

I'm the older brother, yet he holds all the broken pieces of me.

For what might be a century, we sit there in each other's arms and sob.

CHAPTER
FIFTY-FIVE

TITUS

Is it numbness that tugs on my eyelids, forcing me to blink and breathe again?

Vengeance?

Acceptance?

Our tears have stopped, allowing me to look at my brother. I grab his face in my calloused palms. His skin is smoother, like he has this ethereal glow of candlelight. Battles once stained the whites of his eyes weary and red, but now they are a pure, clean white. His hair is thicker, and the ends shine with new health.

I run my hand over his biceps. Did he gain muscle?

He blinks away tears. "I'm okay," he assures me.

"Your shadows..." I look around the cell. If it weren't for the walls, I'd be tricked into thinking we were floating on grey clouds. "You're magic truly has no ending?"

Tristen nods. I wait for a joke that doesn't come.

He's grown into someone who doesn't laugh as much. "My magic is always there, charged and ready to go, just as Elderan said it would be."

Is he relieved or stressed?

"You don't need blood anymore," I surmise.

"I drank it," he corrects me. "Old habits die hard. It tastes like chocolate, but it didn't fuel my magic. It's just an indulgence now." He looks down with apprehension. "Selene asked me to give you something, and I denied her," he blurts out.

My hand drops from him like it's been burned. "What?"

Tristen bites his lip. "She knew," he nods. "It was her way of warning me she was leaving. She wanted me to take care of you, but I slammed the door in her face. I finally saw a future where you were happy, and," he shrugs, "I wanted to keep it that way. So I refused to hear her out. I'm sorry."

My mate wanted to talk to him and not me! Finally, I reach for the bottle of water and take a sip. It burns. The urge to consume it all almost outweighs my knowledge that it would make me sick.

I hug the bottle to my chest. "Your guilt is misplaced. Selene and Everett are to blame."

"I don't expect you to forgive her." His shadow inches closer like an animal trying to comfort me. "But she died so you could live. I'll love her for that." His next breath is sharp. "We had a message sent to us this morning."

"You sure know how to deliver blow after blow," I grunt. My lips crack from the few drops of water I had.

"It's Selene's father."

"What?"

"He's here," Tristen replies. His shadow curls up, creating a second wall to trap me in.

The cell starts to spin, my fangs sharpen for his blood; my ears long for his screams. I don't just picture Selene. I see Sable, too. I hear echoes of everything Hector said as she died. Selene's father is a catalyst; I intend to make him suffer.

"His body is," Tristen clarifies as he runs a hand through his thick hair. "Along with a General Leander who said he was delivering a gift... from Everett."

My mouth dries. Give me a dagger so I can plunge it into my ears. I never want to hear Everett's name again.

"Solaria is being torn apart as we speak; the nobles are fighting for King Aridel's crown, and the army is in pieces. Turns out a portion of the soldiers were in Everett's pocket. They turned on King Aridel, delivering his body to you as a symbol of their wish to join us. King Aridel's got one hundred and twenty-seven arrows in him." The sound of Tristen's whistle is nearly lost in the rhythm of my erratic heartbeat. "He's a thin man too, not a simple task, but fae archers are worth their weight in gold."

Another revelation. I pinch the bridge of my nose. I think I'm going to vomit, but my stomach is empty. Maybe I can purge the shredded pieces of my heart.

Tristen rises and points his open hand towards me. He wiggles his fingers, waiting for me to accept his help to stand. "I'll throw you over my shoulder if I have to." He raises an eyebrow in warning. "Be angry; be numb. Fuck it, if you want to be a shell, be one! Shells are empty homes. I'll reassemble you, and shove you back inside. I can't make a new world without you, brother."

He bends down, interlaces our fingers, and pulls me to my feet. My knees ache as I sway. He has to help me stand.

"Titus, you are the first person to oversee an army of vampires, fae, and mages. We need you."

A shell. I'm a shell. Empty, forced to be filled with all the facts and revelations.

Forced.

Maybe that's what I need, someone to force me, because I'd much rather stay in this cell and rot. But then they all would be right. Selene would be right.

It would all be for nothing.

Nothing.

It's a struggle, but I step back and hold my ground. I'm not doing this for Selene or Everett.

I'm not! I hate them! I want to erase them from history.

My eyes trace Tristen's boots, his strong legs, chest, and his face, which I have loved from the first moment he was placed in my arms as a crying baby. I'm doing this for him. For my other brothers and sister.

Tristen's grin makes him look like a kid again. "Mages?" I mutter.

"Hector's army," Tristen replies, putting an arm around me as we slowly leave the cell. The cuffs chafed my wrist, causing raw, unhealed wounds due to my lack of magic. "They are calling you an emperor. The leader who will unite war-torn lands, a leader who will made kings bend a knee," Tristen adds as we approach the stairs.

I can only make it up five steps before I shake my head. Tristen props me against the wall, pulls out a flask of blood, and brings it to my lips. I drink it down and shake my wrists.

Pulling a key from his pocket, he hesitates, studying my demeanor before unlocking the mage cuffs.

Fire races up and down my veins. It finds my injuries and heals them, except when it reaches my heart. That can't be healed. It's held captive by Selene's magic. Caged until it deems my heart healed.

"I do not want knees bent," I announce as we finish climbing the stairs. "I want a world where we stand side by side, shoulder to shoulder."

～

I look down at the Vitalis. A fucking book was worth so many lives. The sheer power makes our small room feel on the verge of collapse. Reaching out, I press my index finger into the cover.

"Where is the sword?" Is that my voice? It's cavernous, rumbling like a faceless beast that lurks in the shadows.

"I have it. I will hide it once we sort this shit out," Tristen replies sternly. "I haven't tested Elderan's facts, but if he's correct, that sword is the only thing that can kill me."

I close my eyes, hold my breath, and flip the book open. In the dead center of the page is a rune, drawn in a faint black substance, but it's outlined in a shimmering gold thread that moves as magic does. Lighter sketches surround it, preliminary work the artist did before finalizing the design.

"I can't draw," I whisper.

"We once couldn't hold a sword properly, but we learned." Tristen comes to my side. "Does that mean you're doing this?"

"I don't know what I'm doing anymore."

"You thought Selene was your ocean." He gently presses his shoulder against mine. "She was forever, endless, boundless. She was your mate, and by the gods, she was magnificent."

I sink my fangs into my lip until it bleeds. I'll never taste her again.

My fingers itch to feel the silk of her black hair. My eyes water, and I plead to the gods to let me look upon her face just one more time.

"But she wasn't the ocean, Titus. *You* were." He removes my hand from the book and grabs me by the shoulders. "She was a storm that came thrashing into your life; she was wild and free within her locked-up tower."

I wanted to free Selene. But she knew she'd never taste freedom.

She locked me inside with her, forcing me to endure her final days.

Tristen's fingers curl into my skin. "She was whipping winds and harsh glares; she was gentle caresses and strikes of lightning that struck you. No matter how magnificent and wondrous their strength is, storms do not last. Eventually, they die out, and parts of them return to the ocean. Remember the part she gave you, the good memories. Another storm will blow into your life again."

When did he turn into a wise old man?

"I can't survive losing another storm." Why do they want me to suffer this again?

"Sometimes oceans clash with fresh water; you'll meet your match. Hey, I'm not telling you to think about moving on; I'm suggesting that once emotions settle into calmer waters, you will find your purpose. We're all hoping it's this book." He carelessly slaps the Vitalis. "But until then, you have all of us. We will stand in your stead and watch over it; we're here, helping you.

"The world we knew has ended, but the ashes are filled with nutrients that will support the new life. So let's build something. Let's make sure the two boys who lost their parents are not forced to kill so they can eat supper."

My lip trembles. I wish we were those two boys again. Maybe I'd grab a knife and end it. Save us both so much suffering.

What about my other siblings?

What about the good memories we had?

How can one bad event expunge all the joys of life?

It shouldn't, but here I am allowing it to erase the memories on the paper that holds my life's story.

Tristen's eyes soften as he continues. "Let's make a world where a little girl wants a name, where a monster does not enslave a boy." He blinks rapidly. "Let's make a world where there is a branch of warriors who fear nothing."

He pulls me into a hug and presses his lips to my ear.

"Let's make a world the two boys we once were could have been proud of."

I thought Selene's burnt-down field would look different. Like freedom. Victory.

It's just depressing. It's still here. The grass is scorched, the soil dry, but the land underneath remains. The dead roots of Galen's rose bushes still cling to the charred dirt.

It's going to take a long time until all these terrible memories are no longer as detailed in my mind.

"Mind if I join you?"

Yes, I mind.

"I heard you approach an hour ago," I grunt.

Hector thinks it's an invitation. He sits next to me on the outskirts, where the grass is alive. To make life more intolerable, the skies are clear, giving me a view of the last remaining pieces of Caldara's mountains to the far north of us.

Hector rests his tattooed arm on his knee. His runes look the same, but deep within his flesh, their power feeds him. A glance over my shoulder reveals Cyrus, Ryker, Nero, Ember, Tristen, and Adrian.

"Don't tell me Everett had another gift delivered." I shake my wrist, looking at my new bracelet. The rune that wards off Shades is carved into it.

We sent out letters all over the land showing in detail how to draw this rune so it can be activated. We warned kings, queens, and towns ruled by no crown. We told them of the Shades and Phantoms, of the enemy that has united us all; we told them of our power of runes, of the new kingdom we are forming, one that does not care for crowns and glory. We told them we will protect anyone who needs us and those who think they don't.

We are the most powerful, feared, and even loved people in our world.

But I'm still a shell. My mind is so dark, I don't think anyone can see me. It's best they don't.

Hector snorts; his smirk is distant. "No. I think we're on our own."

"What do you want?" I rasp.

He reaches down and grabs a piece of grass. "I don't know. I... I... I just. I loved her."

"Love kills," I bite.

He closes his eyes and hangs his head. "I need you to care," he whispers. "I need people not to think Sable was a monster."

"She was."

His neck turns sharply towards the mountains where he killed Sable. "I was never going to allow it to get to a point where she killed you or Selene."

"Shut up." My fire sizzles the grass under me. Hector shifts an inch.

"Everett never told me Selene would die. He told me if I picked the right path, Sable would."

My fire erupts, covering Hector. I lose control. In a panic, I pull my fire back, lunging to help him, but... he holds up his forearm. "Protection runes. This one repels vampire magic."

I shove him back.

"I'm not telling you this to piss you off. I just need you to know if I knew this was how the new world began, I'd—"

"It doesn't matter." I stand and dig my fingernails into my palms. "What's done is done." I look down my nose at him. "Where is your sister?" I bark. It's time to tell the past to fuck off. I have made my decision.

"Why?"

"I need her to open a portal for me."

His throat rolls. "You're leaving us."

I look at Blackthorn, a castle I vowed to burn. "No. I can't outrun my mistakes. I have to bear the burden of them disfiguring my memory. I want to say goodbye."

"To Selene," he clarifies.

"No. To my old life."

Salt fills my nose, and it stings my face as I approach the crashing waves that invade the shore. Sofia did as I asked; she portaled me to a beach, one near her kingdom.

It's barren, hot, and arid except for a small grove of date palms. The heat is so intense it stirs the air, forcing me to kick off my boots and enter the water. I asked to come alone. But I'm learning that being a ruler is more like being a baby; no one leaves you be.

Tristen lurks down the shore, ready to swim in after me in case I decide to never come back up for air.

"I'm the ocean," I curl my toes into the cool sand. A wave splashes against my knees. "And you..." I tip my chin up. The sun burns my forehead. The ocean mist invades my nose. "You, my mate, were a storm.

You battered me, wrecked me... cleansed me. I'm new. I'm different. You wanted to save me. You did, but I'm dead inside."

My knees shake as I give in and sit in the shallow waters. My armor grows heavier as sand digs in between it. I thrust my hands into the water, pulling up shells.

A bitter smile tugs at my lips. I hold a calico shell between my fingers. "Not all shells can be filled." I turn it around; it's no bigger than a spoon. Not meant to be a home. That was never my fate. I was never meant to love a single person. A ruler has to sacrifice themselves, because everyone wants a piece of them.

I palm the shell, close my fist, and squeeze. Eventually, it cracks. I shake it free, then realize all this sand is broken shells. Vessels shattered by storms that have ravaged them. Slowly chipped them down into grains small enough, smooth enough for others to walk on.

That's what I'm meant to be—a surface, a bridge that's smooth, secure, and safe for those who can't defend themselves.

"I can't forgive you." A wave crashes into me.

I lick the saltwater off my lips.

"But..." I nod and slowly stand. "I can move on. I'll tell you the true reason why I'm agreeing to do this, Selene. If I give up, hide away, and let grief consume me, I'll die, and that means I'll see you again."

I refuse to let my tears join the water.

"And I don't want to see you, Selene. I want to forget you. So I'm going to move on, live, and fight for the world your brother wanted. I'm going to let Tristen change me into what he is. I'm going to be practically immortal, stuck here, where you can't hurt me anymore. I'm going to live an undying life so I never have to see you in the afterlife," My roar causes the waves rushing towards me to flee back to the depths.

"The only way I'll be forced to, is if I fail and one of those rare swords plunges into my heart." I turn coldly. Wave after wave slams into my back. Each of my steps is painful and creaky. I'm an animal forced to change worlds. Swimming is over, and I must now learn to walk and conquer new lands.

"I'm not going to fail."

Immortality might seem like a blessing, but it comes with a curse —a slowly degrading sickness that erases memories. That's exactly what I seek.

I walk to Tristen; his eyes hold a forest of worry I refuse to acknowledge. My lips part as I smile, knowing freedom from Selene's memory is on the horizon. "I'm ready."

Author's Note

Thank you for turning this final page and joining Titus and Selene until the very end. Your dedication and support mean everything.

I know, really I do, this ending might be a shock to some, but an ending means new beginnings can start.

When I first began this series, I started writing Titus's story. But as I explored his past and included glimpses of Selene, brief notes about her quickly flourished into the foundation of the series.

Stay tuned for the second book. I will be dropping clues in my newsletter and on social media. Lots of my art and posts have hints as to what is to come.

I post most often on IG @authoragharris and my newsletter, which you can sign up for on my website. www.authoragharris.com

Please consider leaving a review; they help indie authors immensely.

If you have any questions, I will be doing Q&A, so feel free to submit your questions. You can message me on social media. If you want me to go into the process of writing a book, being an indie author, or more about these characters (I know you must have questions about Sable, too), just message me, and your question might be included.

Thank you all!